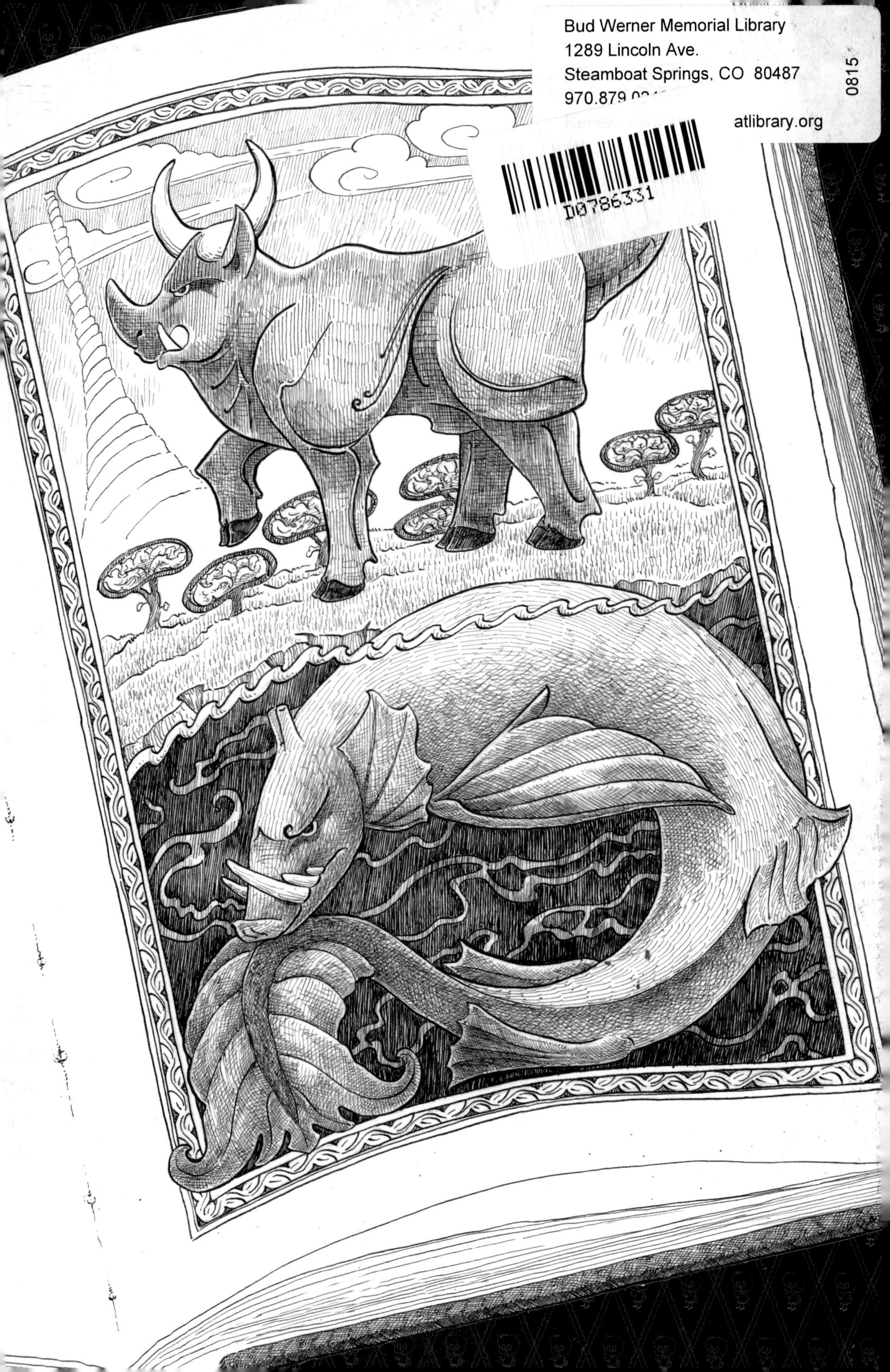

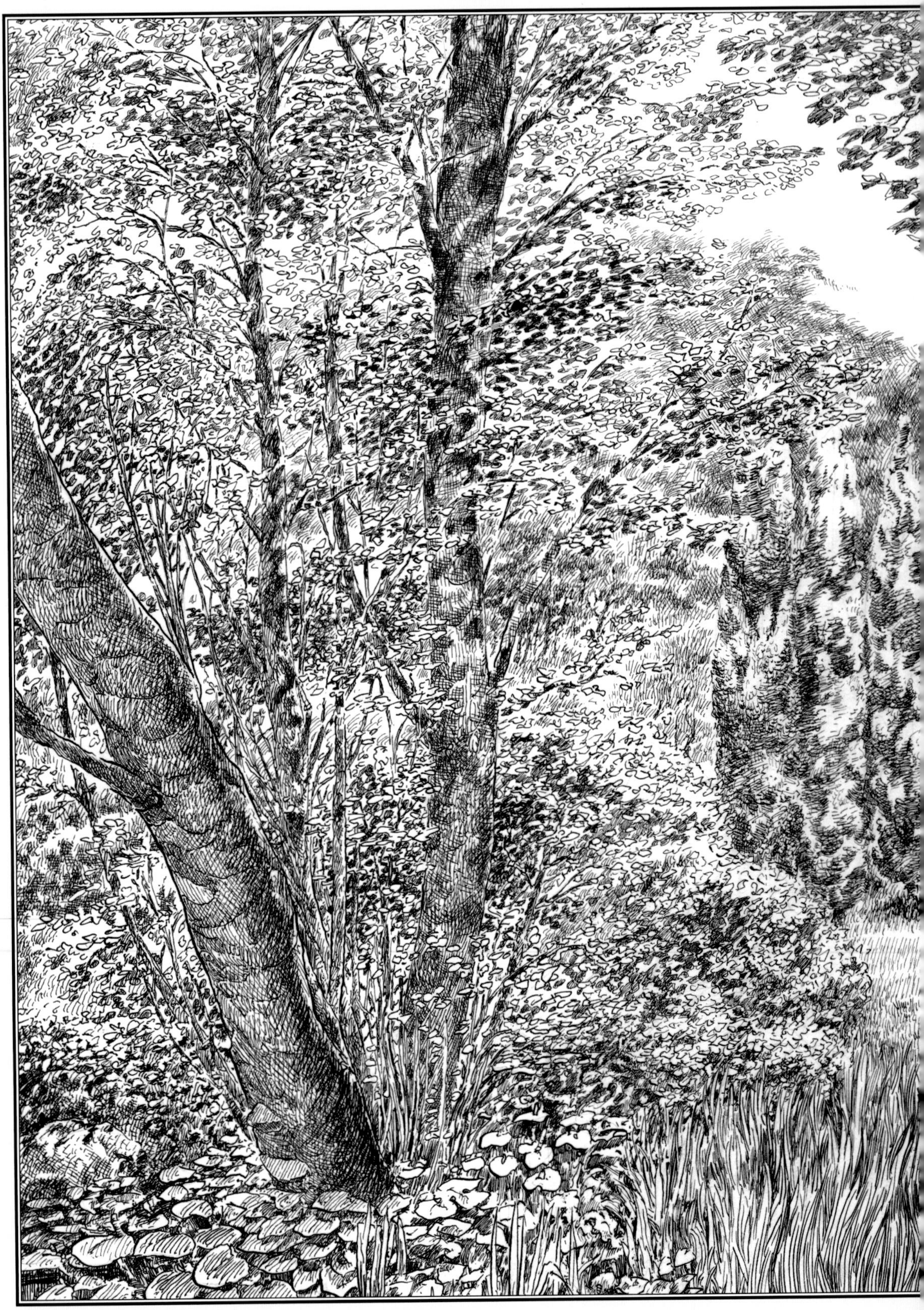

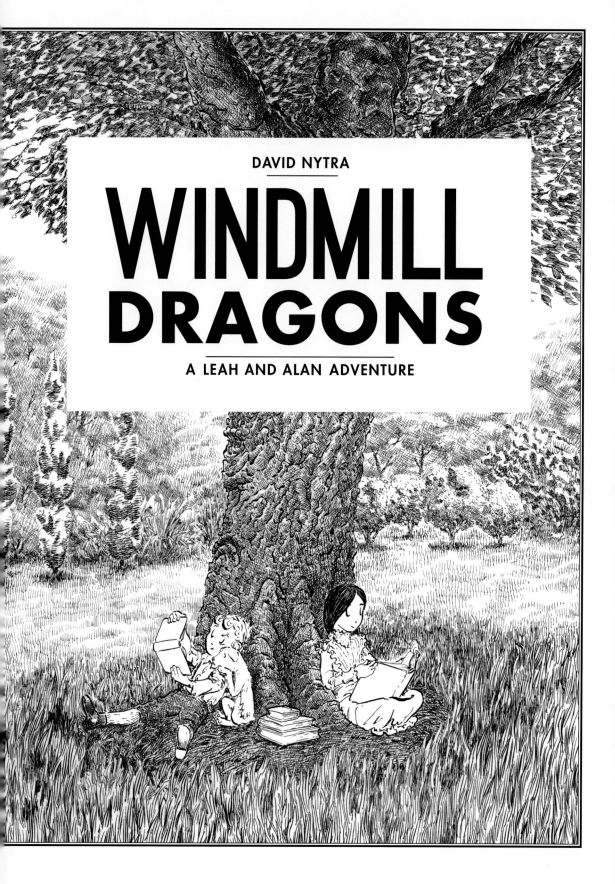

DAVID NYTRA

WINDMILL DRAGONS

A LEAH AND ALAN ADVENTURE

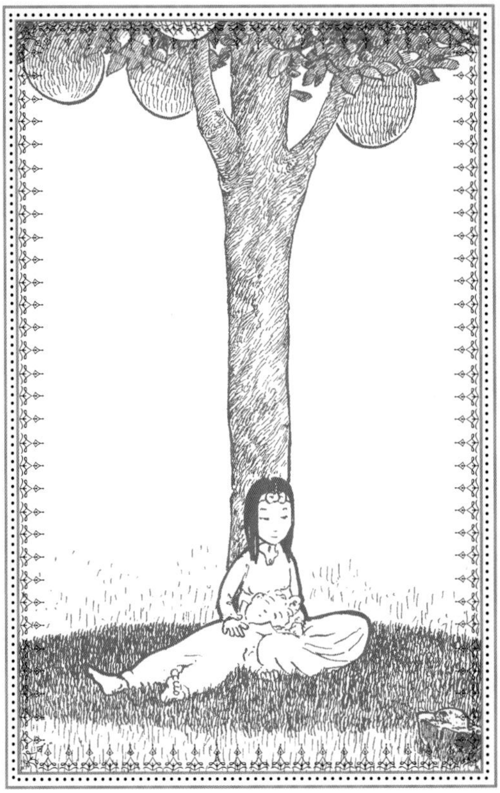

ex libris

· · (**FROM THE LIBRARY OF**) · ·

WINDMILL
DRAGONS

A LEAH AND ALAN ADVENTURE

A TOON GRAPHIC BY

DAVID NYTRA

TOON BOOKS • NEW YORK

A JUNIOR LIBRARY GUILD SELECTION

Editorial Director & Book Design: FRANÇOISE MOULY

Editorial Consultant: DASH

Managing Editor: SASHA STEINBERG

DAVID NYTRA'S artwork was drawn in India ink with a Hunt 104 nib on bristol board.

FOR VISUAL READERS

TOON
GRAPHICS

All our books are Smyth Sewn (the highest library-quality binding available) and printed with soy-based inks on acid-free, woodfree paper harvested from responsible sources. Printed in China by C&C Offset Printing Co., Ltd. Distributed to the trade by Consortium Book Sales and Distribution, Inc.; orders (800) 283-3572 34; orderentry@perseusbooks.com; www.cbsd.com.

Library of Congress Cataloging-in-Publication Data available upon request.

ISBN 978-1-935179-88-7 (hardcover)

15 16 17 18 19 20 C&C 10 9 8 7 6 5 4 3 2 1

WWW.TOON-BOOKS.COM

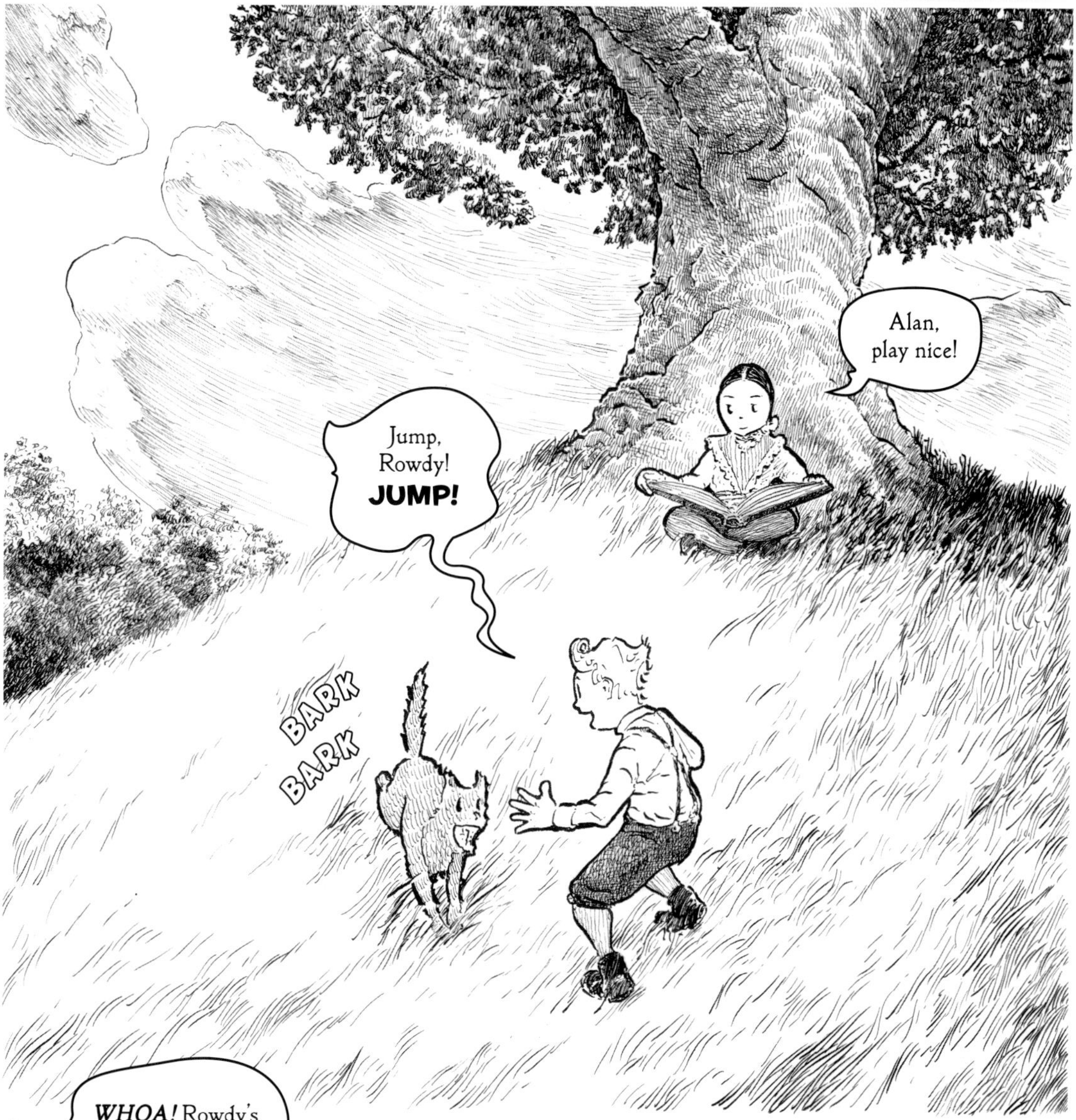
Alan,
play nice!
Jump,
Rowdy!
JUMP!
BARK
BARK

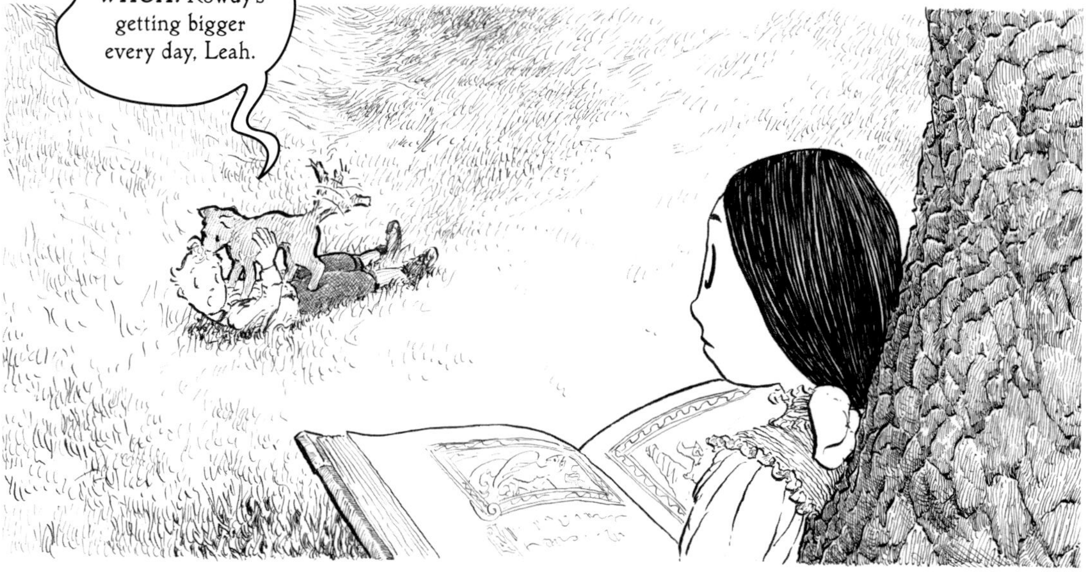
WHOA! Rowdy's
getting bigger
every day, Leah.

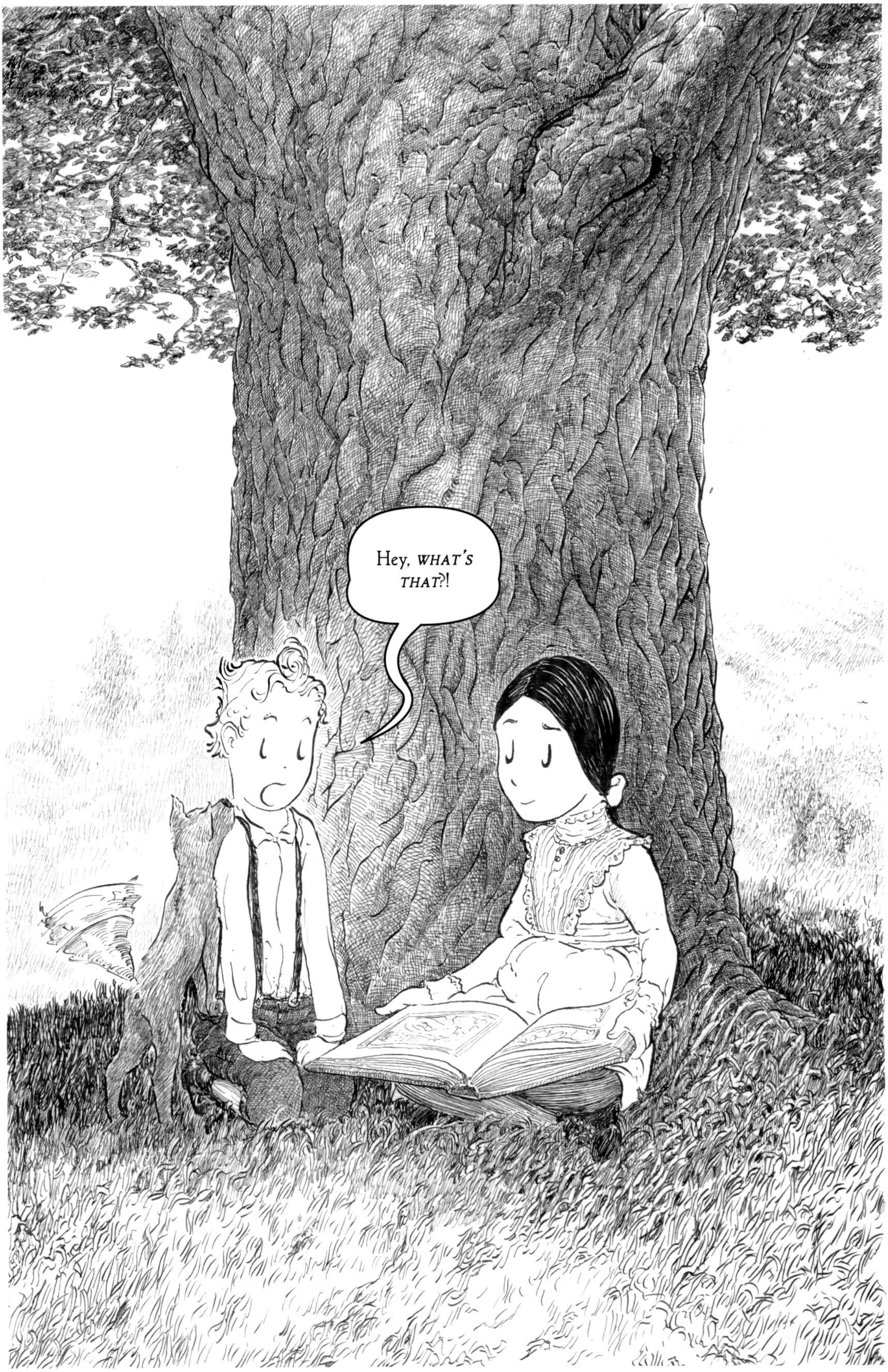
Hey, *WHAT'S THAT?!*

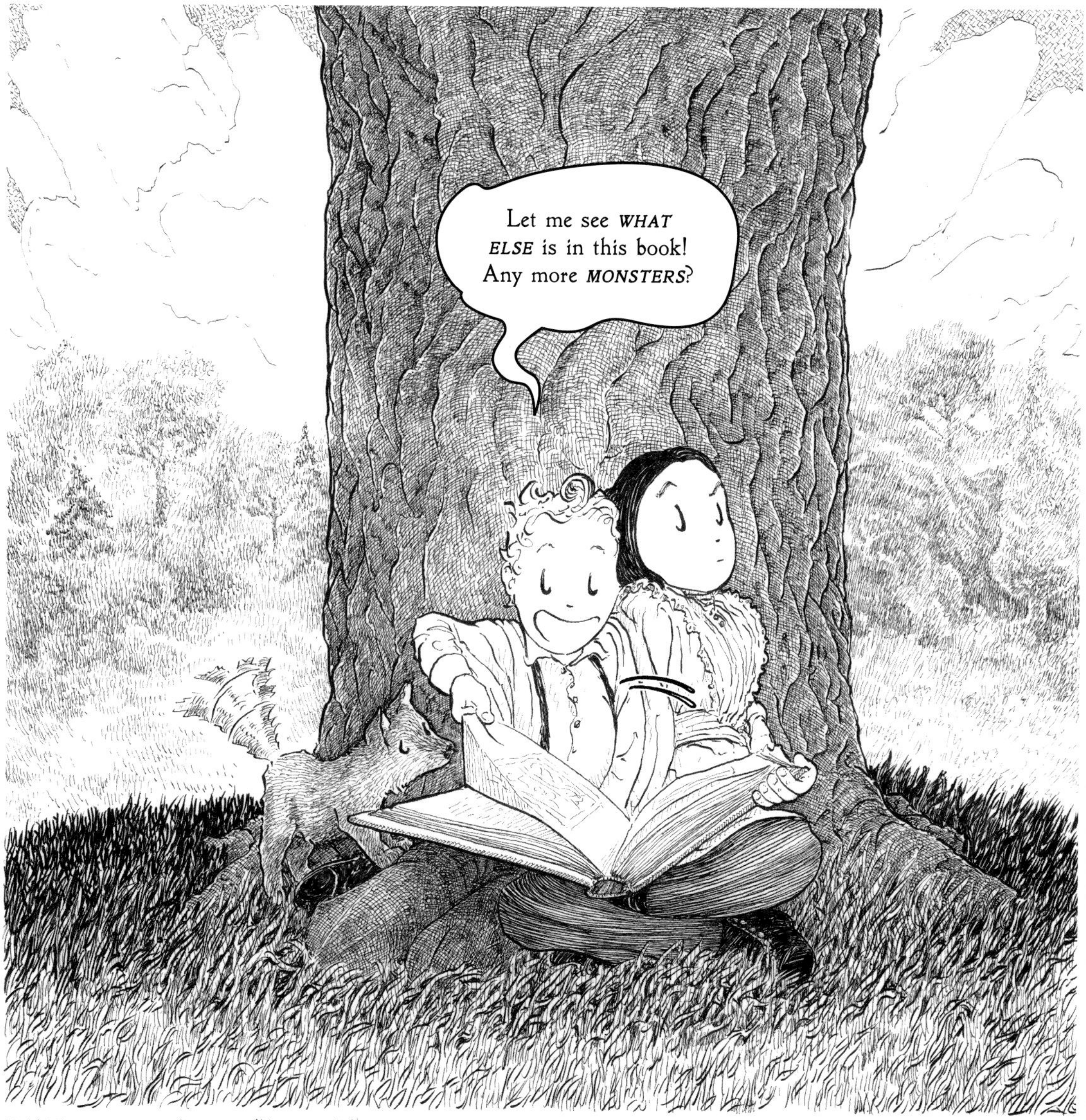
Let me see *WHAT ELSE* is in this book! Any more *MONSTERS*?

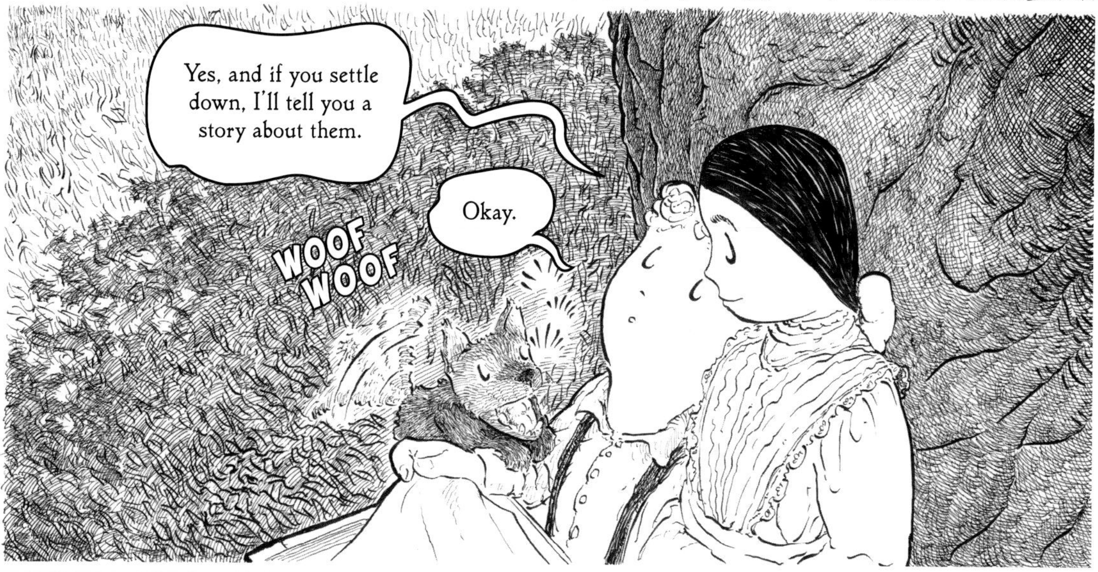
Yes, and if you settle down, I'll tell you a story about them.
Okay.
WOOF WOOF

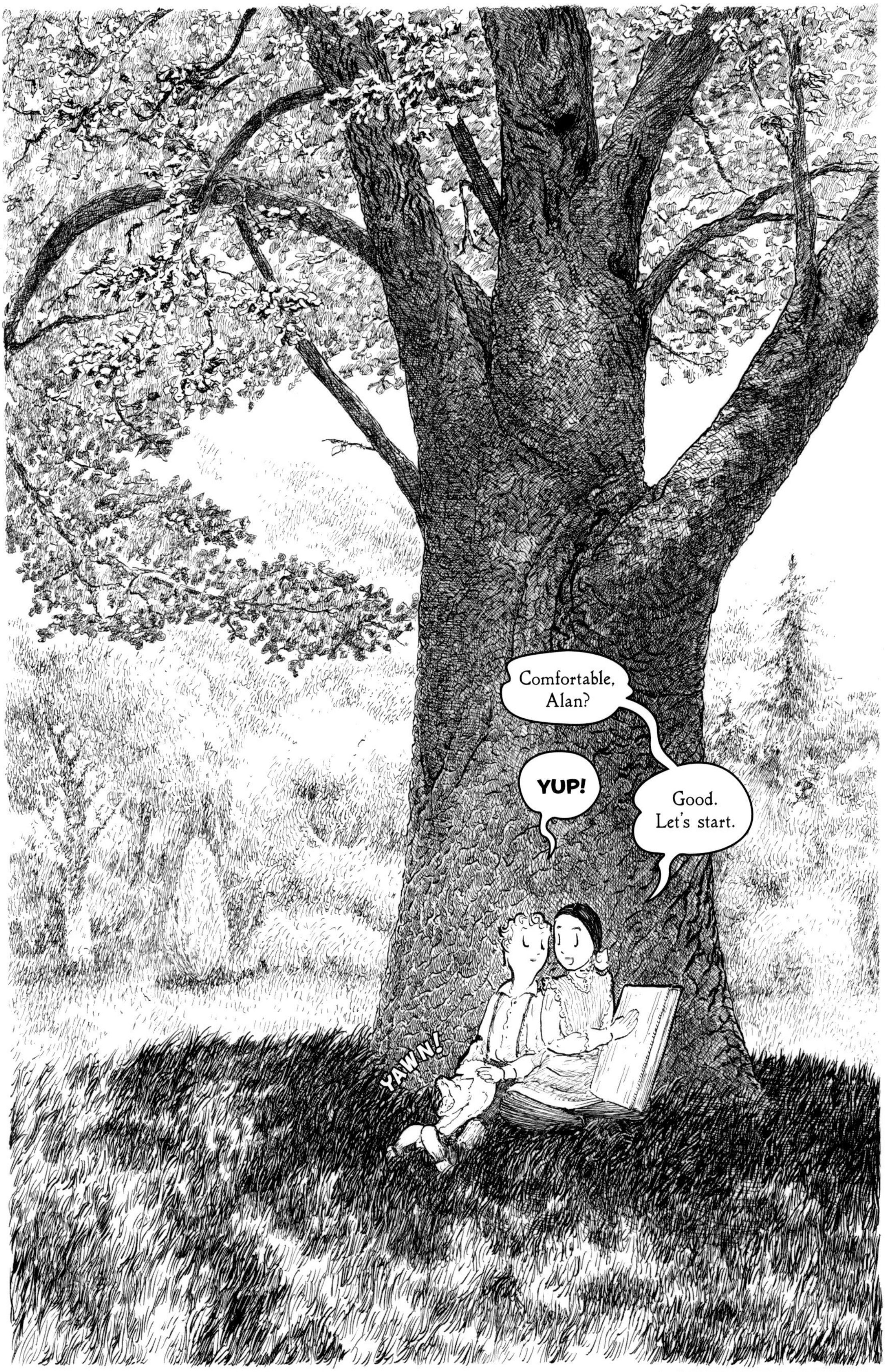
Comfortable,
Alan?
YUP!
Good.
Let's start.
YAWN!

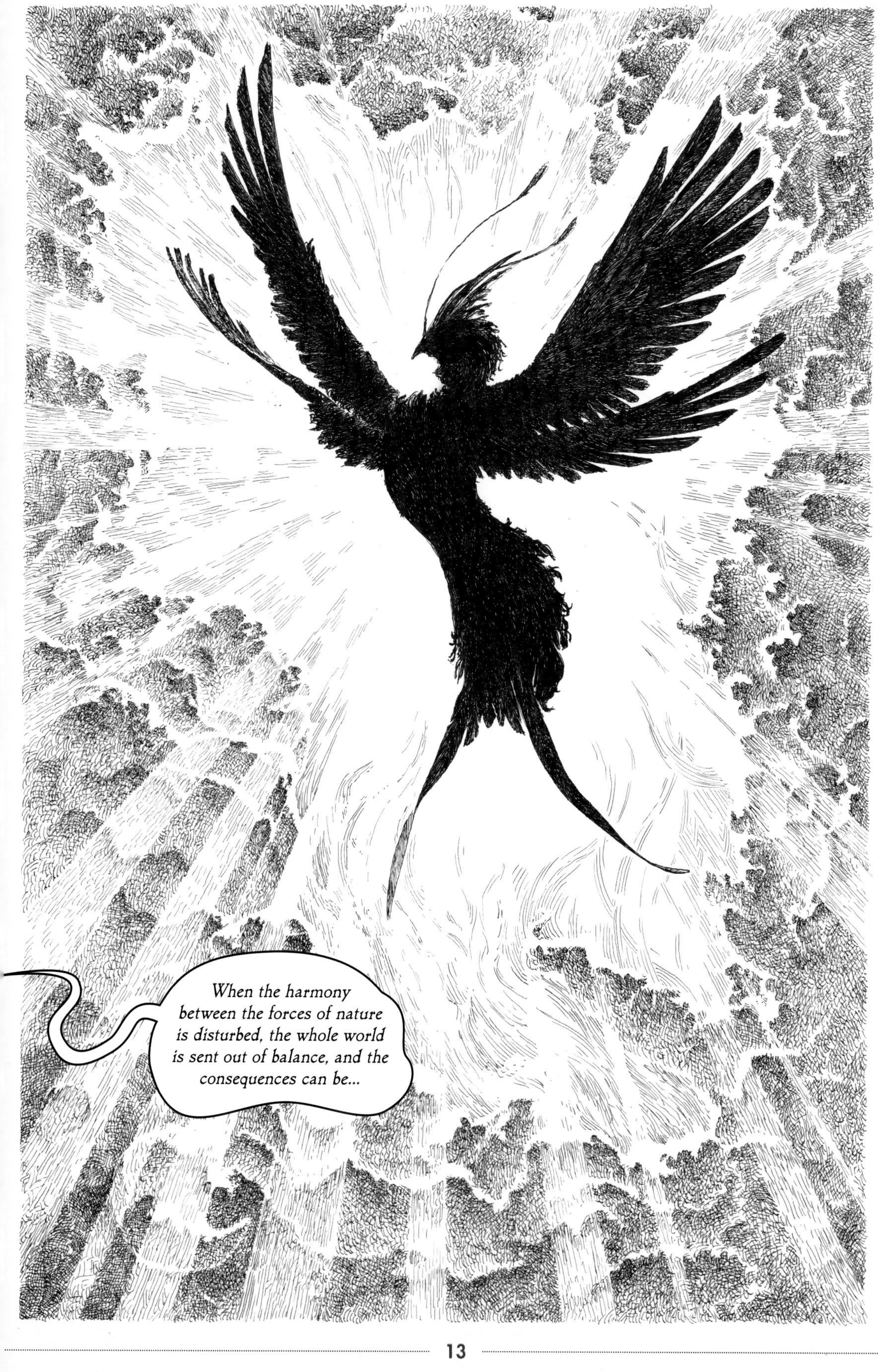
When the harmony between the forces of nature is disturbed, the whole world is sent out of balance, and the consequences can be...

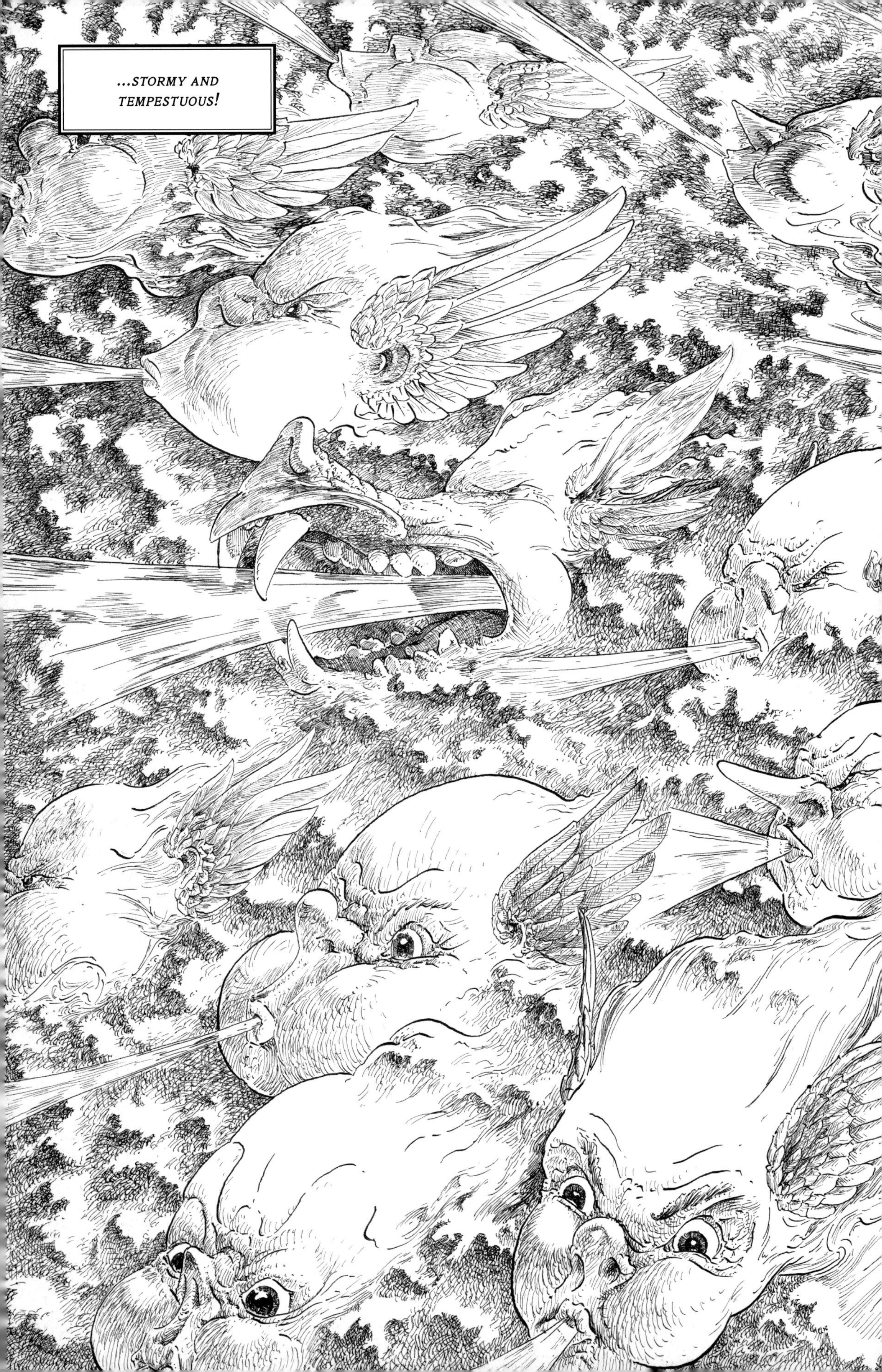
...STORMY AND TEMPESTUOUS!

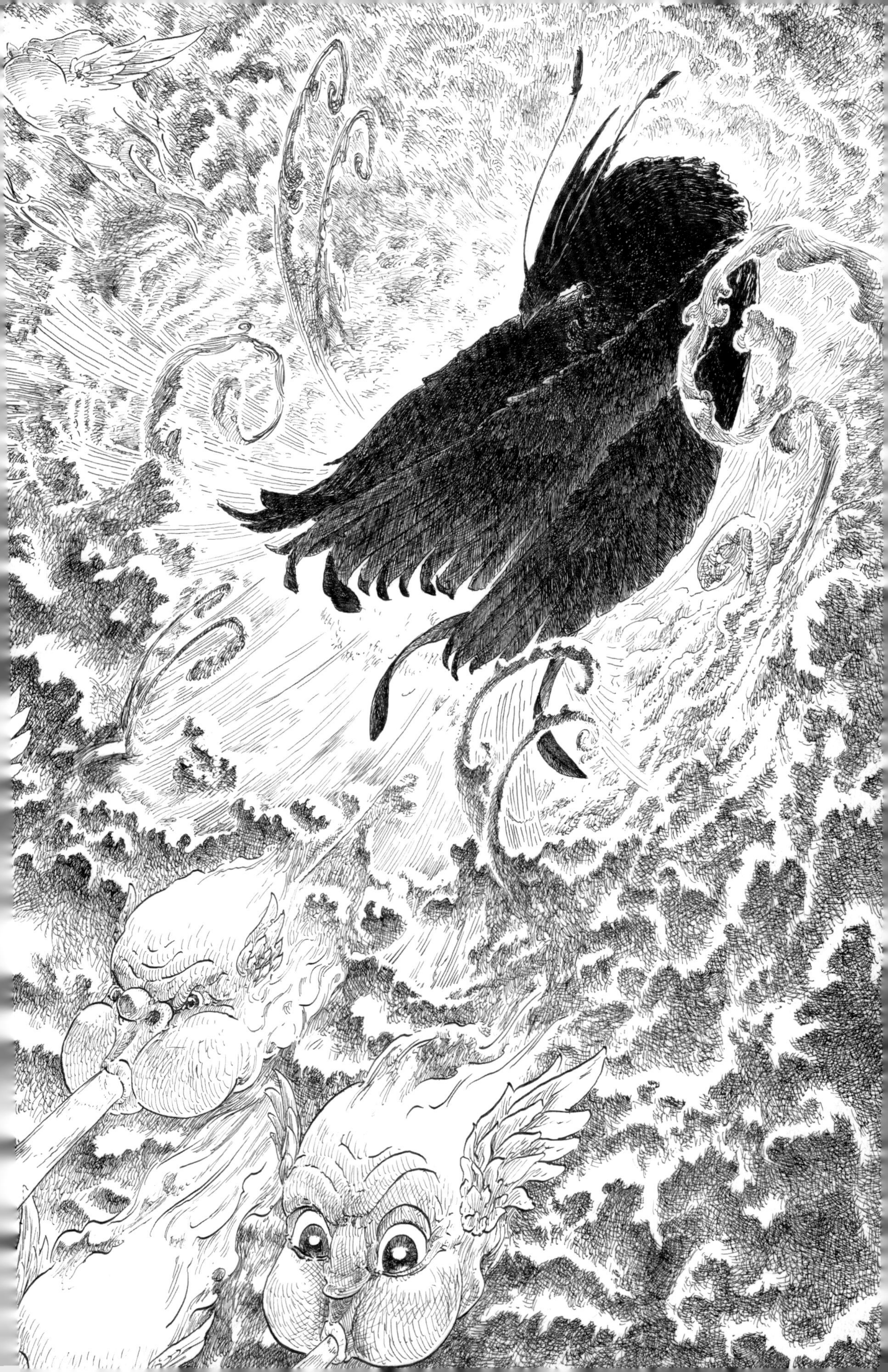

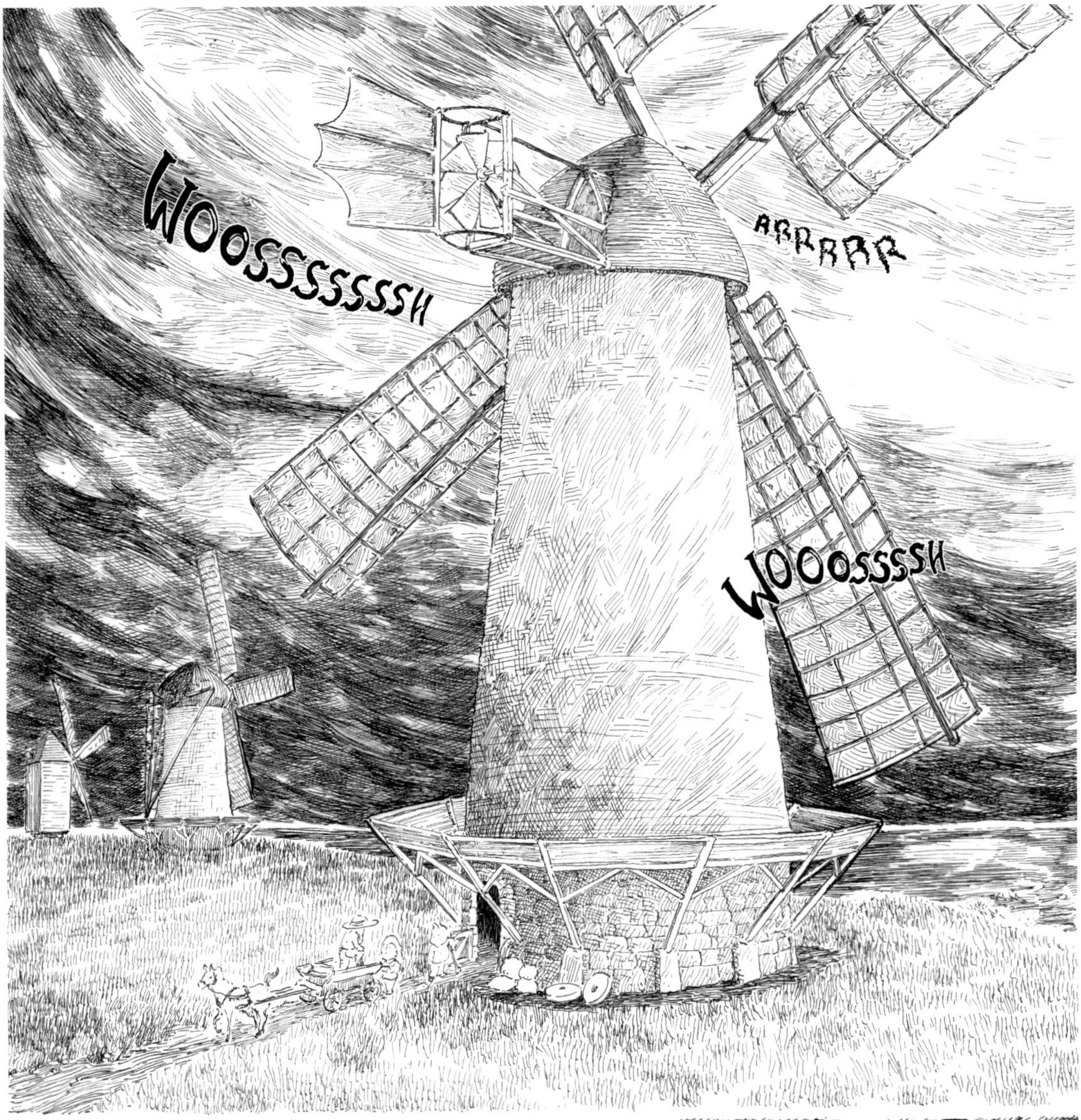
WOOSSSSSSSH
ARRRRRR
WOOOSSSSH

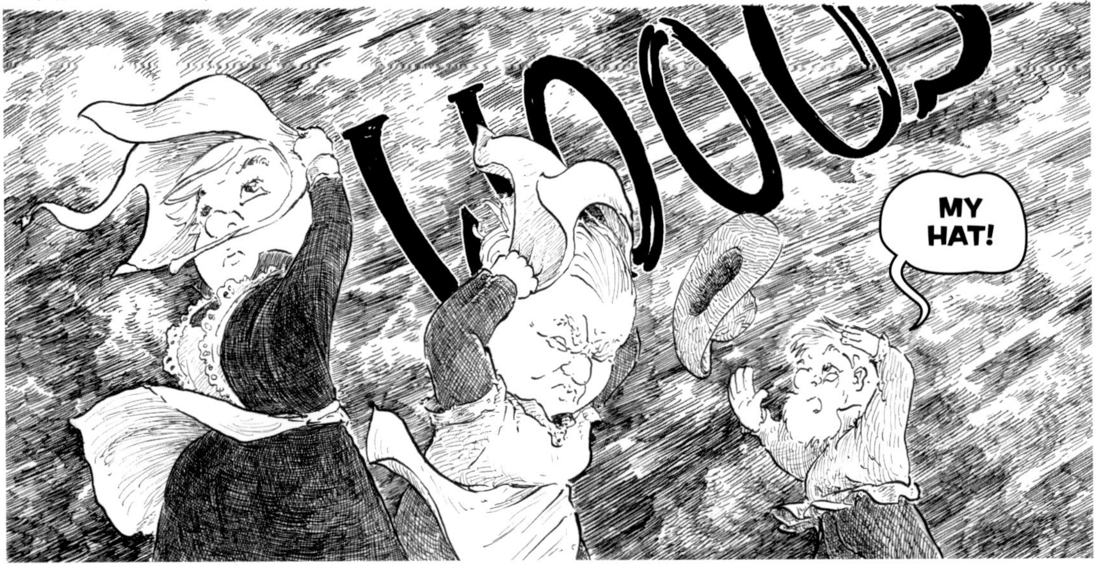
WOOOS
MY HAT!

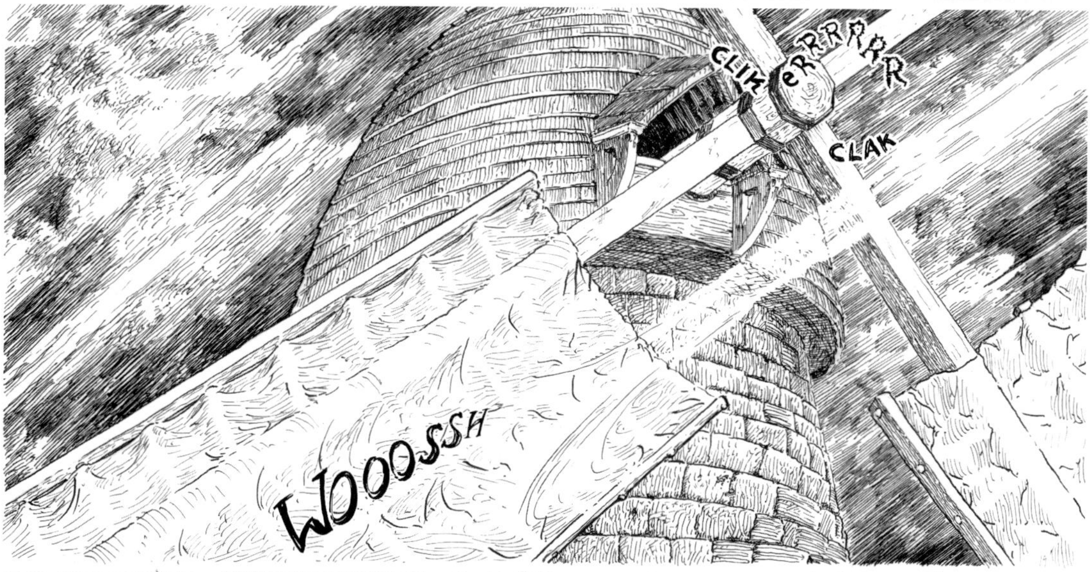
CLIK
eRRRRRR
CLAK
WOOOSSH

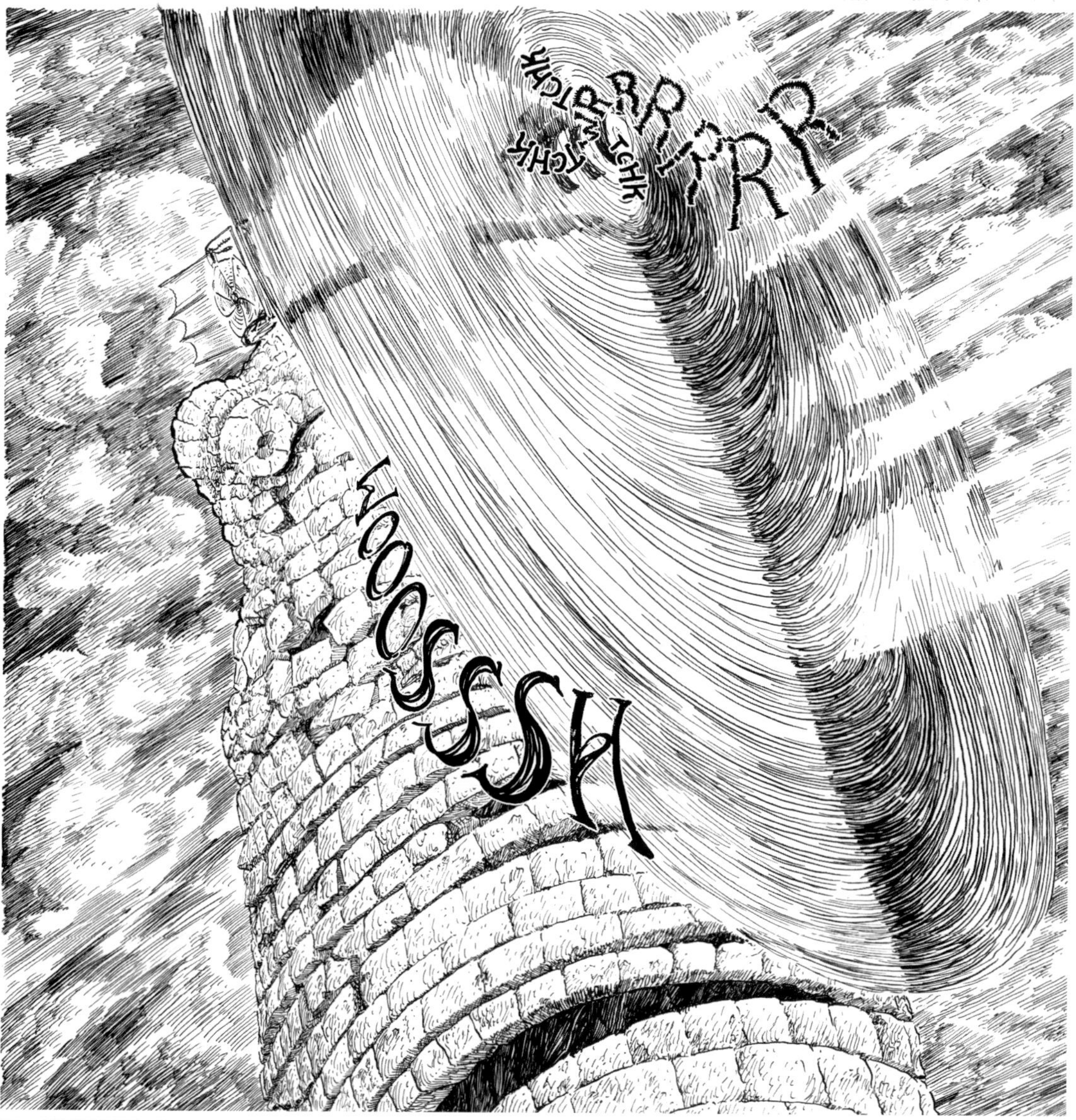
TCHK
TCHK
TCHK
WOOOSSSH

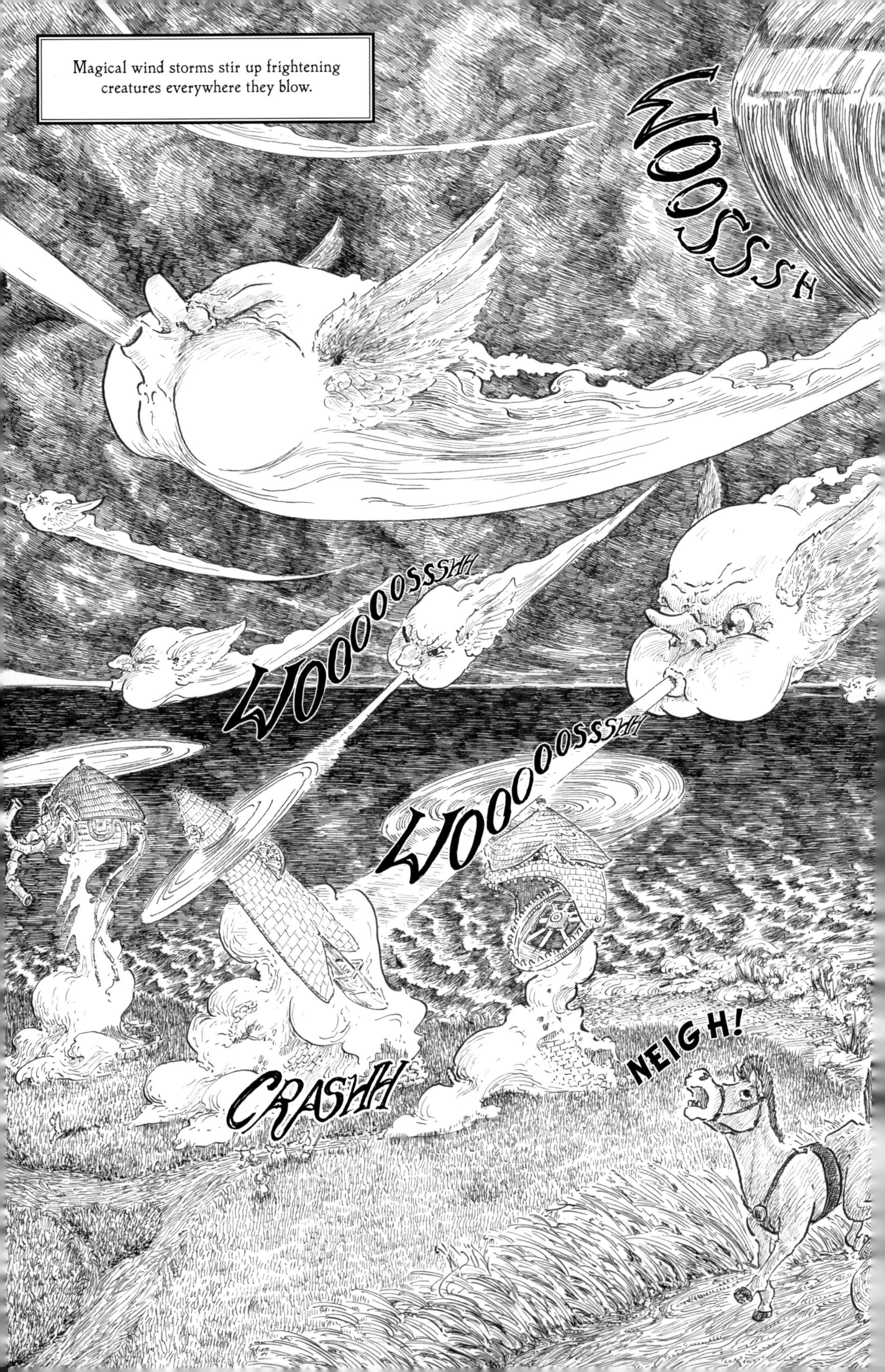
Magical wind storms stir up frightening creatures everywhere they blow.
WOOSSSH
WOOOOOOSSSHH
WOOOOOOSSSHH
CRASHH
NEIGH!

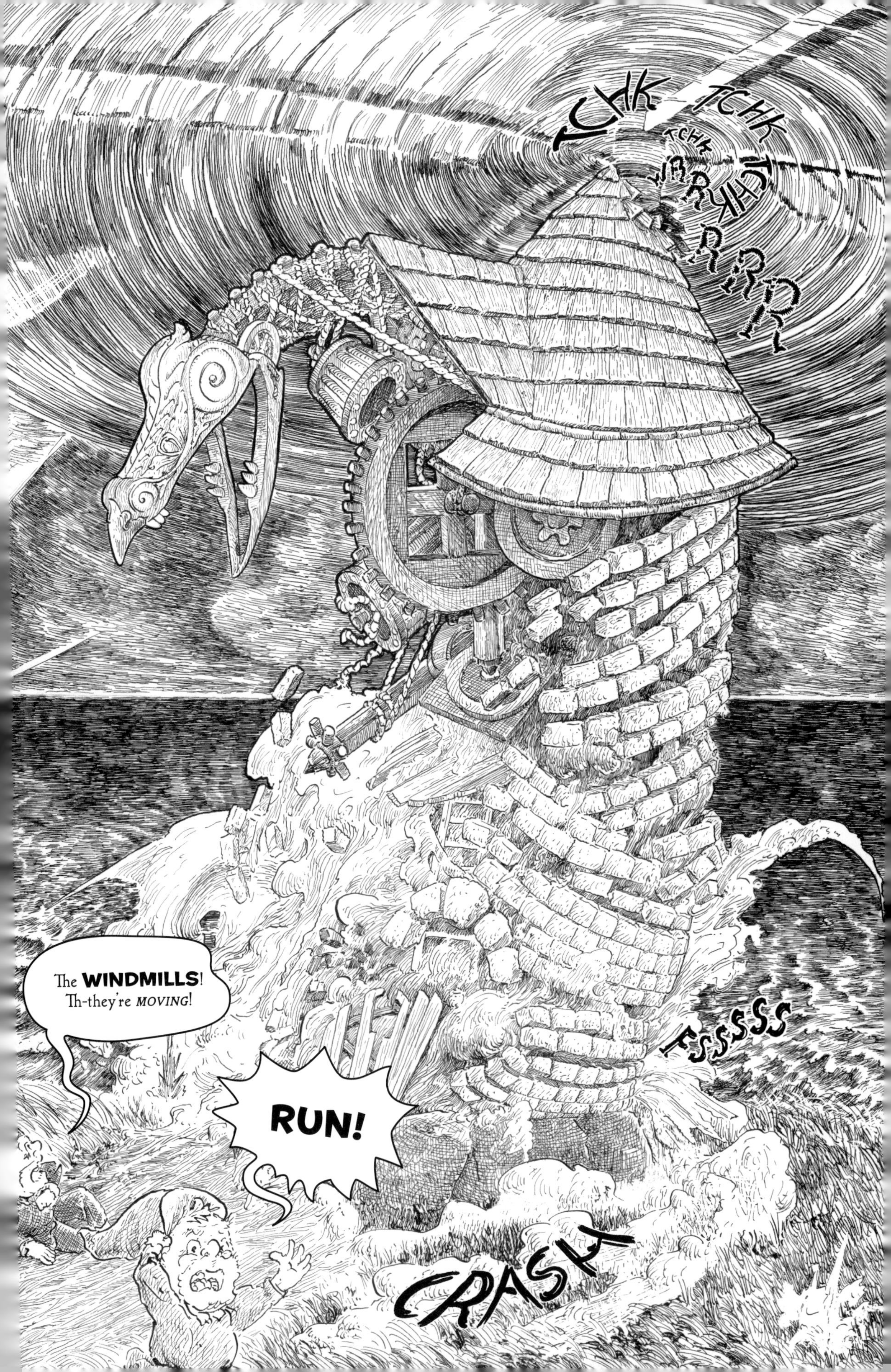
TCHK TCHK
TCHK
TCHKK
WRRRRRRR
The **WINDMILLS**!
Th-they're *MOVING*!
RUN!
FSSSSSS
CRASH

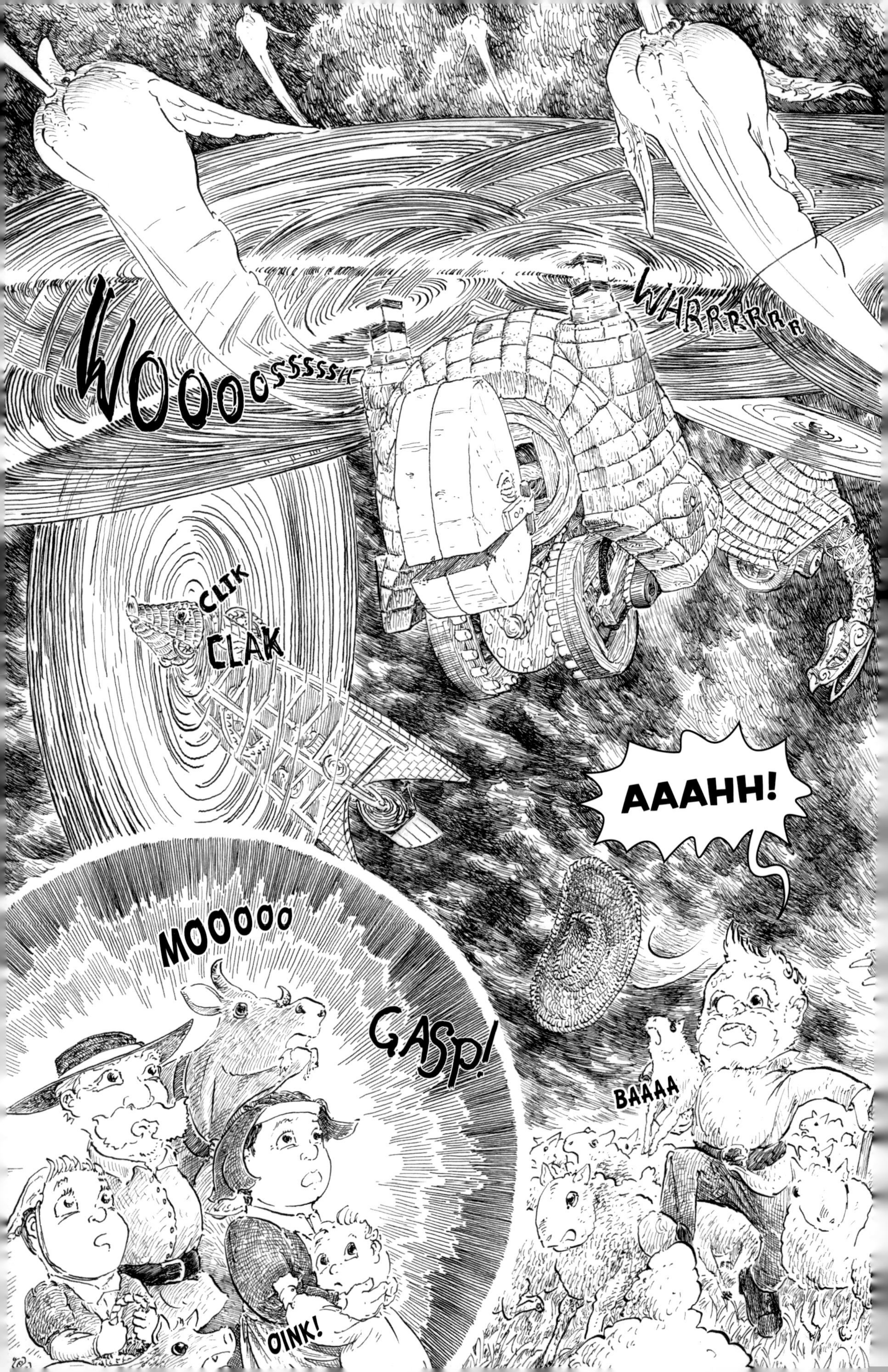
WOOOOSSSSSSH
WHRRRRRRR
CLIK
CLAK
AAAHH!
MOOOOO
GASP!
BAAAA
OINK!

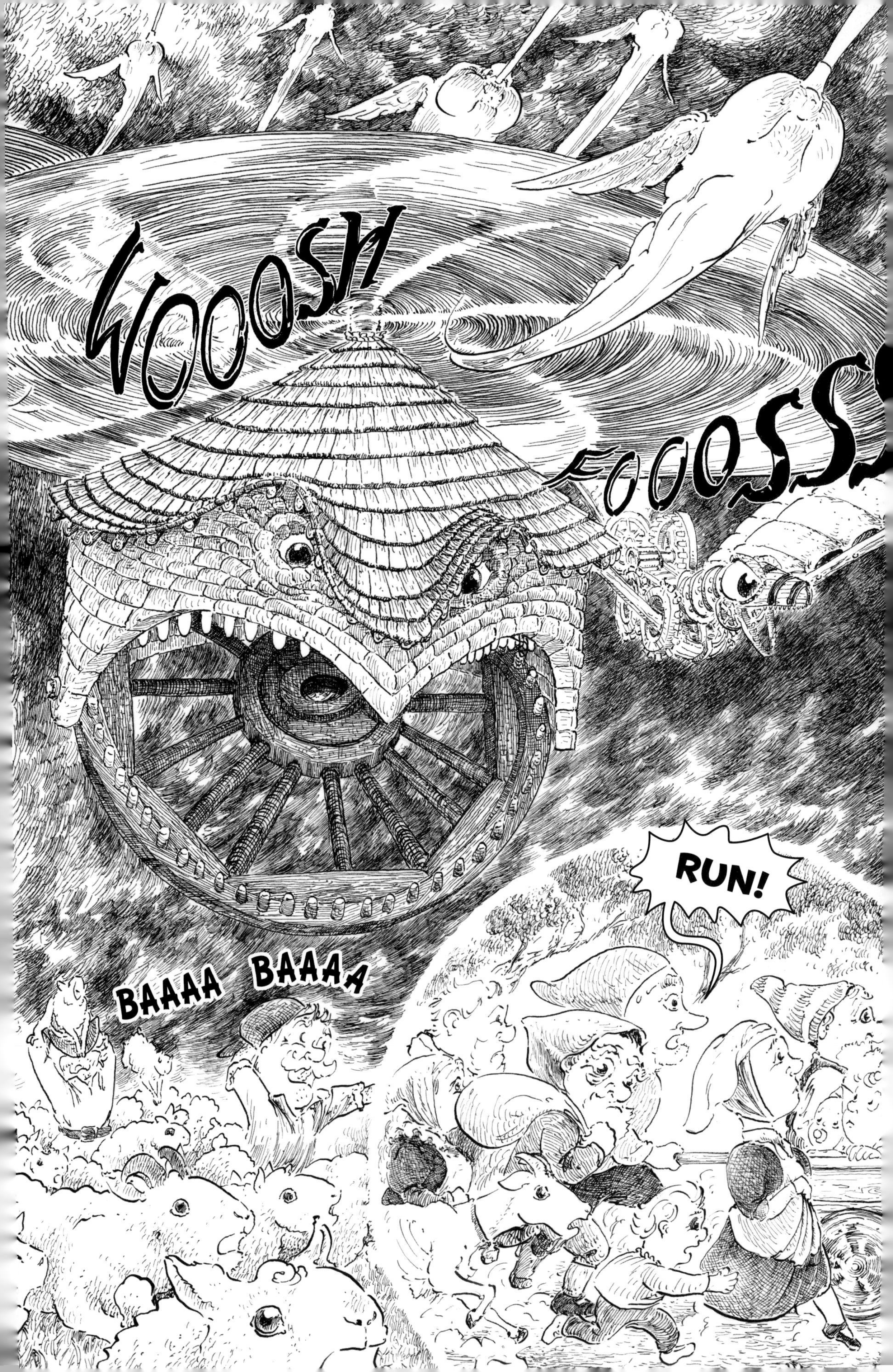
WOOOSH
FOOOSSS
RUN!
BAAAA BAAAA

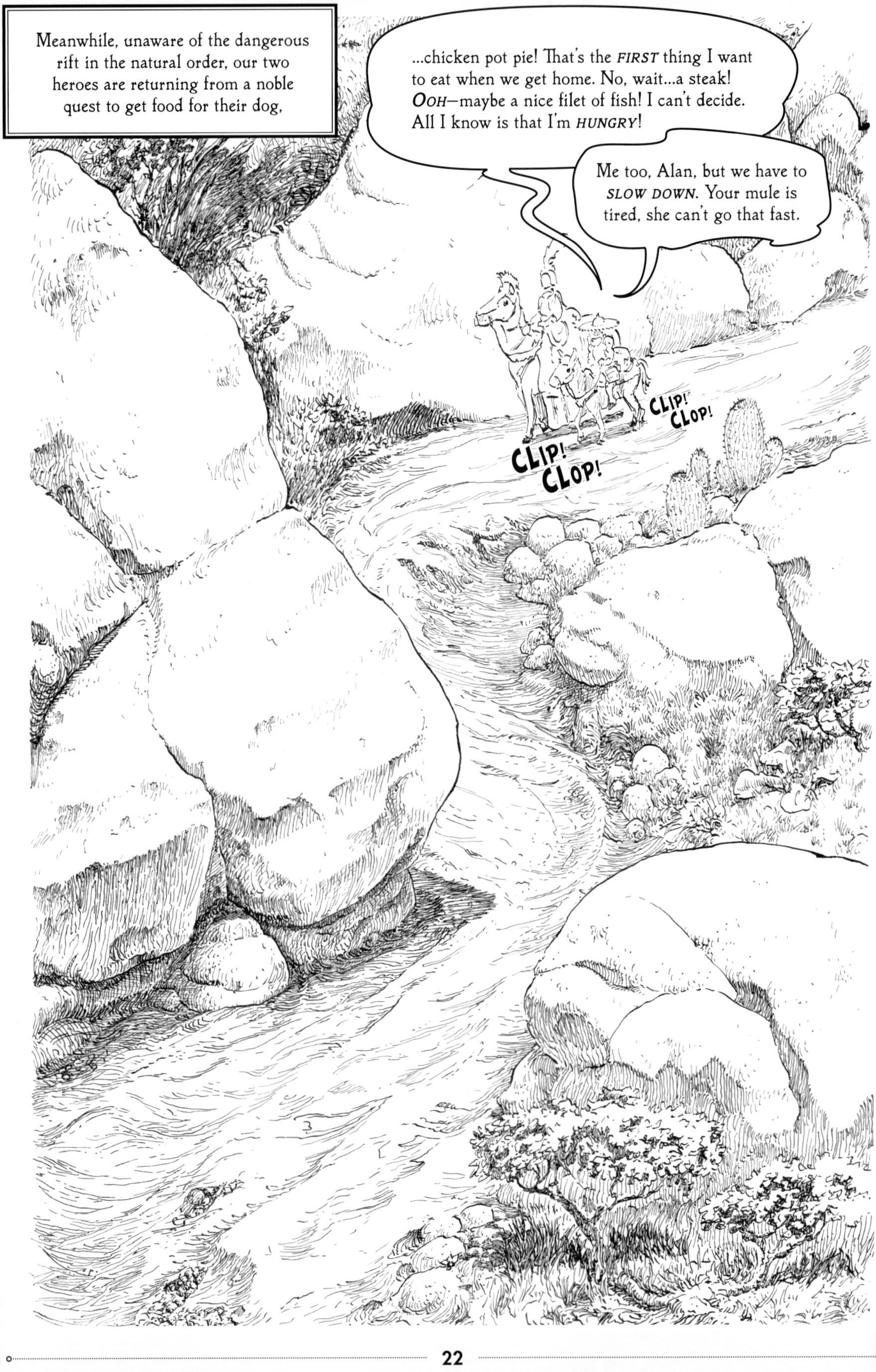

Meanwhile, unaware of the dangerous rift in the natural order, our two heroes are returning from a noble quest to get food for their dog,
...chicken pot pie! That's the FIRST thing I want to eat when we get home. No, wait...a steak! OOH—maybe a nice filet of fish! I can't decide. All I know is that I'm HUNGRY!
Me too, Alan, but we have to SLOW DOWN. Your mule is tired, she can't go that fast.
CLIP! CLOP!
CLIP! CLOP!

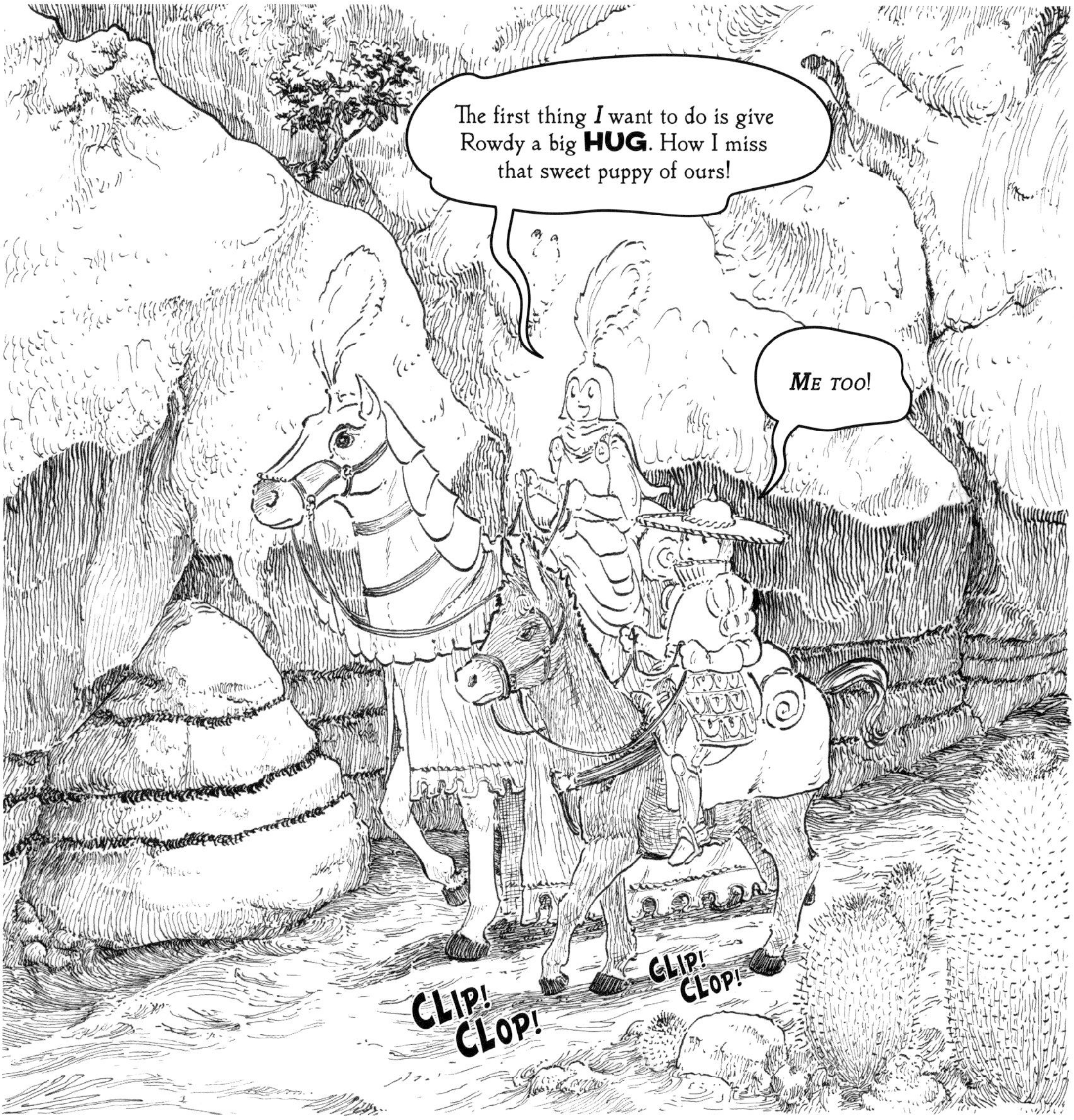
The first thing *I* want to do is give Rowdy a big **HUG**. How I miss that sweet puppy of ours!
ME TOO!
CLIP! CLOP!
CLIP! CLOP!

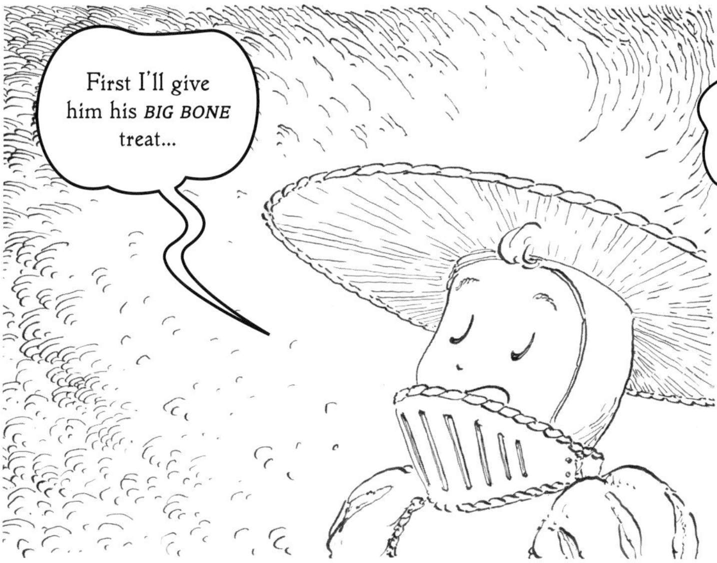
First I'll give him his *BIG BONE* treat...

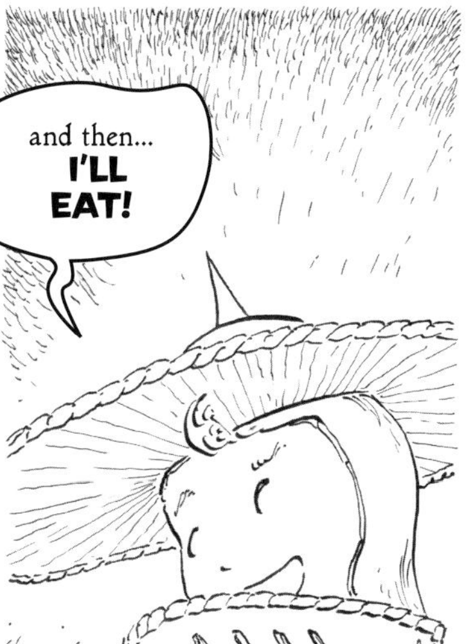
and then... **I'LL EAT!**
RUMBLE RUMBLE

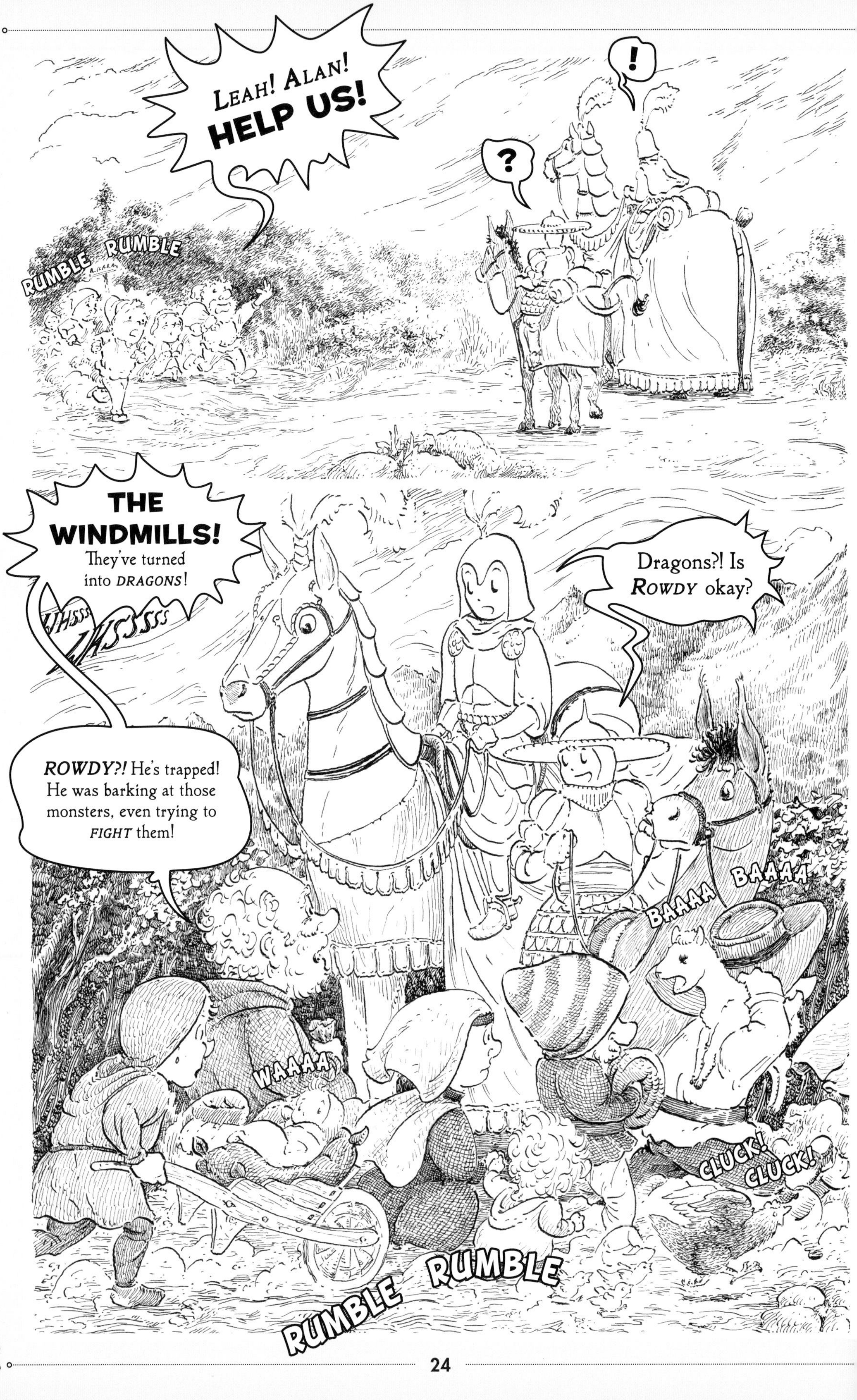
LEAH! ALAN! HELP US!
RUMBLE RUMBLE
?
!
THE WINDMILLS! They've turned into DRAGONS!
Dragons?! Is ROWDY okay?
ROWDY?! He's trapped! He was barking at those monsters, even trying to FIGHT them!
BAAAA BAAAA
WAAAA
CLUCK! CLUCK!
RUMBLE RUMBLE

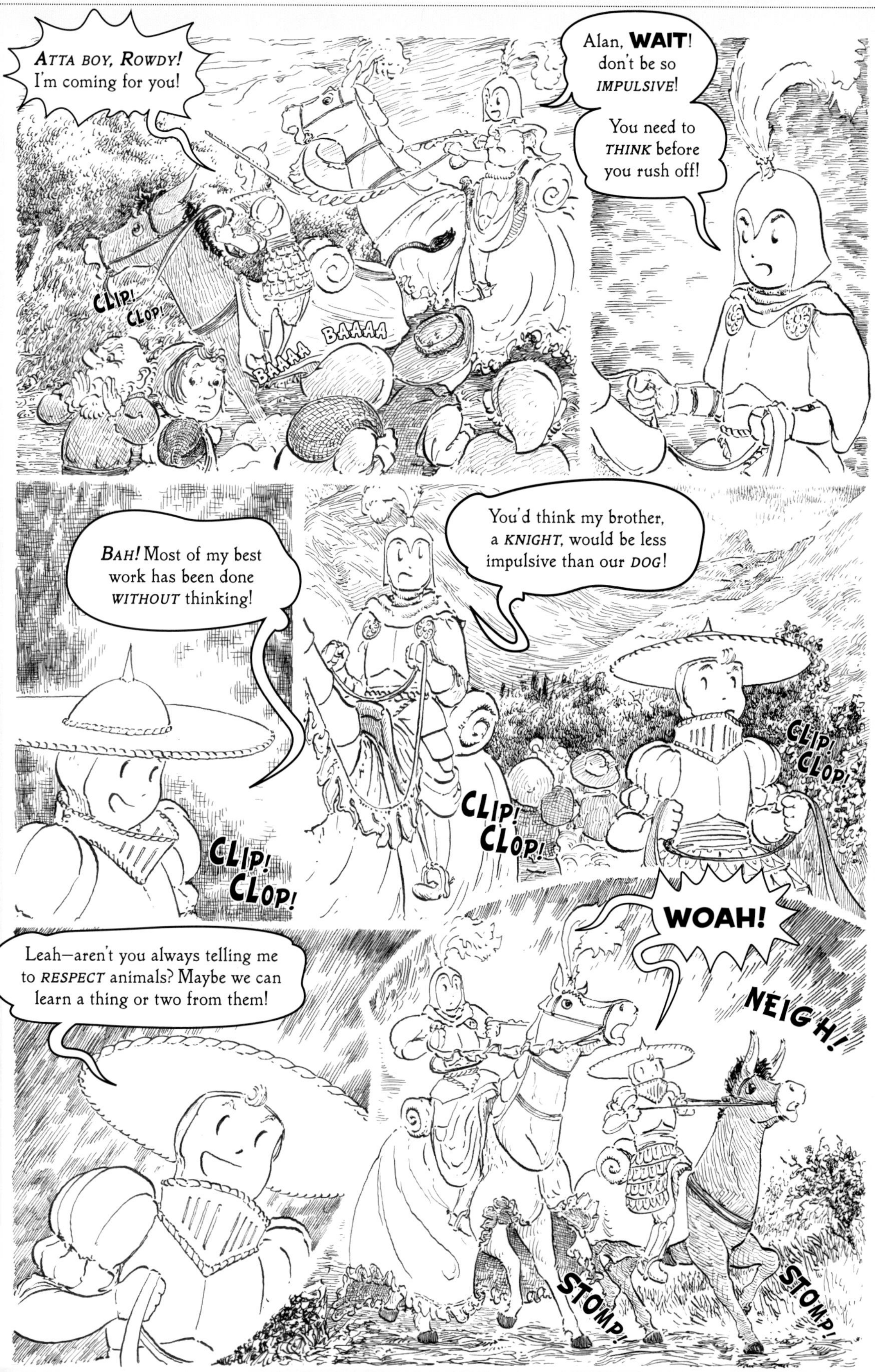

Atta boy, Rowdy! I'm coming for you!
CLIP! CLOP!
BAAAA BAAAA
Alan, **WAIT**! don't be so *IMPULSIVE*!
You need to *THINK* before you rush off!
Bah! Most of my best work has been done *WITHOUT* thinking!
CLIP! CLOP!
You'd think my brother, a *KNIGHT*, would be less impulsive than our *DOG*!
CLIP! CLOP!
CLIP! CLOP!
Leah—aren't you always telling me to *RESPECT* animals? Maybe we can learn a thing or two from them!
WOAH!
NEIGH!
STOMP!
STOMP!

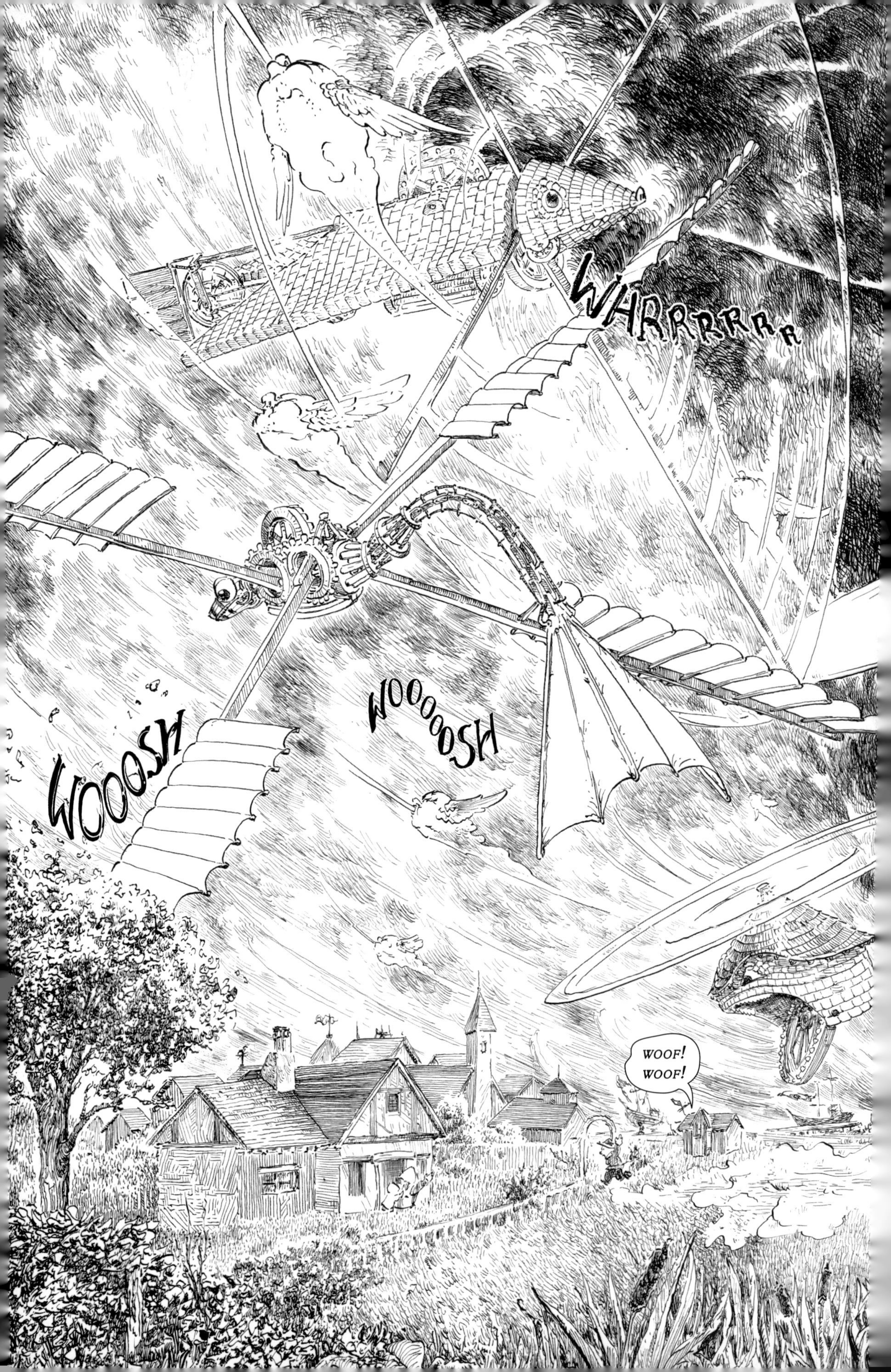
WHRRRRRRR
WOOOSH
WOOOOOSH
WOOF! WOOF!

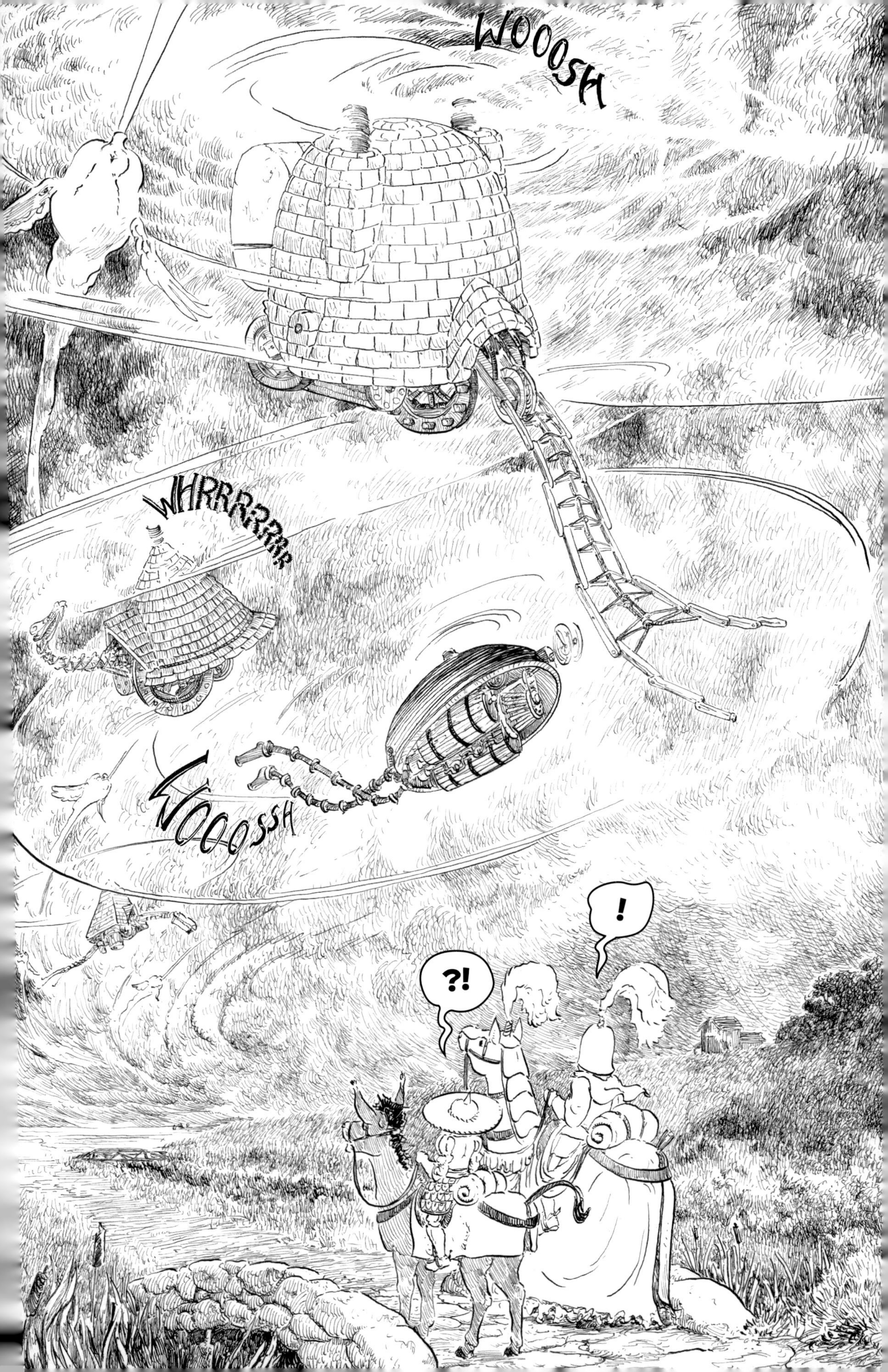
WOOOSH
WHRRRRRRR
WOOOSSH
?!
!

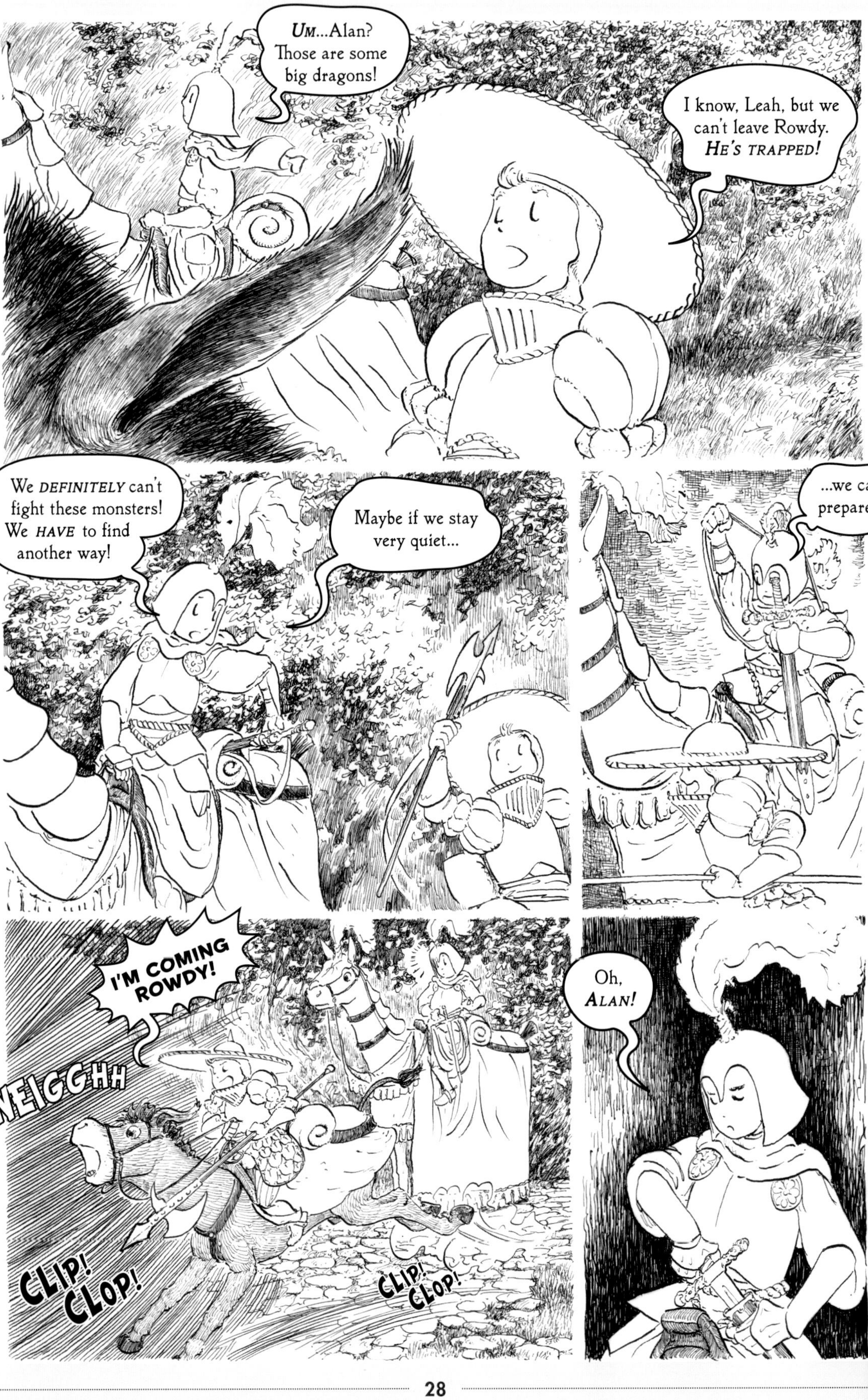
UM...Alan? Those are some big dragons!
I know, Leah, but we can't leave Rowdy. HE'S TRAPPED!
We DEFINITELY can't fight these monsters! We HAVE to find another way!
Maybe if we stay very quiet...
...we can prepare—
I'M COMING ROWDY!
NEIGGHH
CLIP! CLOP!
CLIP! CLOP!
Oh, ALAN!

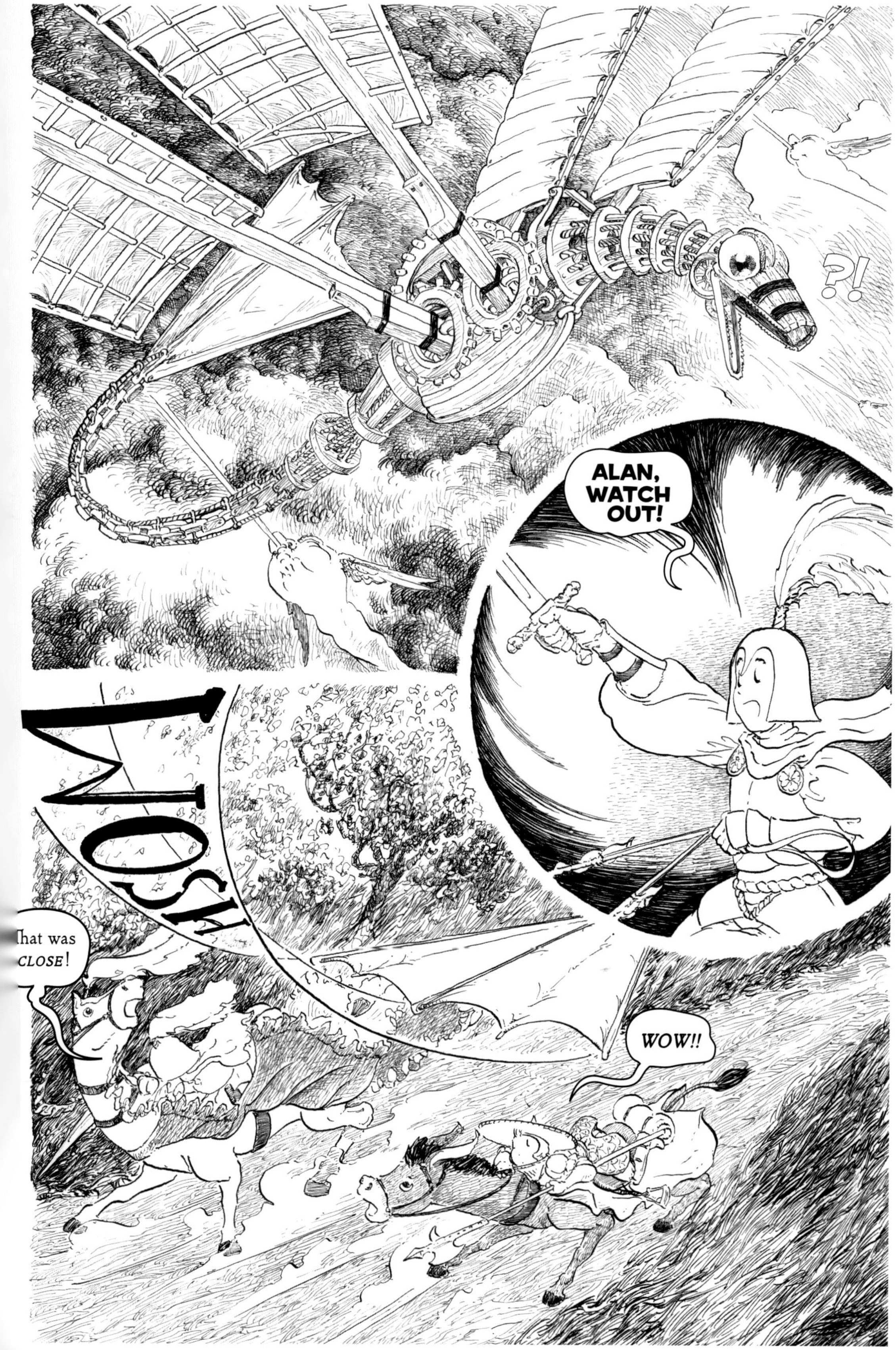
?!
ALAN, WATCH OUT!
WOSH
That was CLOSE!
WOW!!

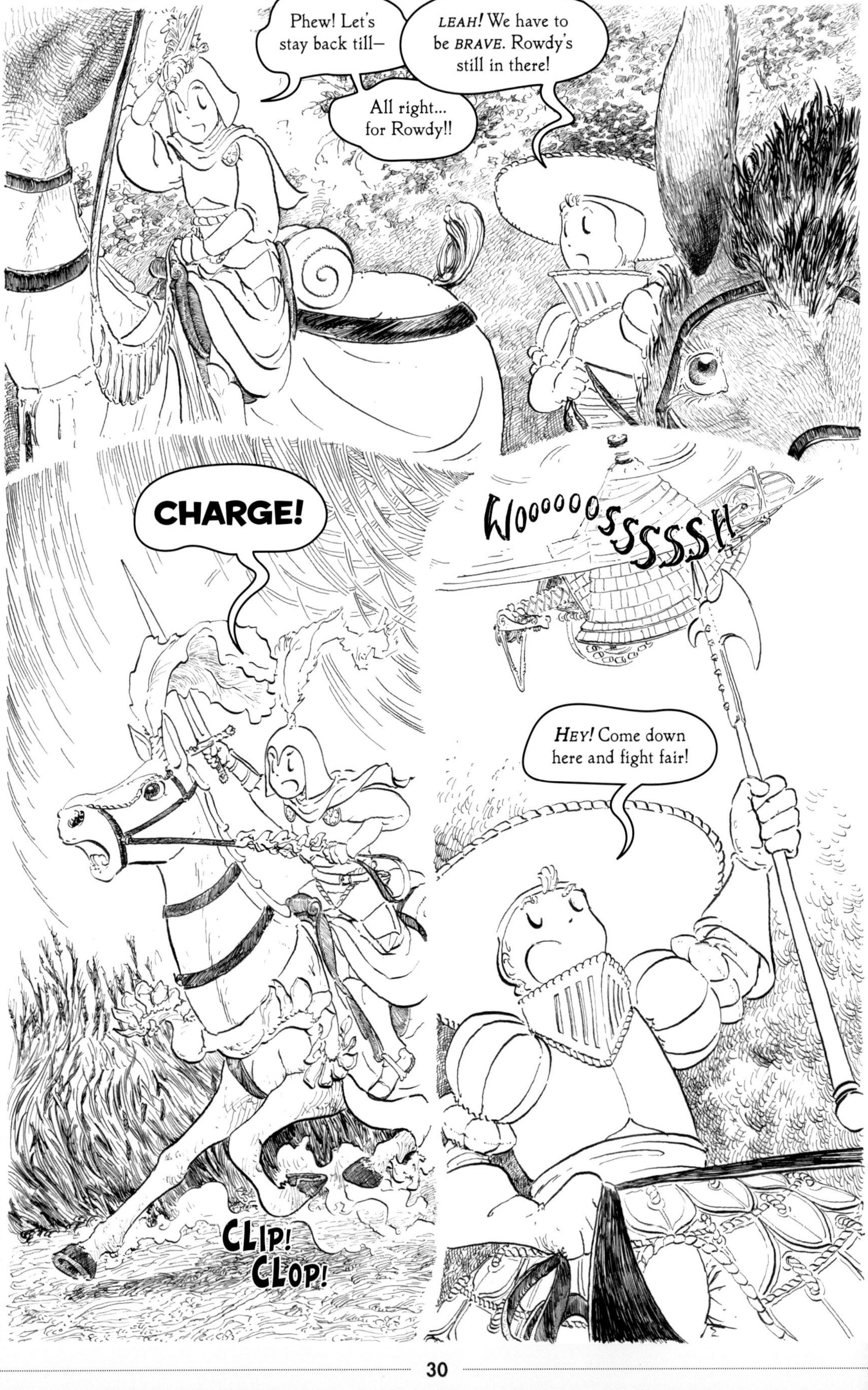
Phew! Let's stay back till—
LEAH! We have to be BRAVE. Rowdy's still in there!
All right... for Rowdy!!
CHARGE!
WOOOOOOOSSSSSH!
HEY! Come down here and fight fair!
CLIP! CLOP!

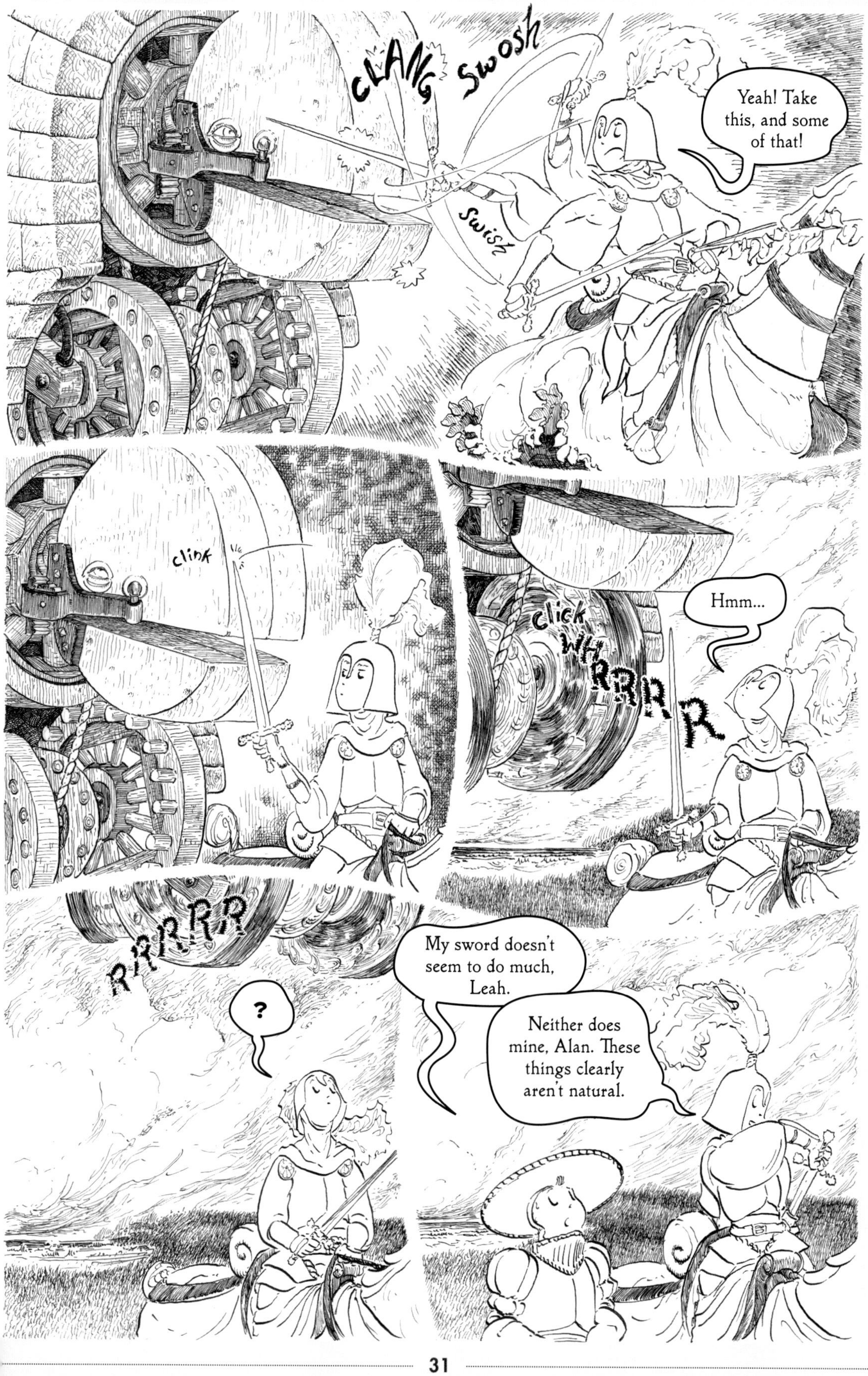
CLANG
Swosh
Yeah! Take this, and some of that!
Swish
clink
Hmm...
click
WHRRRRR
RRRRRR
My sword doesn't seem to do much, Leah.
?
Neither does mine, Alan. These things clearly aren't natural.

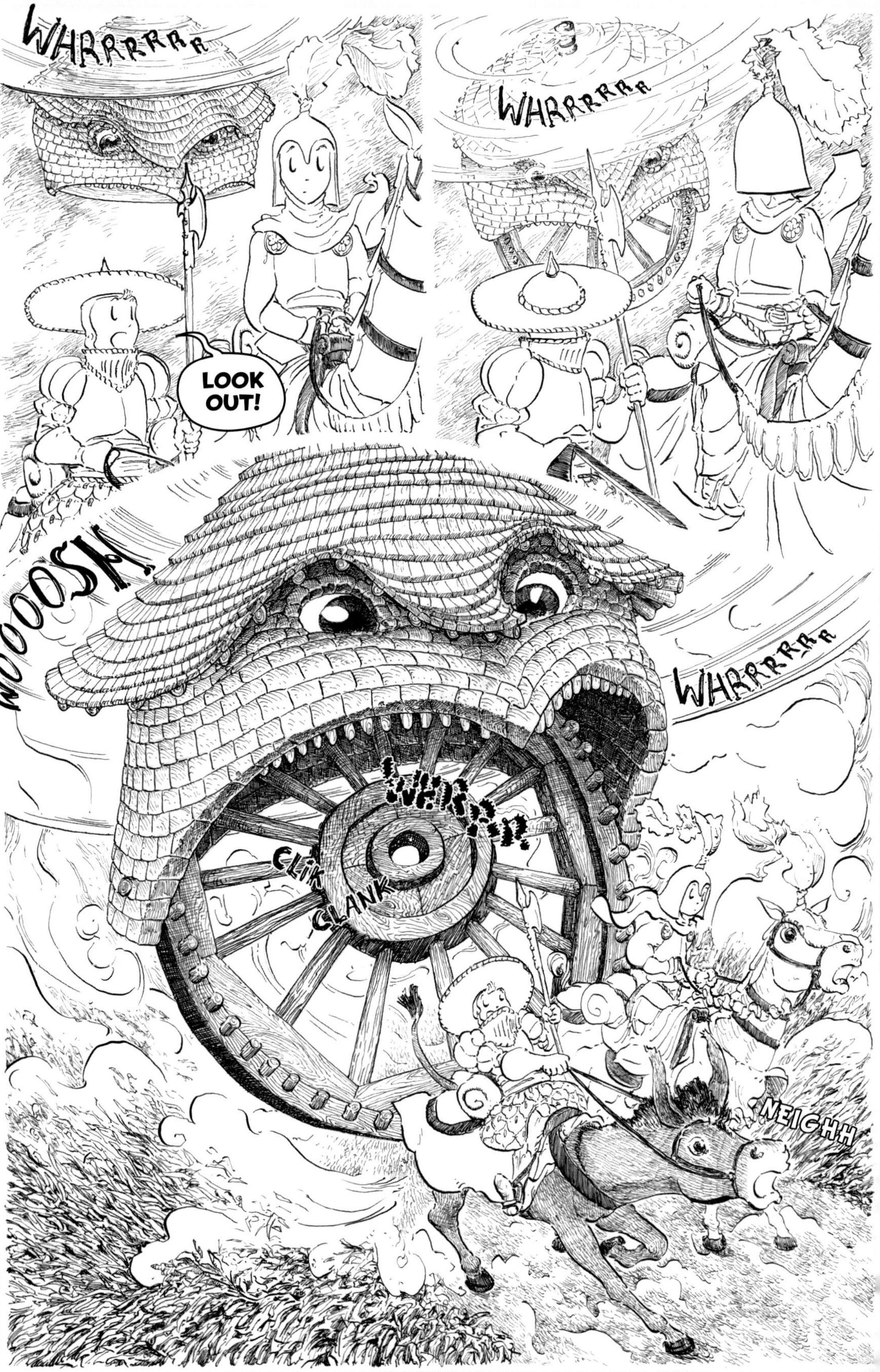
WHRRRRRR
LOOK OUT!
WHRRRRRR
WOOOOSH
WHRRRRRR
CLIK
CLANK
NEIGHH

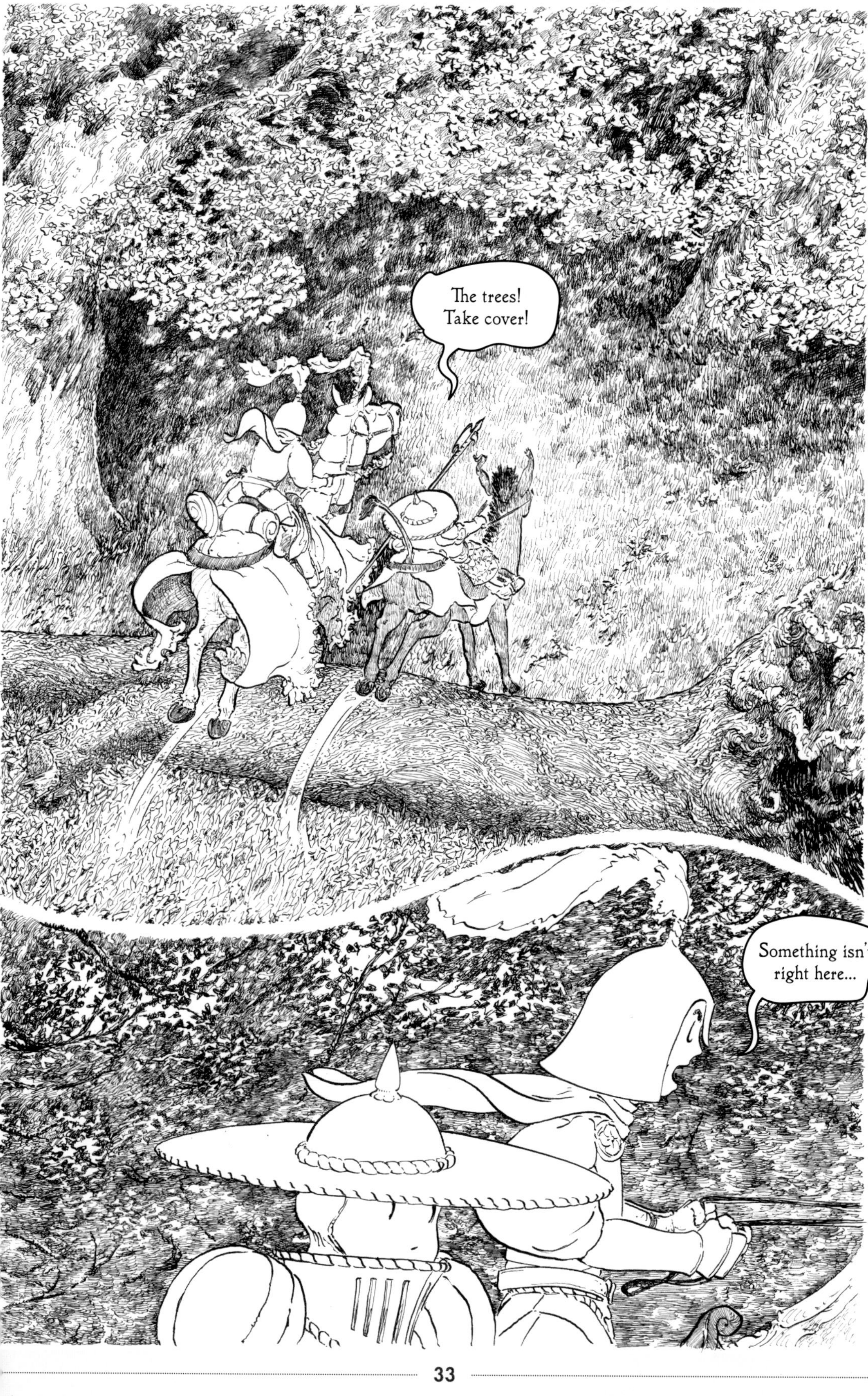
The trees!
Take cover!
Something isn't
right here...

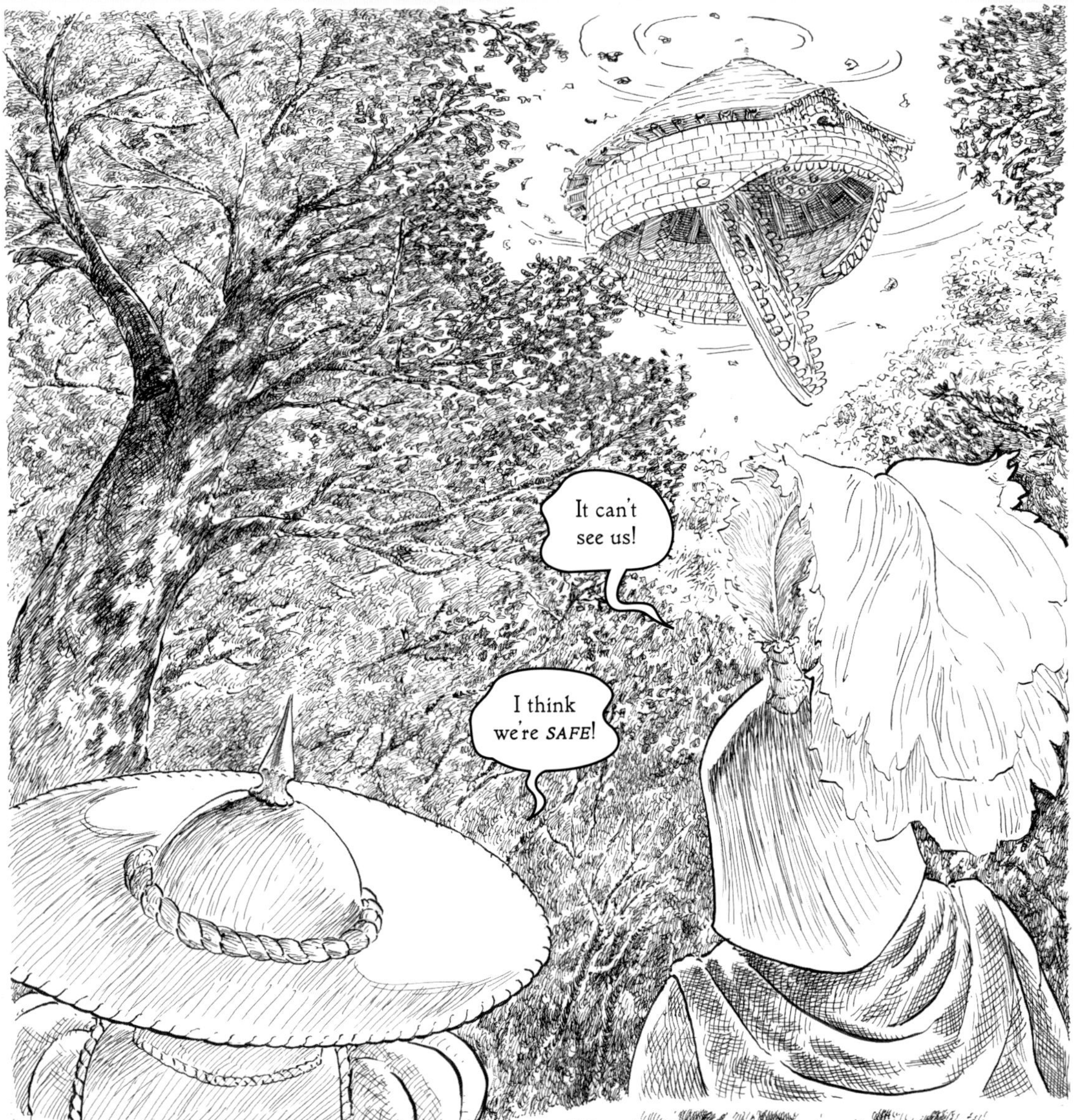
It can't see us!
I think we're *SAFE*!
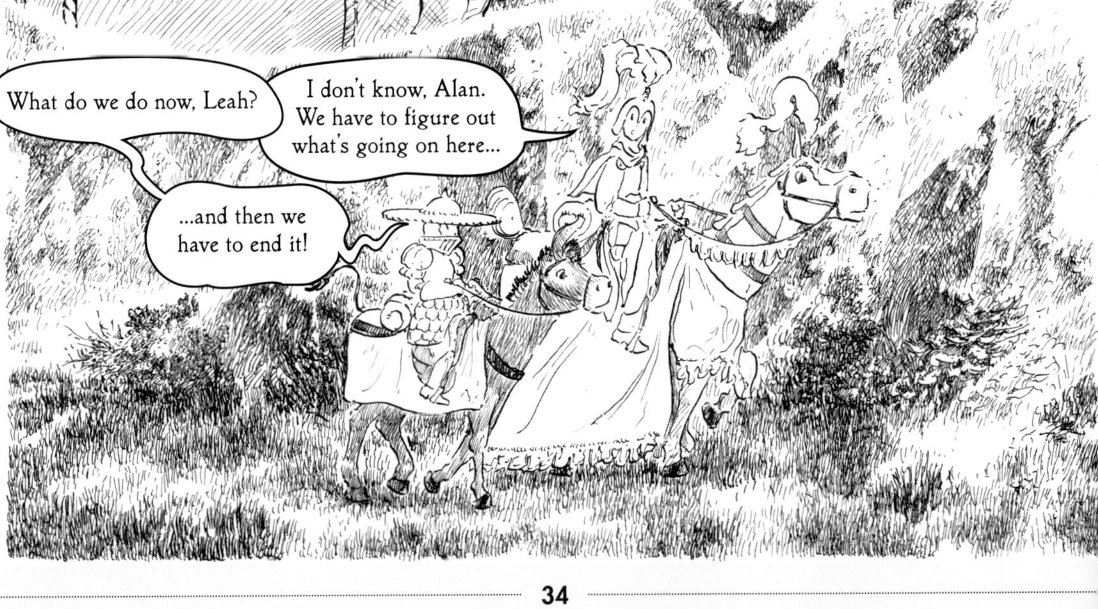
What do we do now, Leah?
I don't know, Alan. We have to figure out what's going on here...
...and then we have to end it!

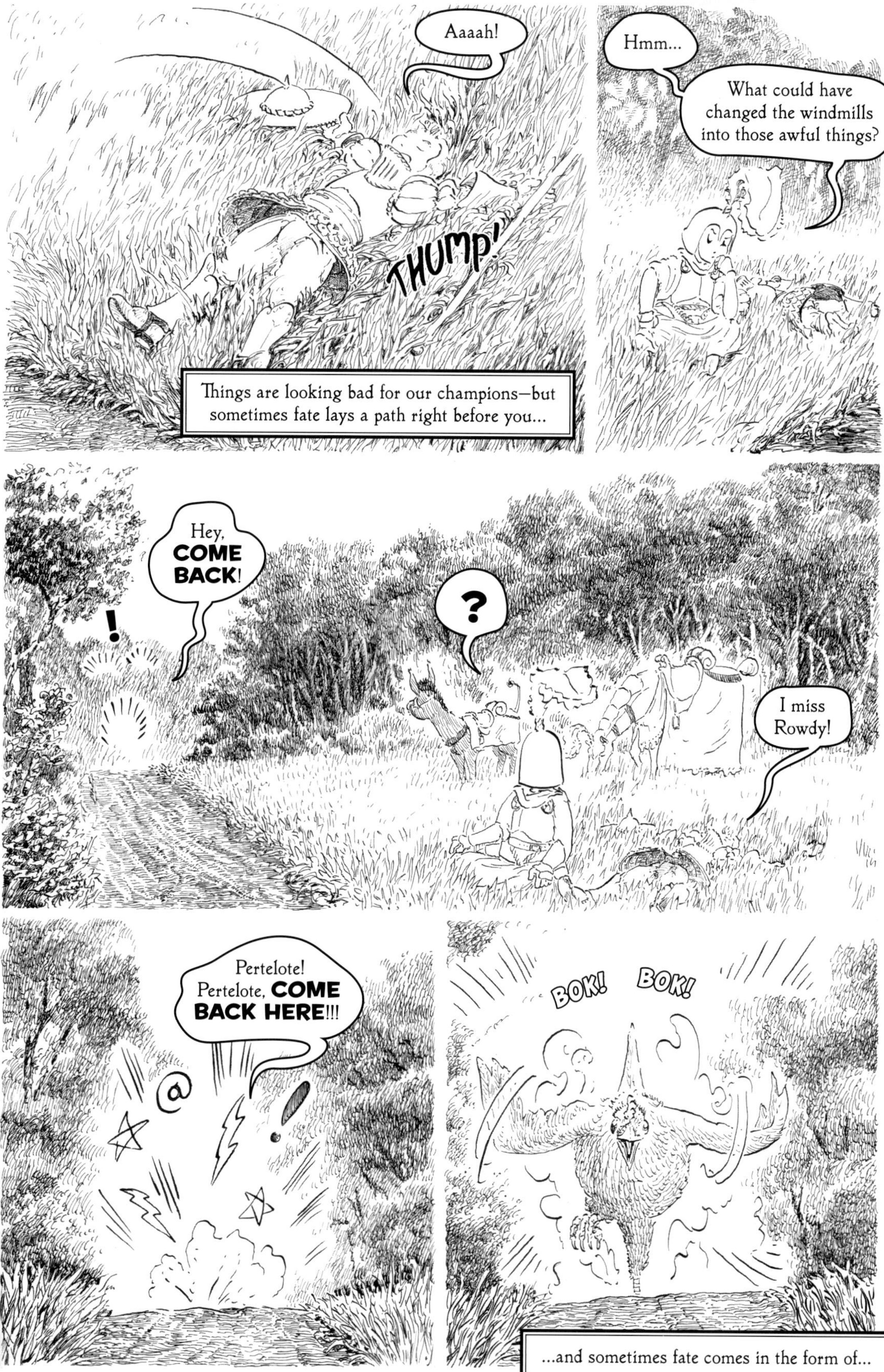

Aaaah!
THUMP!
Things are looking bad for our champions—but sometimes fate lays a path right before you...
Hmm...
What could have changed the windmills into those awful things?
Hey, **COME BACK**!
!
?
I miss Rowdy!
Pertelote! Pertelote, **COME BACK HERE**!!!
BOK! BOK!
...and sometimes fate comes in the form of...

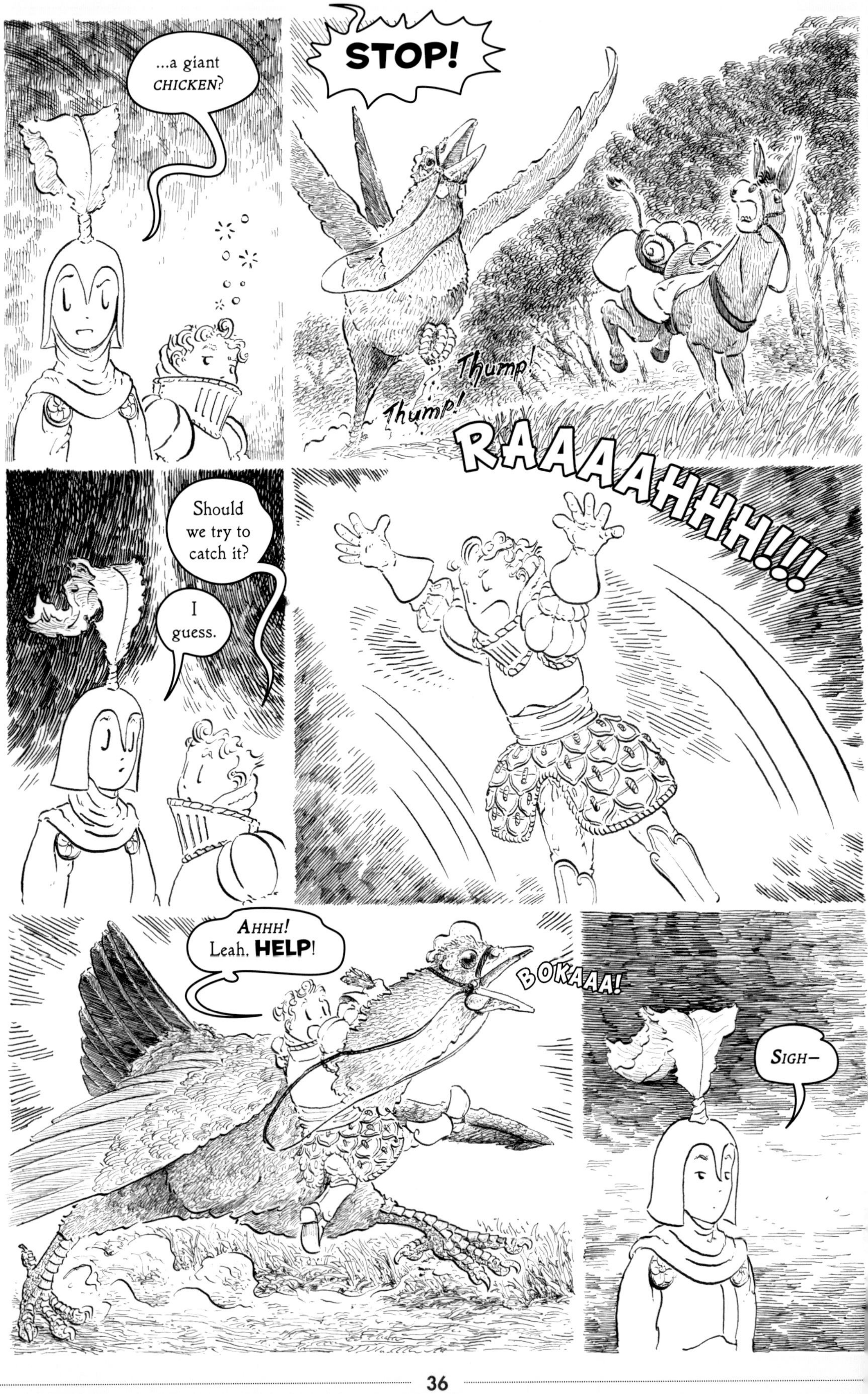

...a giant *CHICKEN*?
STOP!
Thump!
Thump!
RAAAAAHHHH!!!
Should we try to catch it?
I guess.
AHHH! Leah, **HELP**!
BOKAAA!
SIGH—

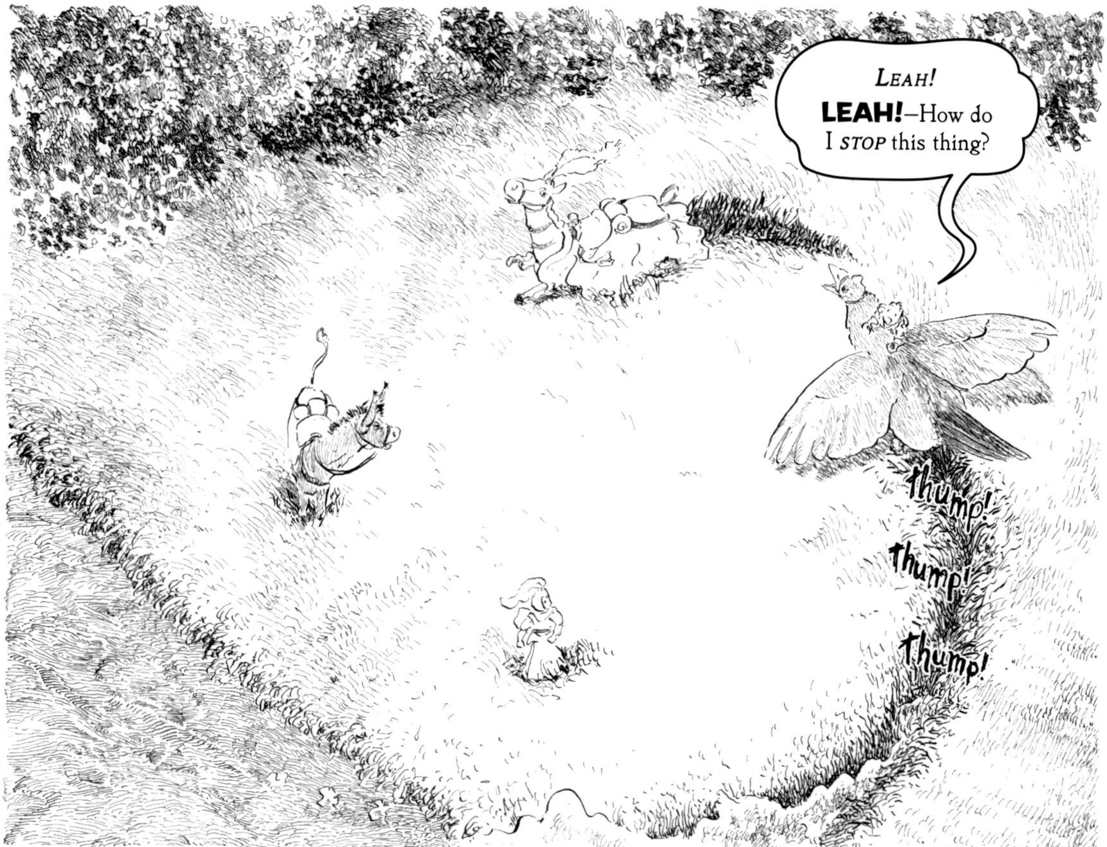
LEAH!
LEAH!—How do I STOP this thing?
thump! thump! thump!

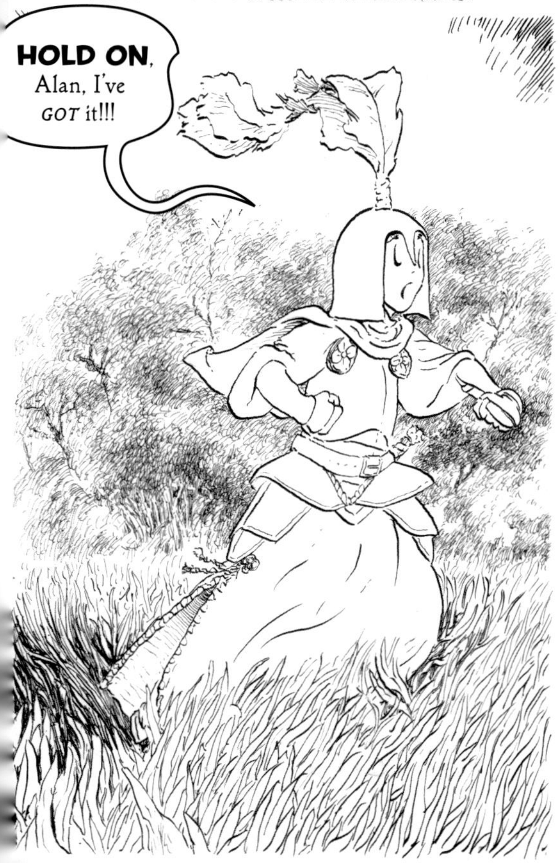
HOLD ON, Alan, I've GOT it!!!

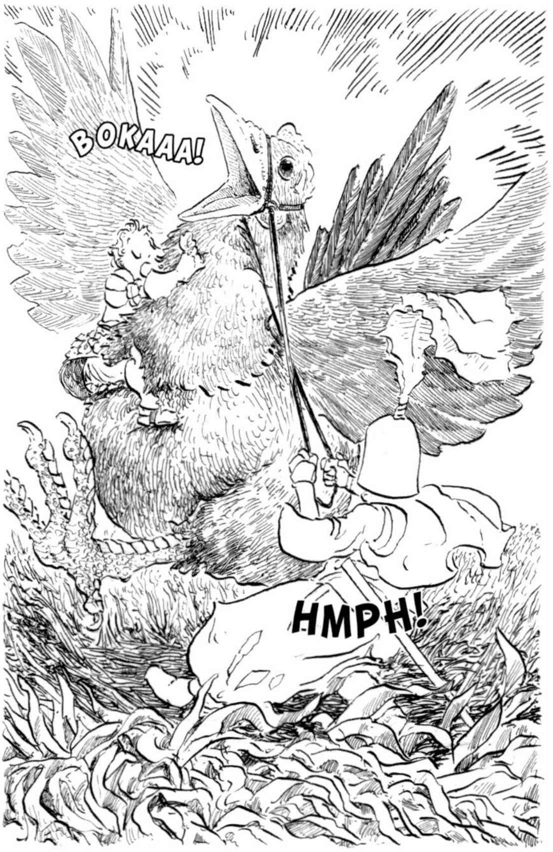
BOKAAA!
HMPH!

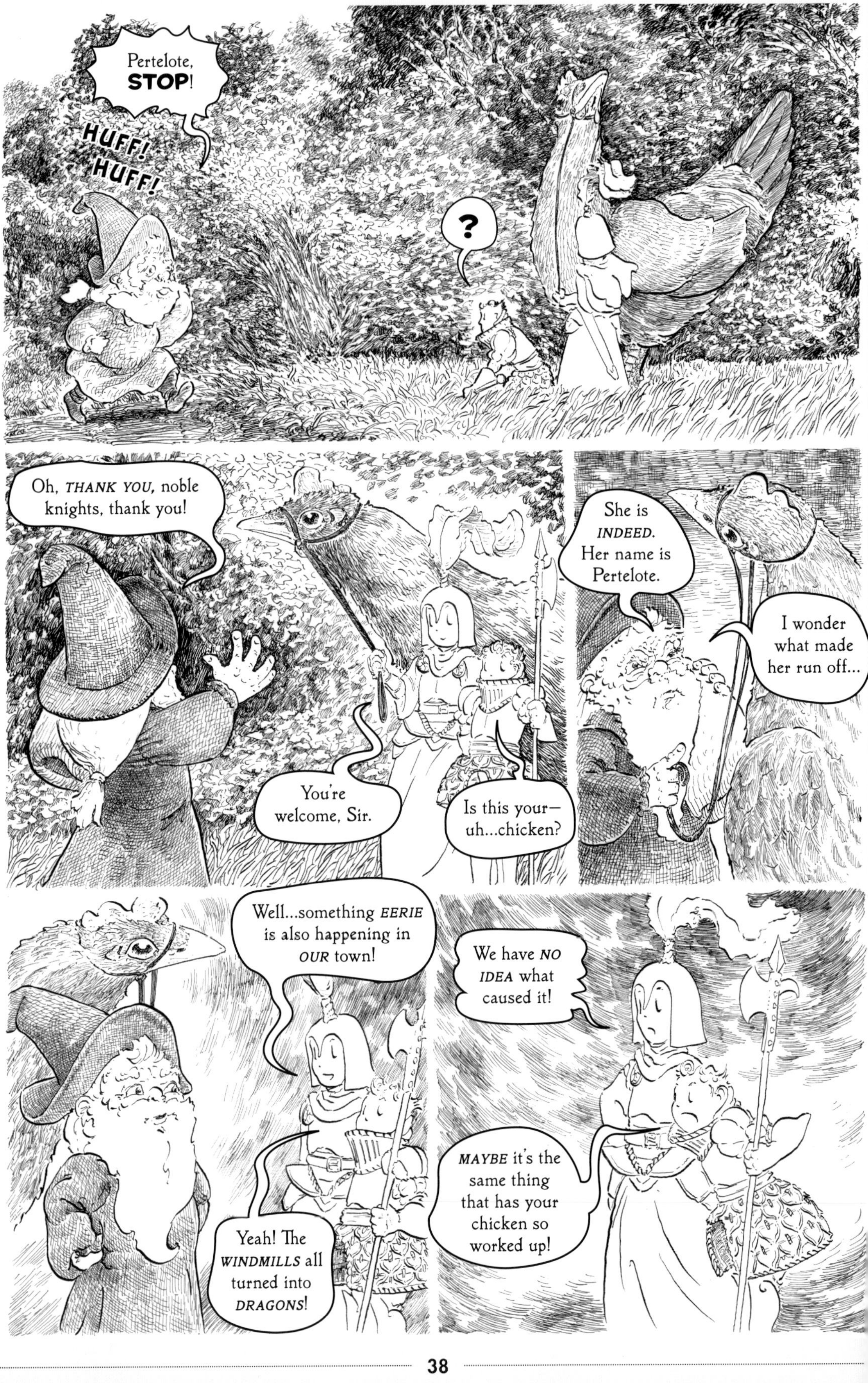

Pertelote, STOP!
HUFF! HUFF!
?
Oh, THANK YOU, noble knights, thank you!
You're welcome, Sir.
Is this your—uh...chicken?
She is INDEED. Her name is Pertelote.
I wonder what made her run off...
Well...something EERIE is also happening in OUR town!
Yeah! The WINDMILLS all turned into DRAGONS!
We have NO IDEA what caused it!
MAYBE it's the same thing that has your chicken so worked up!

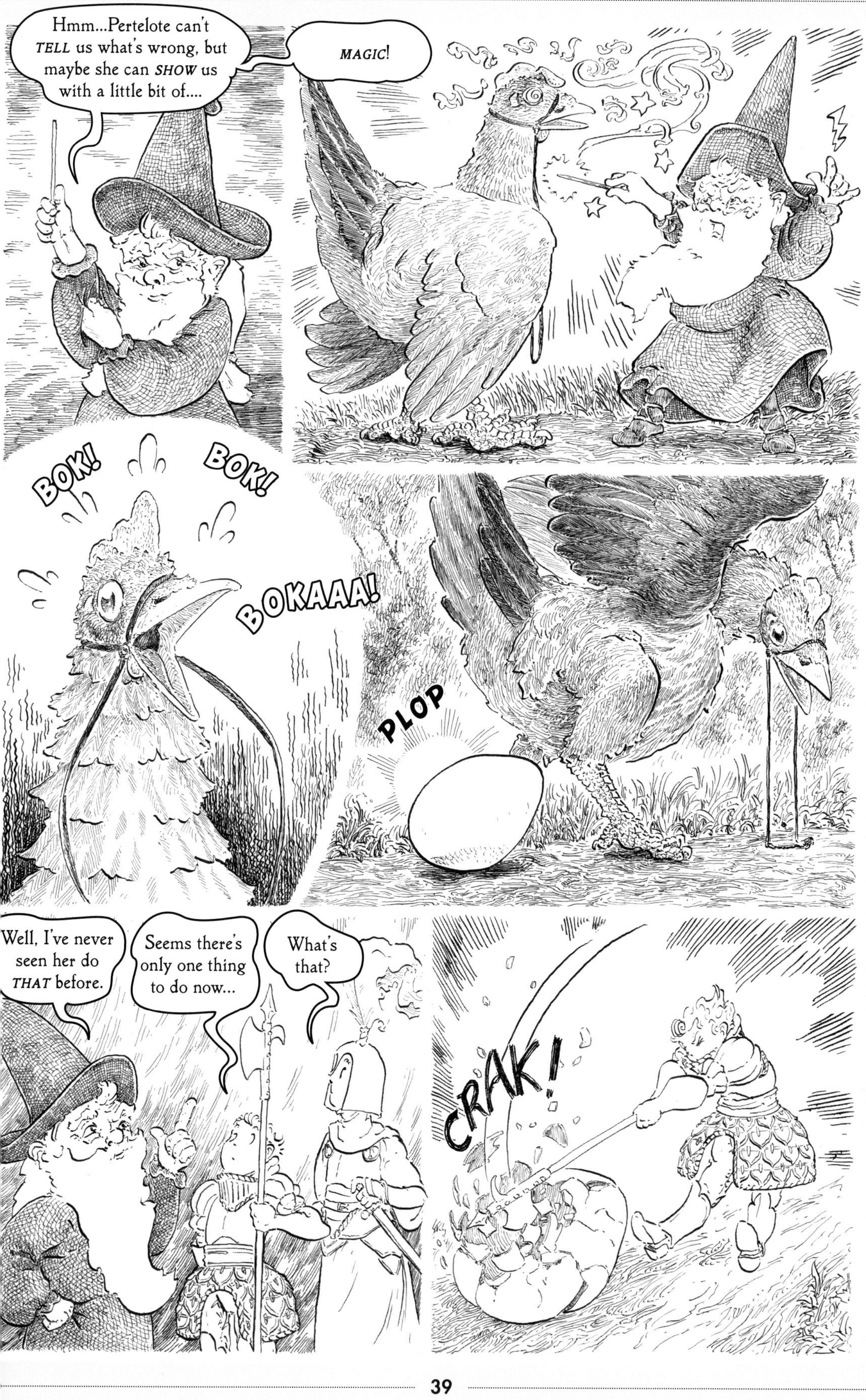
Hmm...Pertelote can't *TELL* us what's wrong, but maybe she can *SHOW* us with a little bit of....
MAGIC!
BOK!
BOK!
BOKAAA!
PLOP
Well, I've never seen her do *THAT* before.
Seems there's only one thing to do now...
What's that?
CRAK!

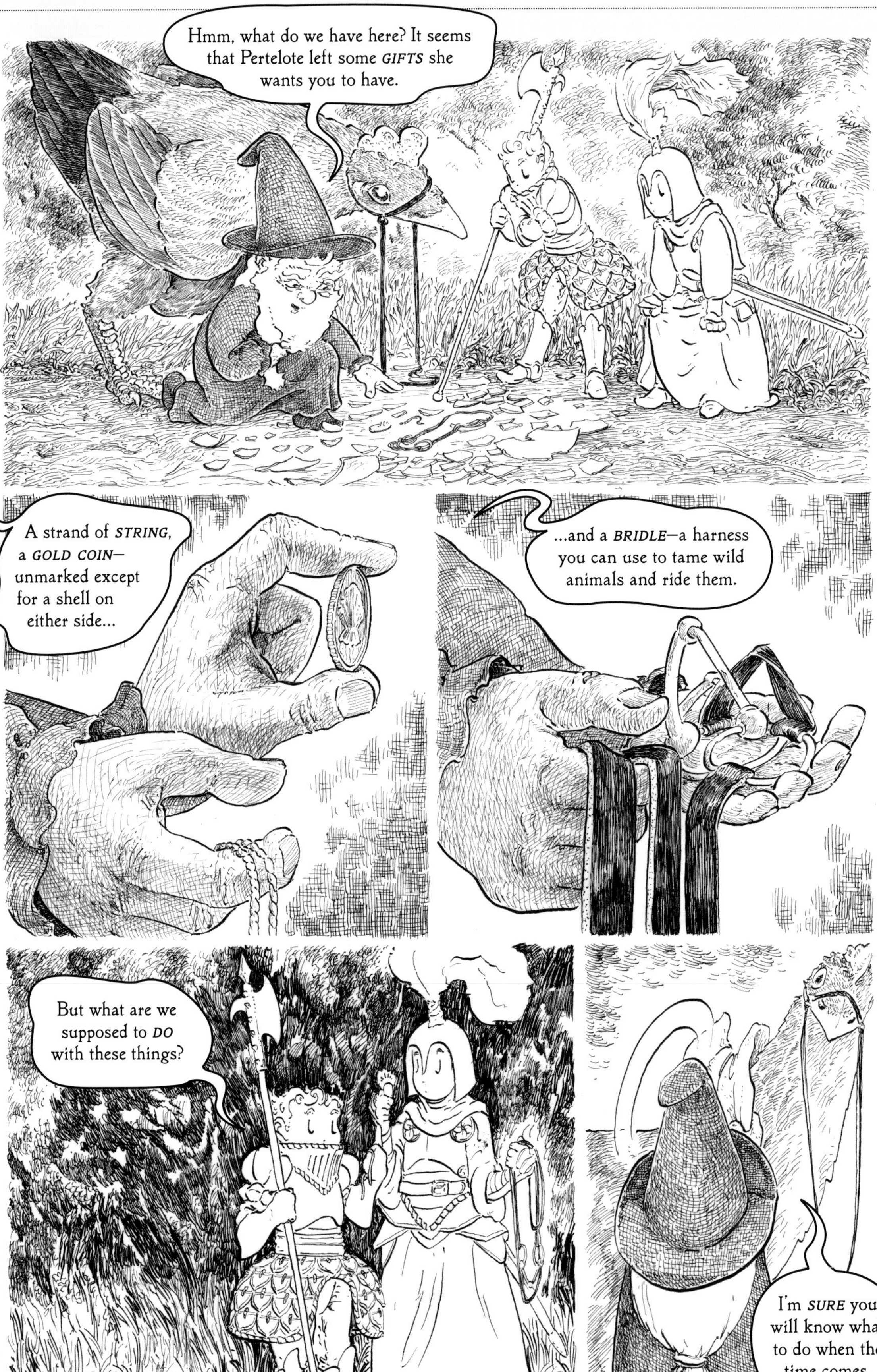
Hmm, what do we have here? It seems that Pertelote left some GIFTS she wants you to have.
A strand of STRING, a GOLD COIN—unmarked except for a shell on either side...
...and a BRIDLE—a harness you can use to tame wild animals and ride them.
But what are we supposed to DO with these things?
I'm SURE you will know wha to do when th time comes.

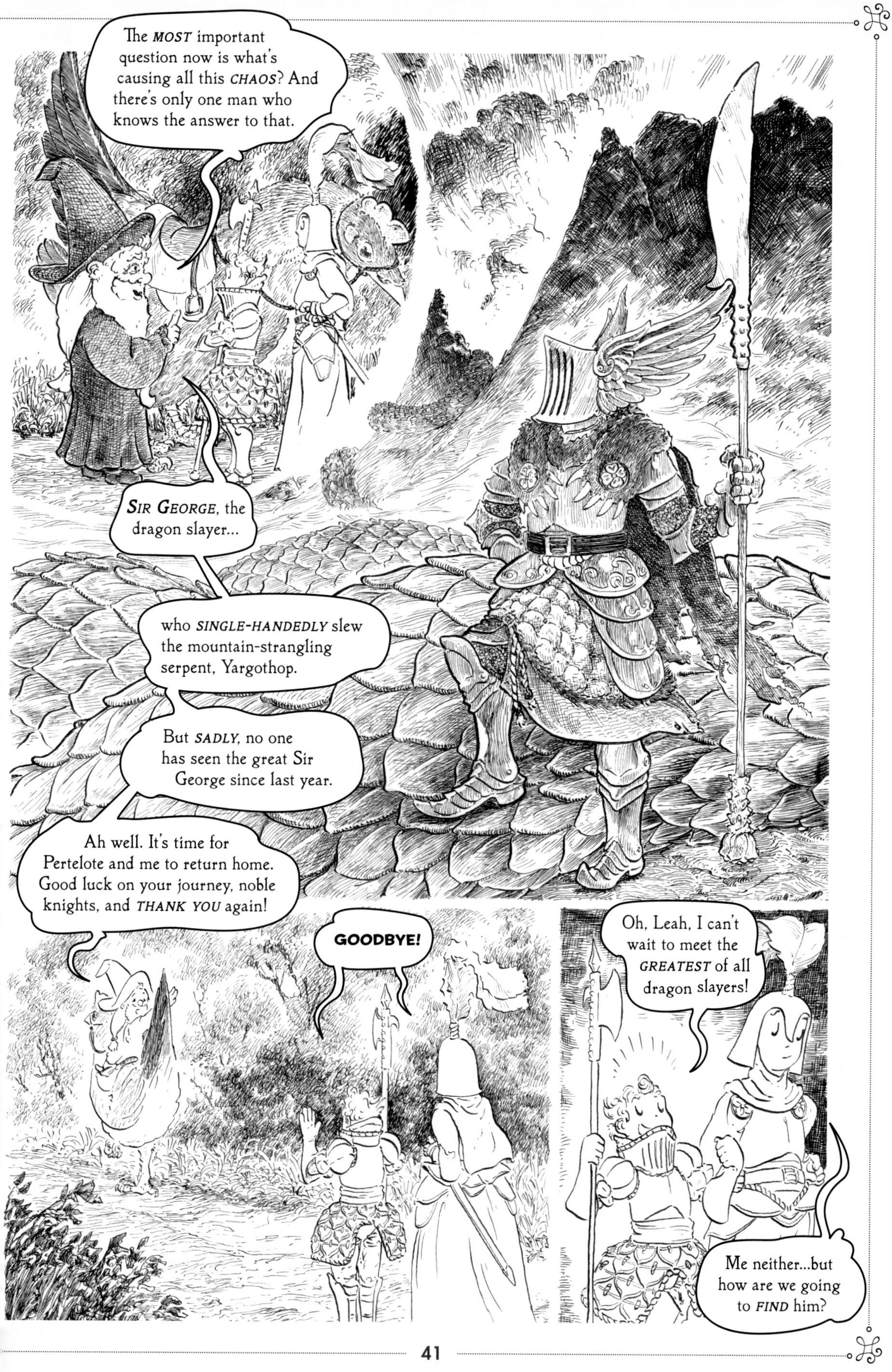
The MOST important question now is what's causing all this CHAOS? And there's only one man who knows the answer to that.
SIR GEORGE, the dragon slayer...
who SINGLE-HANDEDLY slew the mountain-strangling serpent, Yargothop.
But SADLY, no one has seen the great Sir George since last year.
Ah well. It's time for Pertelote and me to return home. Good luck on your journey, noble knights, and THANK YOU again!
GOODBYE!
Oh, Leah, I can't wait to meet the GREATEST of all dragon slayers!
Me neither...but how are we going to FIND him?

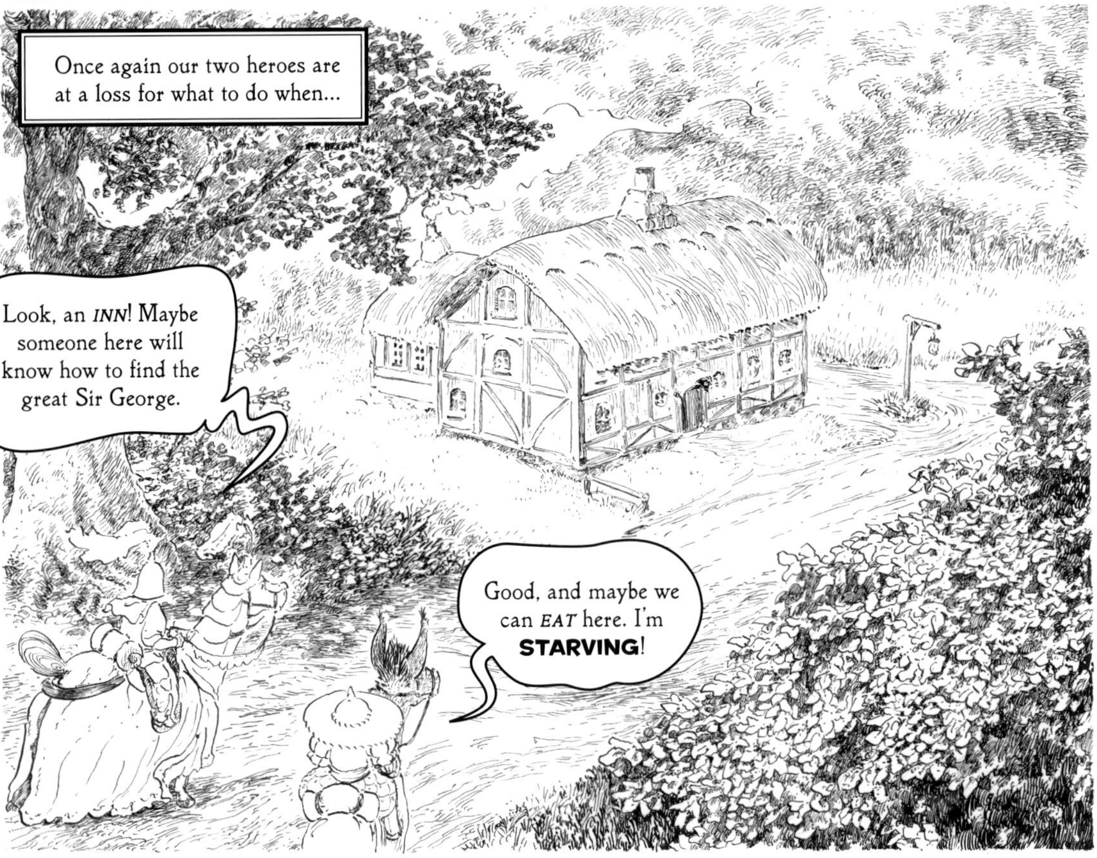
Once again our two heroes are at a loss for what to do when...
Look, an *INN*! Maybe someone here will know how to find the great Sir George.
Good, and maybe we can *EAT* here. I'm **STARVING**!

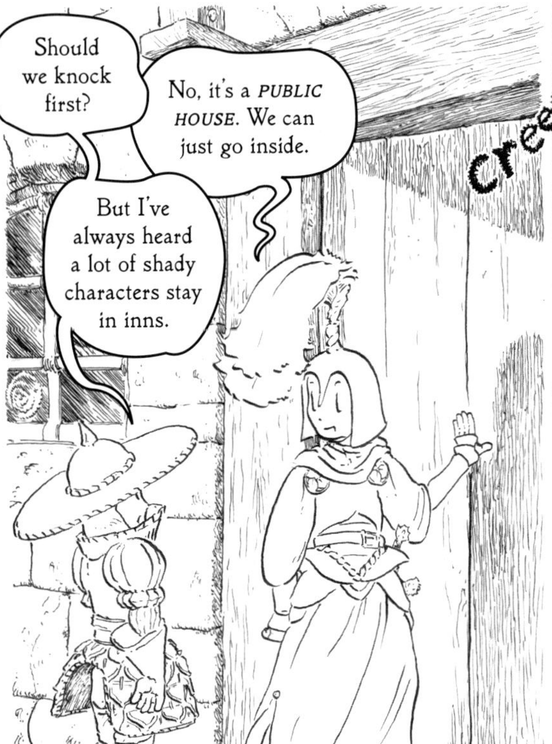
Should we knock first?
No, it's a *PUBLIC HOUSE*. We can just go inside.
But I've always heard a lot of shady characters stay in inns.
Creeeeeeeeak!

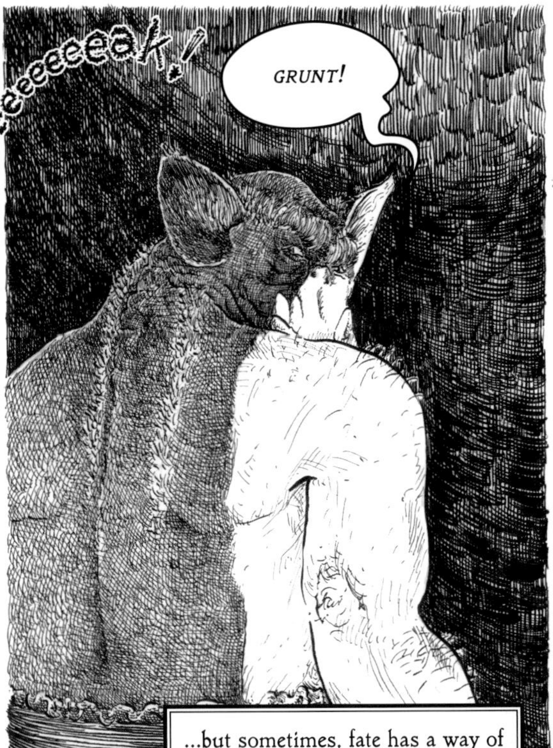
GRUNT!
...but sometimes, fate has a way of tying everything together.

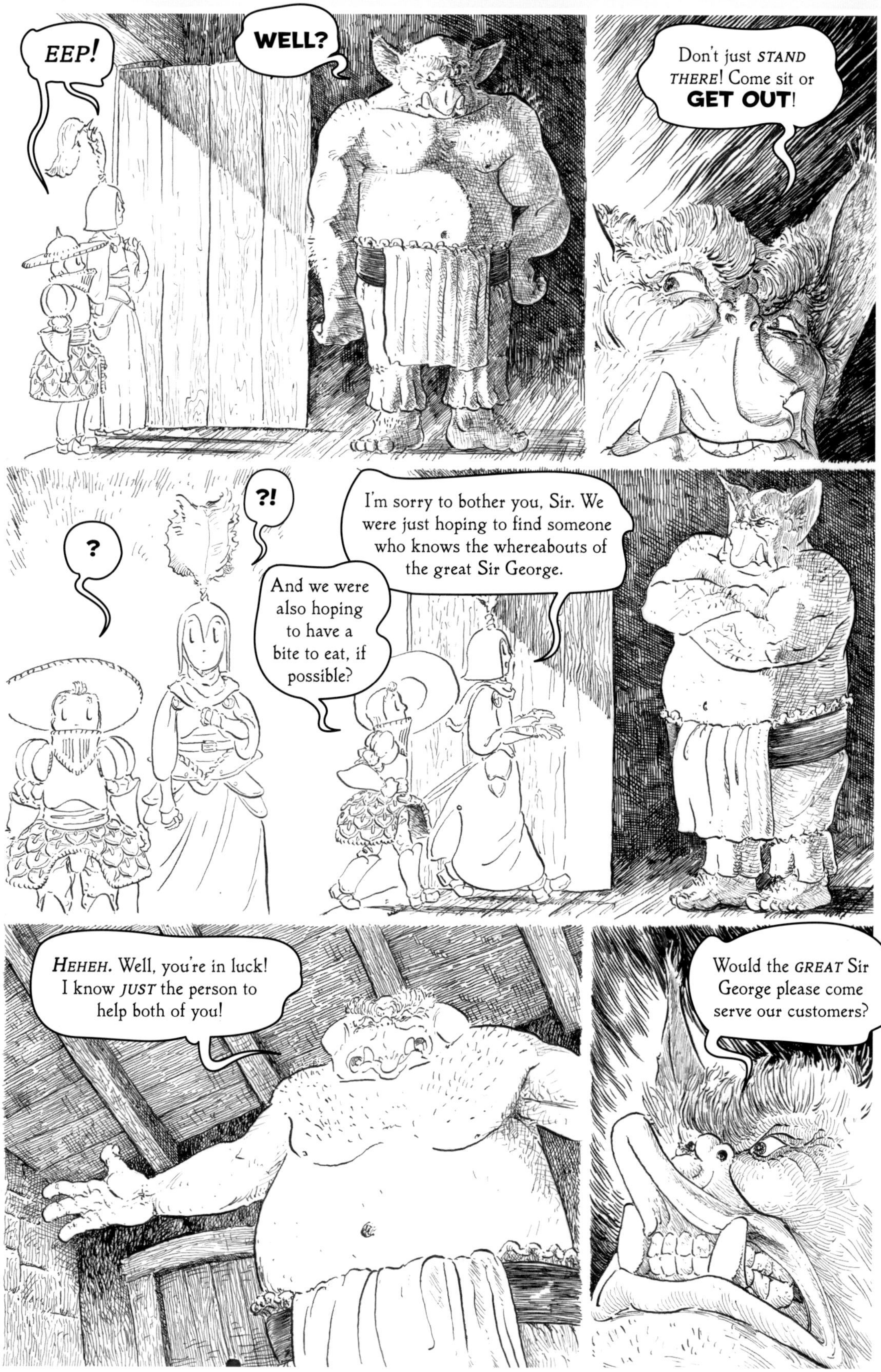
EEP!
WELL?
Don't just STAND THERE! Come sit or GET OUT!
?
?!
I'm sorry to bother you, Sir. We were just hoping to find someone who knows the whereabouts of the great Sir George.
And we were also hoping to have a bite to eat, if possible?
HEHEH. Well, you're in luck! I know JUST the person to help both of you!
Would the GREAT Sir George please come serve our customers?

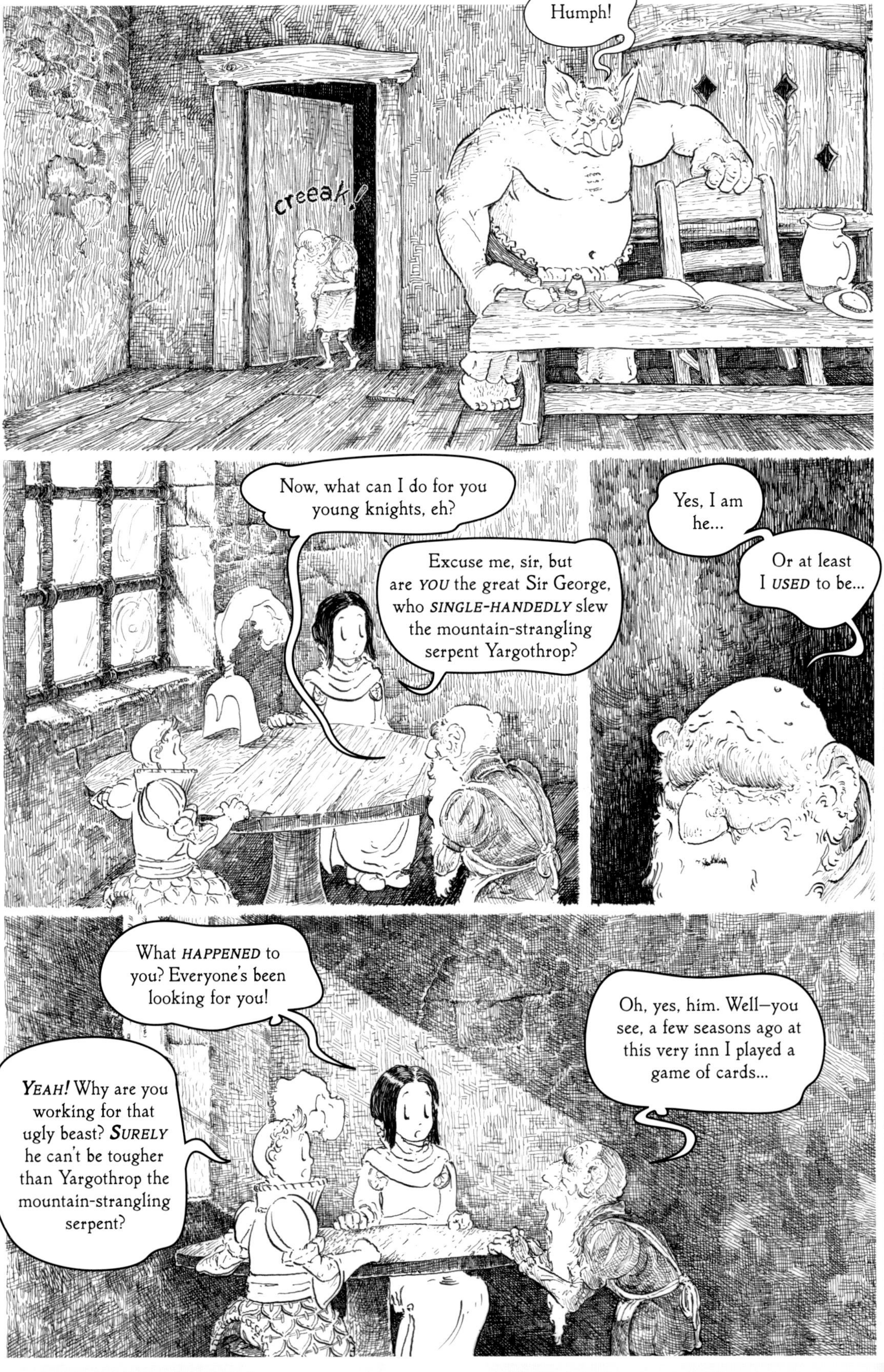
Humph!
creeak!
Now, what can I do for you young knights, eh?
Excuse me, sir, but are YOU the great Sir George, who SINGLE-HANDEDLY slew the mountain-strangling serpent Yargothrop?
Yes, I am he...
Or at least I USED to be...
What HAPPENED to you? Everyone's been looking for you!
YEAH! Why are you working for that ugly beast? SURELY he can't be tougher than Yargothrop the mountain-strangling serpent?
Oh, yes, him. Well—you see, a few seasons ago at this very inn I played a game of cards...

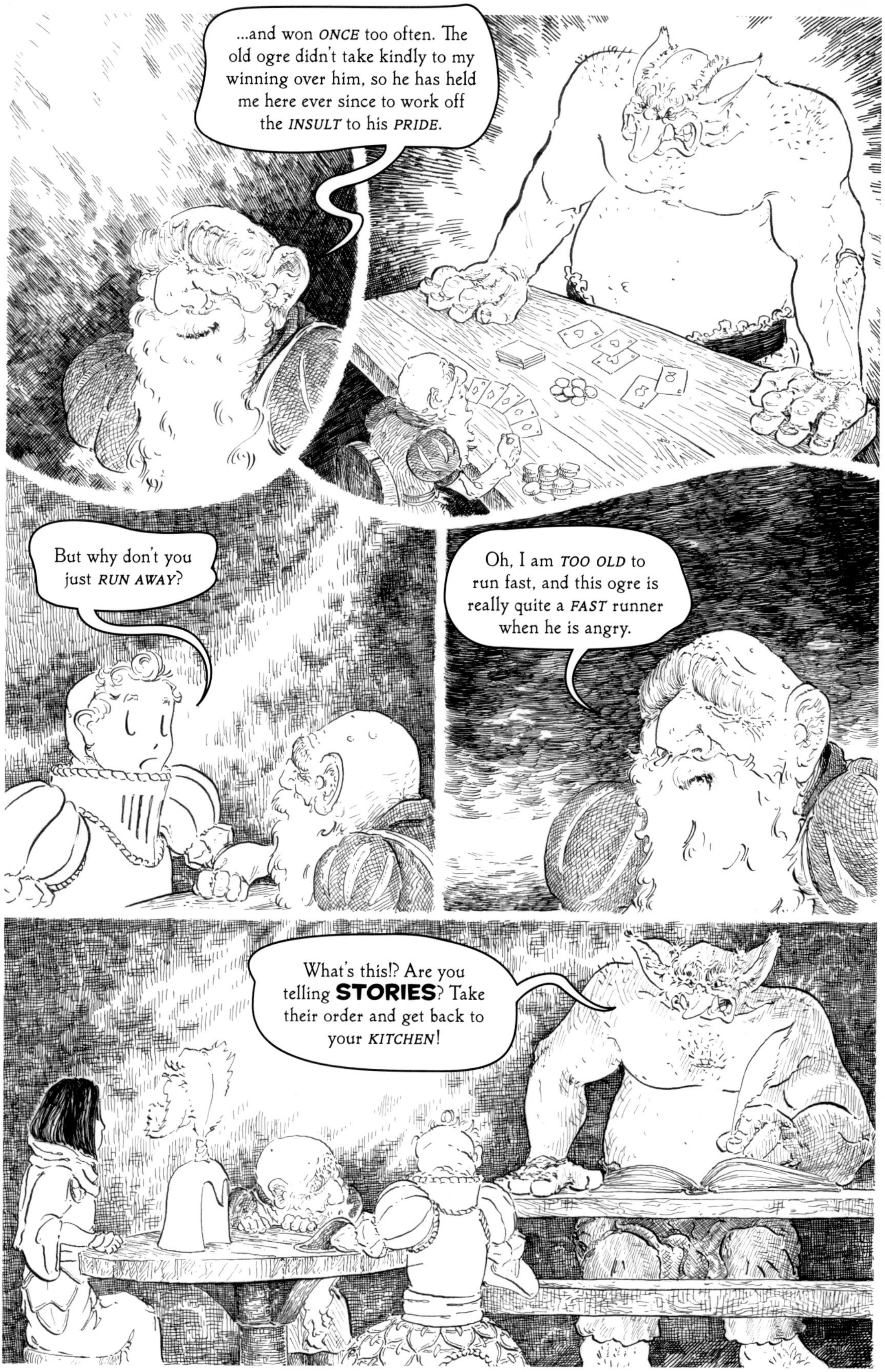
...and won *ONCE* too often. The old ogre didn't take kindly to my winning over him, so he has held me here ever since to work off the *INSULT* to his *PRIDE*.
But why don't you just *RUN AWAY*?
Oh, I am *TOO OLD* to run fast, and this ogre is really quite a *FAST* runner when he is angry.
What's this!? Are you telling **STORIES**? Take their order and get back to your *KITCHEN*!

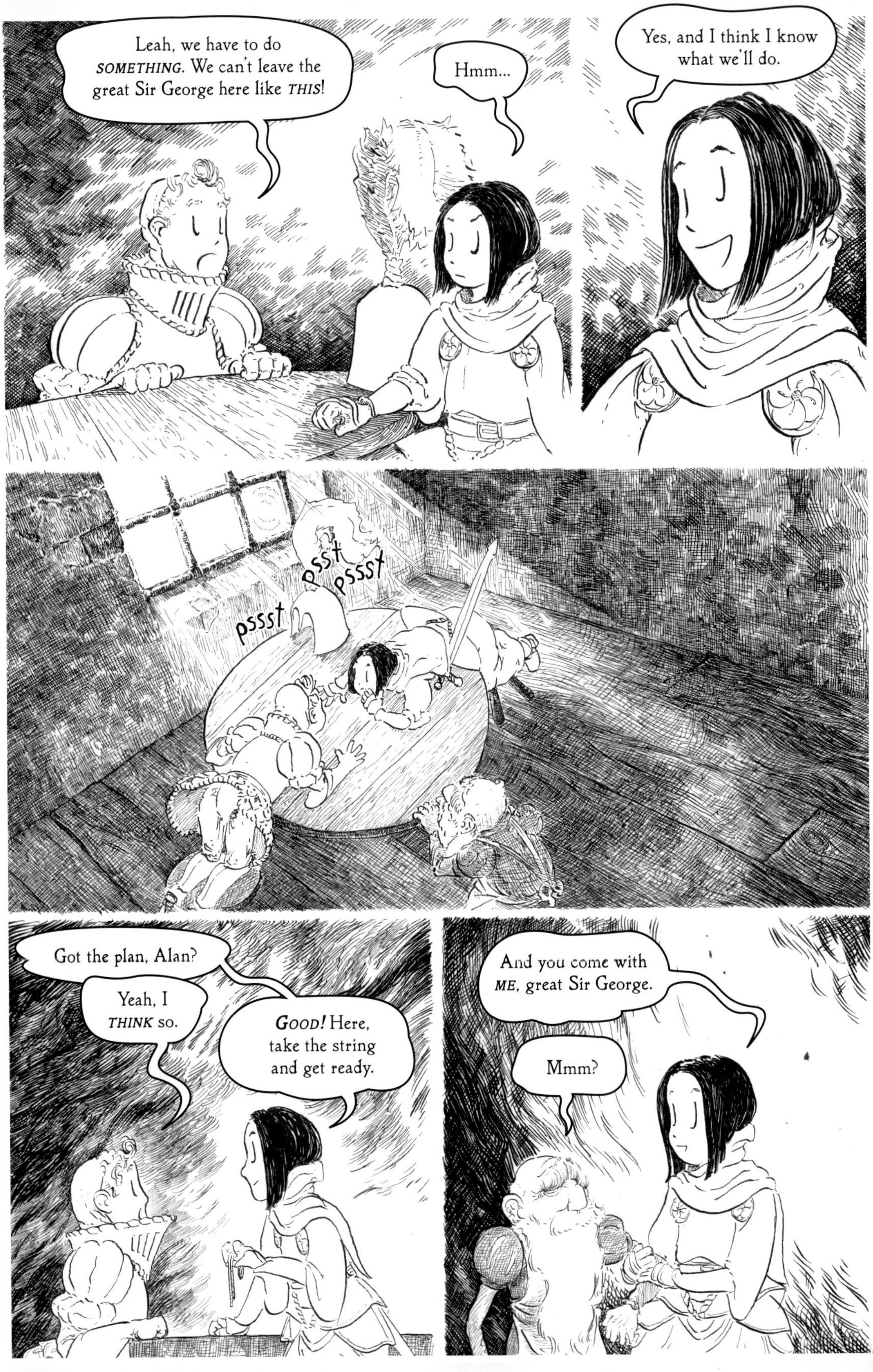
Leah, we have to do SOMETHING. We can't leave the great Sir George here like THIS!
Hmm...
Yes, and I think I know what we'll do.
pssst
pssst
psssst
Got the plan, Alan?
Yeah, I THINK so.
GOOD! Here, take the string and get ready.
And you come with ME, great Sir George.
Mmm?

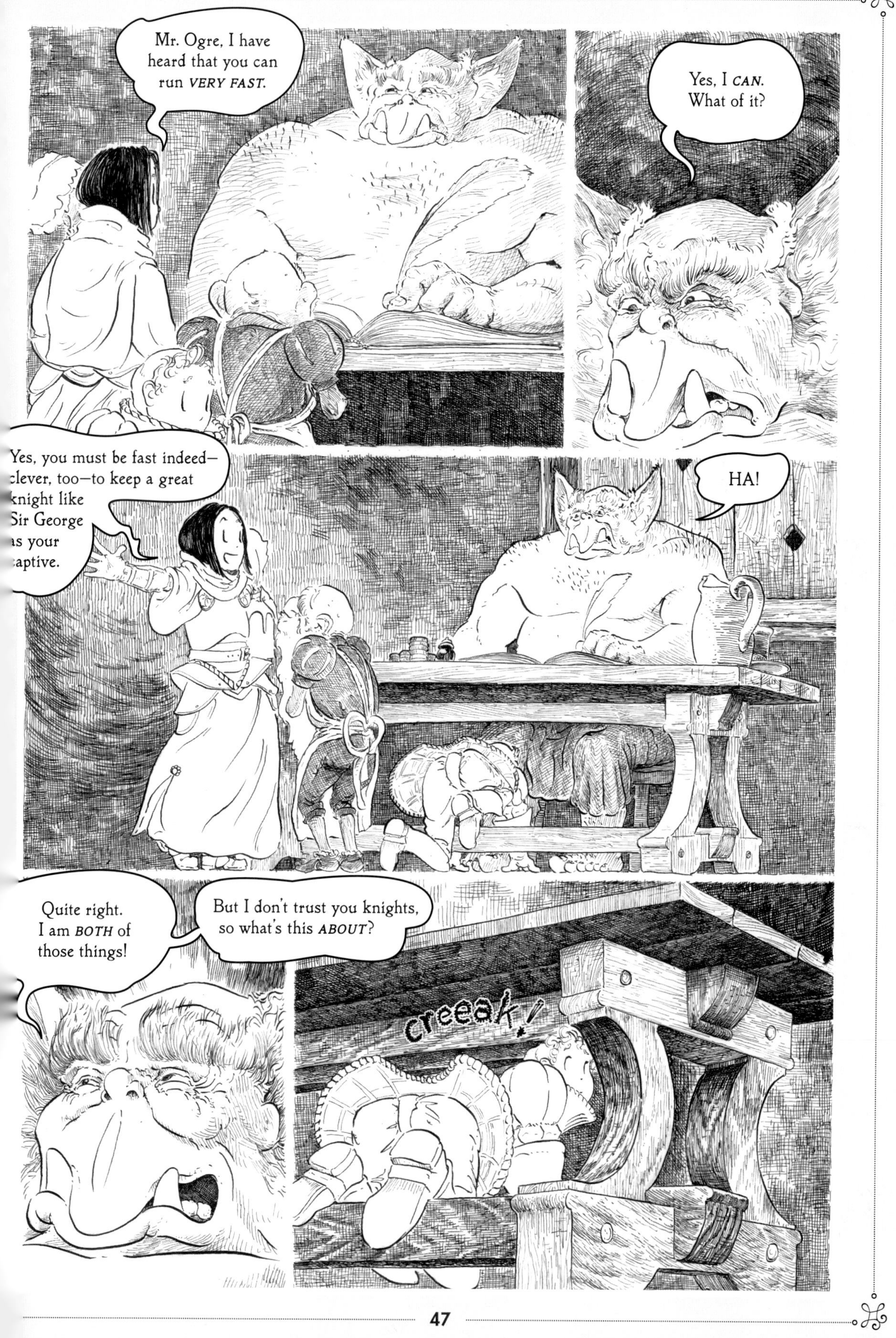
Mr. Ogre, I have heard that you can run VERY FAST.
Yes, I CAN. What of it?
Yes, you must be fast indeed—clever, too—to keep a great knight like Sir George as your captive.
HA!
Quite right. I am BOTH of those things!
But I don't trust you knights, so what's this ABOUT?
creeak!

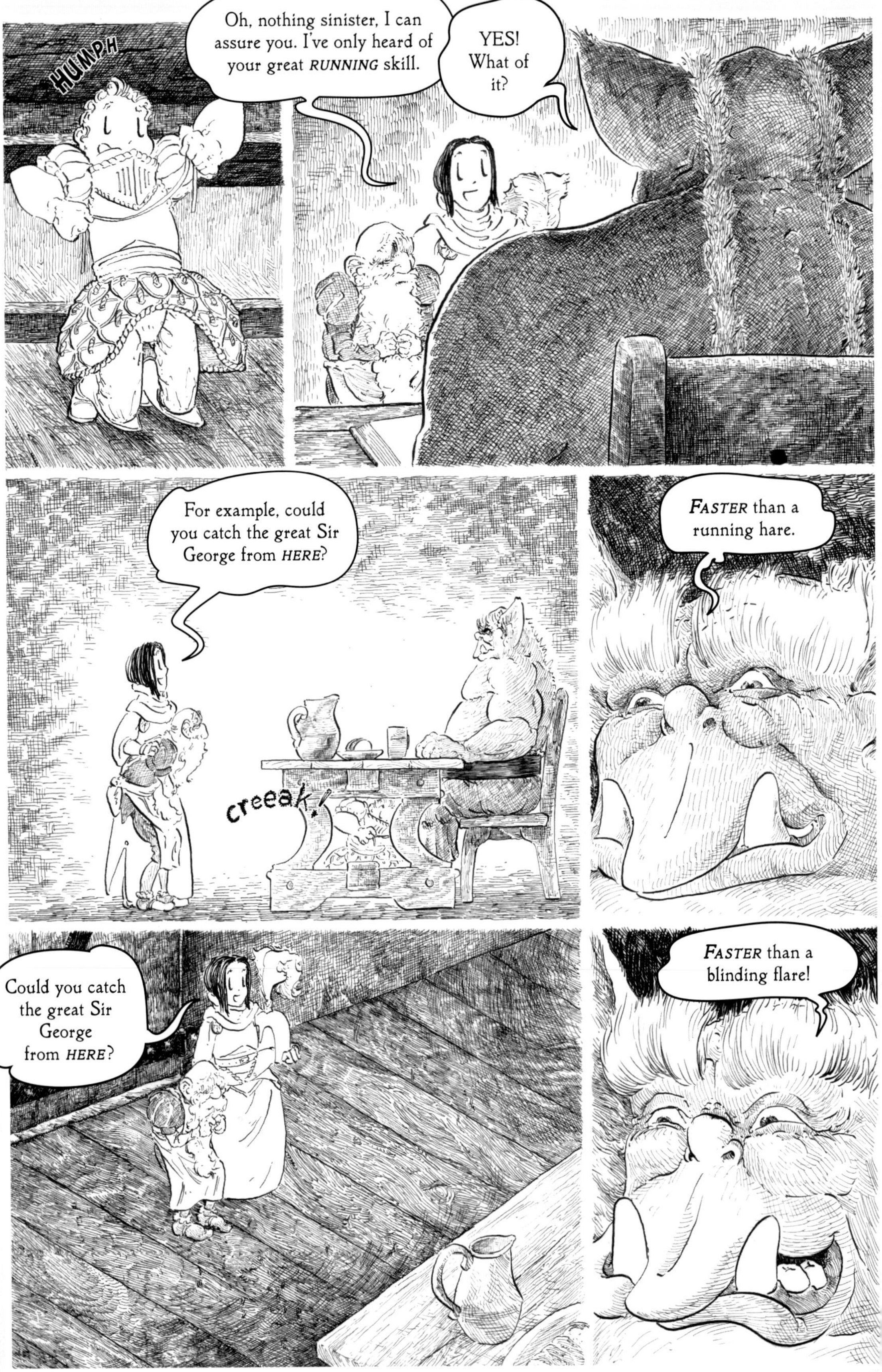
HUMPH
Oh, nothing sinister, I can assure you. I've only heard of your great RUNNING skill.
YES! What of it?
For example, could you catch the great Sir George from HERE?
creeak!
FASTER than a running hare.
Could you catch the great Sir George from HERE?
FASTER than a blinding flare!

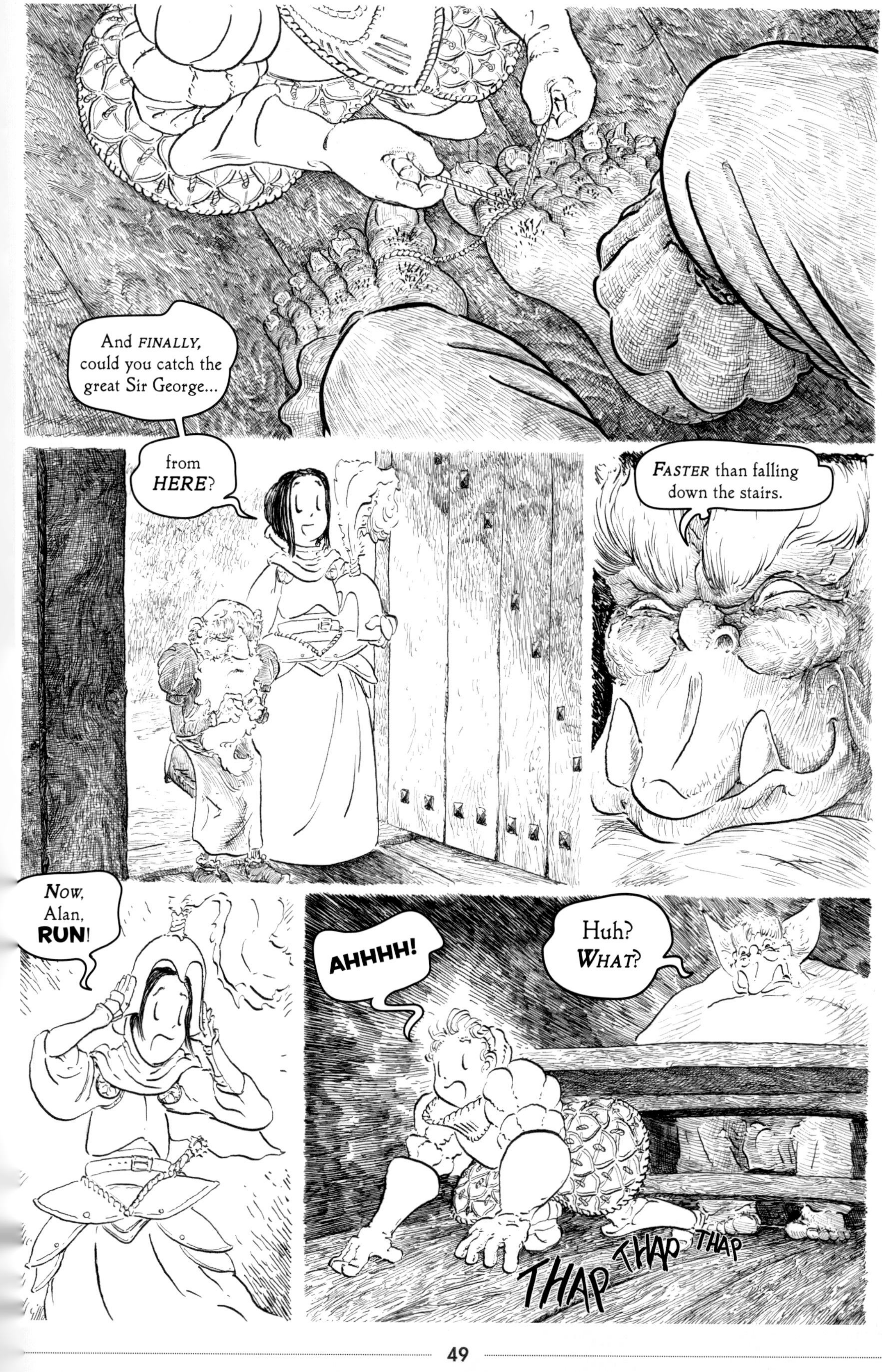
And *FINALLY,* could you catch the great Sir George...
from **HERE**?
FASTER than falling down the stairs.
NOW, Alan, **RUN**!
AHHHH!
Huh? *WHAT*?
THAP THAP THAP

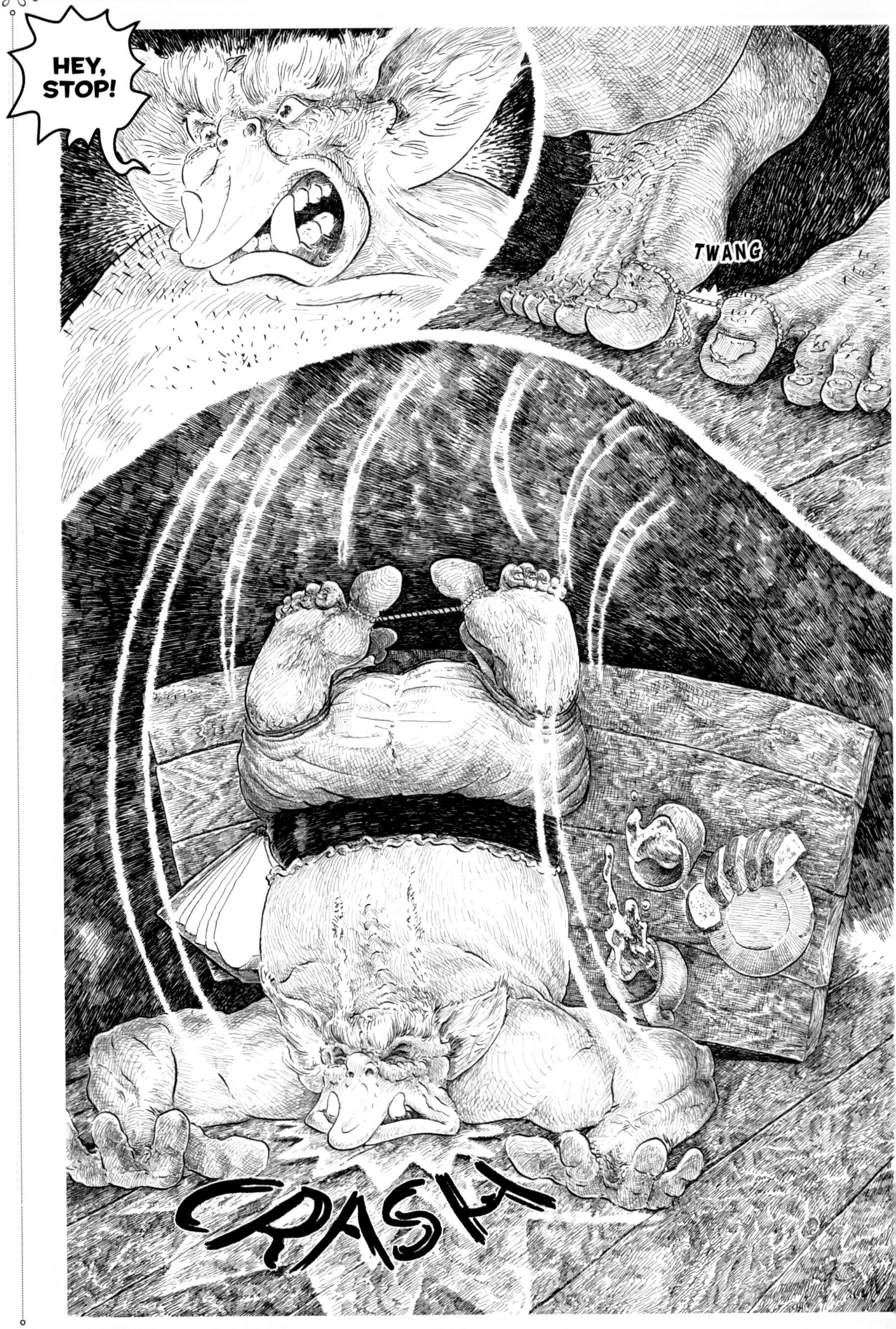
HEY, STOP!
TWANG
CRASH

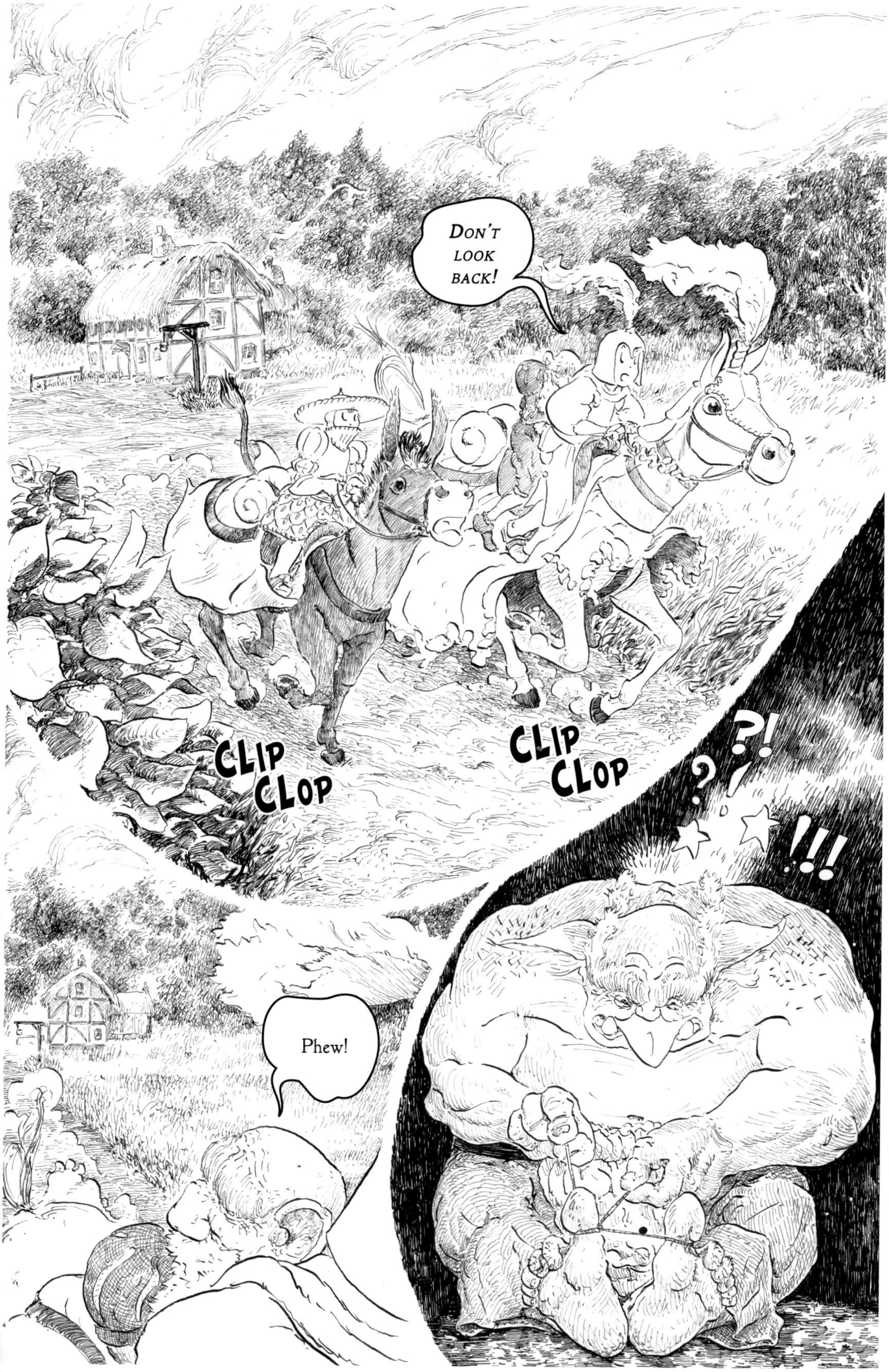
DON'T LOOK BACK!
CLIP CLOP
CLIP CLOP
?!
?
!!!
Phew!

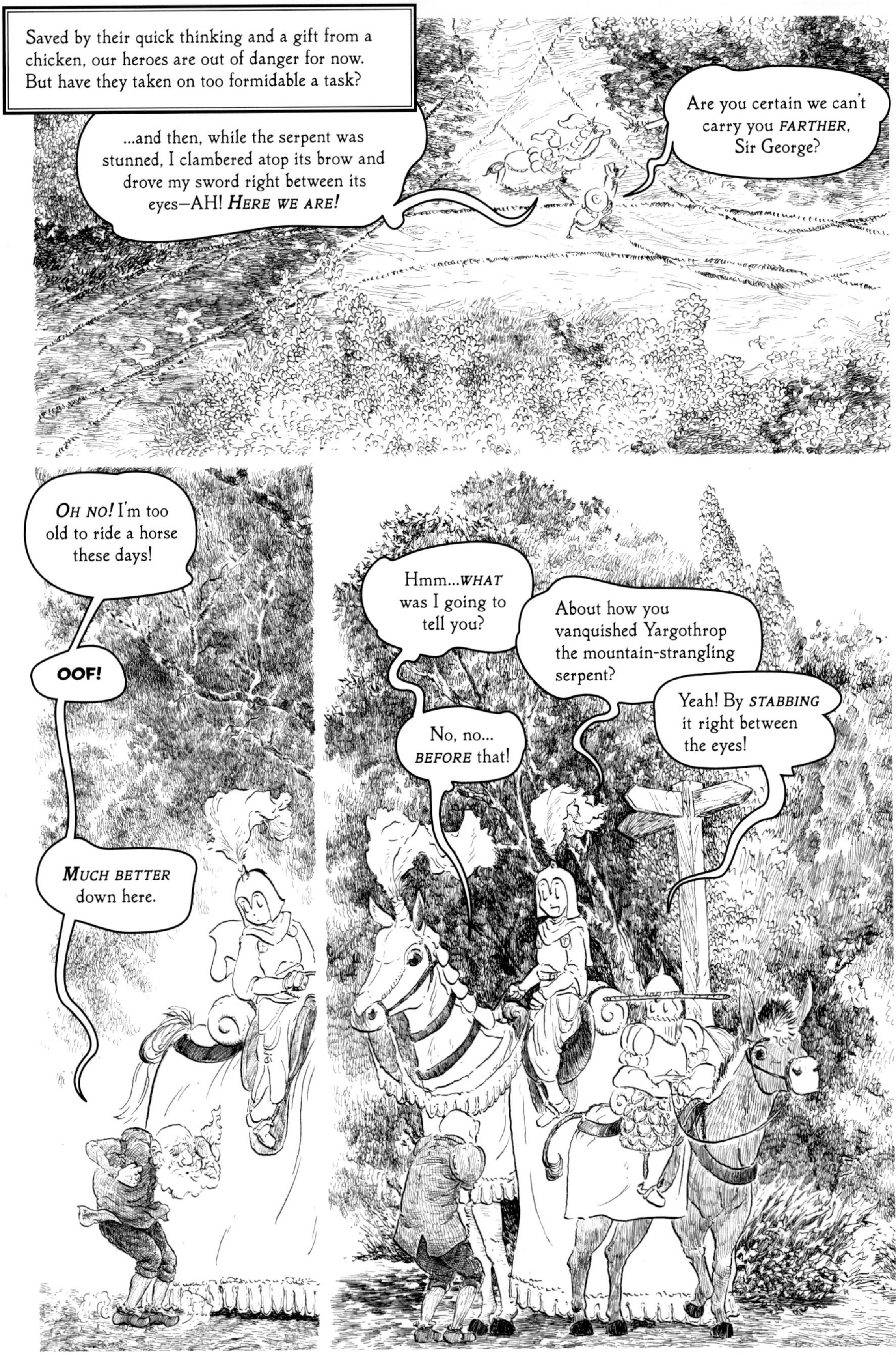
Saved by their quick thinking and a gift from a chicken, our heroes are out of danger for now. But have they taken on too formidable a task?
...and then, while the serpent was stunned, I clambered atop its brow and drove my sword right between its eyes—AH! HERE WE ARE!
Are you certain we can't carry you FARTHER, Sir George?
OH NO! I'm too old to ride a horse these days!
OOF!
MUCH BETTER down here.
Hmm...WHAT was I going to tell you?
About how you vanquished Yargothrop the mountain-strangling serpent?
No, no... BEFORE that!
Yeah! By STABBING it right between the eyes!

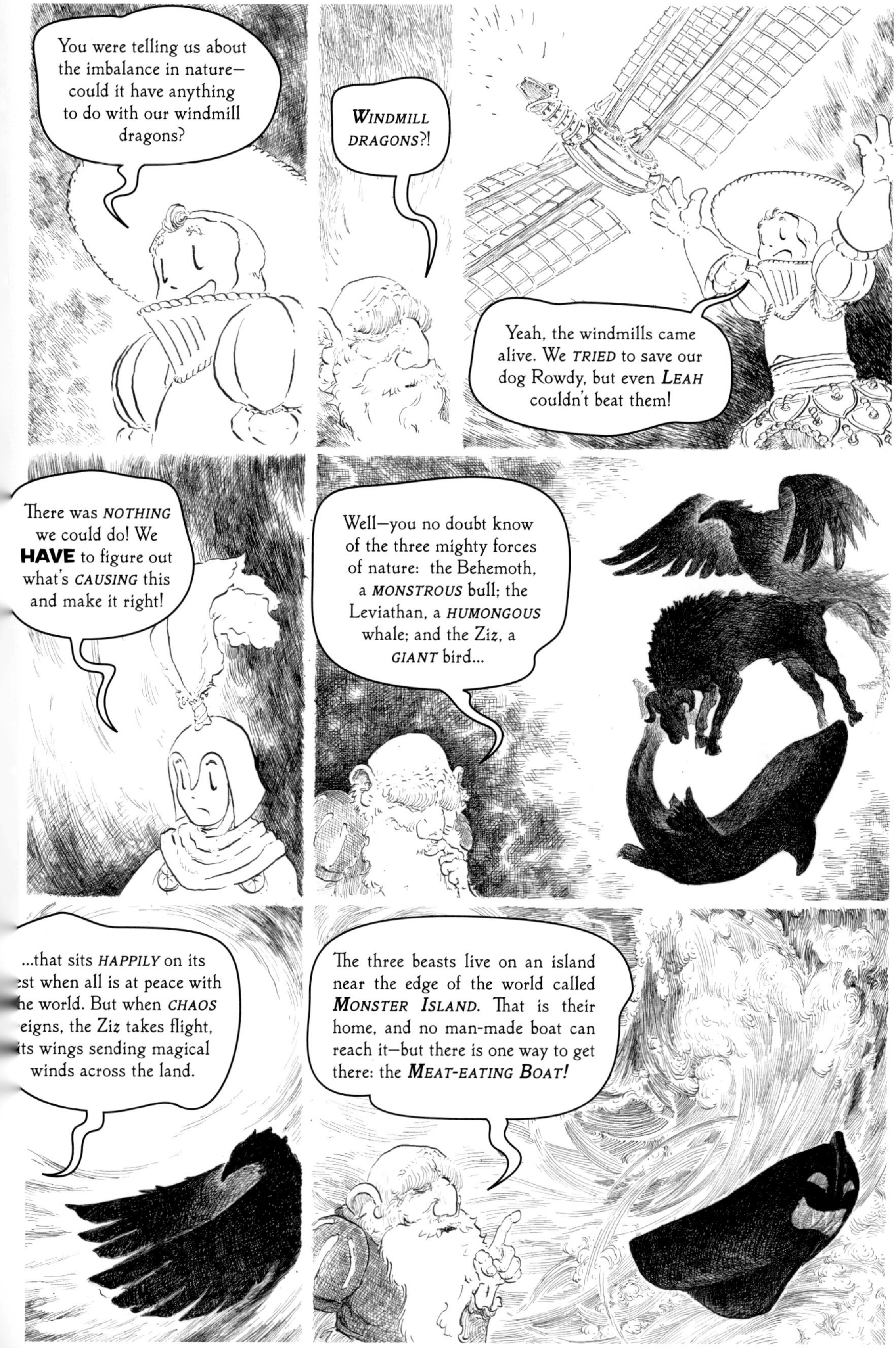
You were telling us about the imbalance in nature—could it have anything to do with our windmill dragons?
WINDMILL DRAGONS?!
Yeah, the windmills came alive. We TRIED to save our dog Rowdy, but even LEAH couldn't beat them!
There was NOTHING we could do! We HAVE to figure out what's CAUSING this and make it right!
Well—you no doubt know of the three mighty forces of nature: the Behemoth, a MONSTROUS bull; the Leviathan, a HUMONGOUS whale; and the Ziz, a GIANT bird...
...that sits HAPPILY on its est when all is at peace with he world. But when CHAOS eigns, the Ziz takes flight, its wings sending magical winds across the land.
The three beasts live on an island near the edge of the world called MONSTER ISLAND. That is their home, and no man-made boat can reach it—but there is one way to get there: the MEAT-EATING BOAT!

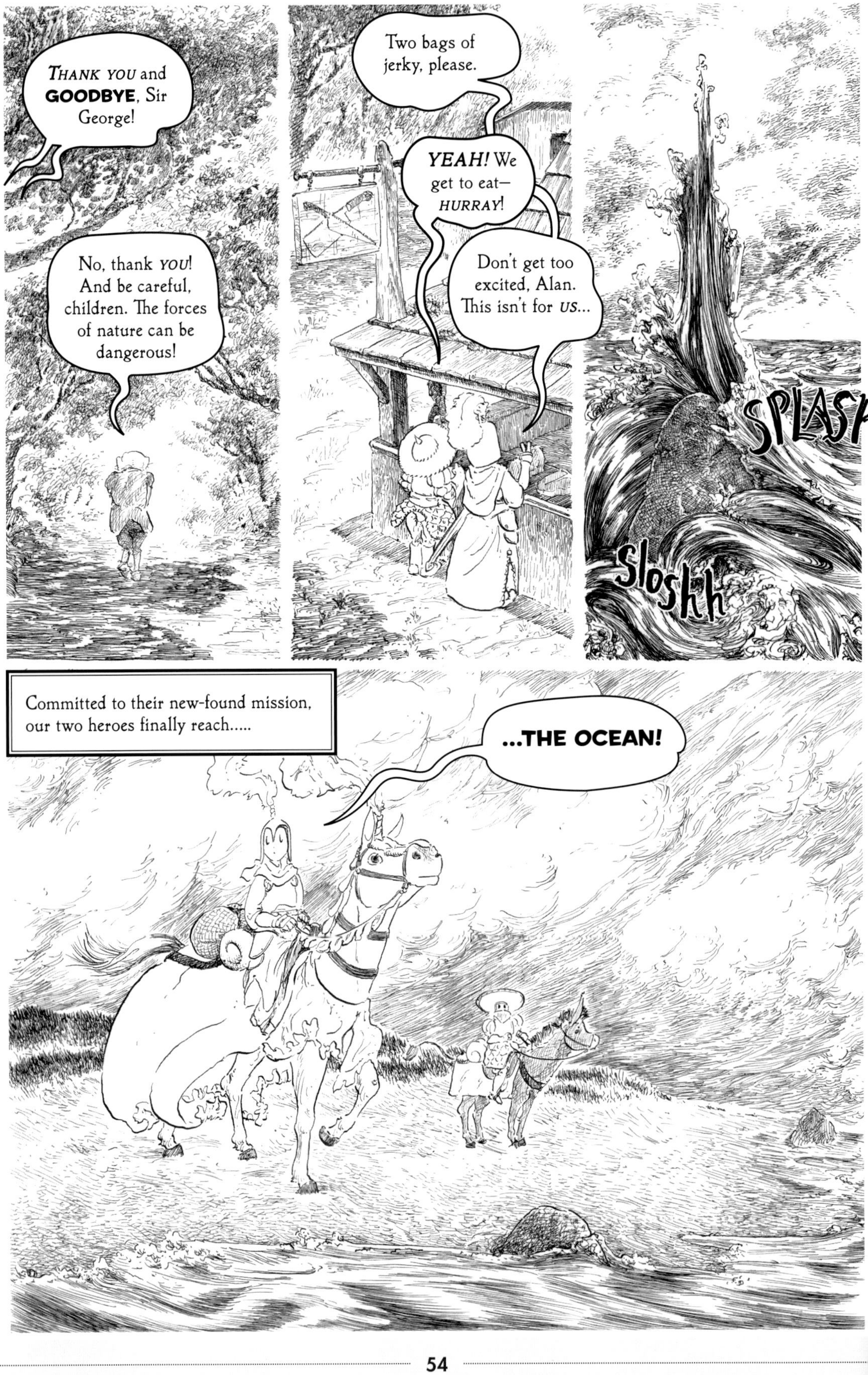
THANK YOU and GOODBYE, Sir George!
No, thank YOU! And be careful, children. The forces of nature can be dangerous!
Two bags of jerky, please.
YEAH! We get to eat—HURRAY!
Don't get too excited, Alan. This isn't for US...
SPLASH
Sloshh
Committed to their new-found mission, our two heroes finally reach.....
...THE OCEAN!

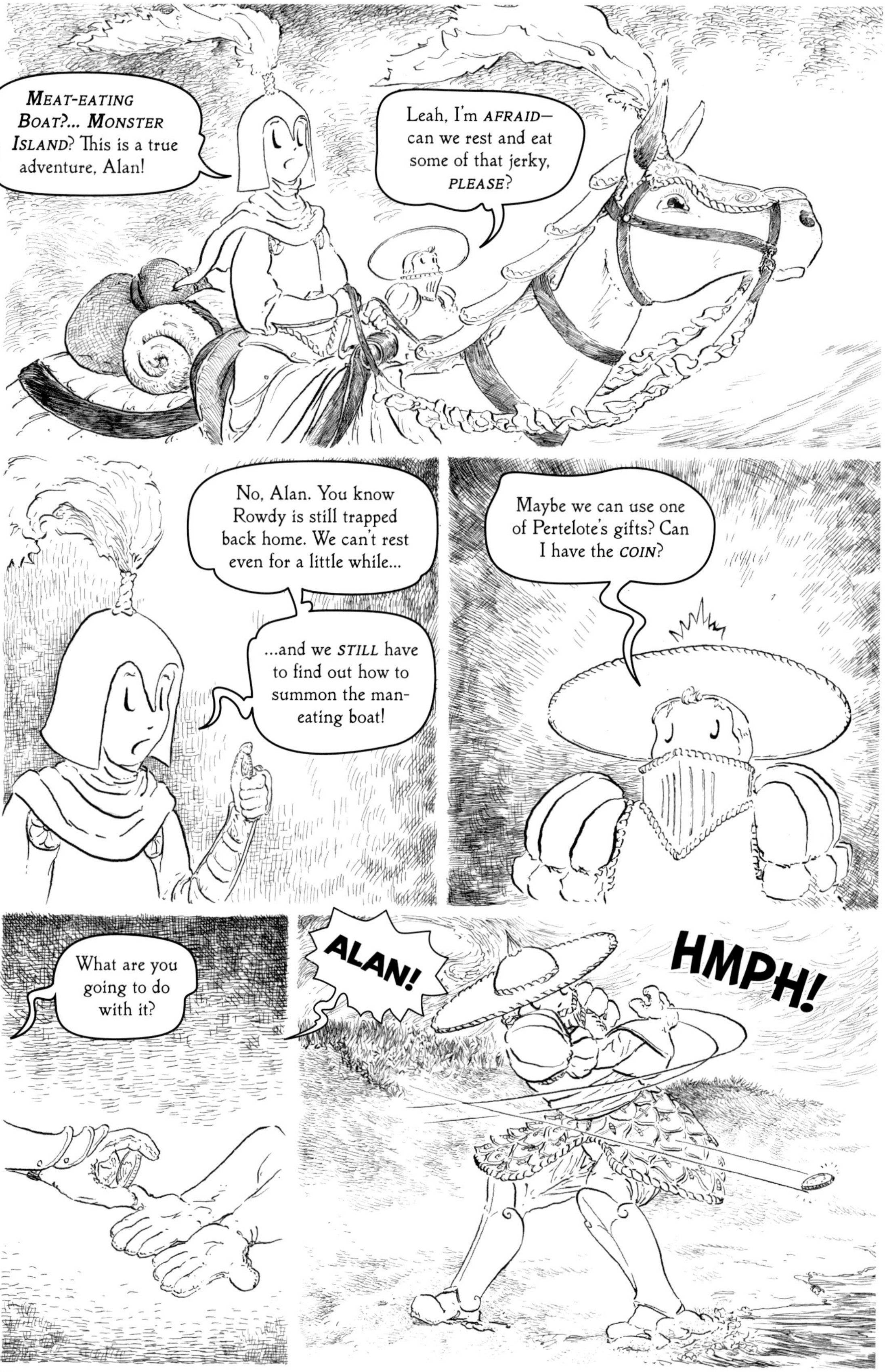
MEAT-EATING BOAT?... MONSTER ISLAND? This is a true adventure, Alan!
Leah, I'm AFRAID— can we rest and eat some of that jerky, PLEASE?
No, Alan. You know Rowdy is still trapped back home. We can't rest even for a little while...
...and we STILL have to find out how to summon the man-eating boat!
Maybe we can use one of Pertelote's gifts? Can I have the COIN?
What are you going to do with it?
ALAN!
HMPH!

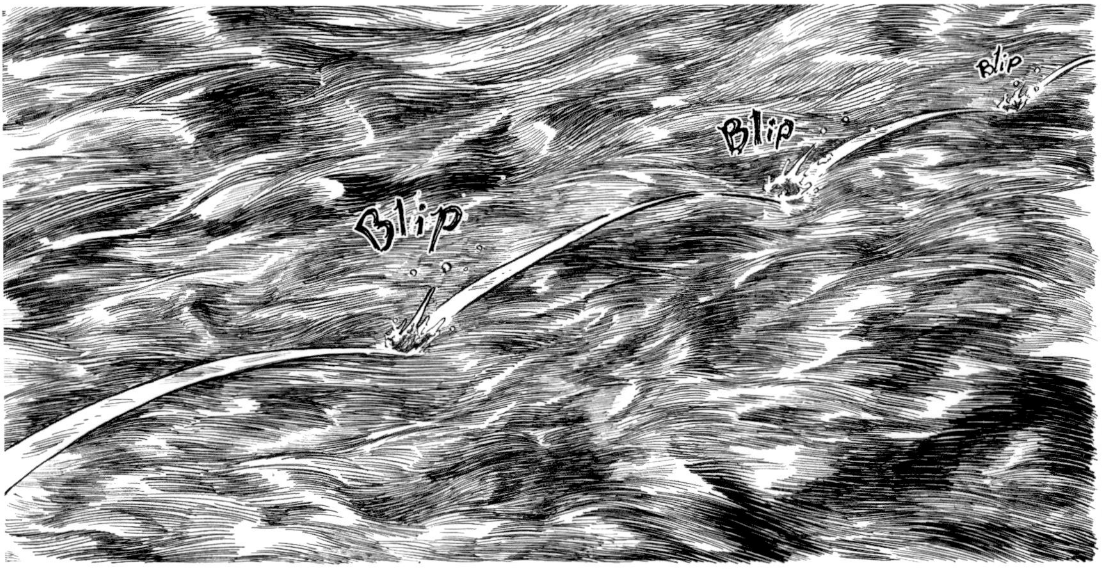
Blip
Blip
Blip

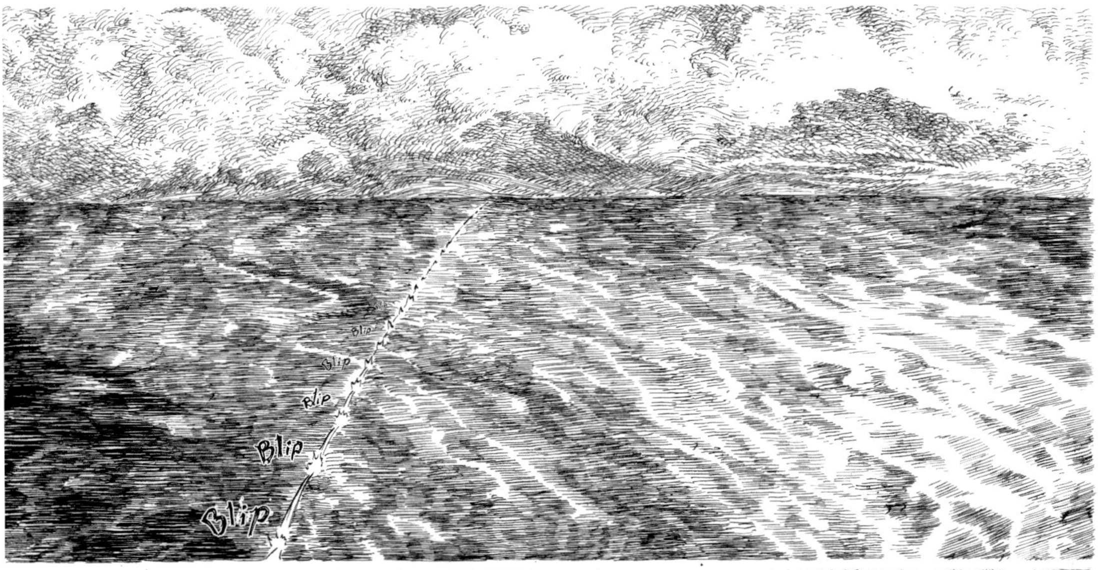
Blip
Blip
Blip
Blip
Blip

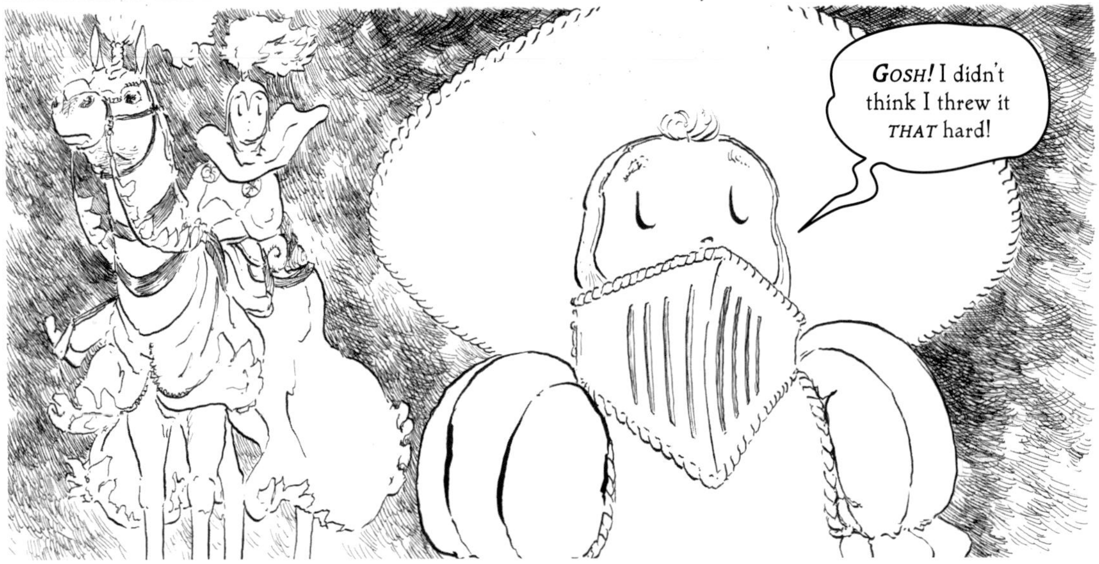
GOSH! I didn't think I threw it THAT hard!

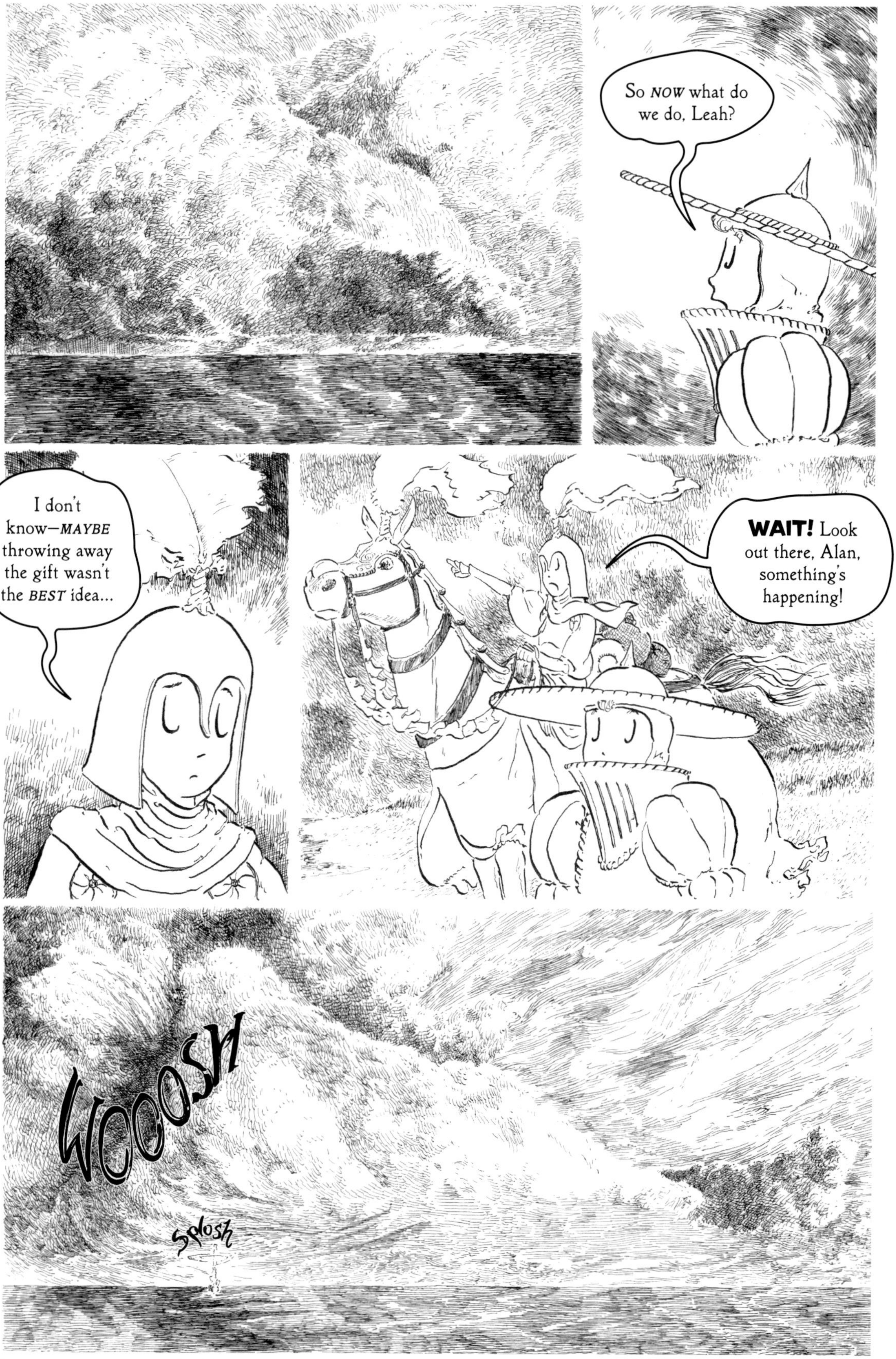
So *NOW* what do we do, Leah?
I don't know—*MAYBE* throwing away the gift wasn't the *BEST* idea...
WAIT! Look out there, Alan, something's happening!
WOOOSH
Splosh

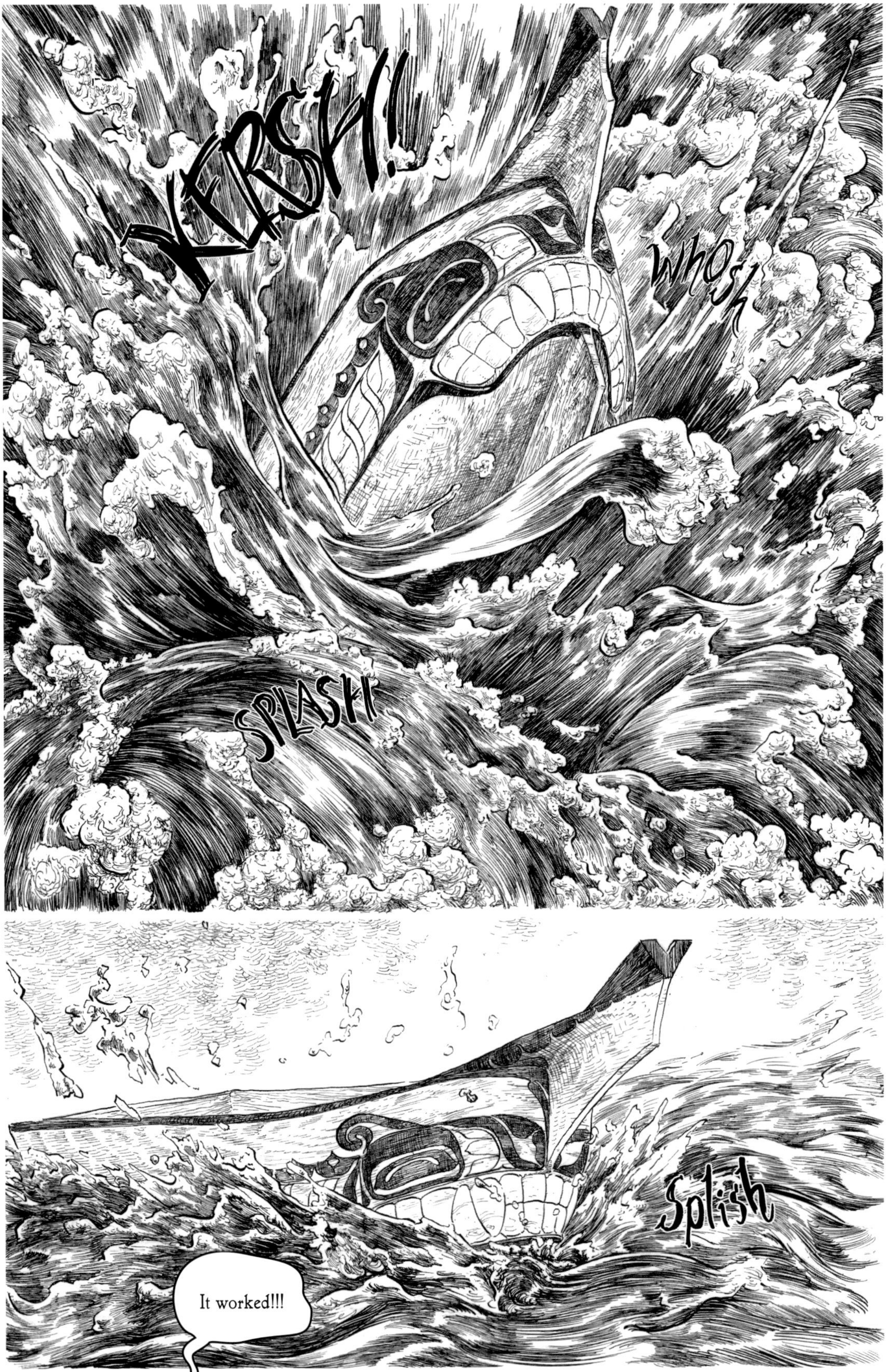
KERSH!!
whoosh
SPLASH
Splish
It worked!!!

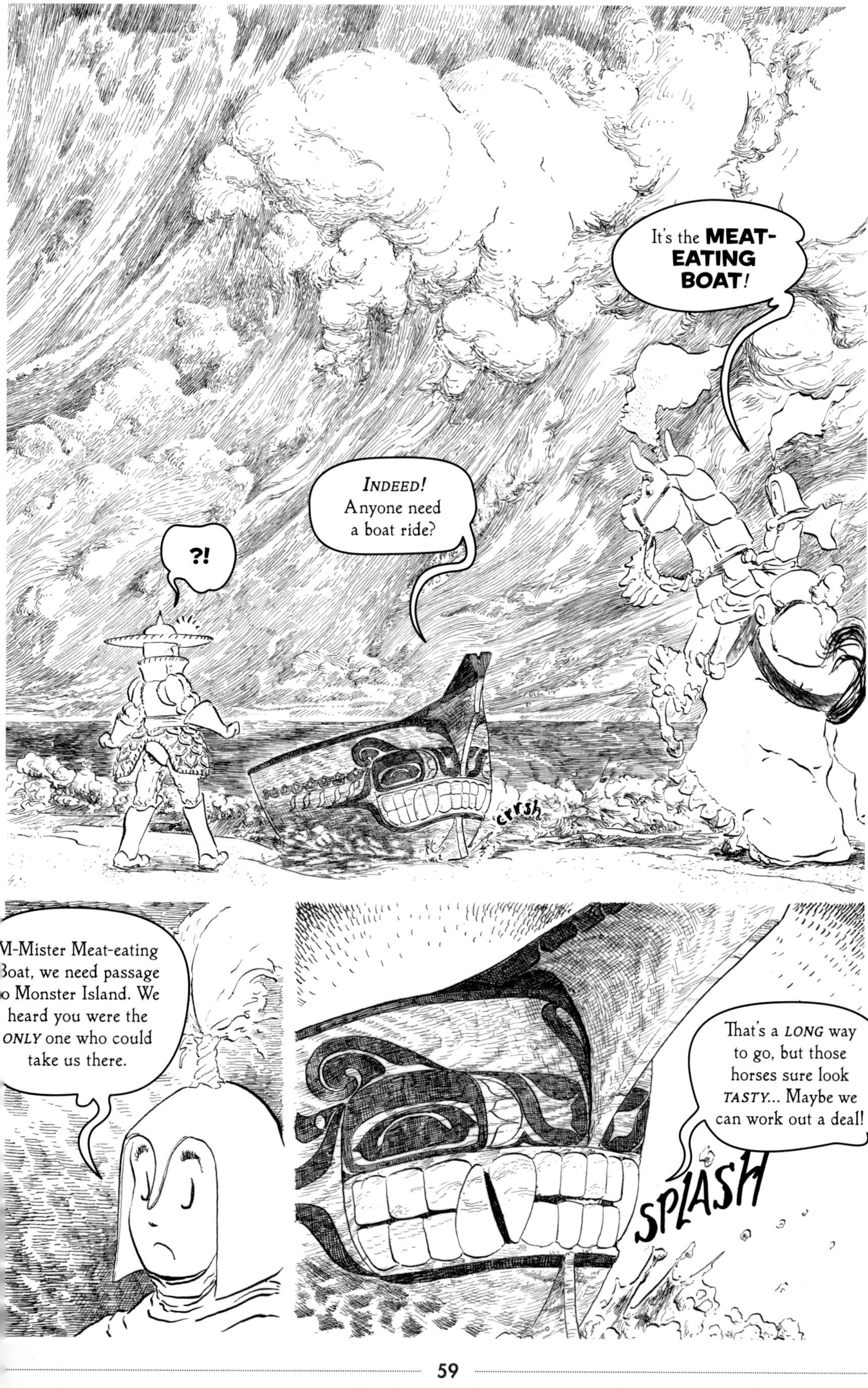

It's the **MEAT-EATING BOAT**!
?!
INDEED! Anyone need a boat ride?
crrsh
M-Mister Meat-eating Boat, we need passage to Monster Island. We heard you were the *ONLY* one who could take us there.
That's a *LONG* way to go, but those horses sure look *TASTY*... Maybe we can work out a deal!
SPLASH

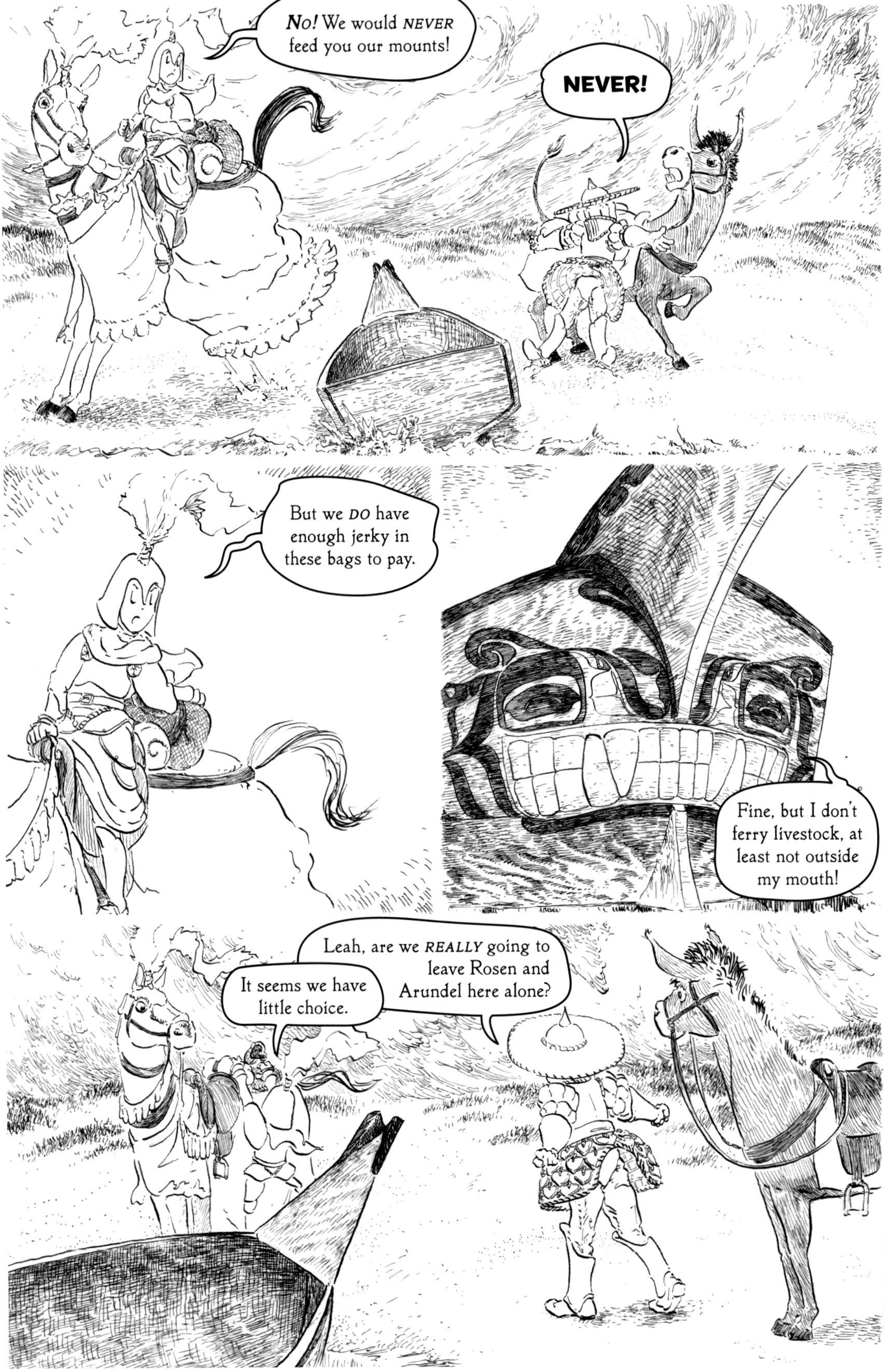
NO! We would NEVER feed you our mounts!
NEVER!
But we DO have enough jerky in these bags to pay.
Fine, but I don't ferry livestock, at least not outside my mouth!
Leah, are we REALLY going to leave Rosen and Arundel here alone?
It seems we have little choice.

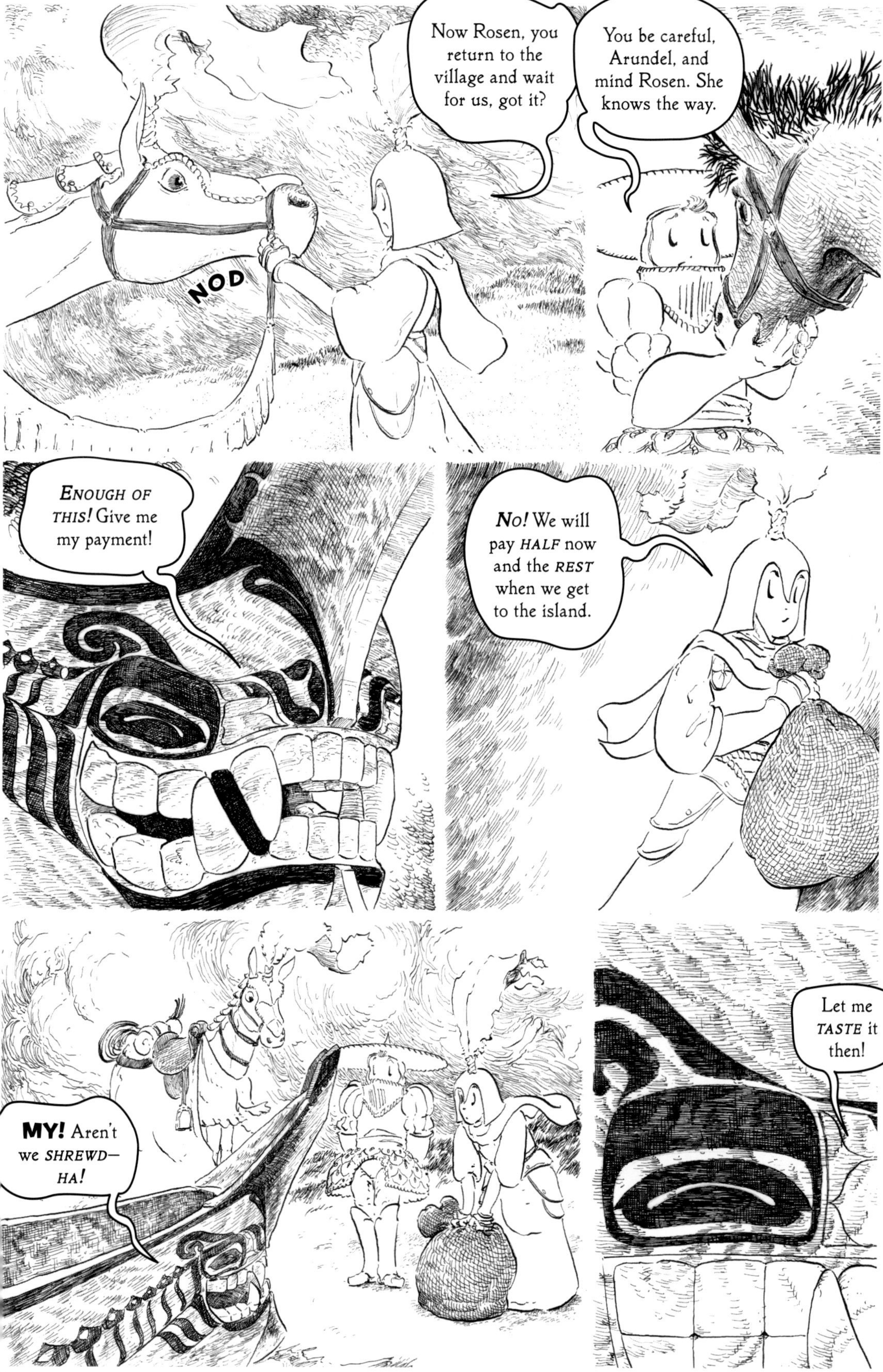
NOD
Now Rosen, you return to the village and wait for us, got it?
You be careful, Arundel, and mind Rosen. She knows the way.
ENOUGH OF THIS! Give me my payment!
NO! We will pay HALF now and the REST when we get to the island.
MY! Aren't we SHREWD—HA!
Let me TASTE it then!

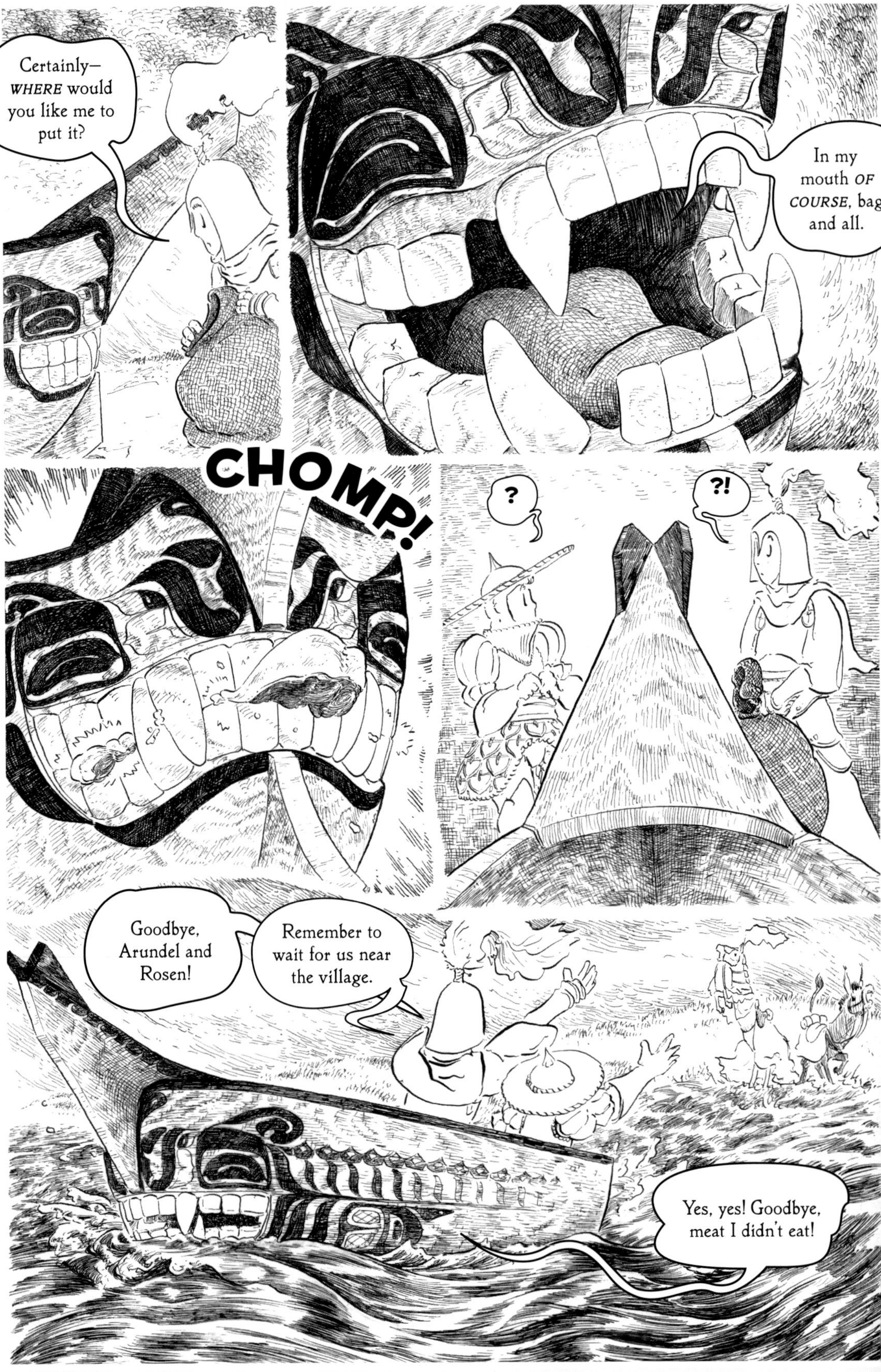
Certainly— *WHERE* would you like me to put it?
In my mouth *OF COURSE*, bag and all.
CHOMP!
?
?!
Goodbye, Arundel and Rosen!
Remember to wait for us near the village.
Yes, yes! Goodbye, meat I didn't eat!

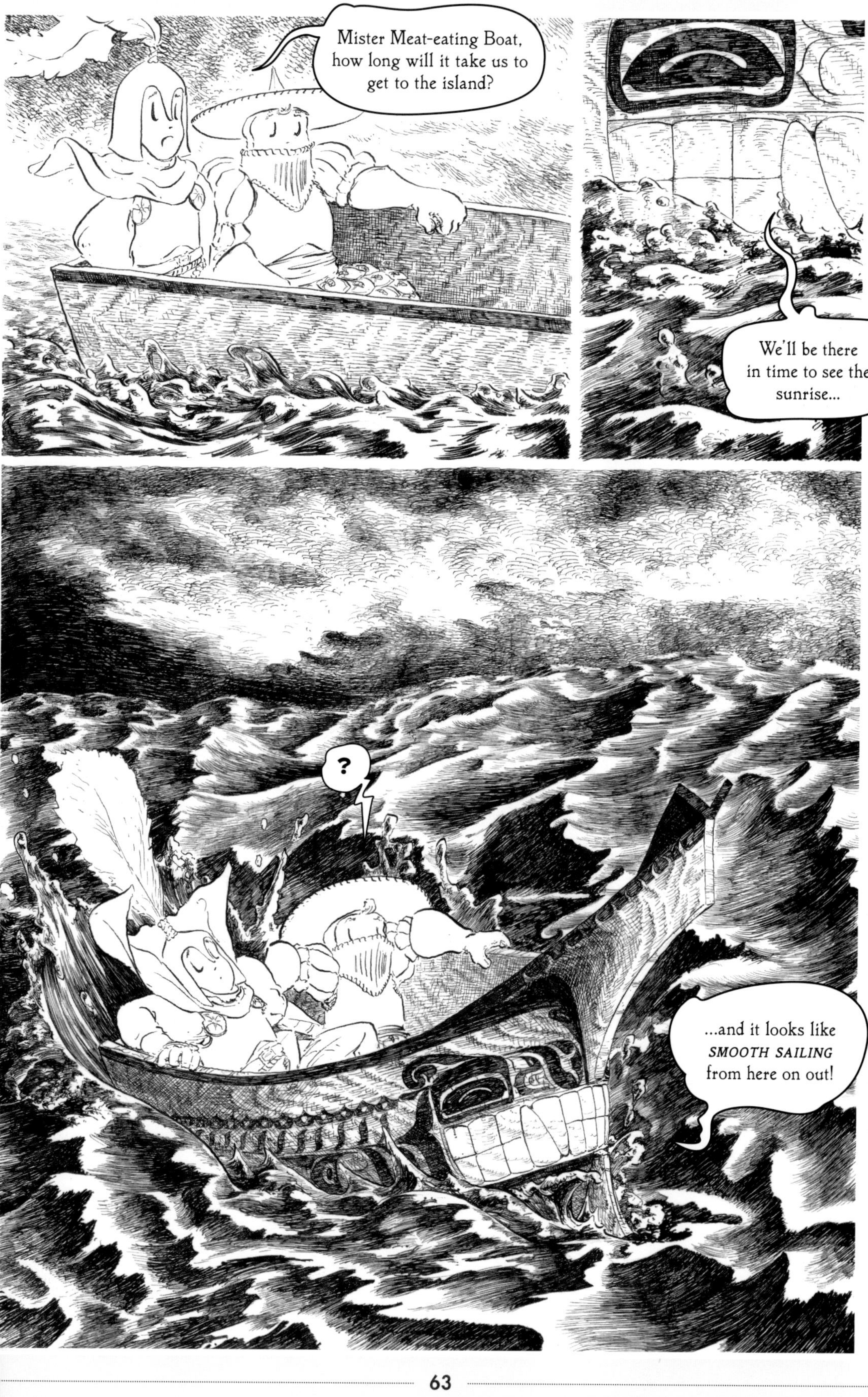
Mister Meat-eating Boat, how long will it take us to get to the island?
We'll be there in time to see the sunrise...
?
...and it looks like *SMOOTH SAILING* from here on out!

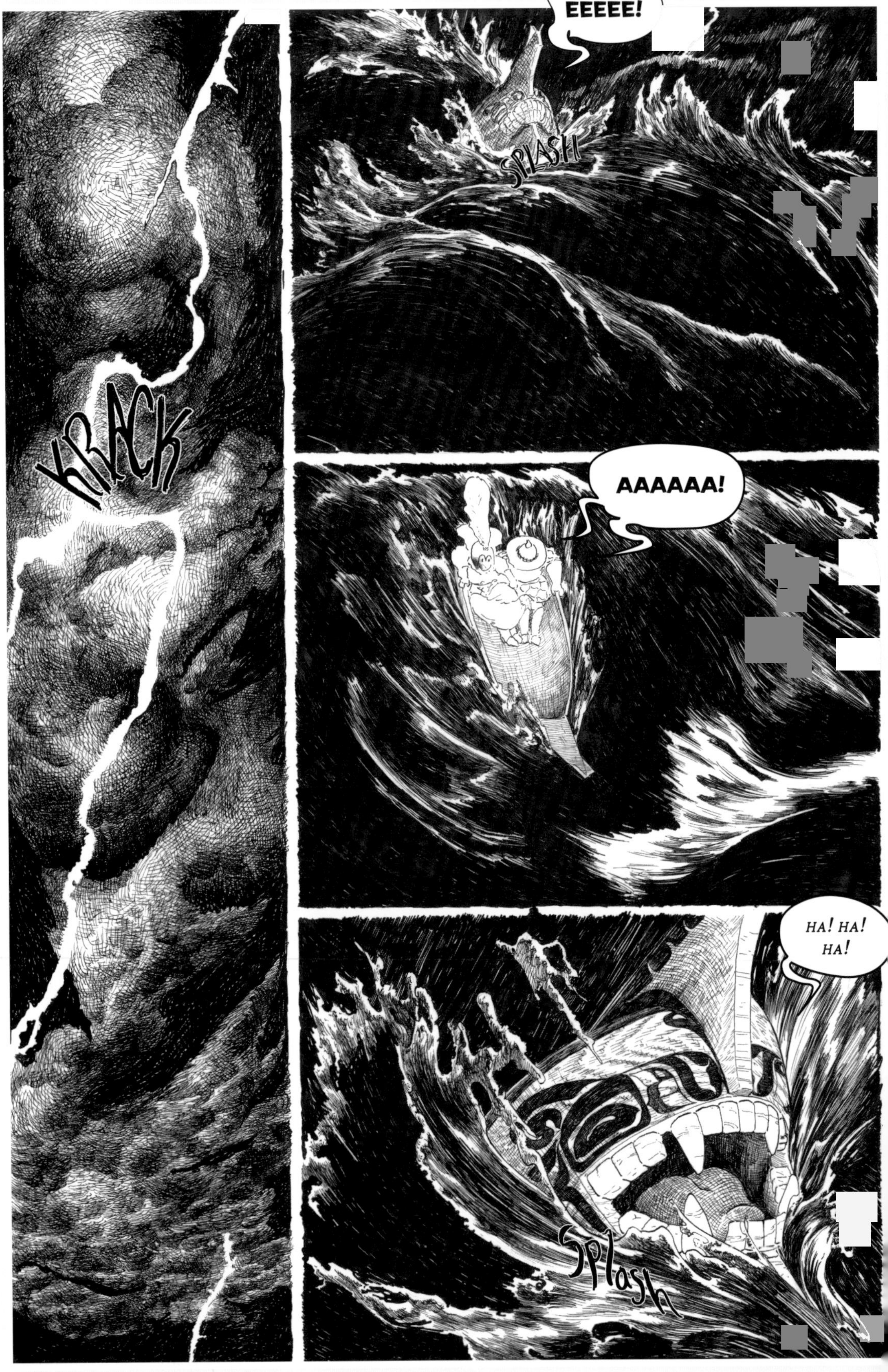
KRACK
EEEEE!
SPLASH
AAAAAA!
HA! HA! HA!
SPLASH

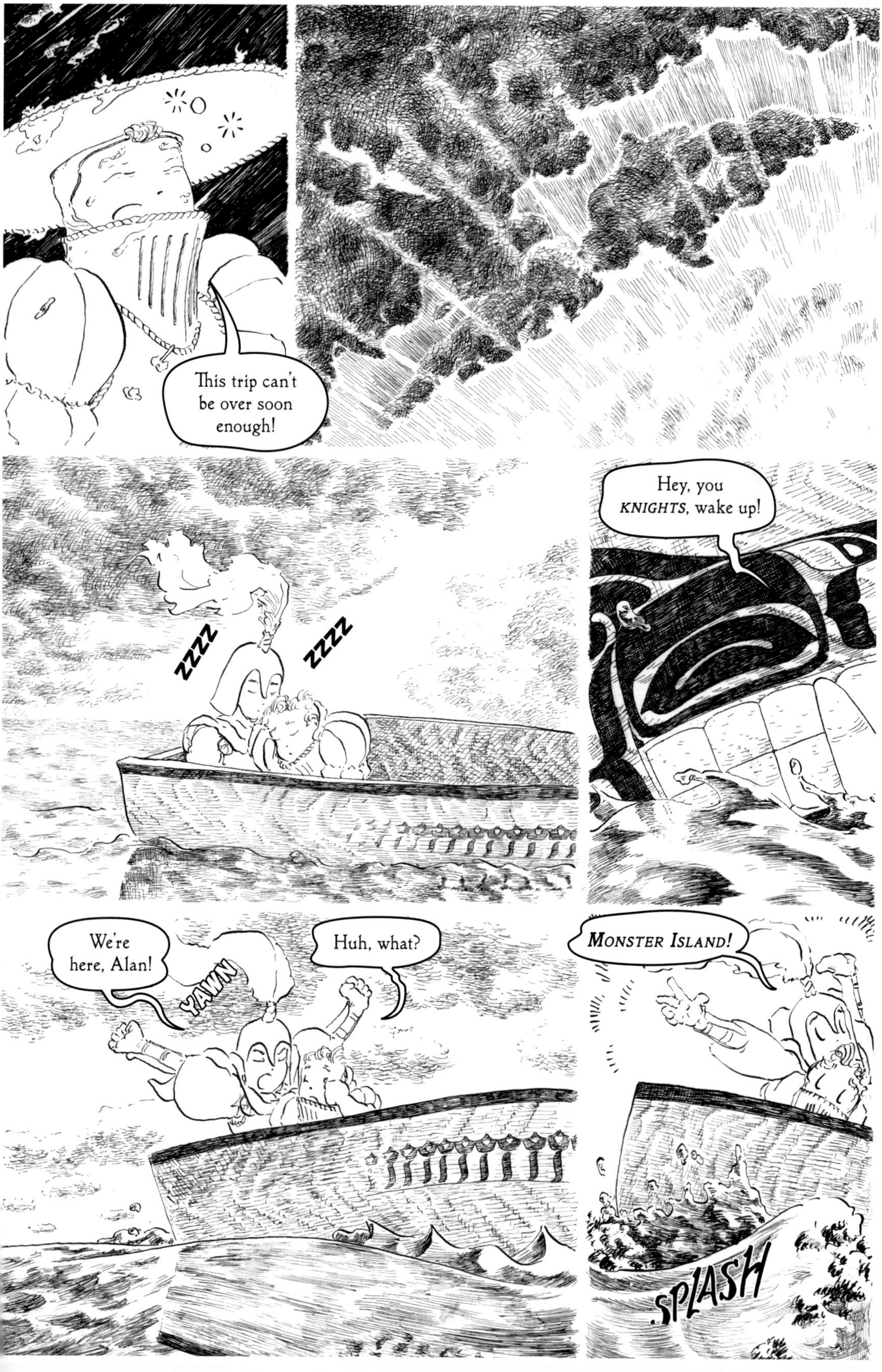
This trip can't be over soon enough!
ZZZZ
ZZZZ
Hey, you KNIGHTS, wake up!
We're here, Alan!
YAWN
Huh, what?
MONSTER ISLAND!
SPLASH

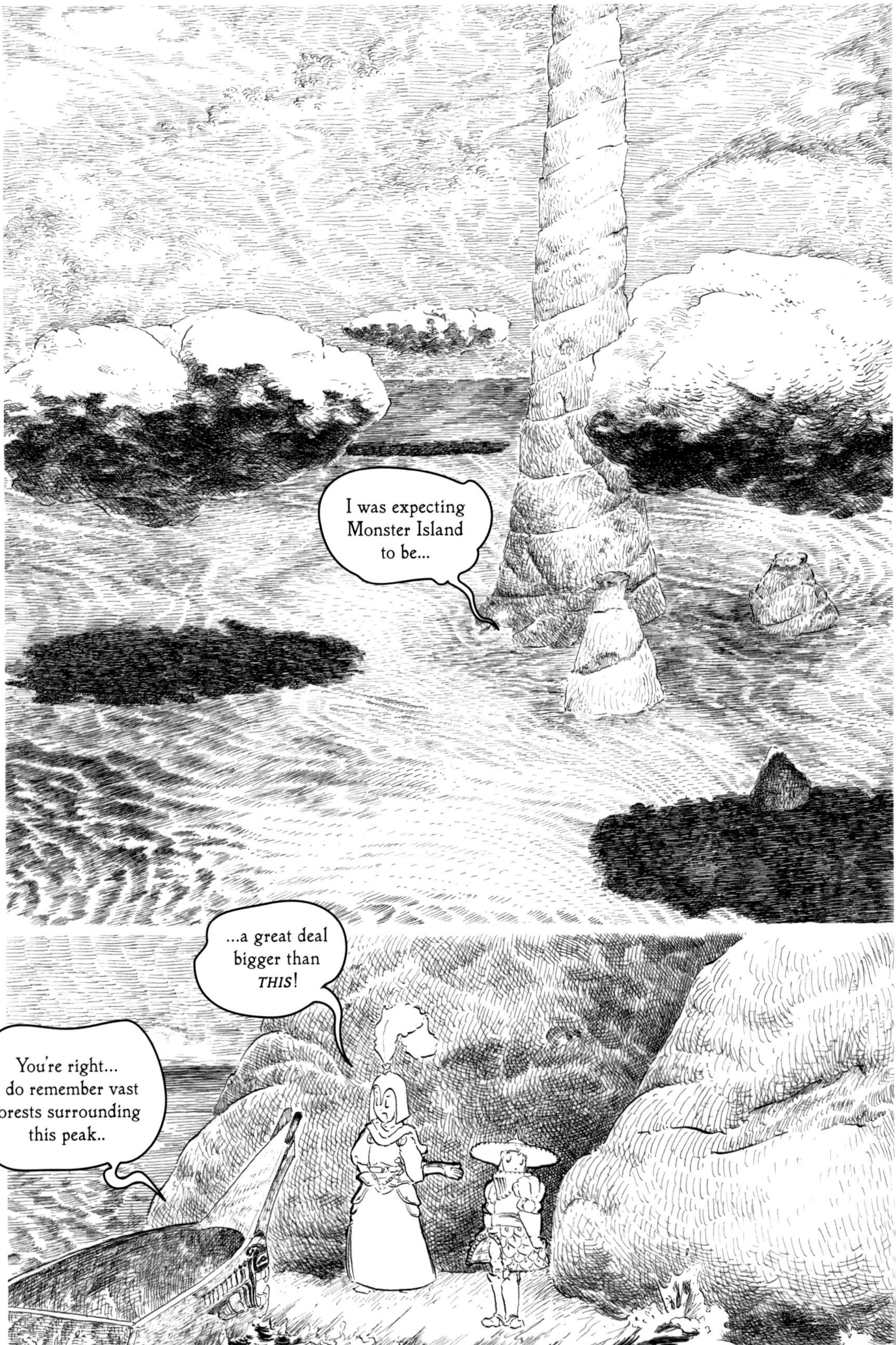
I was expecting Monster Island to be...
...a great deal bigger than *THIS*!
You're right... I do remember vast forests surrounding this peak..

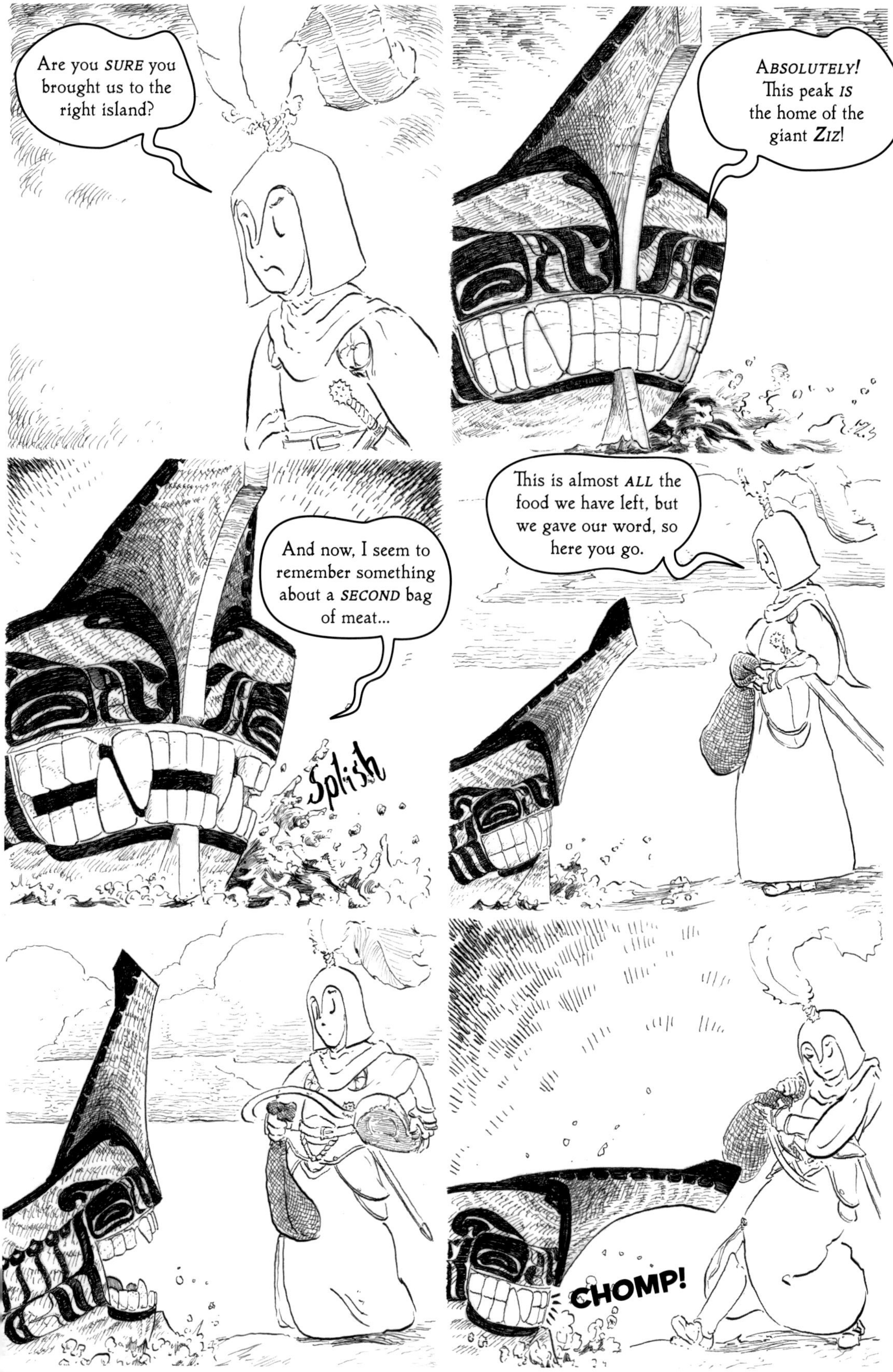
Are you SURE you brought us to the right island?
ABSOLUTELY! This peak IS the home of the giant ZIZ!
And now, I seem to remember something about a SECOND bag of meat...
Splish
This is almost ALL the food we have left, but we gave our word, so here you go.
CHOMP!

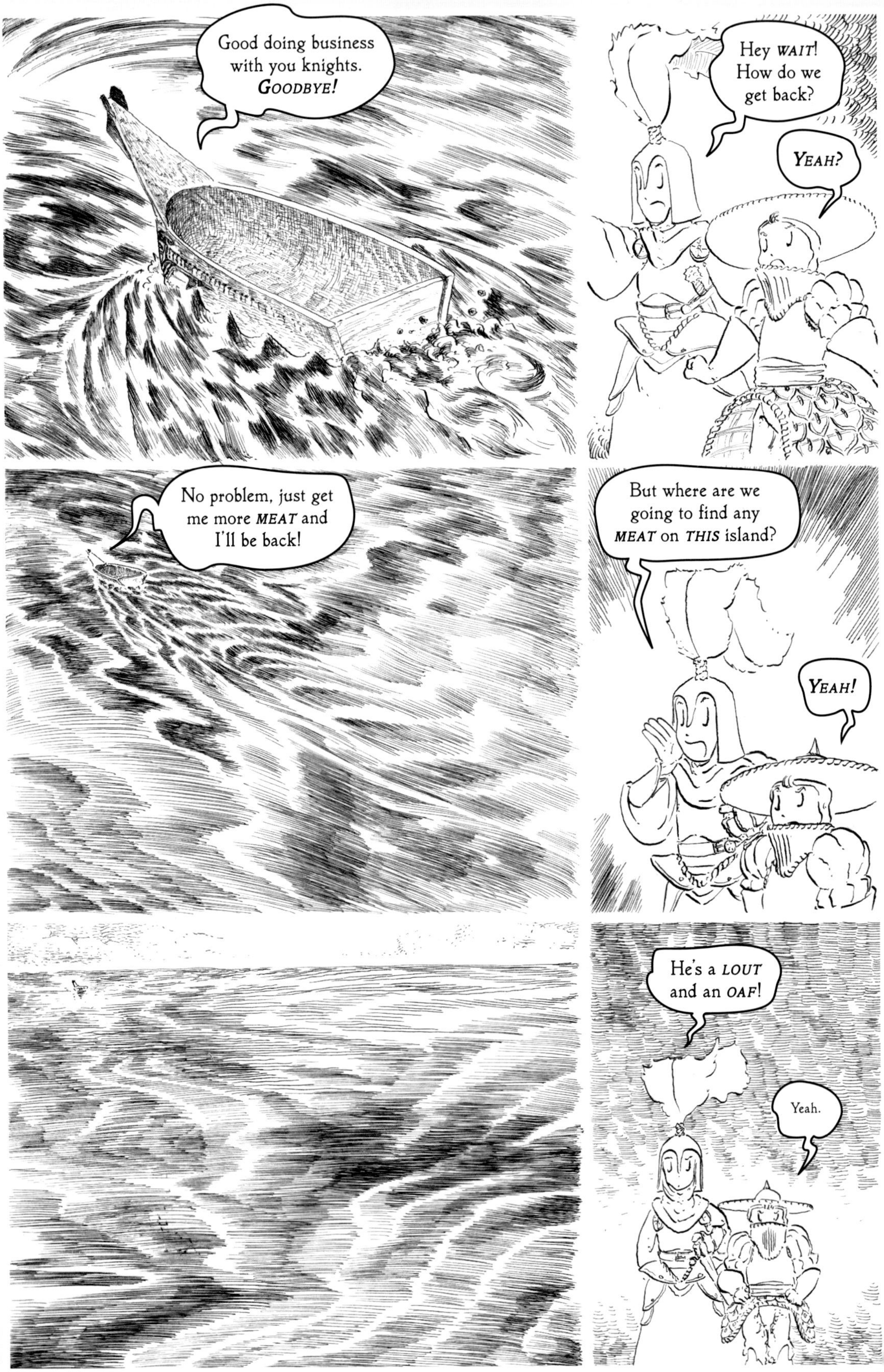
Good doing business with you knights. GOODBYE!
Hey WAIT! How do we get back?
YEAH?
No problem, just get me more MEAT and I'll be back!
But where are we going to find any MEAT on THIS island?
YEAH!
He's a LOUT and an OAF!
Yeah.

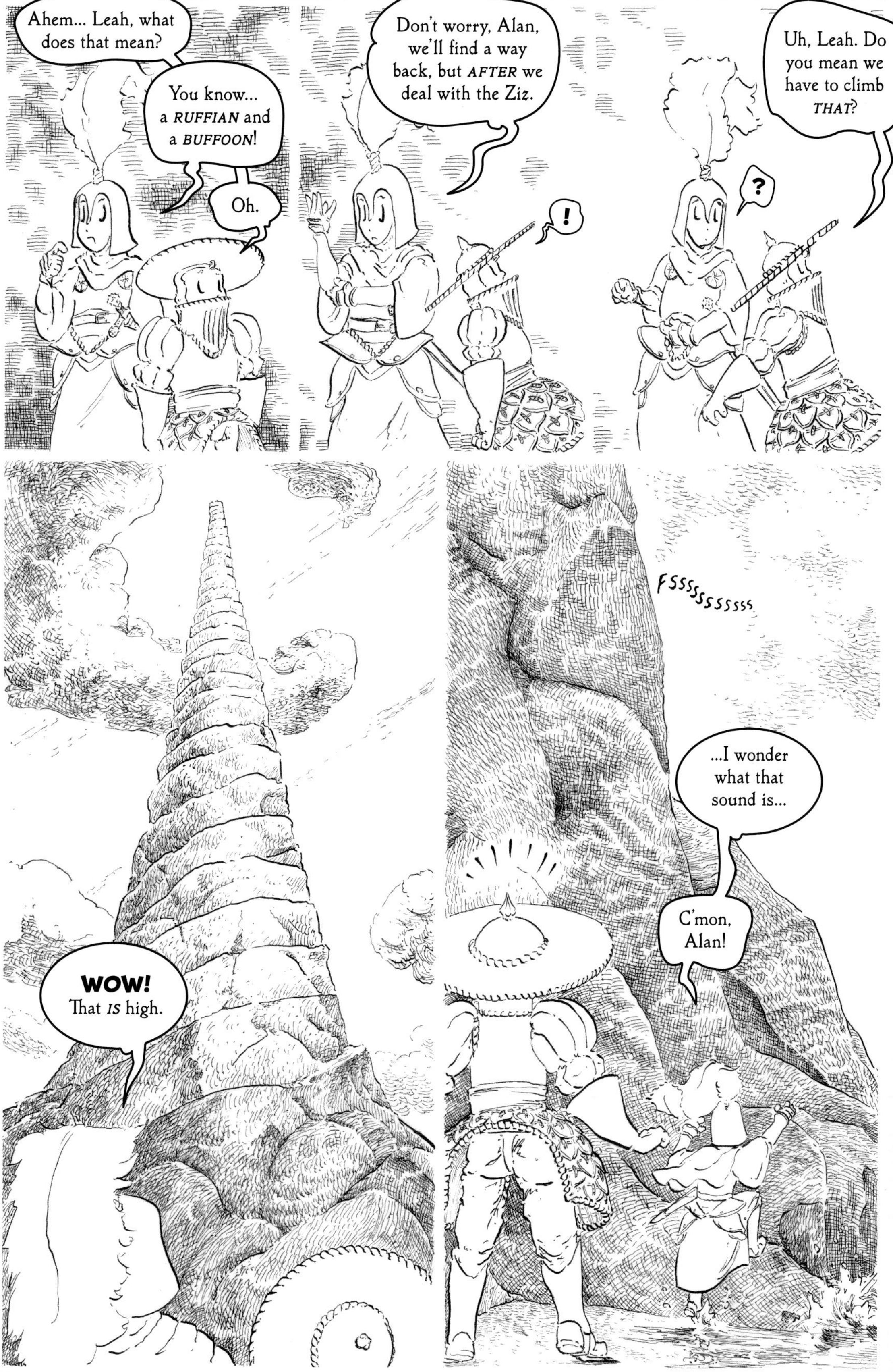
Ahem... Leah, what does that mean?
You know... a RUFFIAN and a BUFFOON!
Oh.
Don't worry, Alan, we'll find a way back, but AFTER we deal with the Ziz.
!
Uh, Leah. Do you mean we have to climb THAT?
?
WOW! That IS high.
FSSSSSSSSSSS
...I wonder what that sound is...
C'mon, Alan!

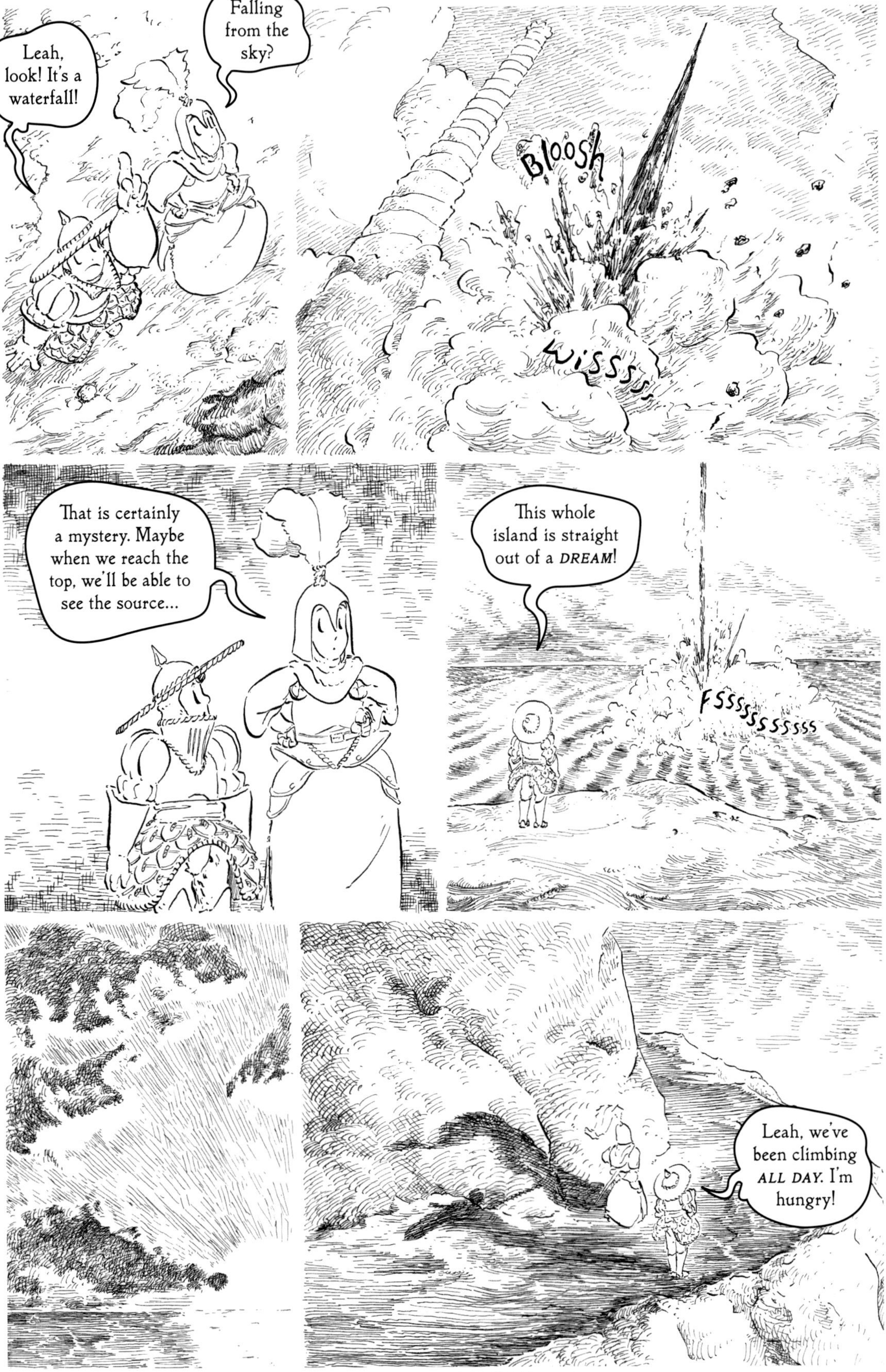
Leah, look! It's a waterfall!
Falling from the sky?
BLOOSH
WISSSSS
That is certainly a mystery. Maybe when we reach the top, we'll be able to see the source...
This whole island is straight out of a *DREAM*!
FSSSSSSSSSSSS
Leah, we've been climbing *ALL DAY*. I'm hungry!

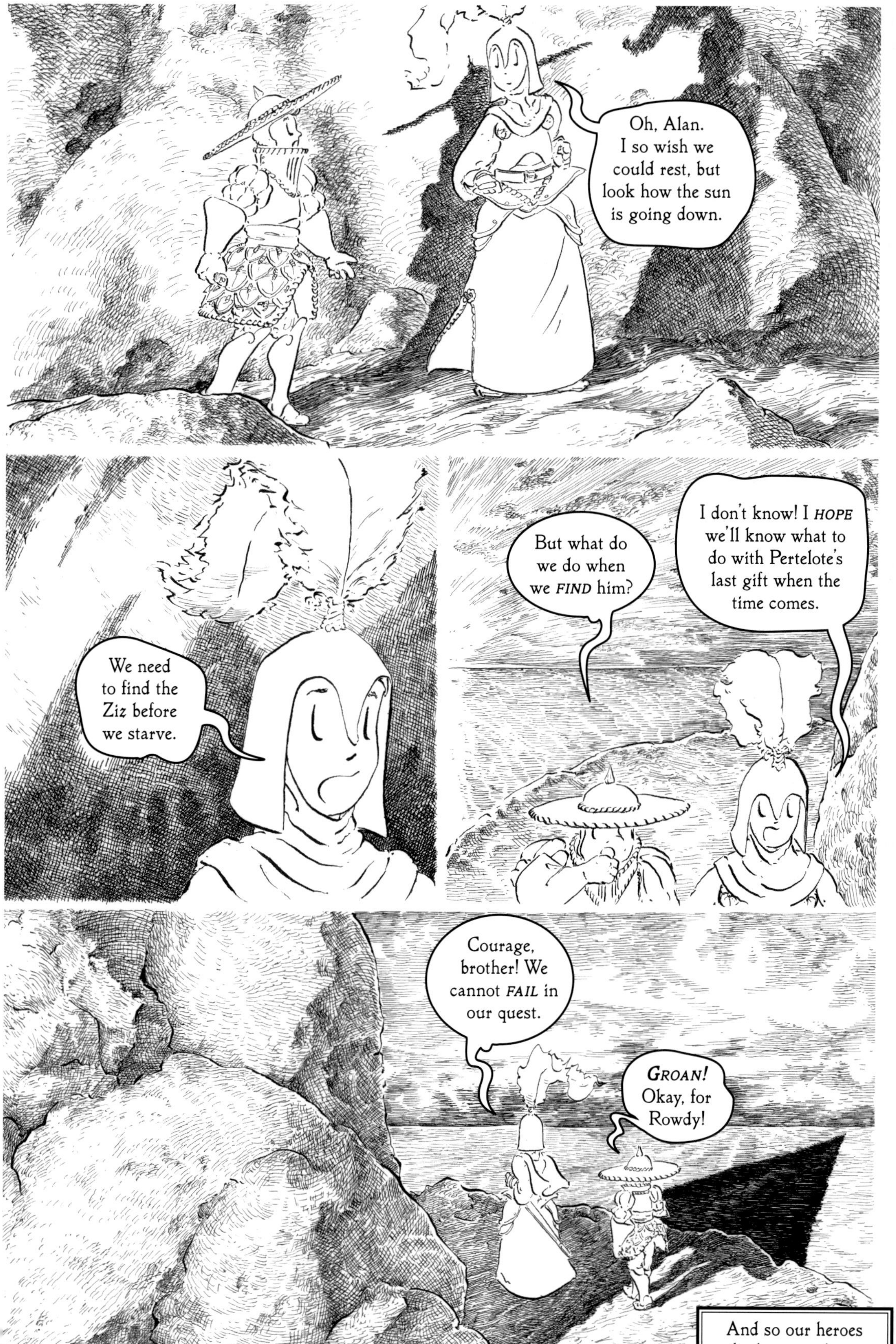
Oh, Alan. I so wish we could rest, but look how the sun is going down.
We need to find the Ziz before we starve.
But what do we do when we *FIND* him?
I don't know! I *HOPE* we'll know what to do with Pertelote's last gift when the time comes.
Courage, brother! We cannot *FAIL* in our quest.
GROAN! Okay, for Rowdy!
And so our heroes climb on...and on...

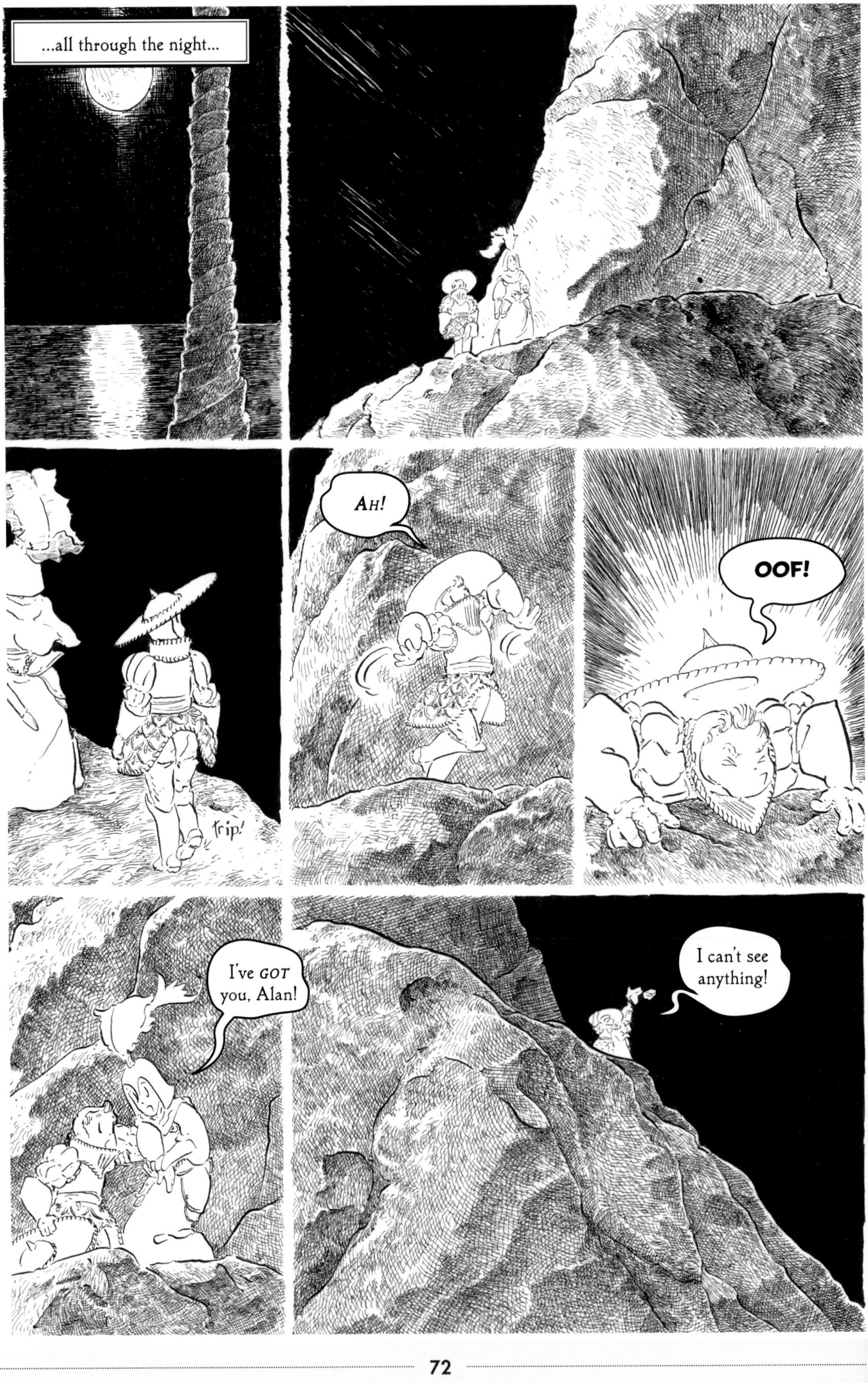
...all through the night...
AH!
trip!
OOF!
I've GOT you, Alan!
I can't see anything!

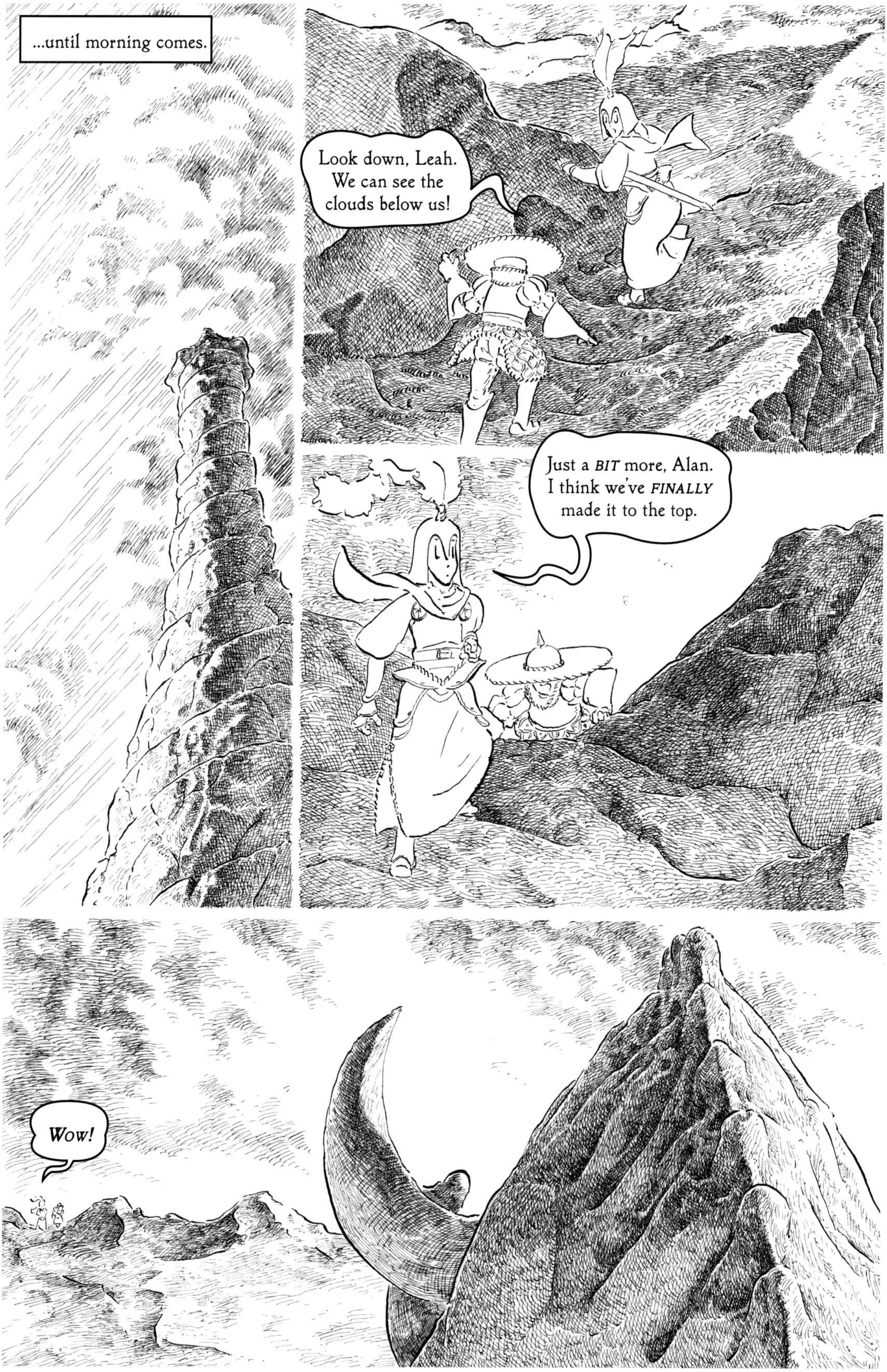
...until morning comes.
Look down, Leah. We can see the clouds below us!
Just a BIT more, Alan. I think we've FINALLY made it to the top.
Wow!

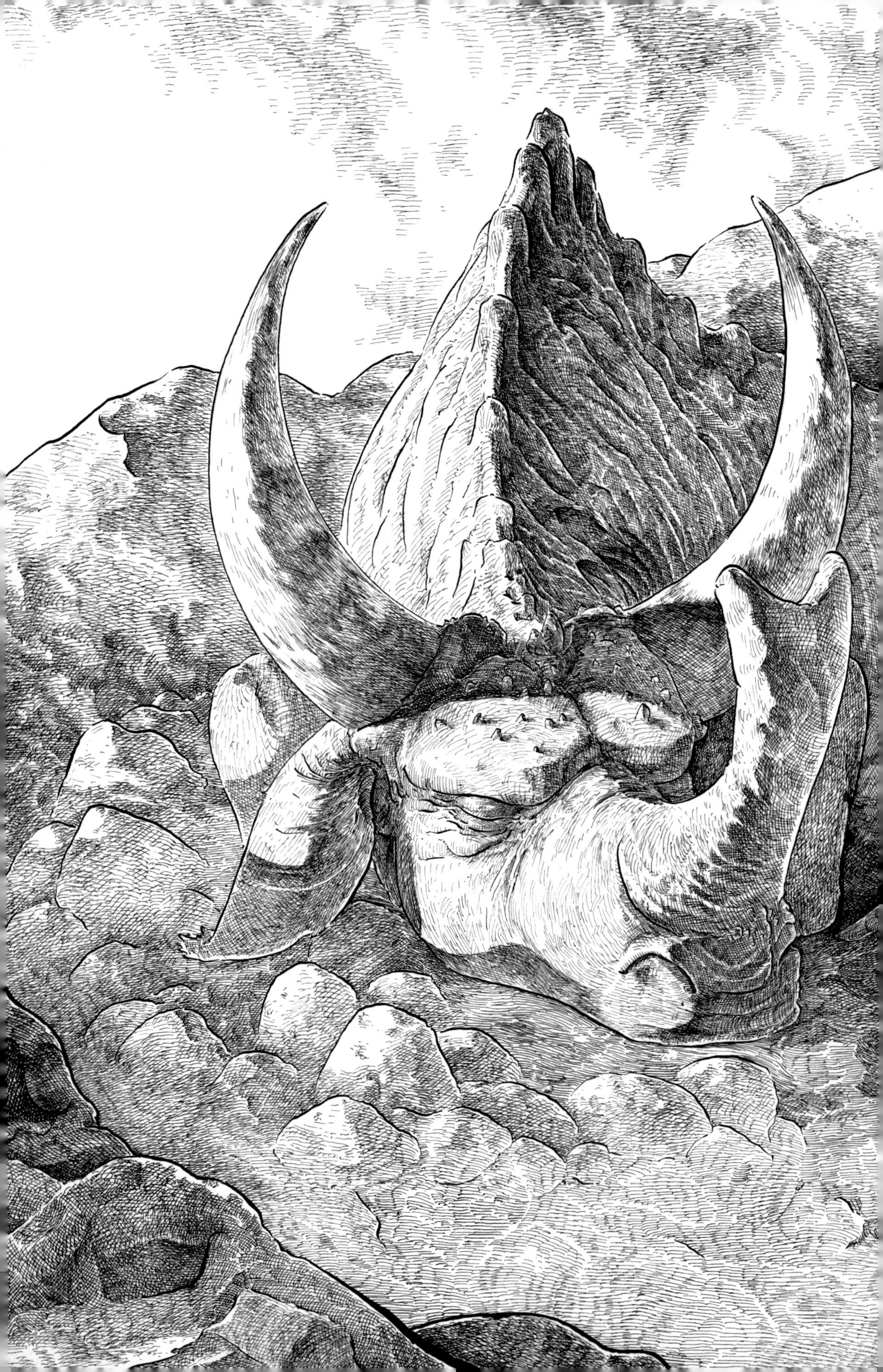

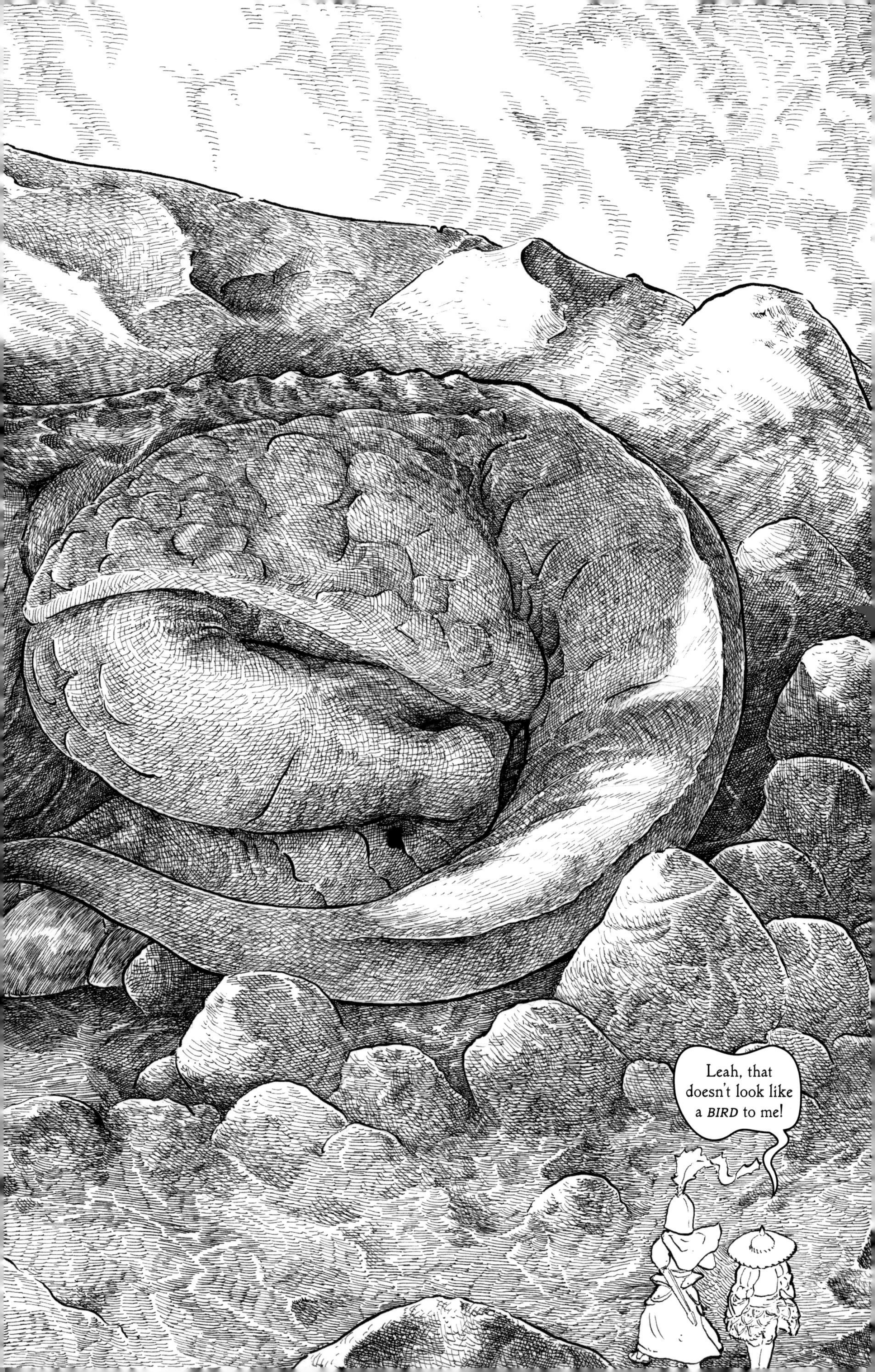
Leah, that doesn't look like a *BIRD* to me!

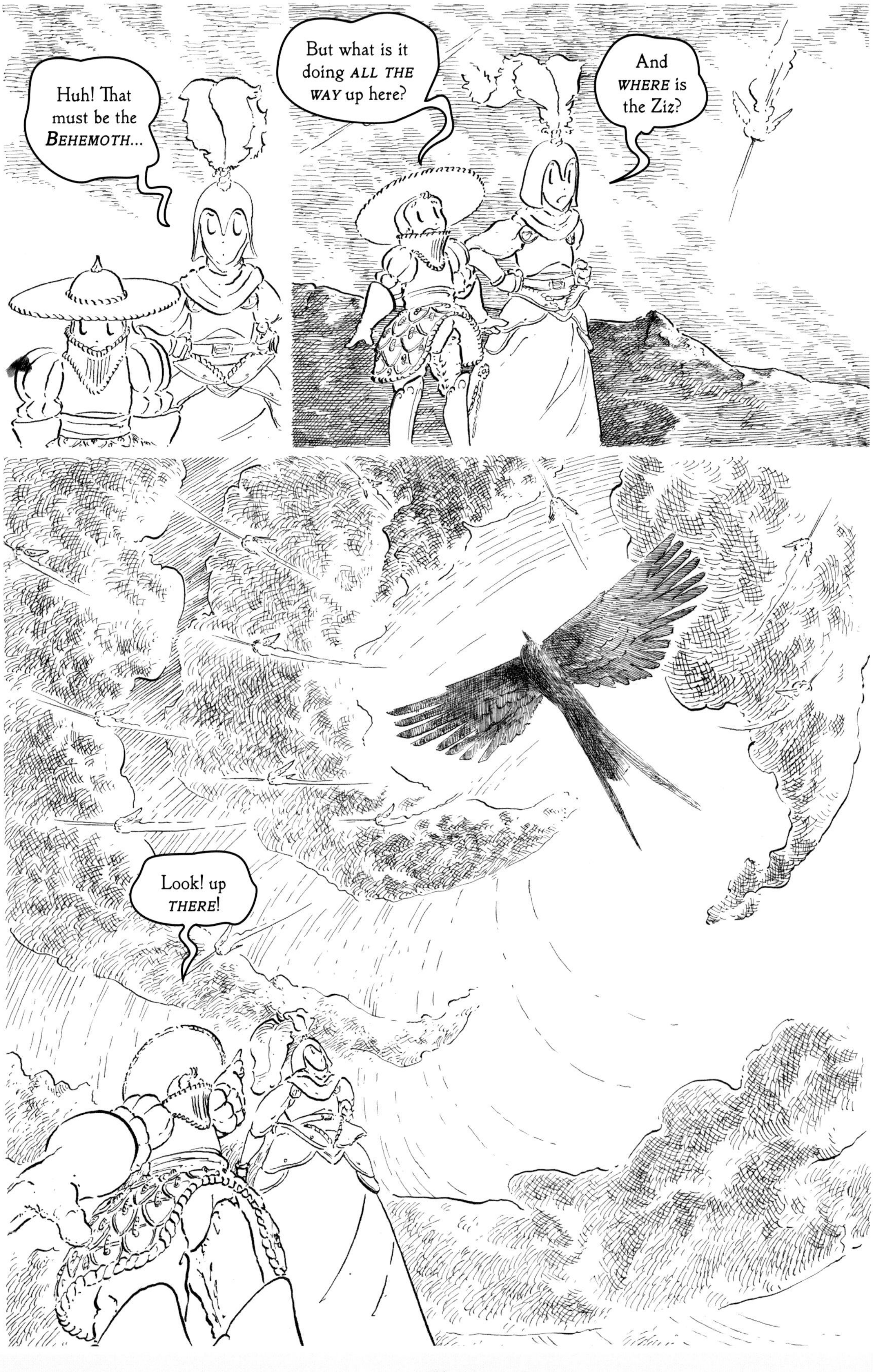
Huh! That must be the BEHEMOTH...
But what is it doing ALL THE WAY up here?
And WHERE is the Ziz?
Look! up THERE!

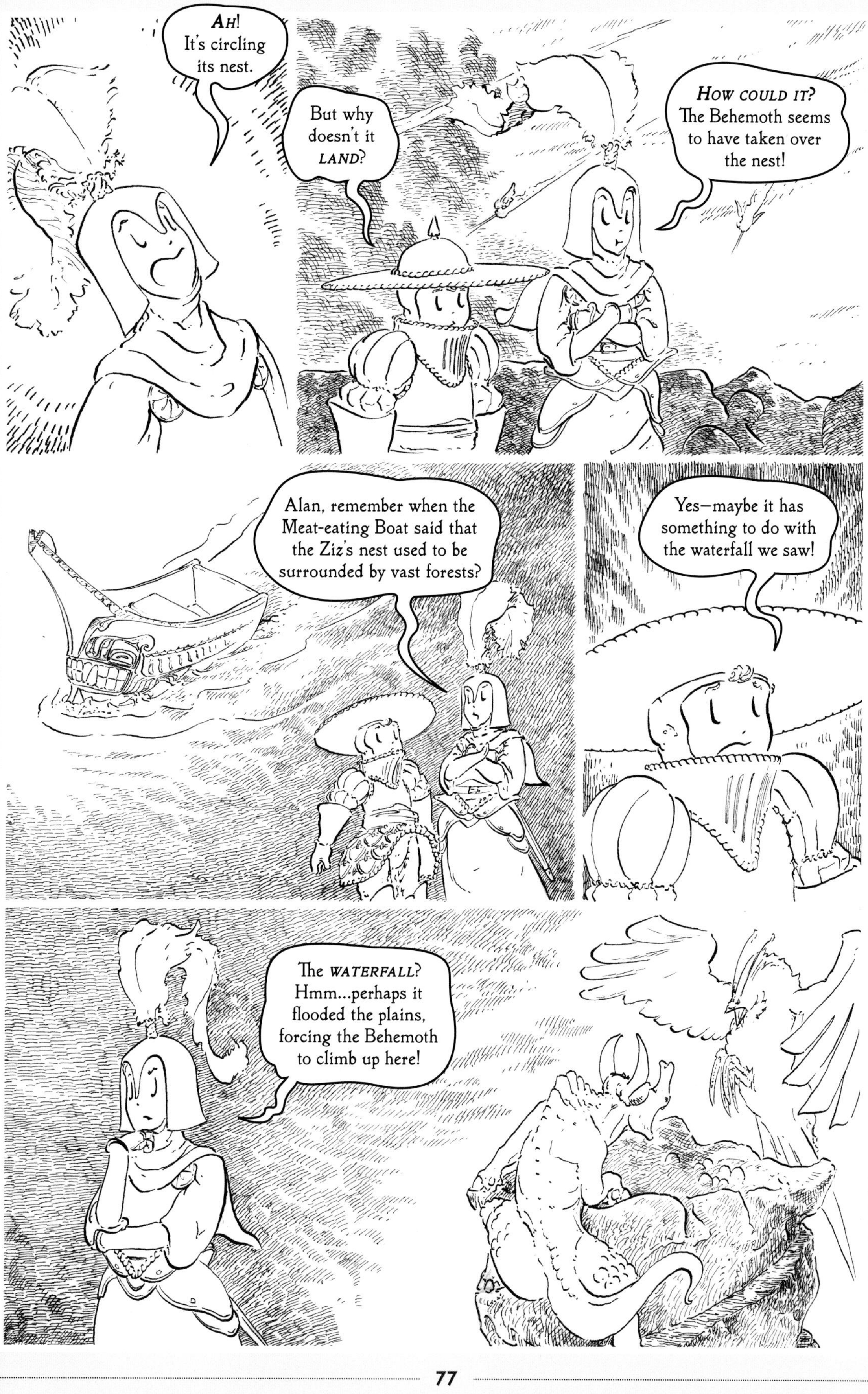

Ah! It's circling its nest.
But why doesn't it *LAND*?
HOW COULD IT? The Behemoth seems to have taken over the nest!
Alan, remember when the Meat-eating Boat said that the Ziz's nest used to be surrounded by vast forests?
Yes—maybe it has something to do with the waterfall we saw!
The *WATERFALL*? Hmm...perhaps it flooded the plains, forcing the Behemoth to climb up here!

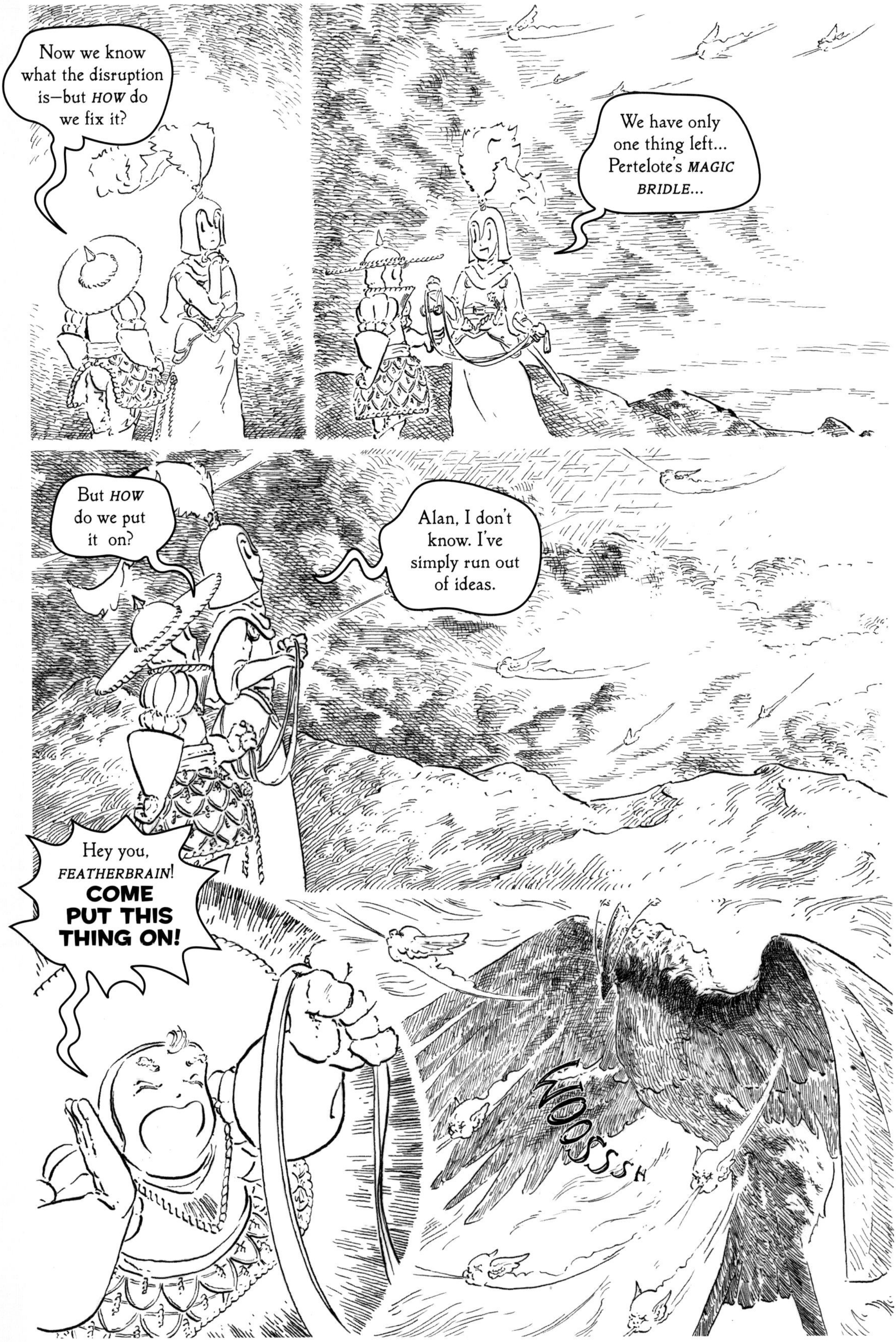
Now we know what the disruption is—but *HOW* do we fix it?
We have only one thing left... Pertelote's *MAGIC BRIDLE*...
But *HOW* do we put it on?
Alan, I don't know. I've simply run out of ideas.
Hey you, *FEATHERBRAIN*! **COME PUT THIS THING ON!**
WOOSSSH

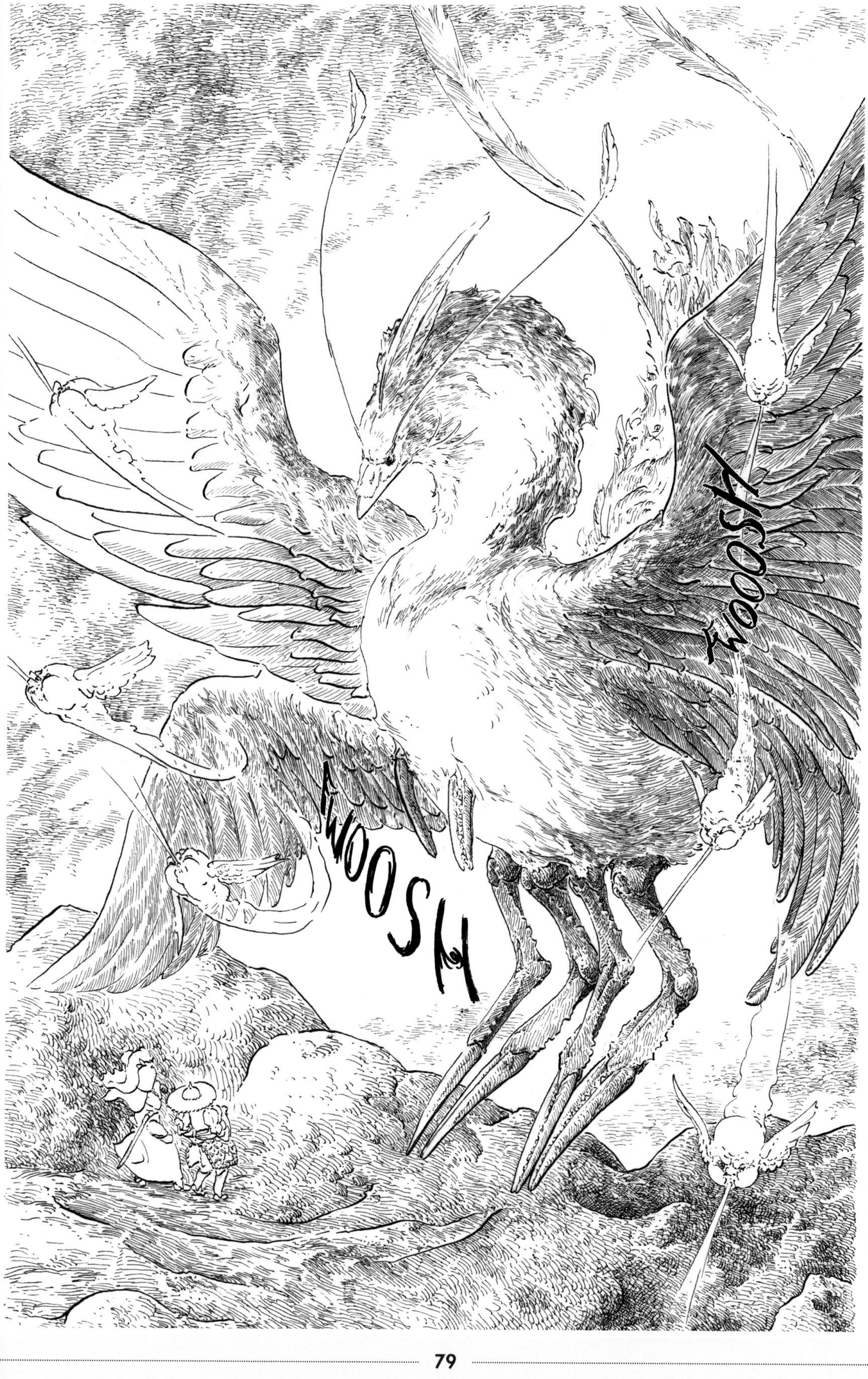
WOOOSH
WOOSH

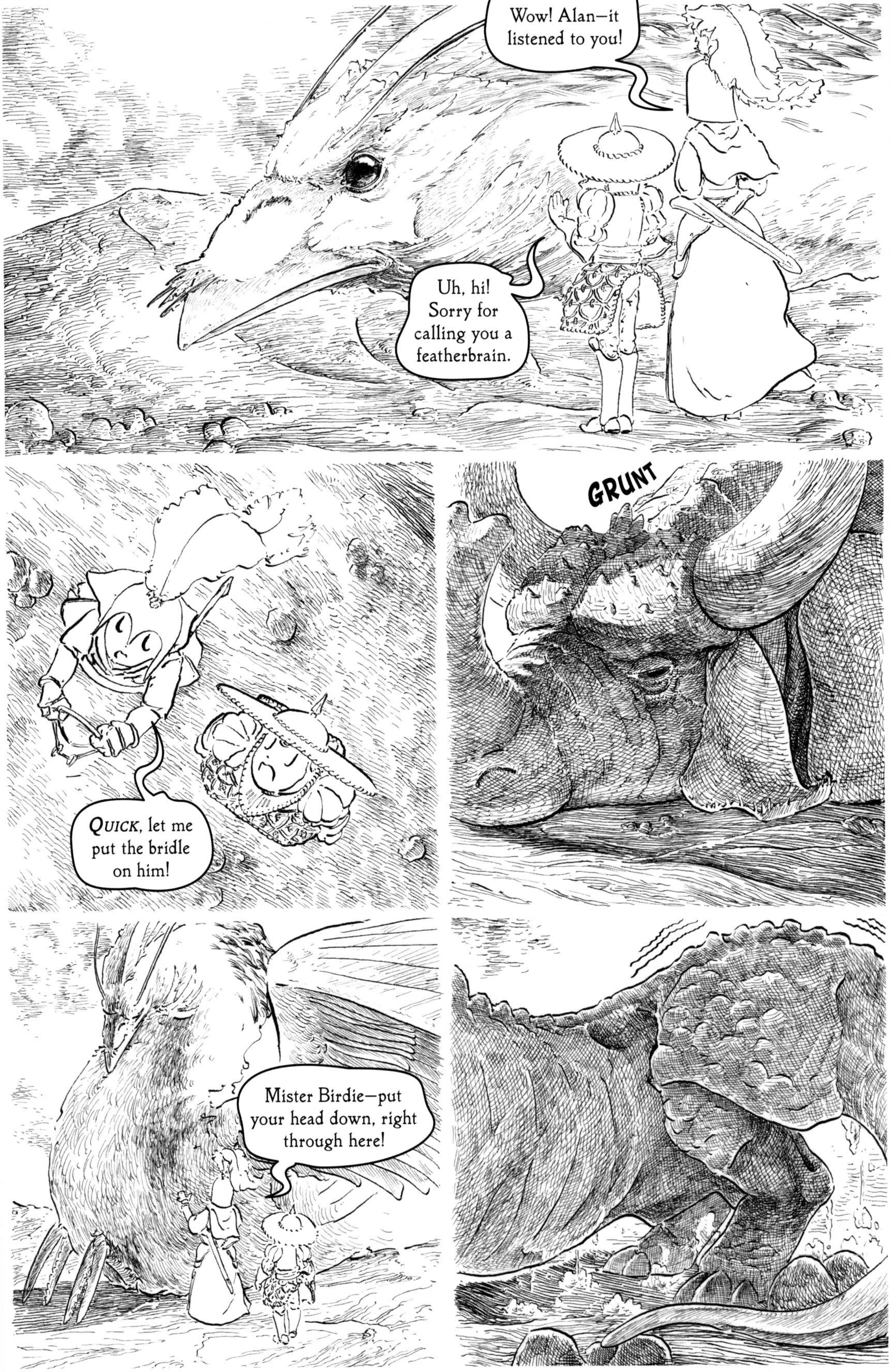
Wow! Alan—it listened to you!
Uh, hi! Sorry for calling you a featherbrain.
Quick, let me put the bridle on him!
GRUNT
Mister Birdie—put your head down, right through here!

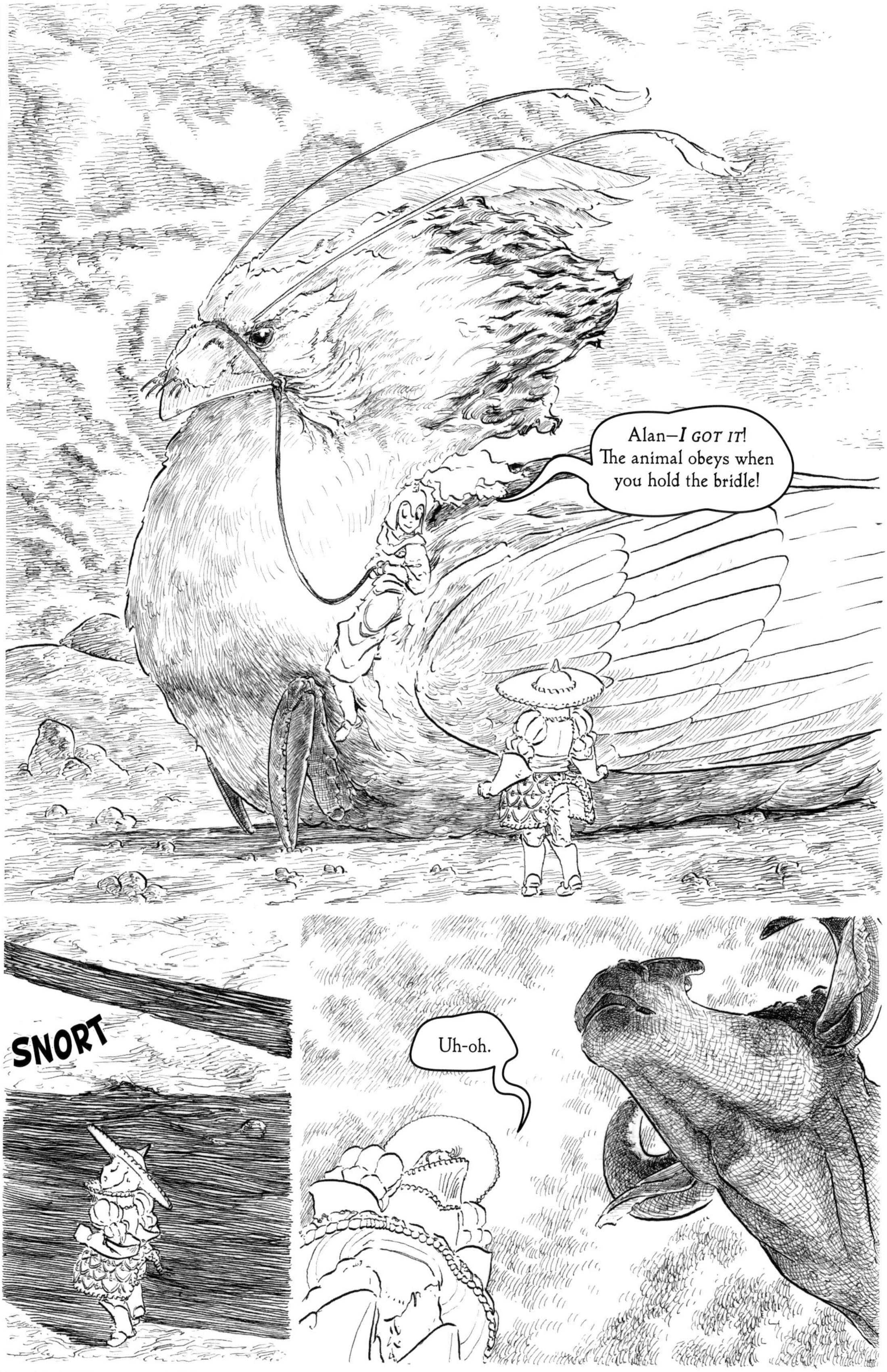

Alan—*I GOT IT*! The animal obeys when you hold the bridle!
SNORT
Uh-oh.

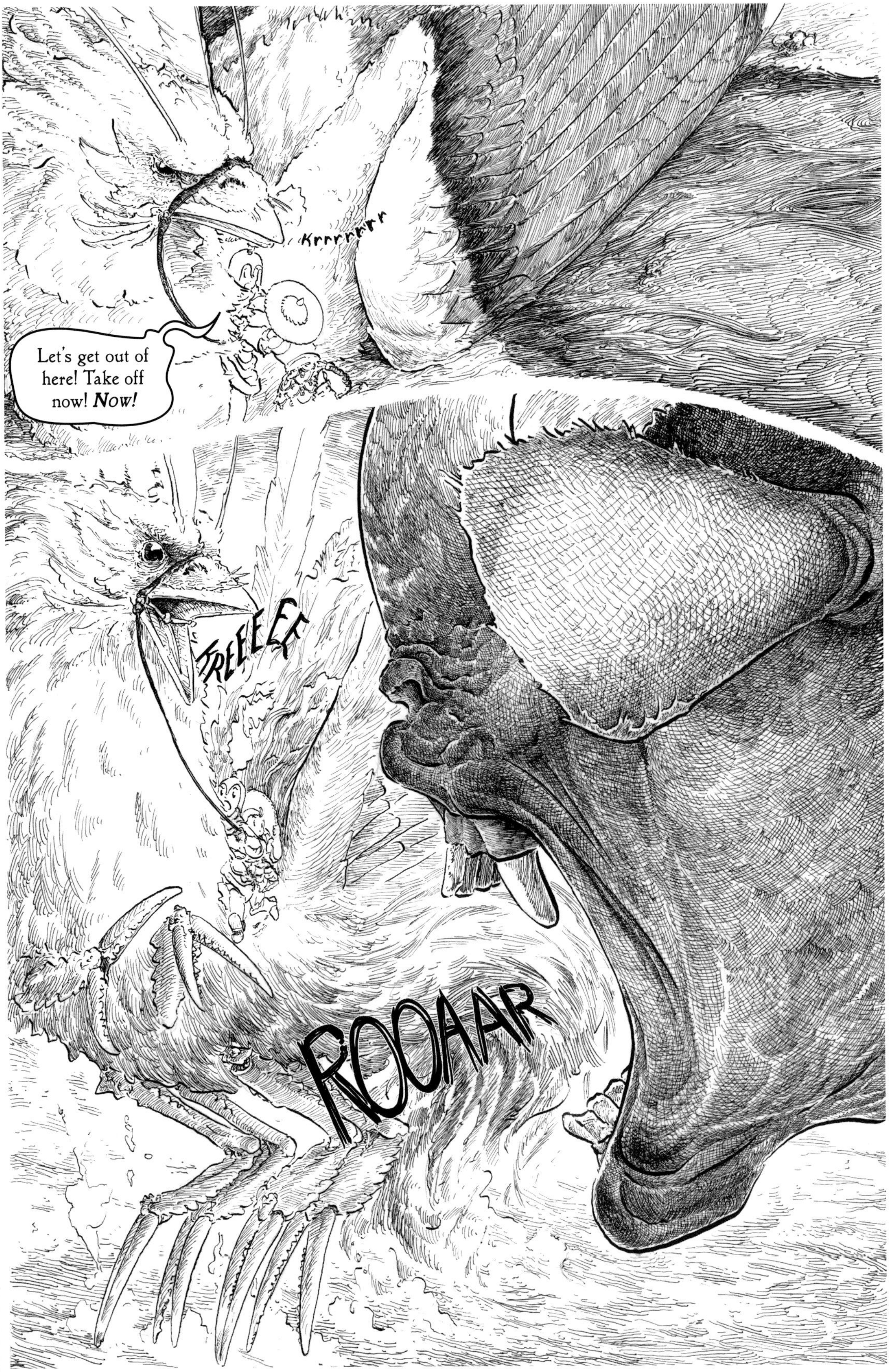
Krrrrrrr
Let's get out of here! Take off now! *Now!*
TREEEEE
ROOAAR

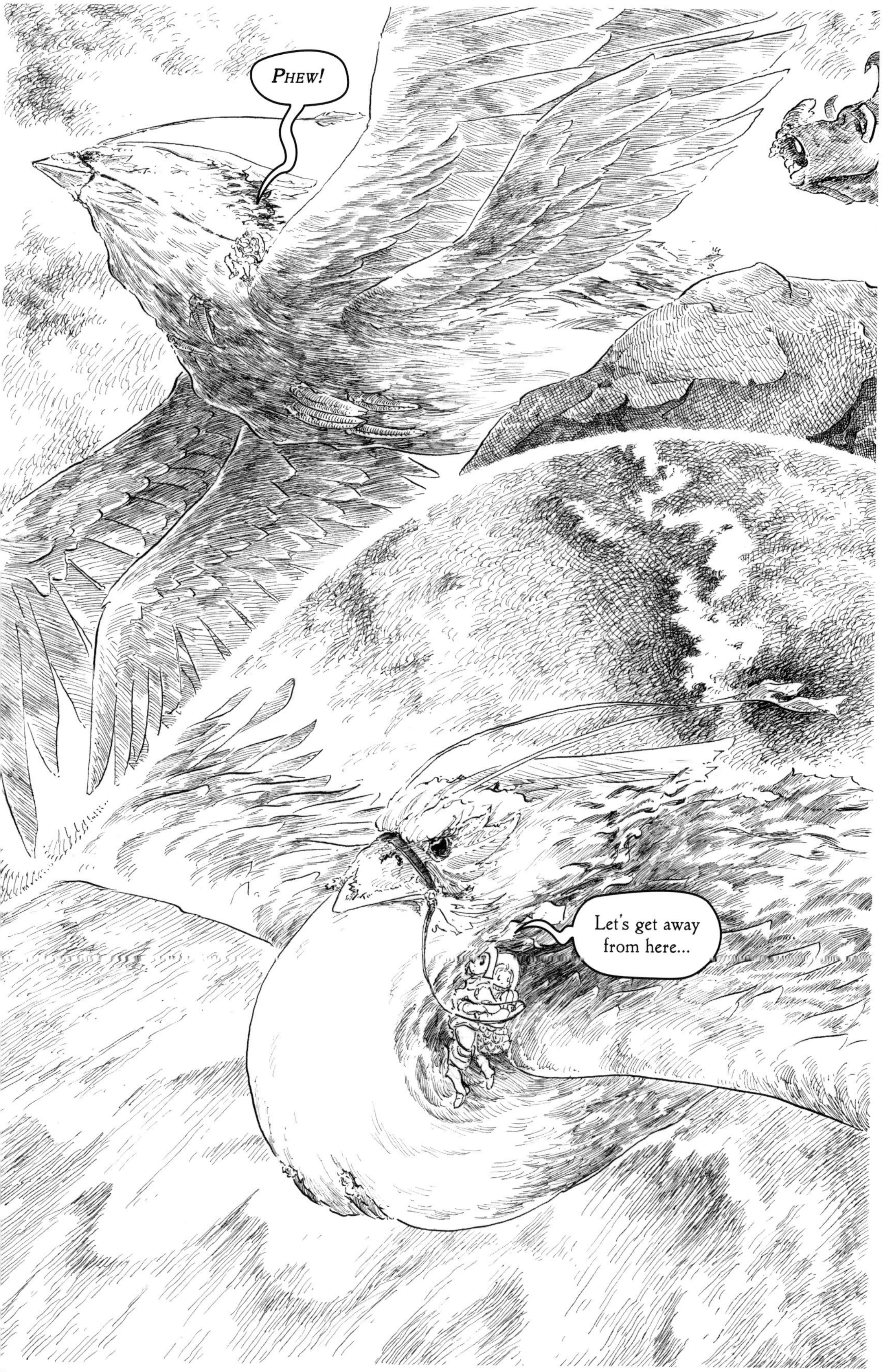
PHEW!
Let's get away from here...

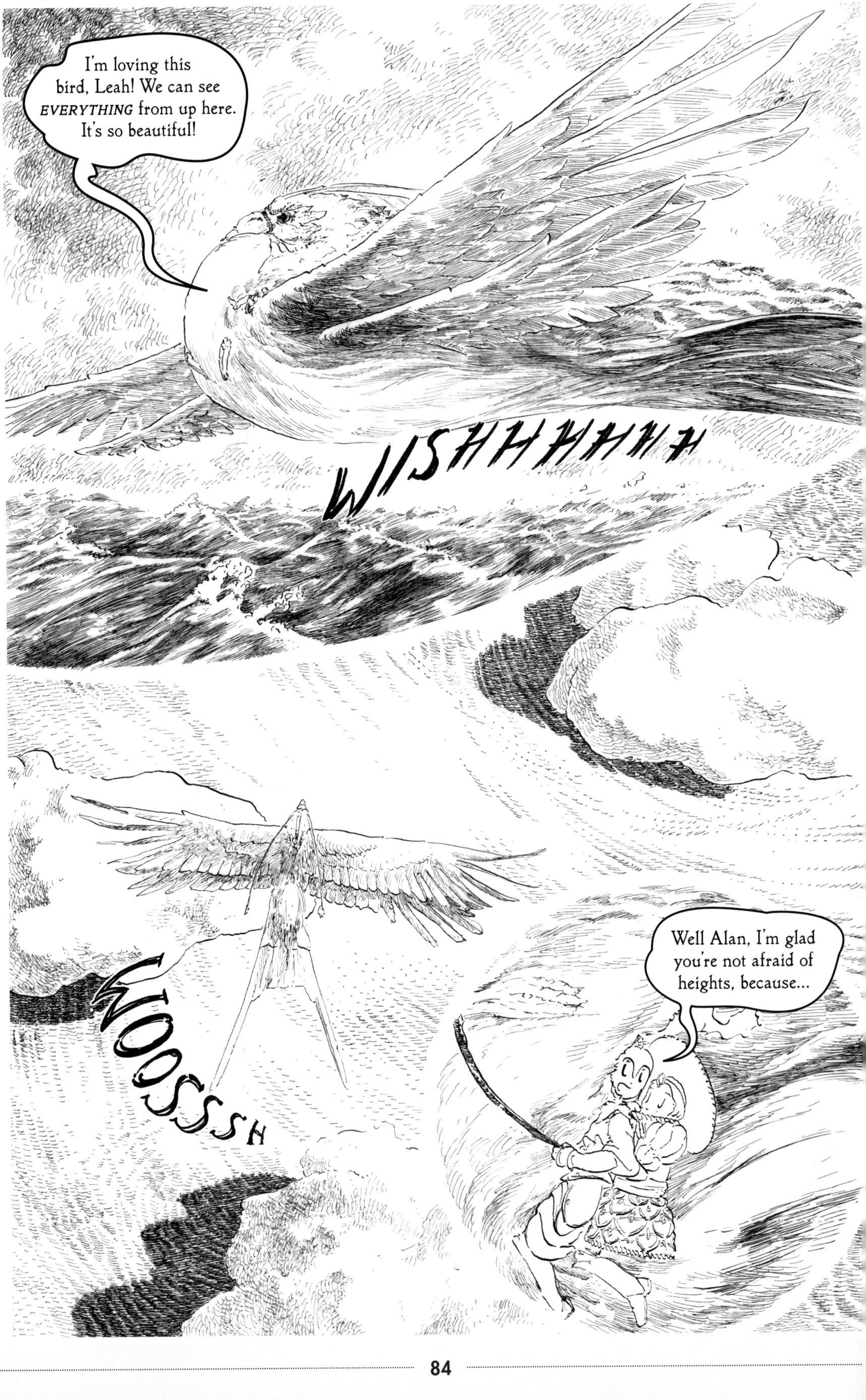
I'm loving this bird, Leah! We can see EVERYTHING from up here. It's so beautiful!
WISHHHHHH
WOOSSSH
Well Alan, I'm glad you're not afraid of heights, because...

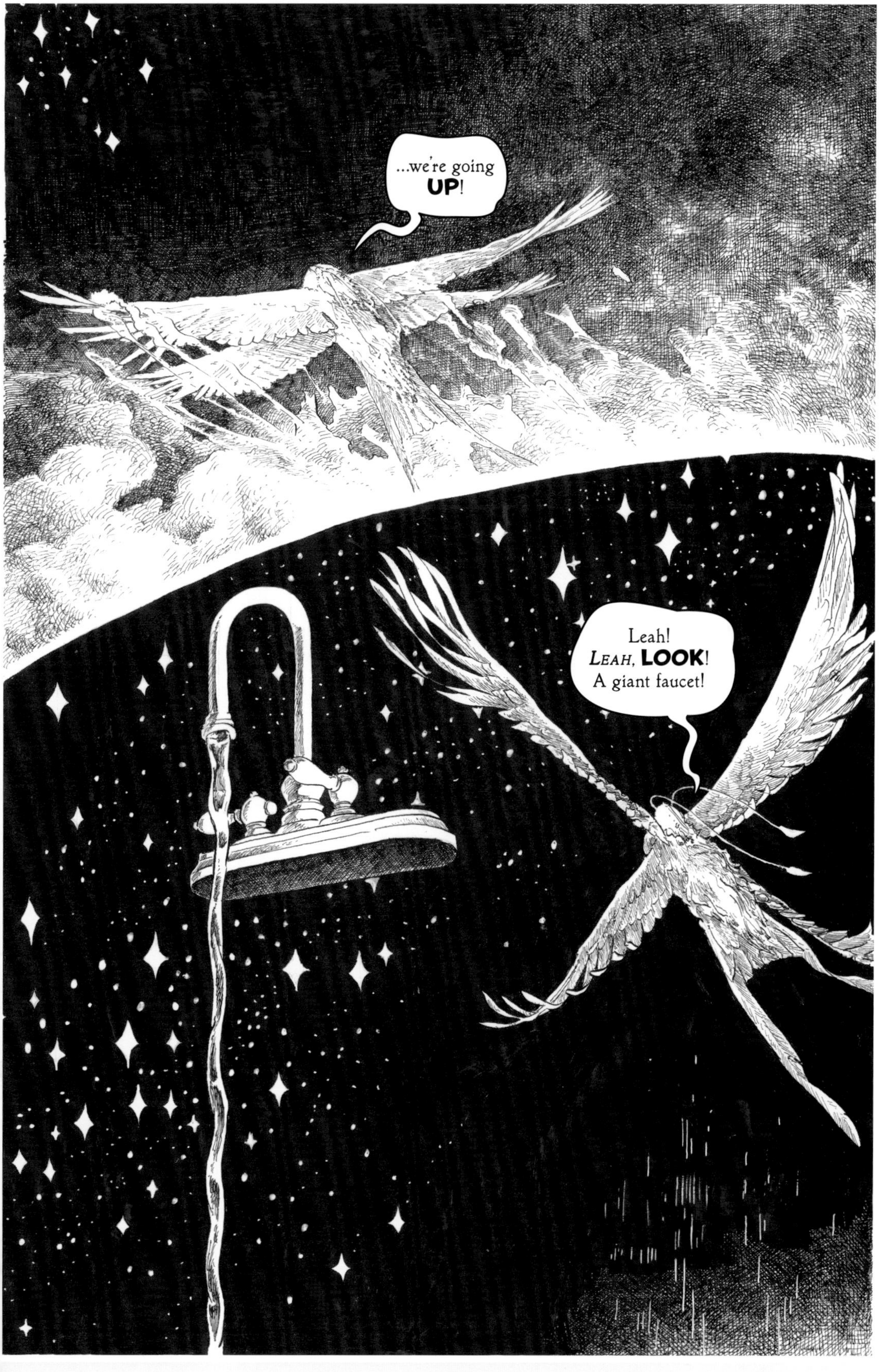
...we're going **UP**!
Leah! *Leah*, **LOOK**! A giant faucet!

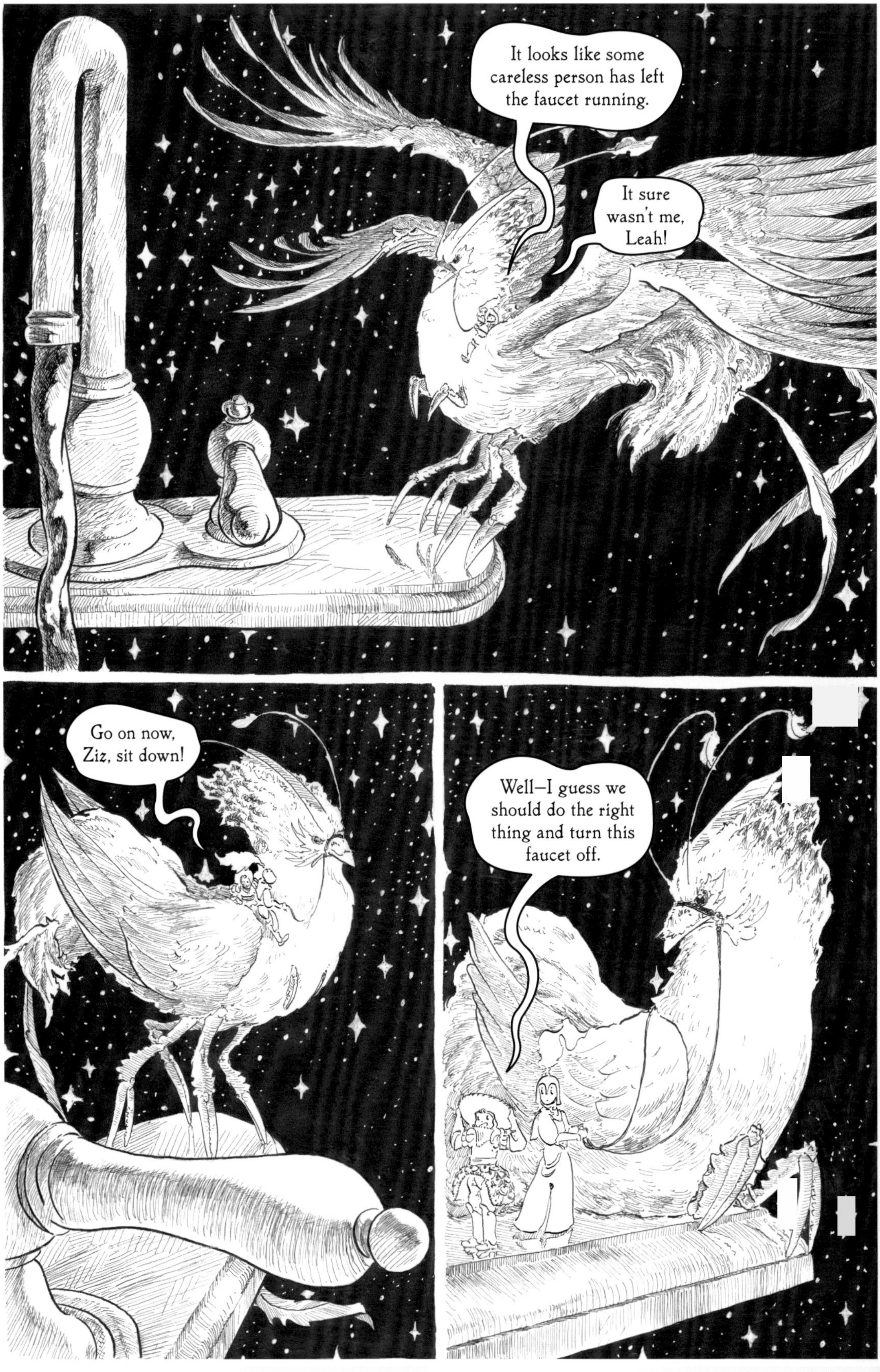
It looks like some careless person has left the faucet running.
It sure wasn't me, Leah!
Go on now, Ziz, sit down!
Well—I guess we should do the right thing and turn this faucet off.

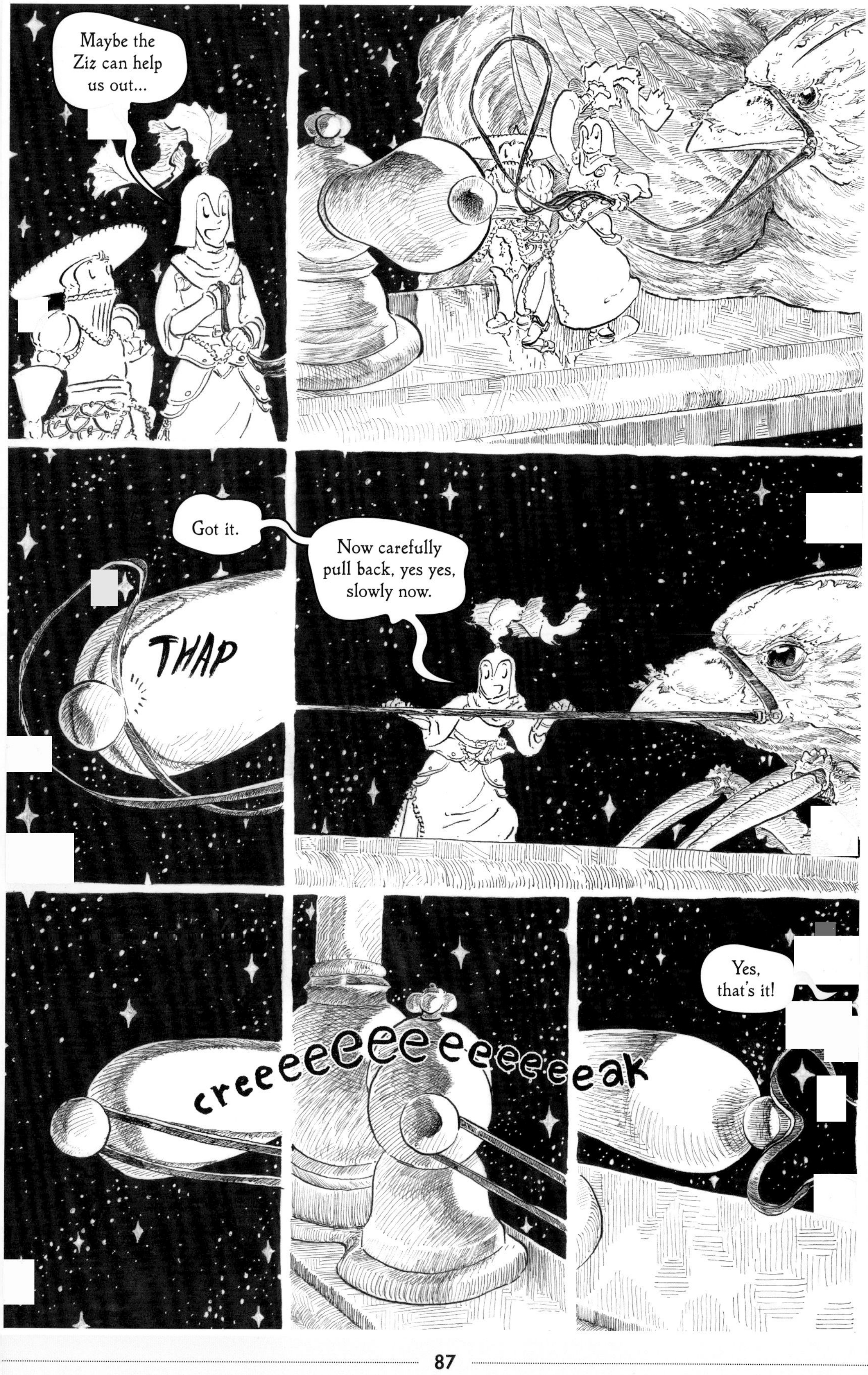
Maybe the Ziz can help us out...
Got it.
Now carefully pull back, yes yes, slowly now.
THAP
creeeeeeeeeeeeeak
Yes, that's it!

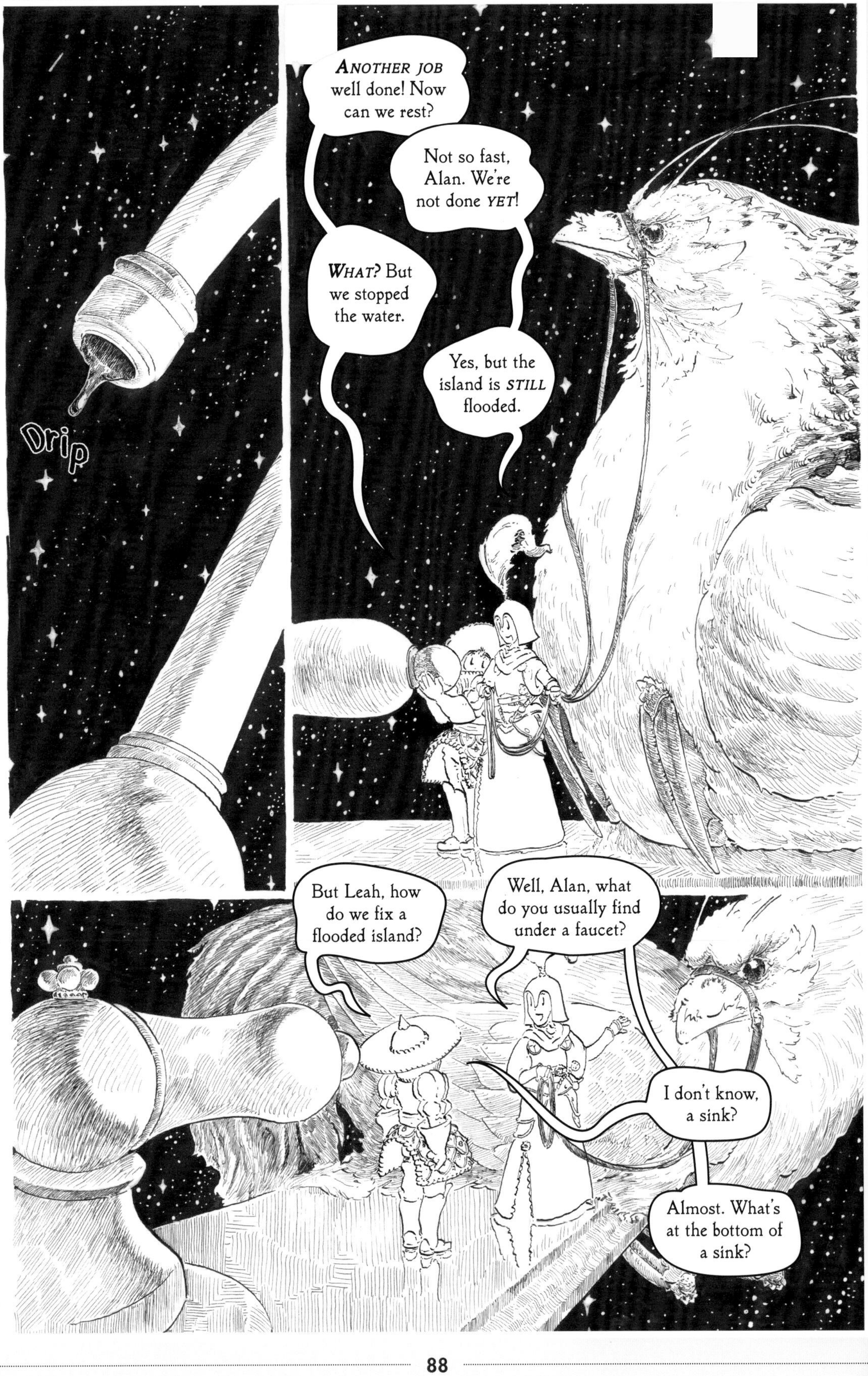
Drip
ANOTHER JOB well done! Now can we rest?
Not so fast, Alan. We're not done YET!
WHAT? But we stopped the water.
Yes, but the island is STILL flooded.
But Leah, how do we fix a flooded island?
Well, Alan, what do you usually find under a faucet?
I don't know, a sink?
Almost. What's at the bottom of a sink?

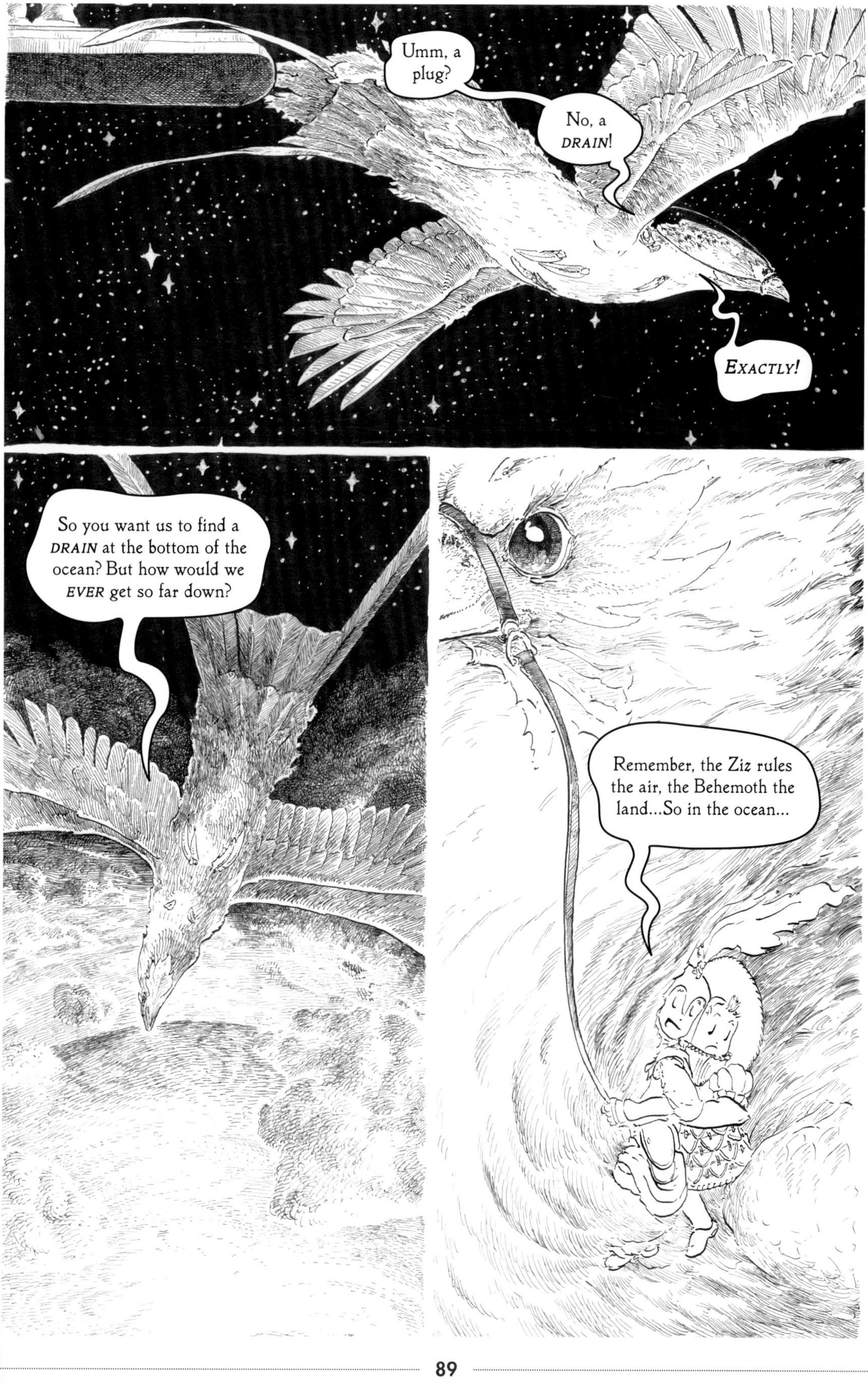
Umm, a plug?
No, a DRAIN!
EXACTLY!
So you want us to find a DRAIN at the bottom of the ocean? But how would we EVER get so far down?
Remember, the Ziz rules the air, the Behemoth the land...So in the ocean...

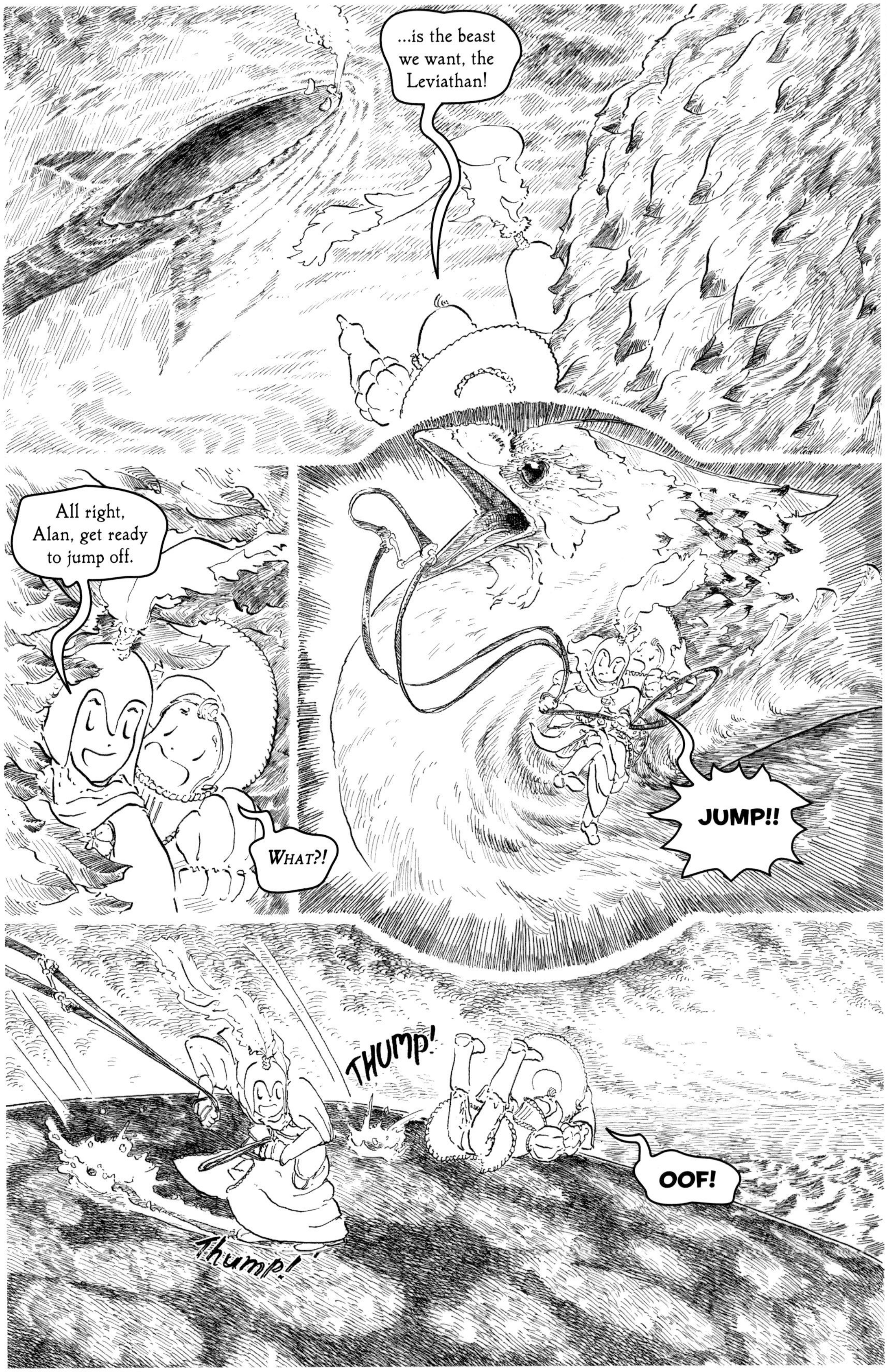
...is the beast we want, the Leviathan!
All right, Alan, get ready to jump off.
WHAT?!
JUMP!!
THUMP!
Thump!
OOF!

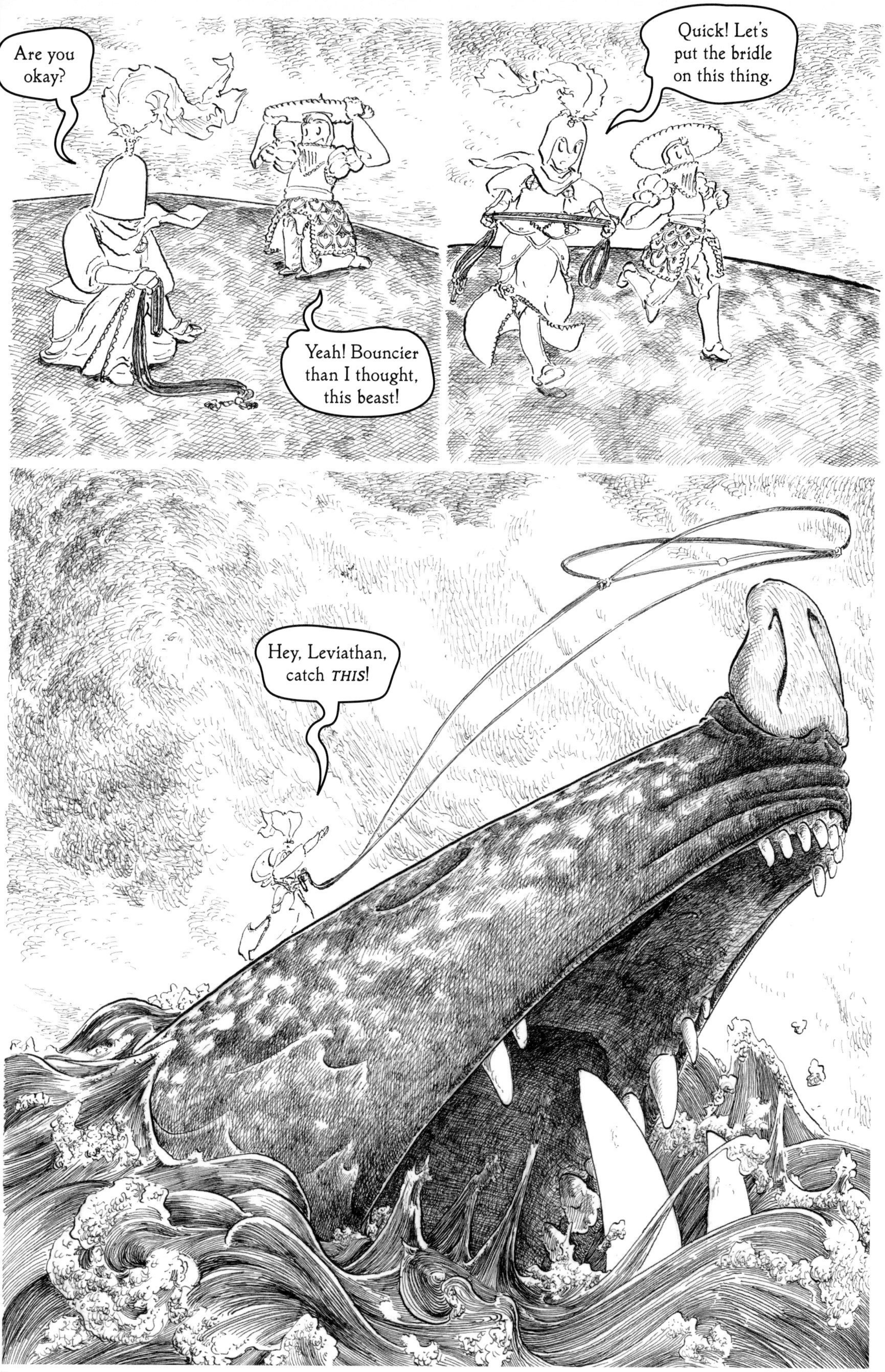
Are you okay?
Yeah! Bouncier than I thought, this beast!
Quick! Let's put the bridle on this thing.
Hey, Leviathan, catch *THIS*!

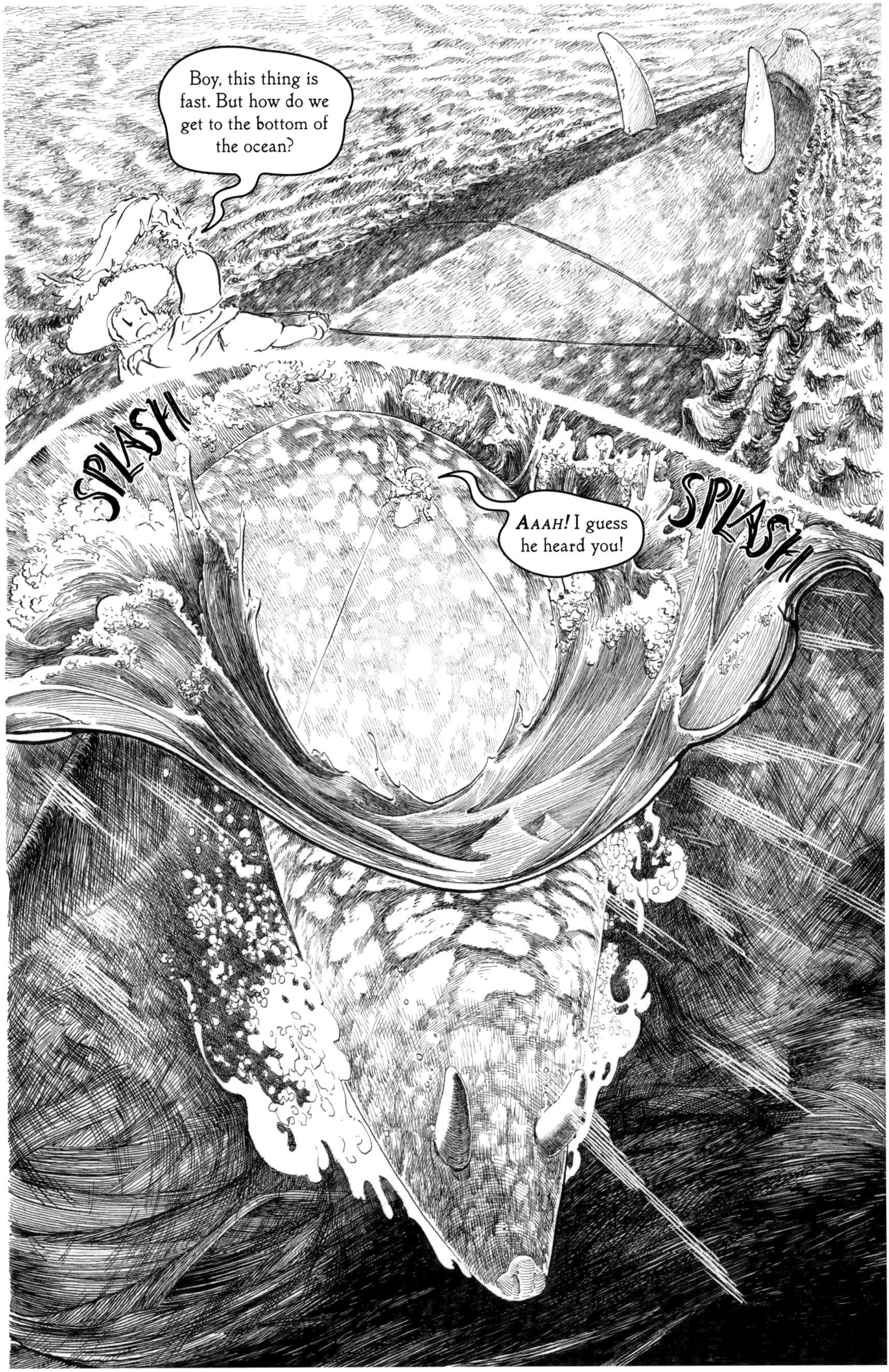
Boy, this thing is fast. But how do we get to the bottom of the ocean?
SPLASH
AAAH! I guess he heard you!
SPLASH

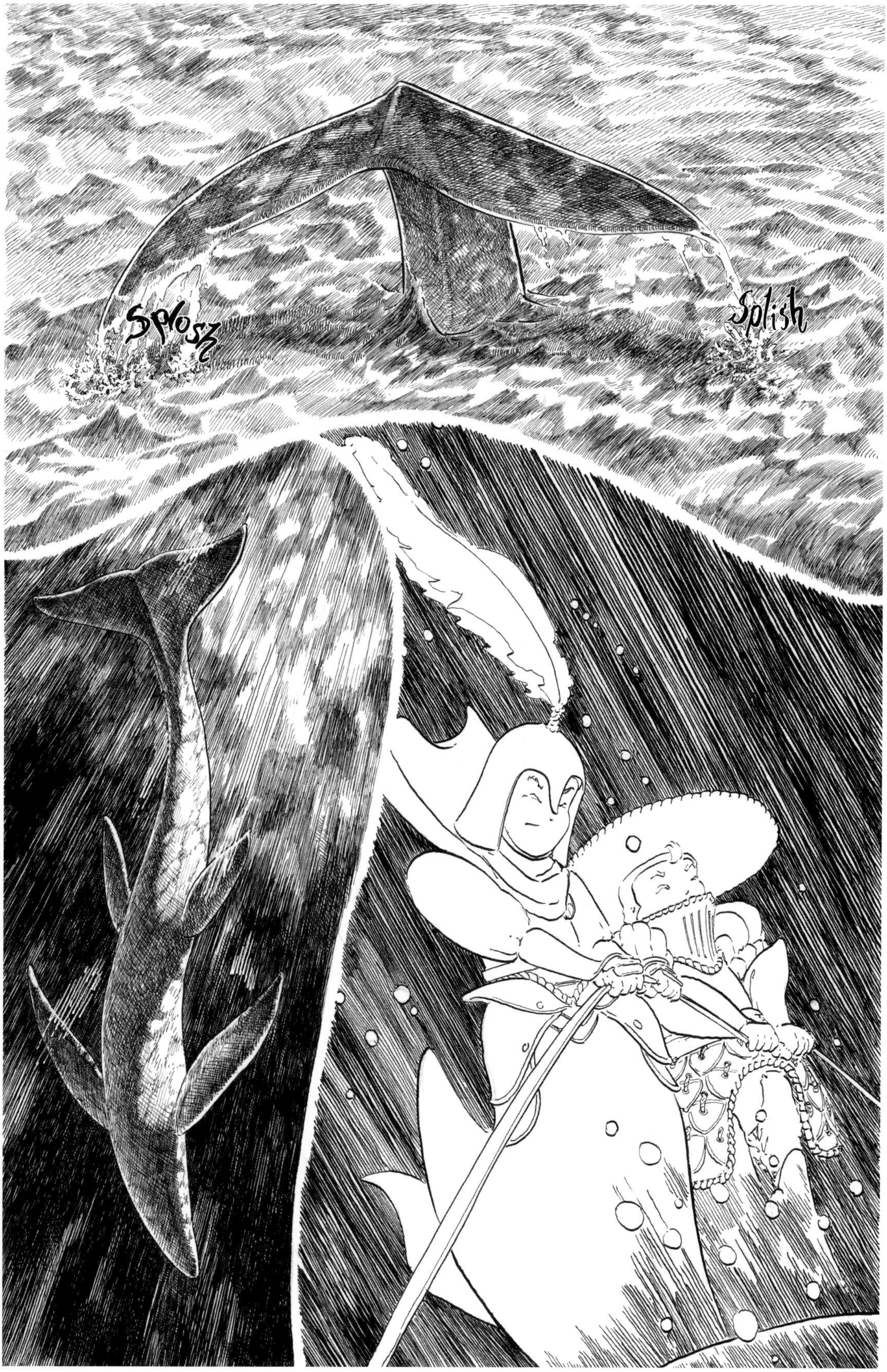
Sprosh
Splish

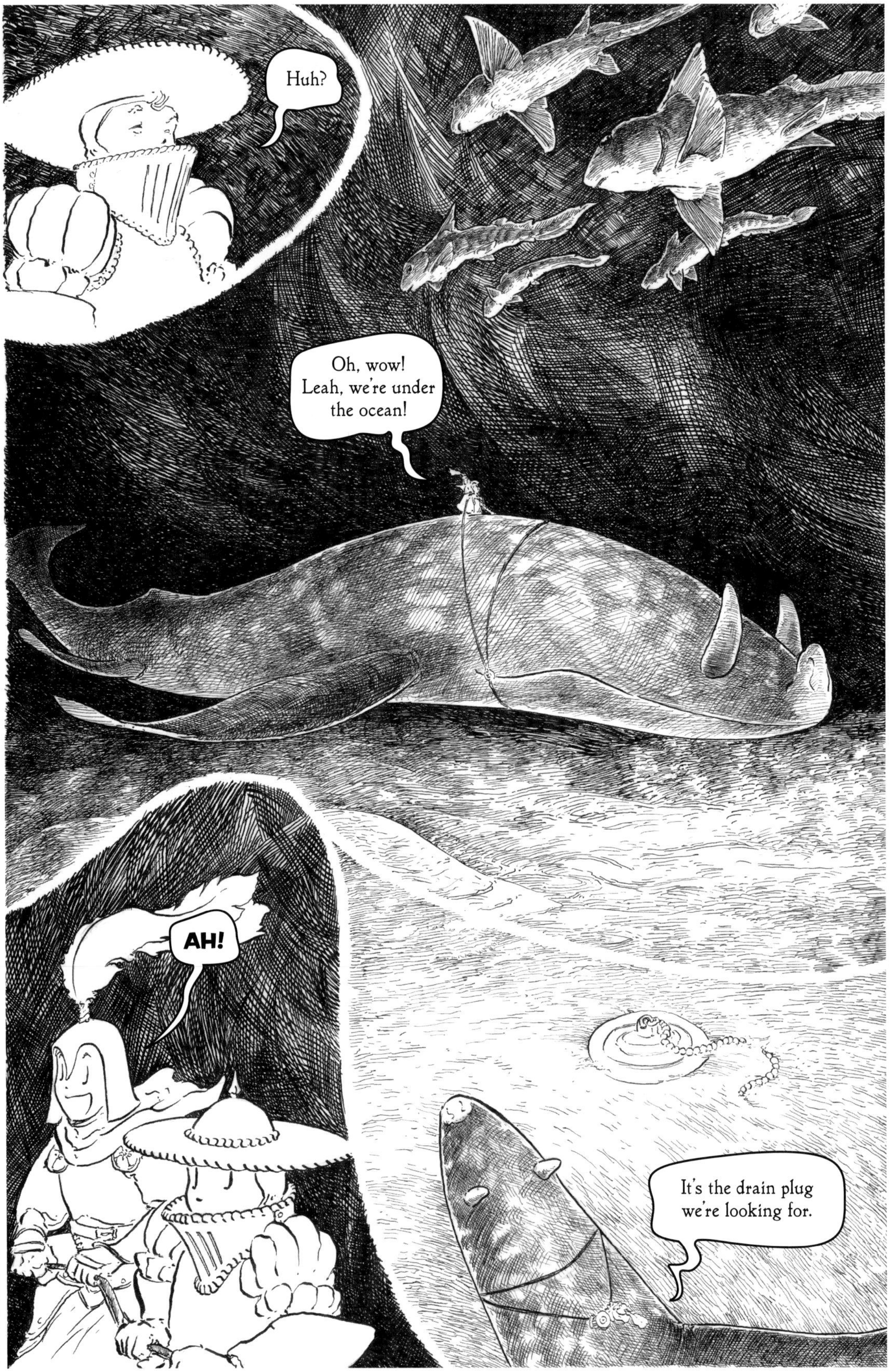
Huh?
Oh, wow! Leah, we're under the ocean!
AH!
It's the drain plug we're looking for.

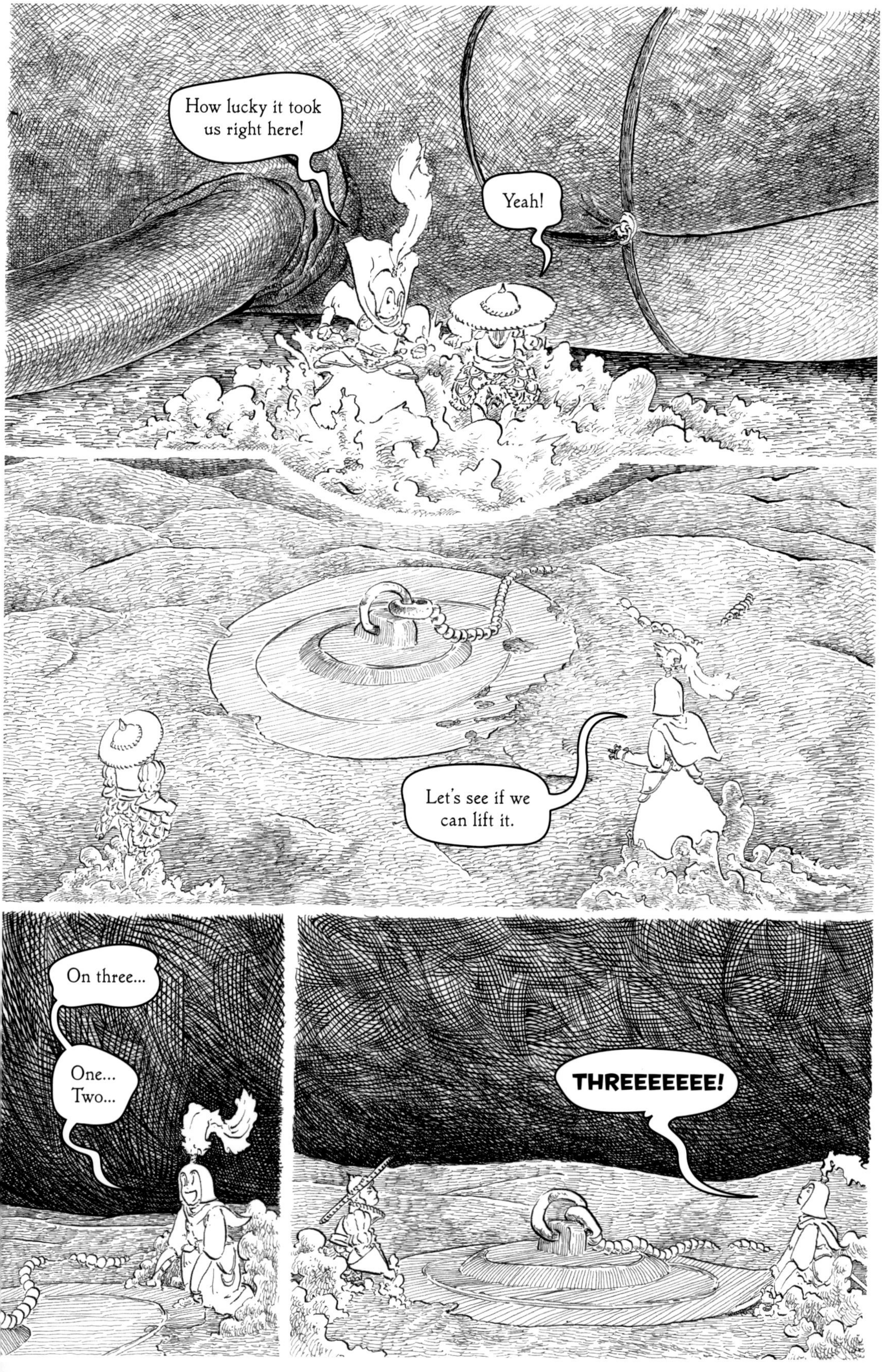

How lucky it took us right here!
Yeah!
Let's see if we can lift it.
On three...
One... Two...
THREEEEEEE!

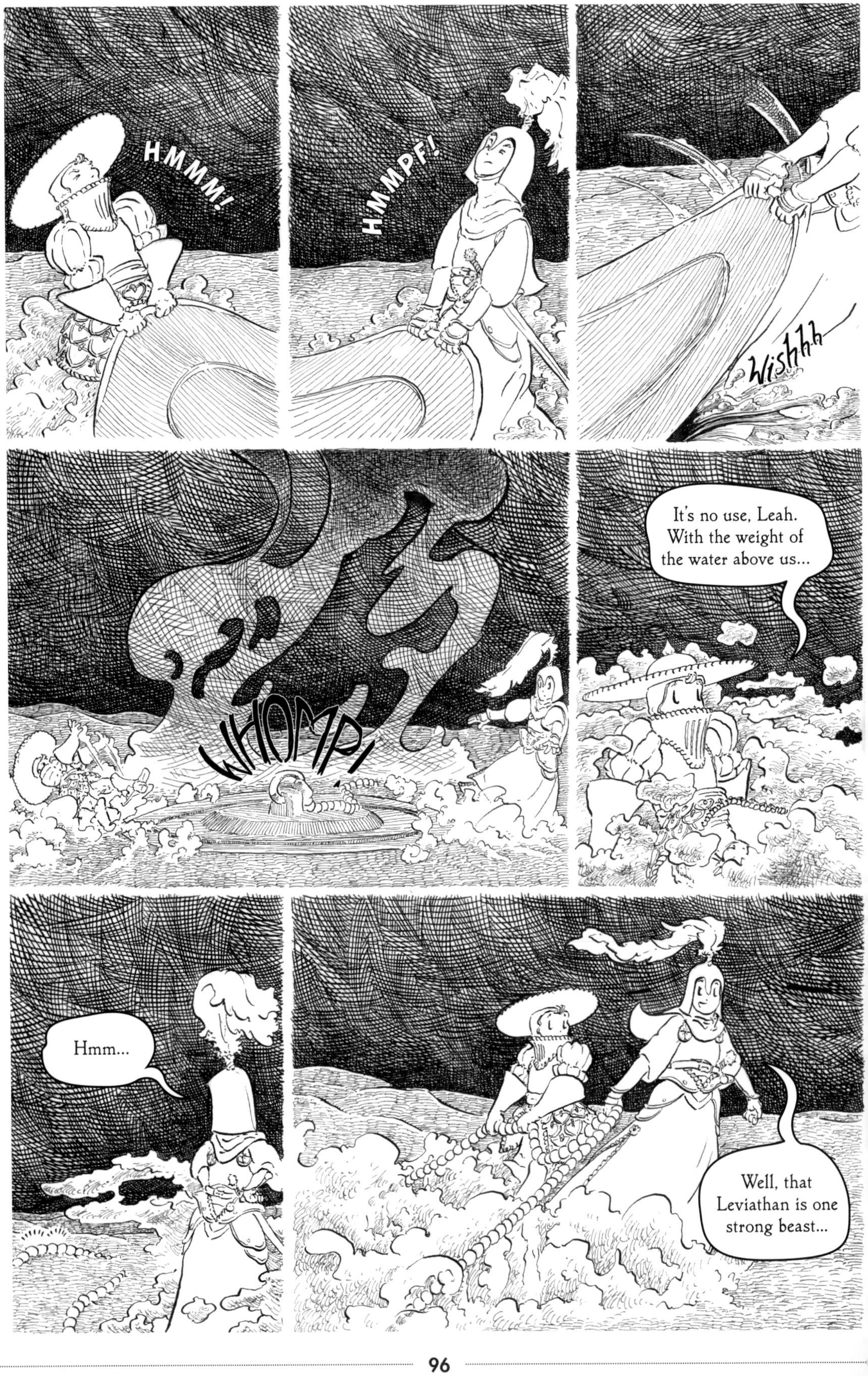
HMMM!
HMMPF!
Wishhh
WHOMP!
It's no use, Leah. With the weight of the water above us...
Hmm...
Well, that Leviathan is one strong beast...

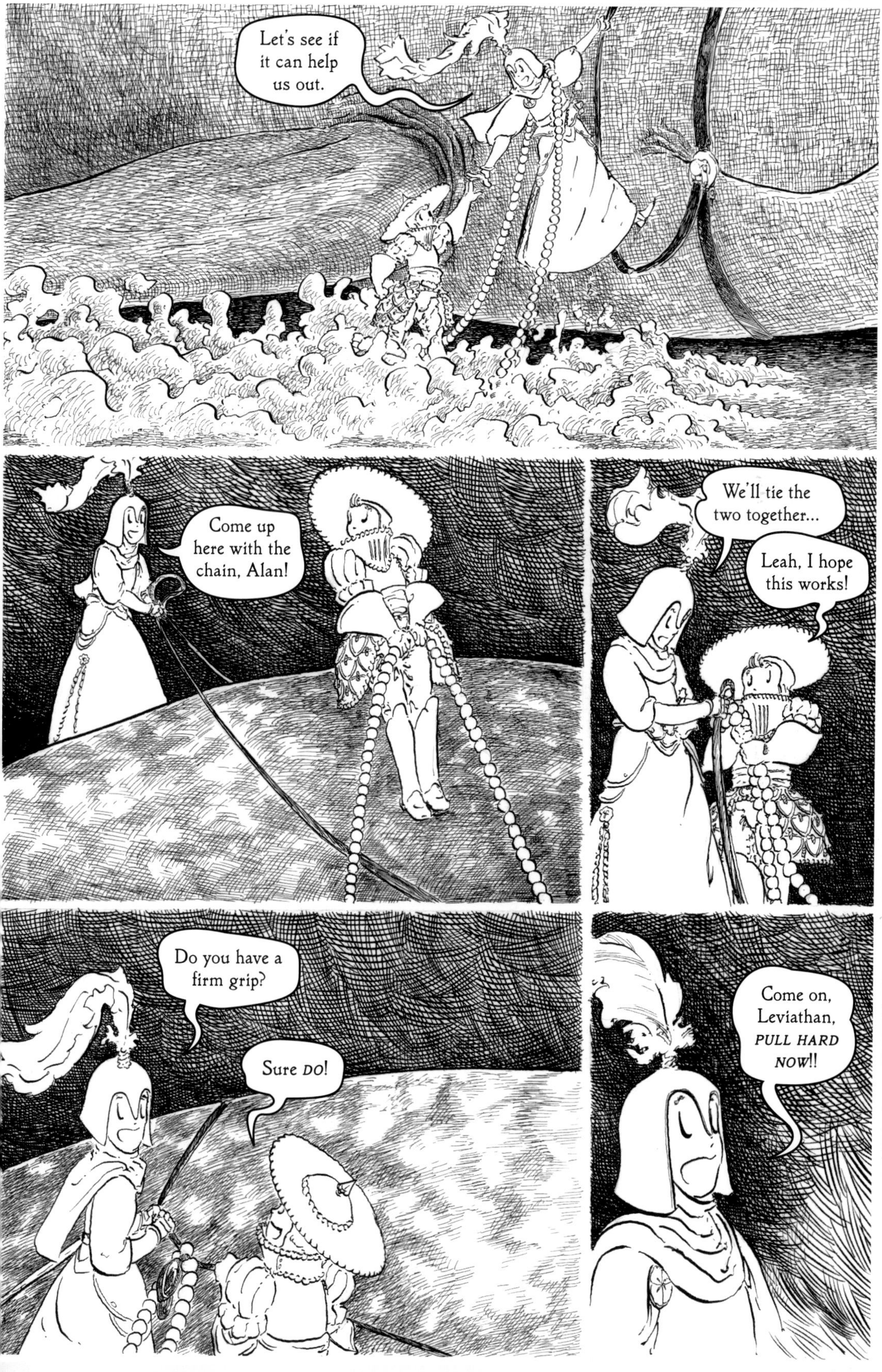
Let's see if it can help us out.
Come up here with the chain, Alan!
We'll tie the two together...
Leah, I hope this works!
Do you have a firm grip?
Sure DO!
Come on, Leviathan, PULL HARD NOW!!

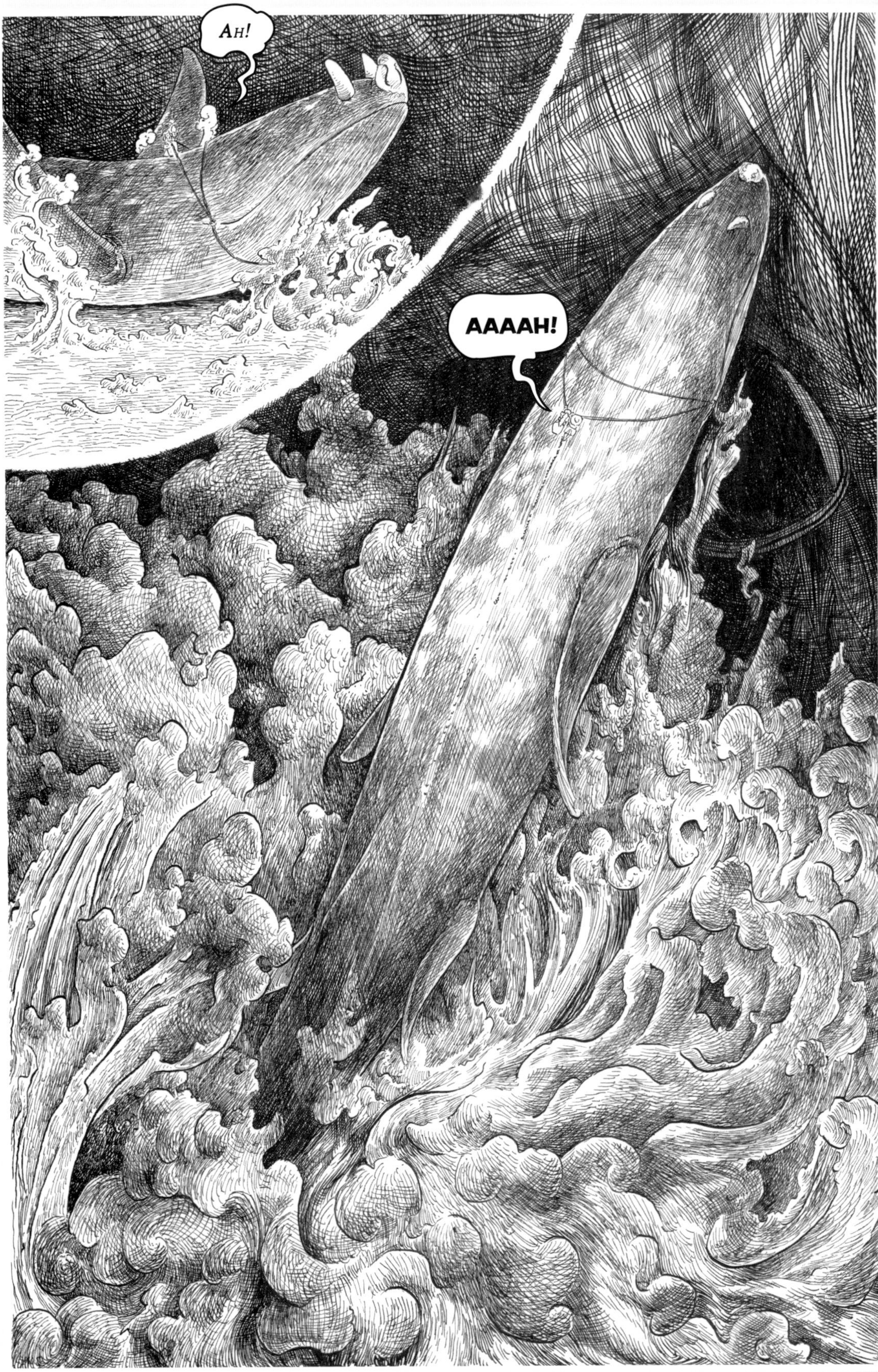
AH!
AAAAH!

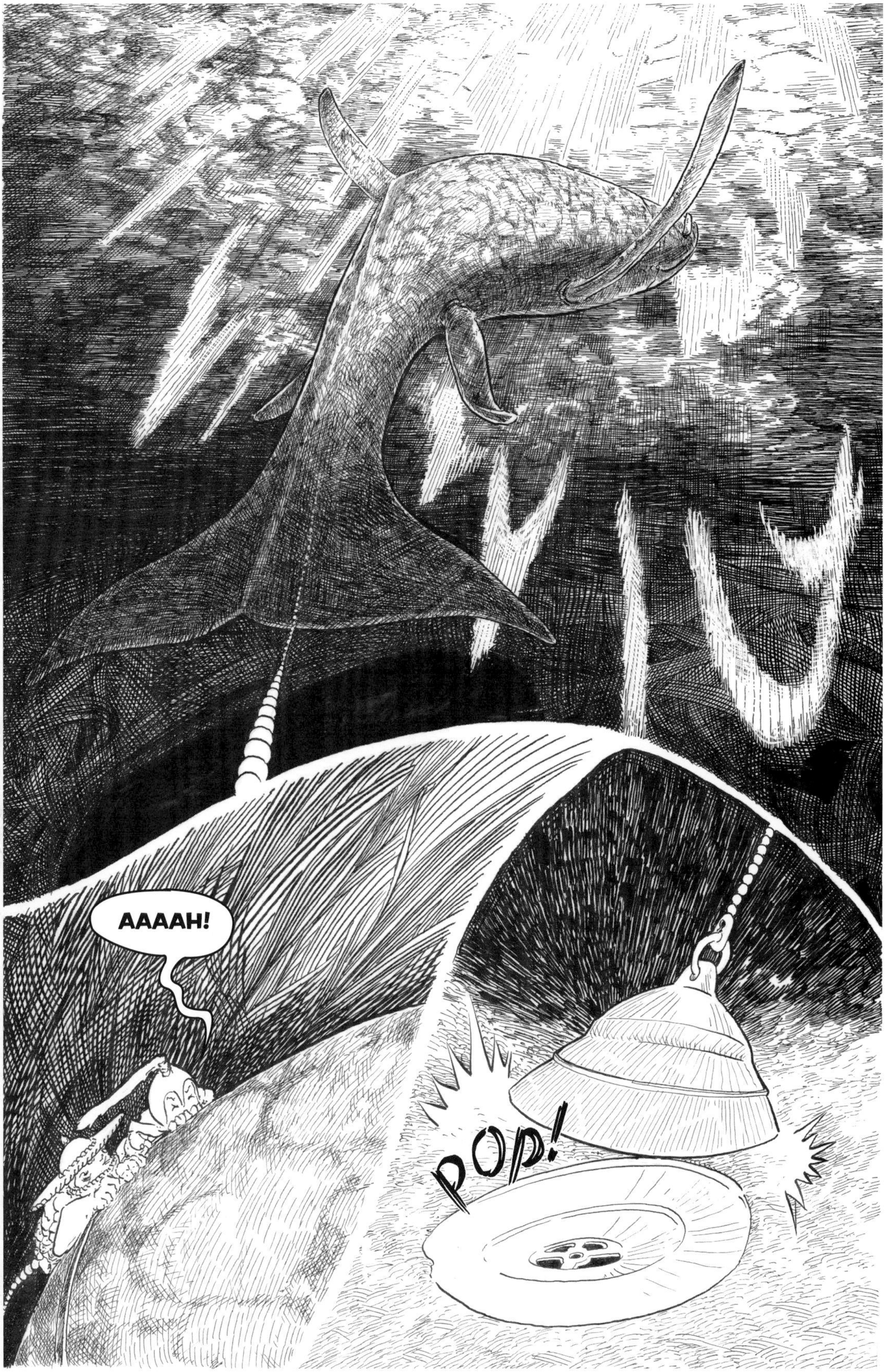
AAAAH!
POP!

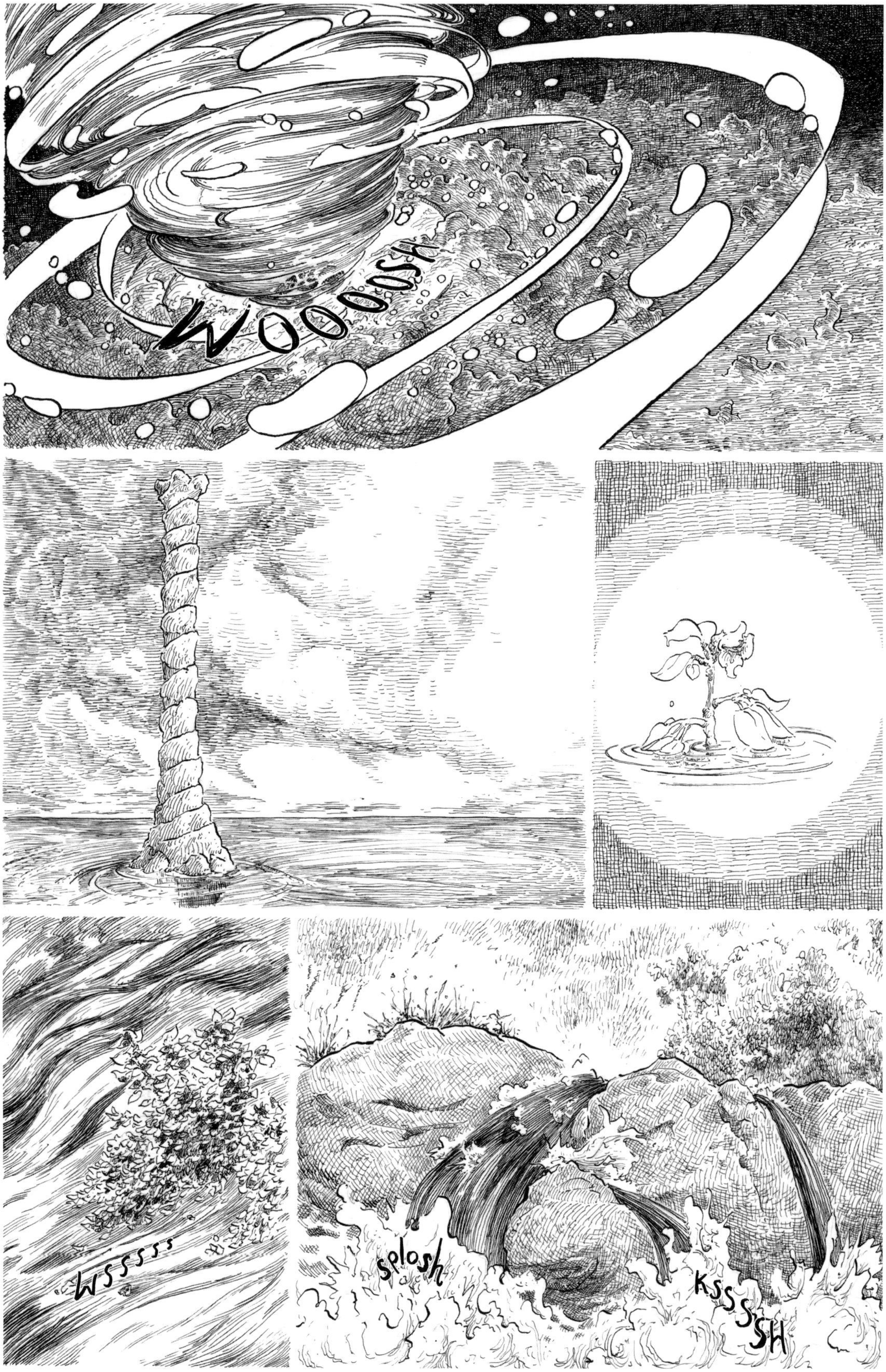
WOOOOSH
WSSSSS
splosh
KSSSSH

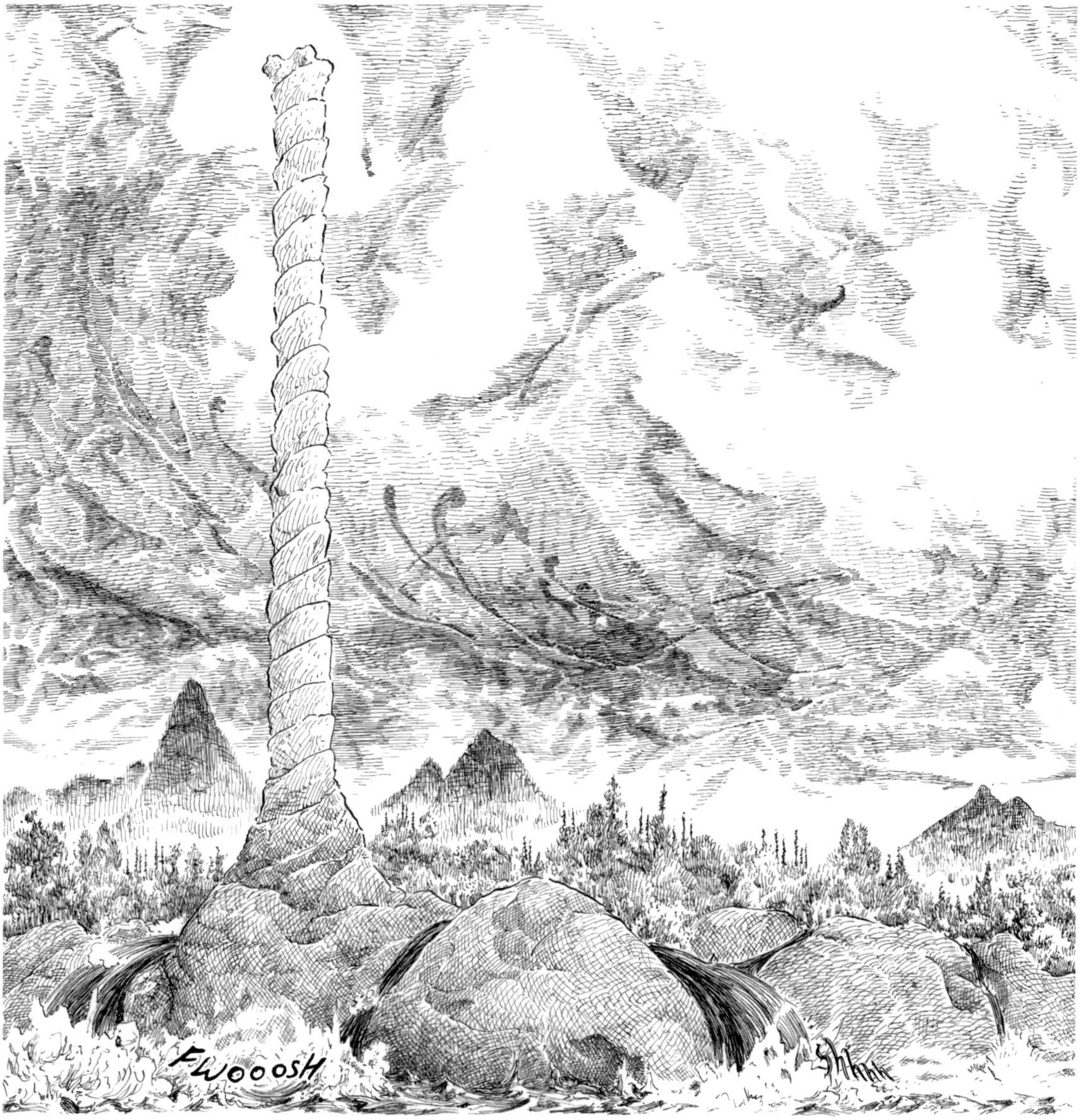
FWOOOSH
SHHHH

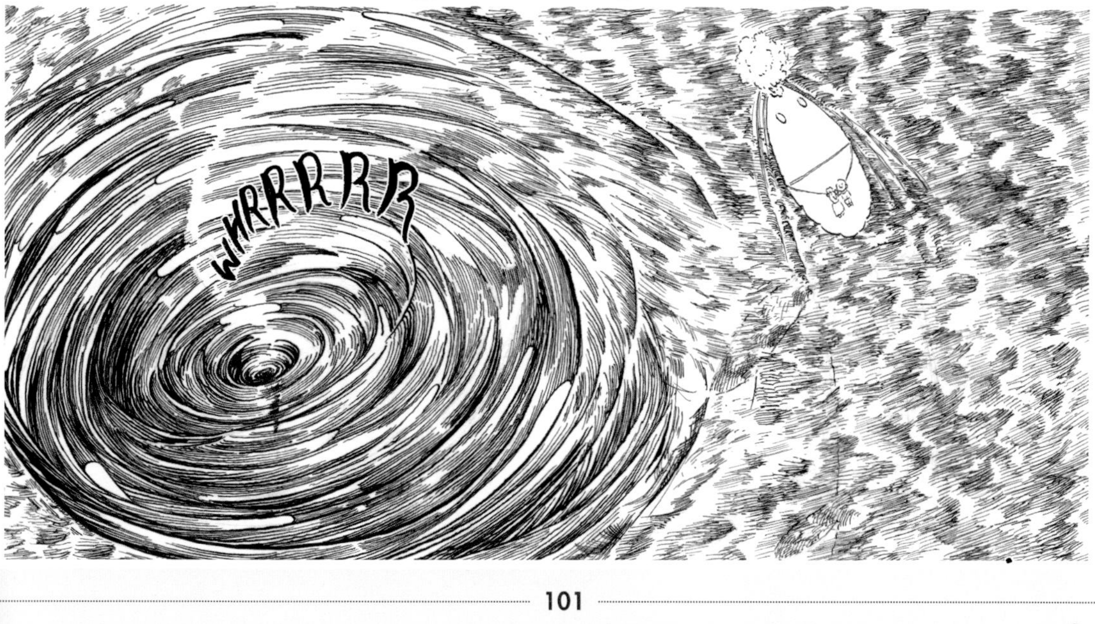
WHRRRRR

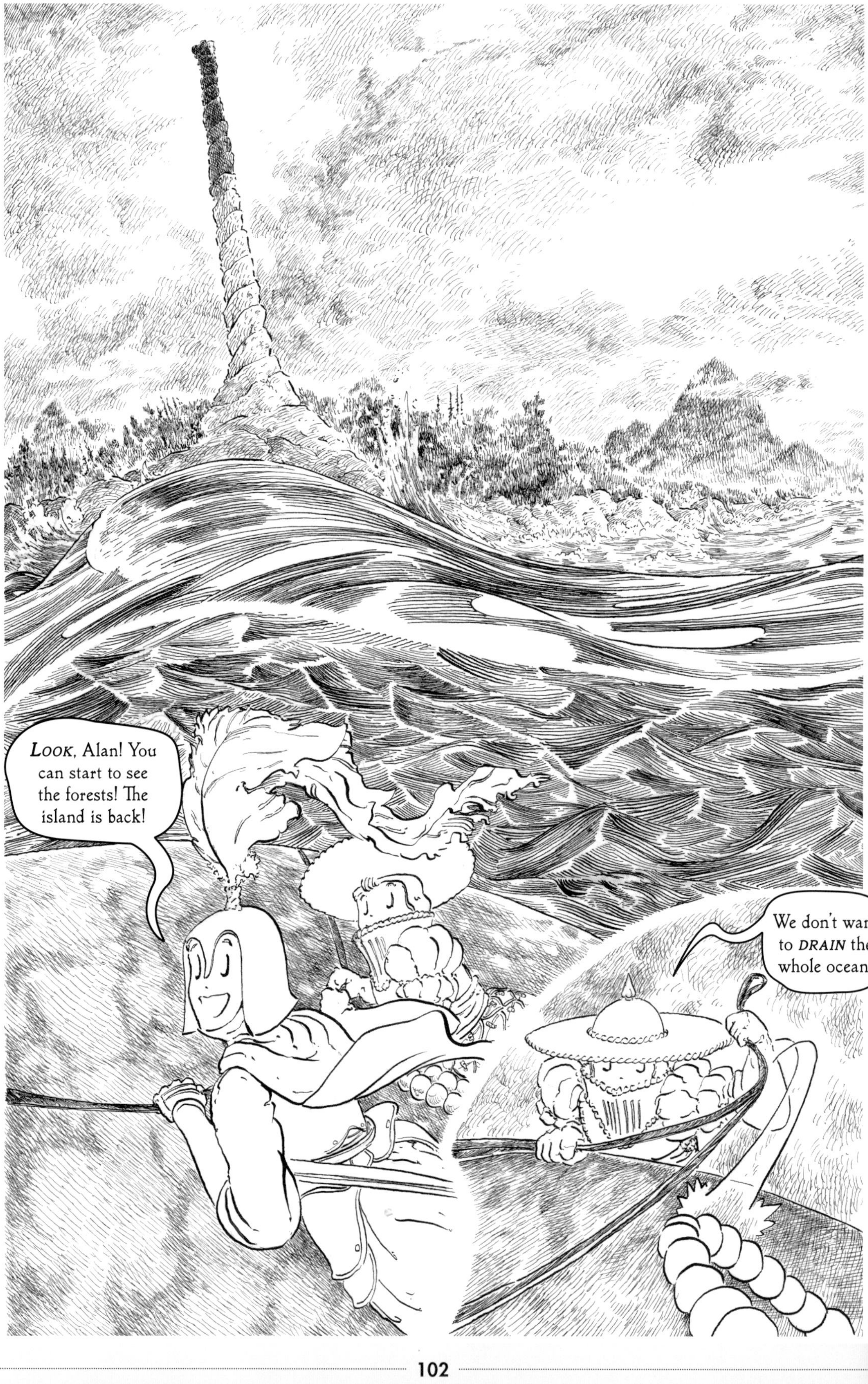
LOOK, Alan! You can start to see the forests! The island is back!
We don't war to DRAIN th whole ocean

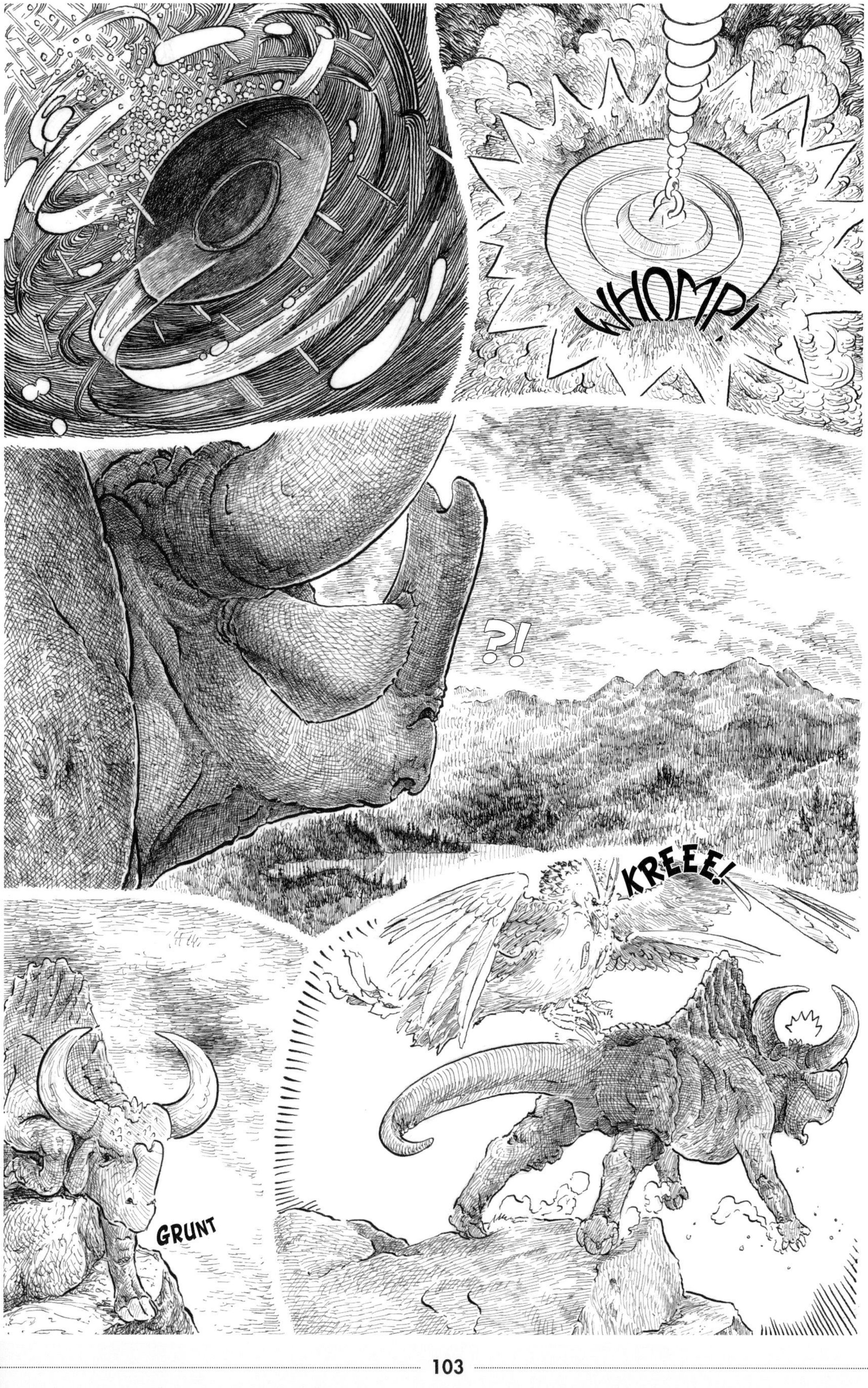
WHOMP!
?!
KREEE!
GRUNT

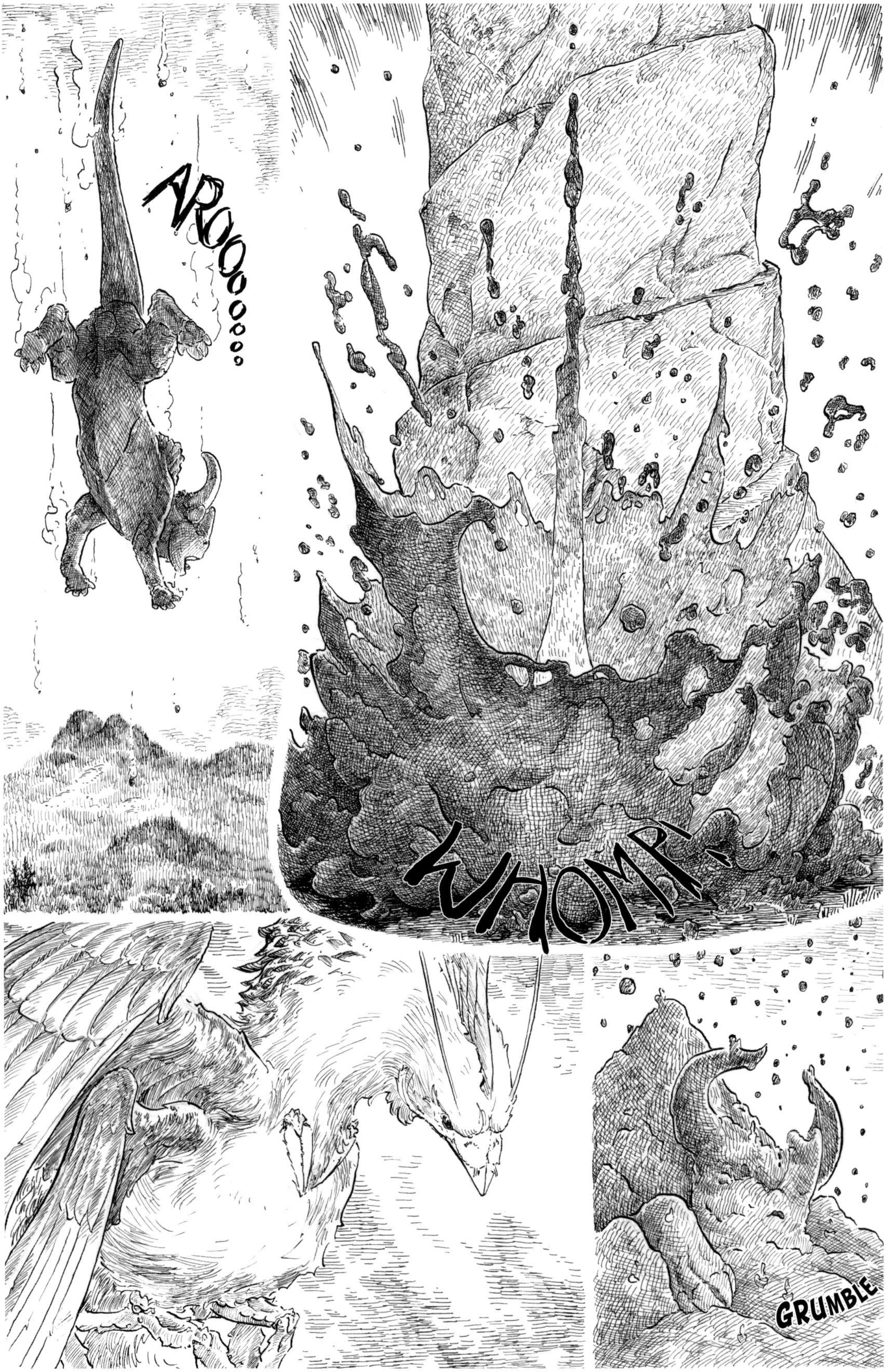
AROOOOOOOOO
WHOMP!
GRUMBLE

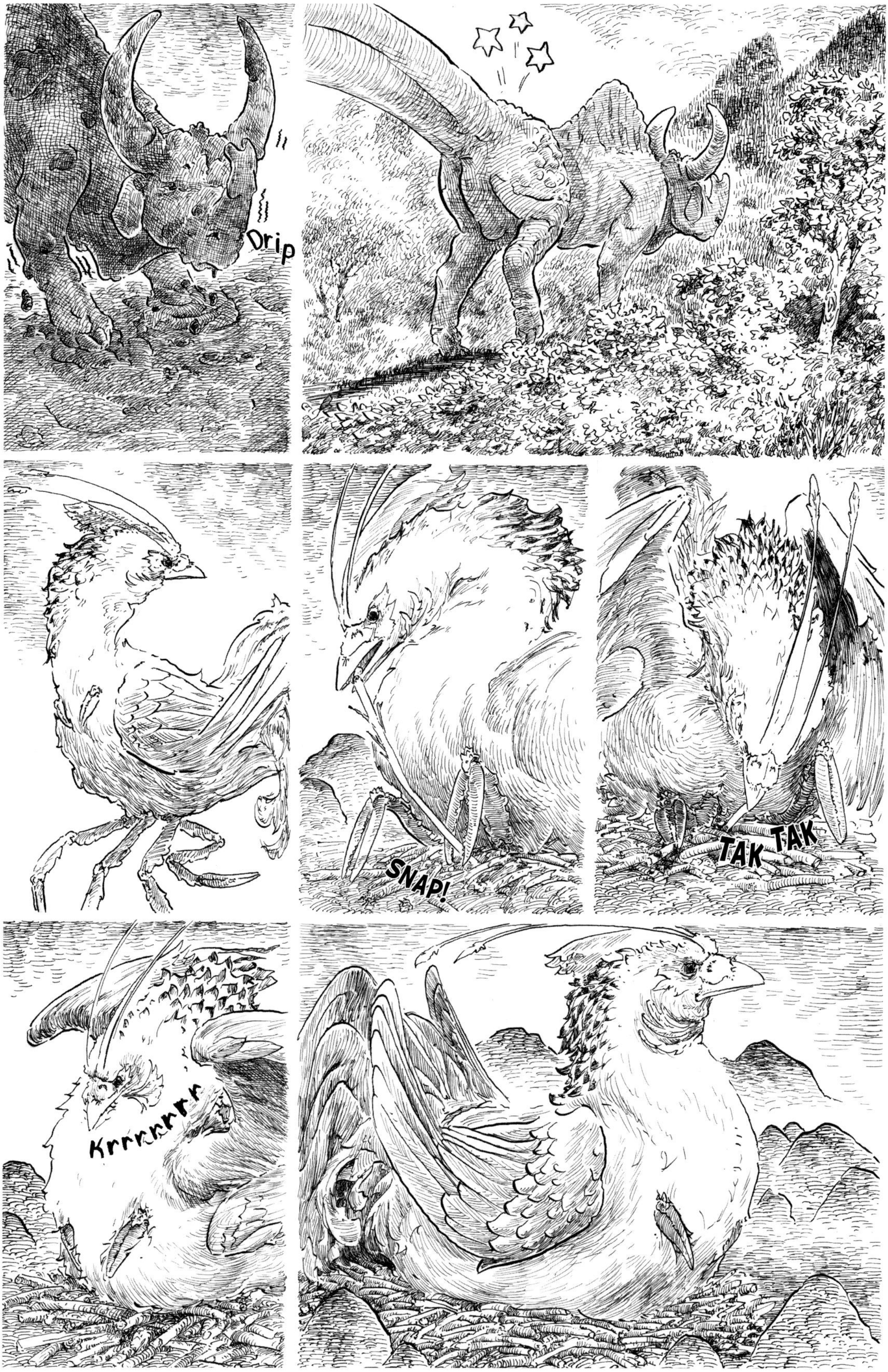
Drip
SNAP!
TAK TAK
Krrrrrrr

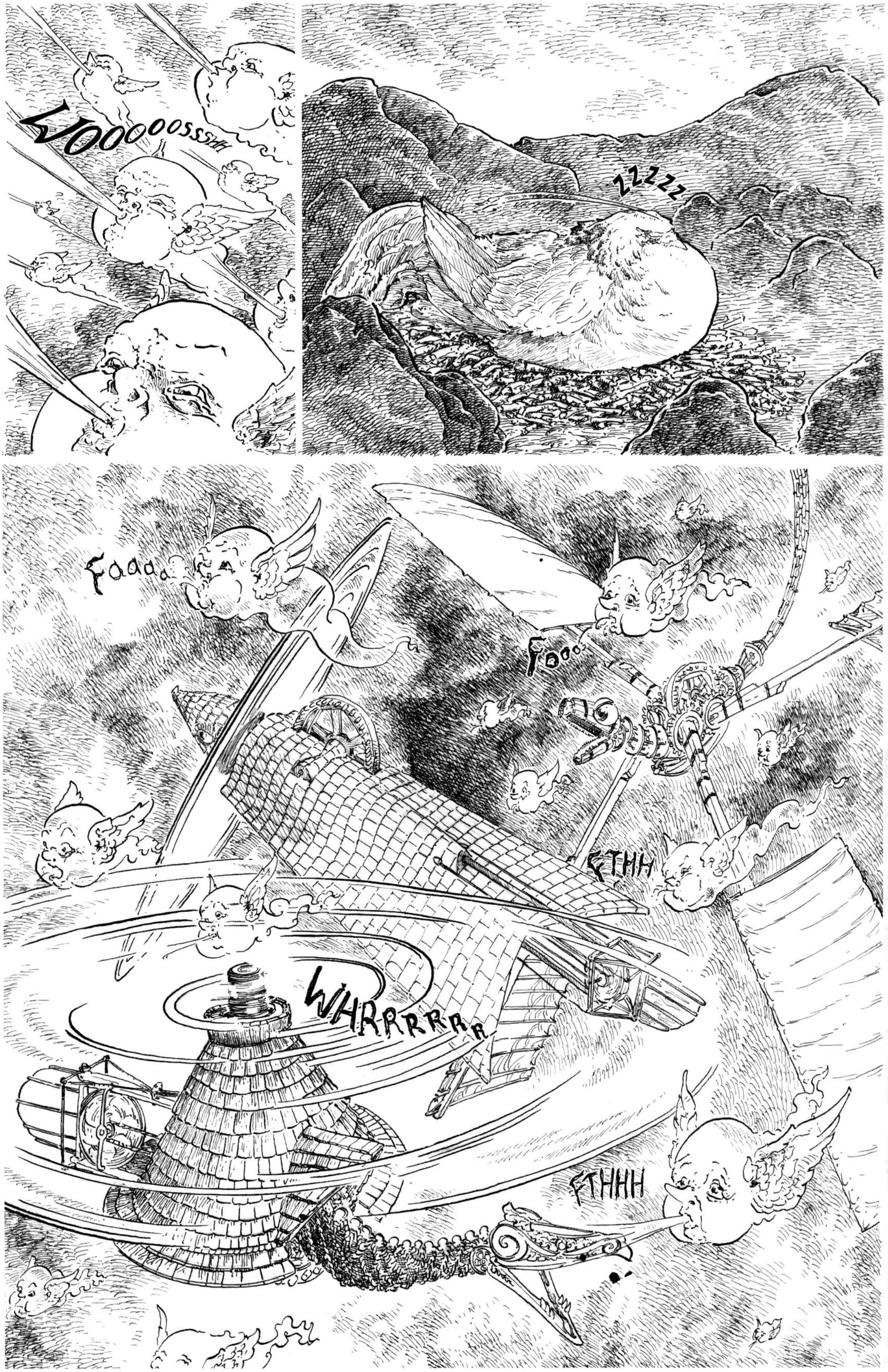

WOOOOOSSSH
ZZZZZ
Faaa..
Fooo
FTHH
WHRRRRRRR
FTHHH

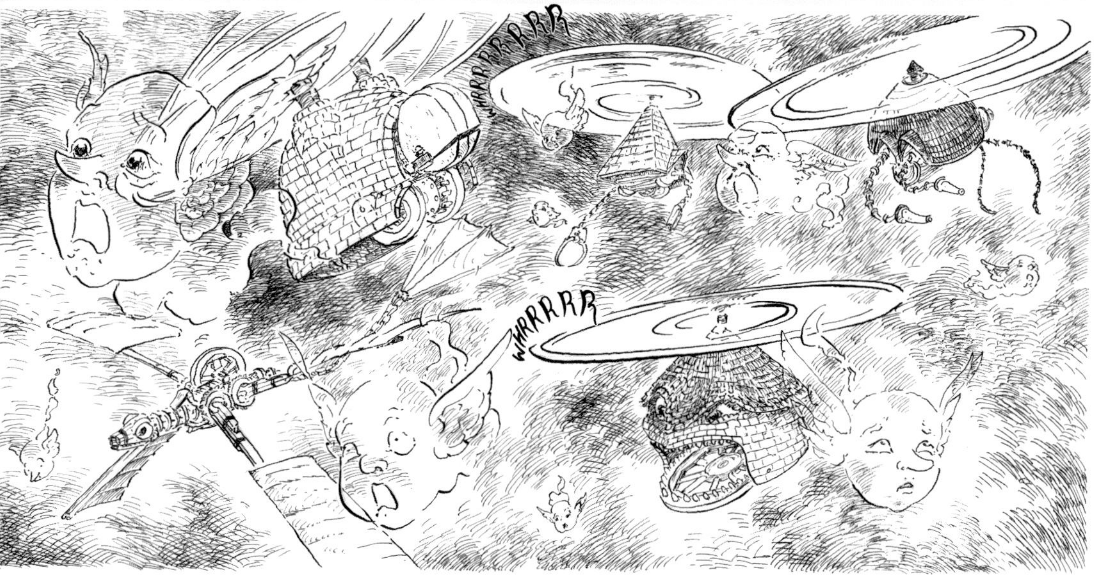
WHRRRRRRRR
WHRRRRR

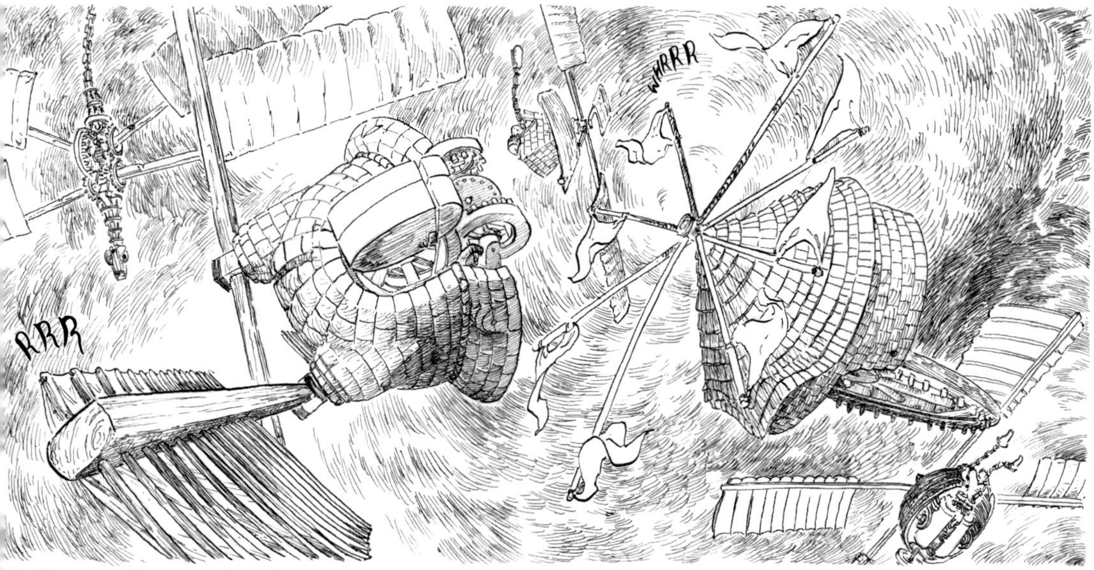
WHRRR
RRR

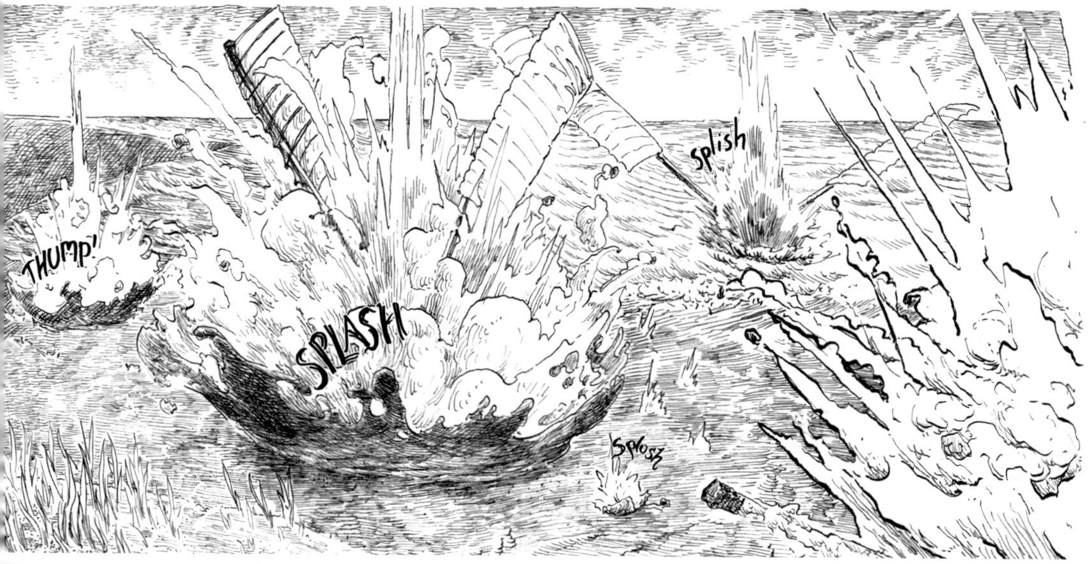
THUMP!
SPLASH
splish

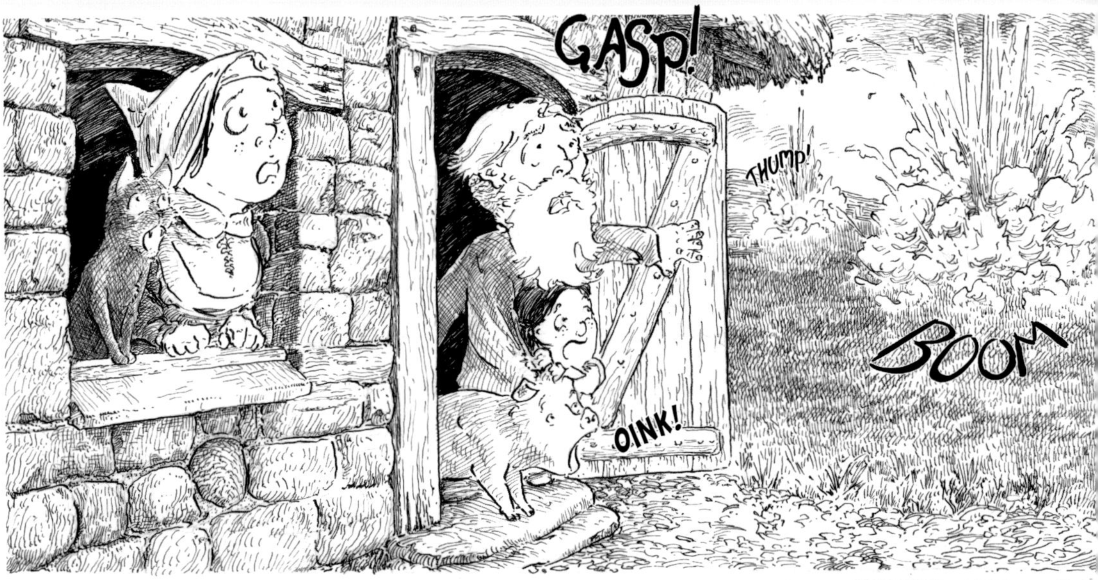
GASP!
THUMP!
BOOM
OINK!

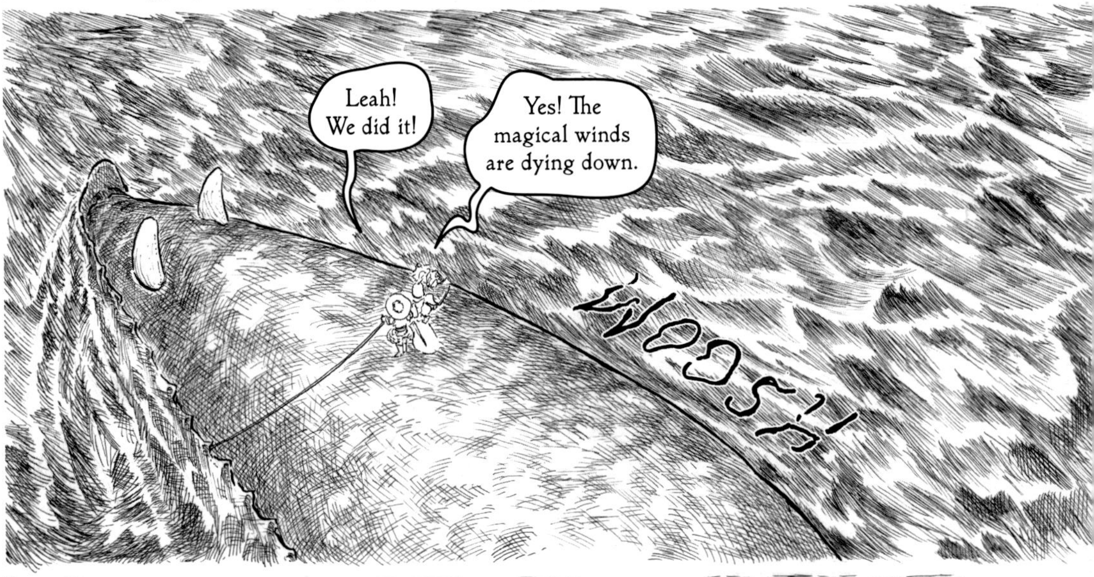
Leah! We did it!
Yes! The magical winds are dying down.
WOOSH!

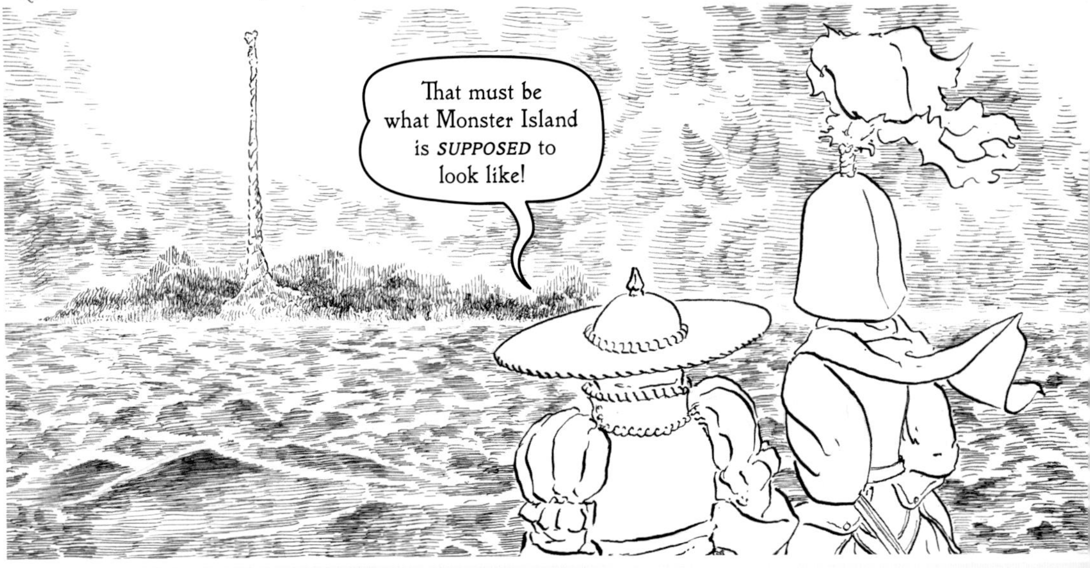
That must be what Monster Island is *SUPPOSED* to look like!

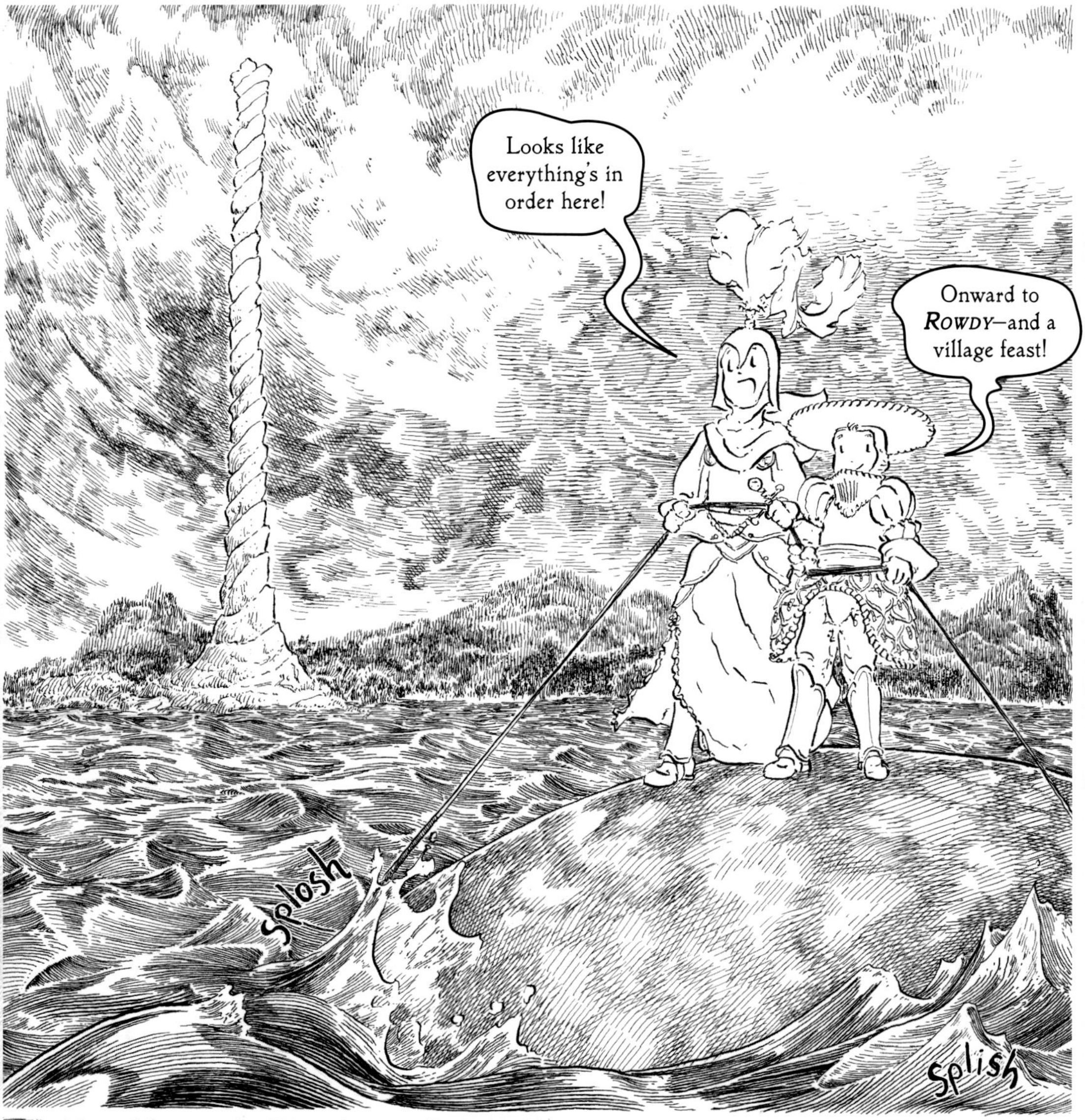
Looks like everything's in order here!
Onward to *ROWDY*—and a village feast!
Splosh
Splish

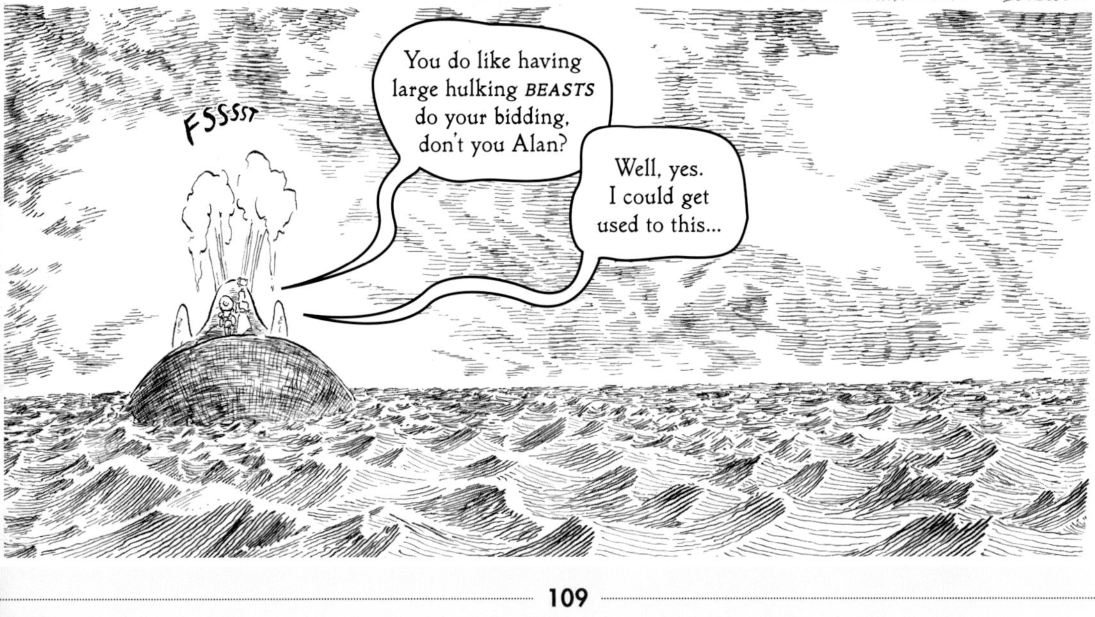
FSSSST
You do like having large hulking *BEASTS* do your bidding, don't you Alan?
Well, yes. I could get used to this...

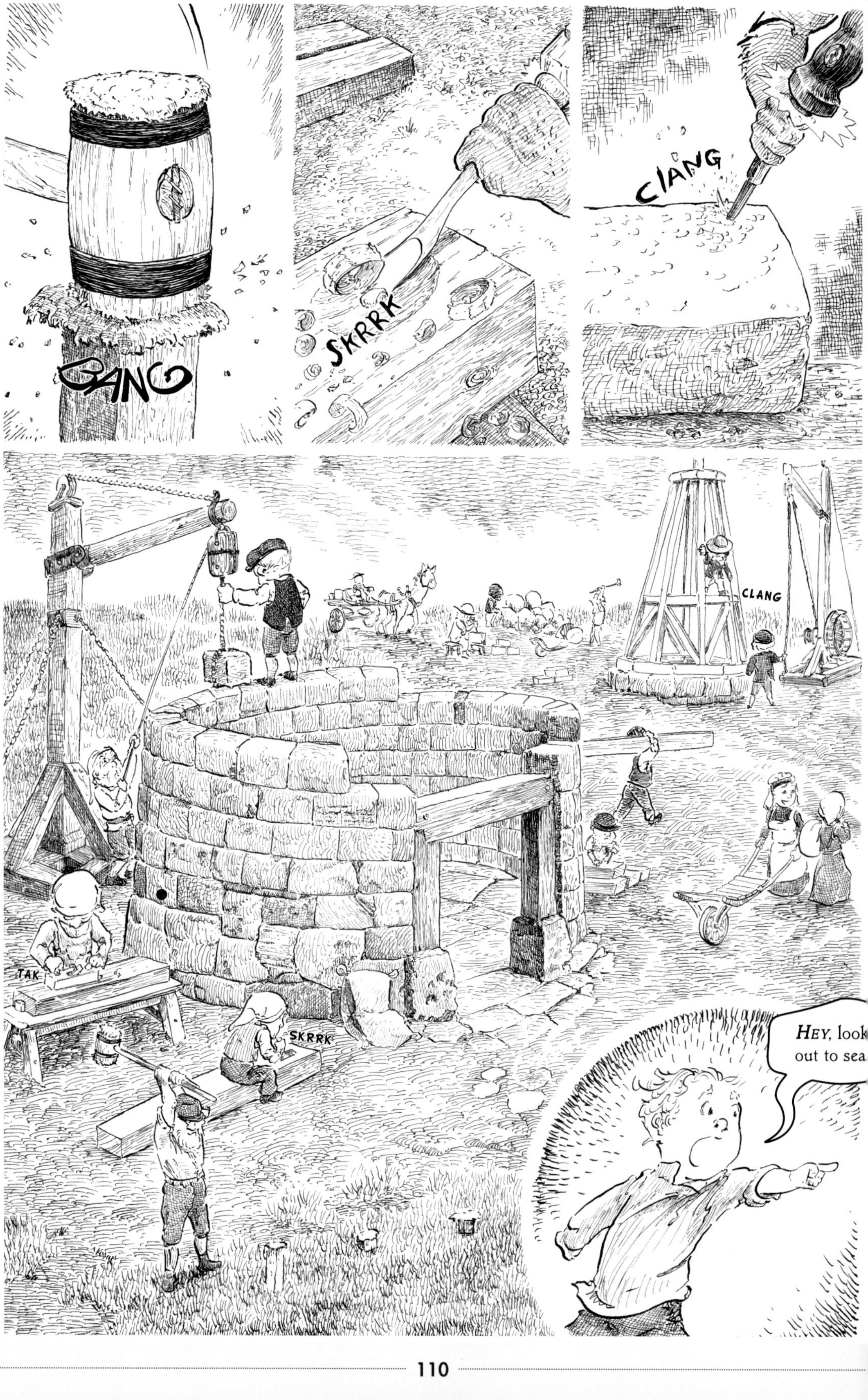
BANG
SKRRK
CLANG
CLANG
TAK
SKRRK
HEY, look
out to sea

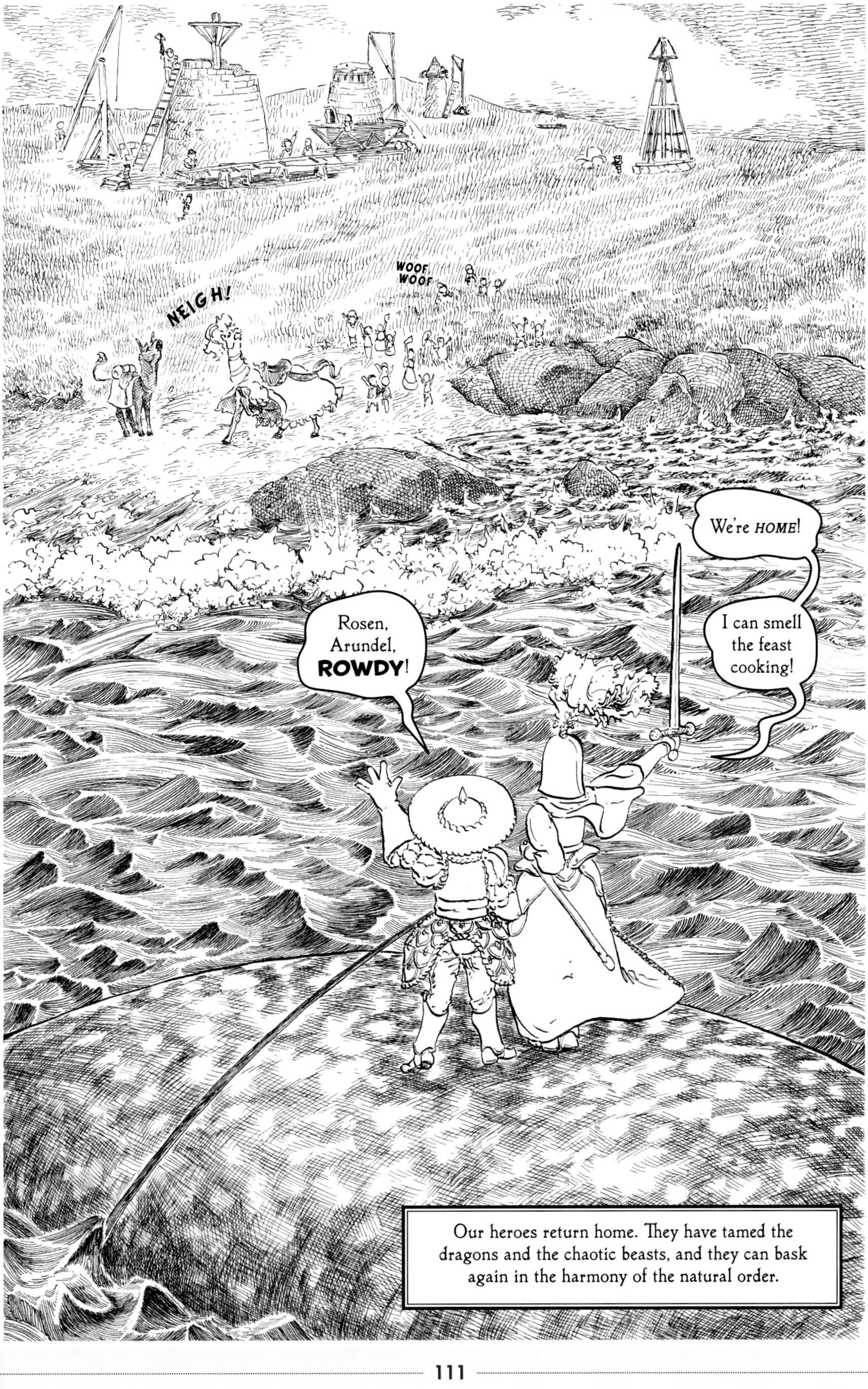
NEIGH!
WOOF WOOF
Rosen, Arundel, **ROWDY**!
We're *HOME*!
I can smell the feast cooking!
Our heroes return home. They have tamed the dragons and the chaotic beasts, and they can bask again in the harmony of the natural order.

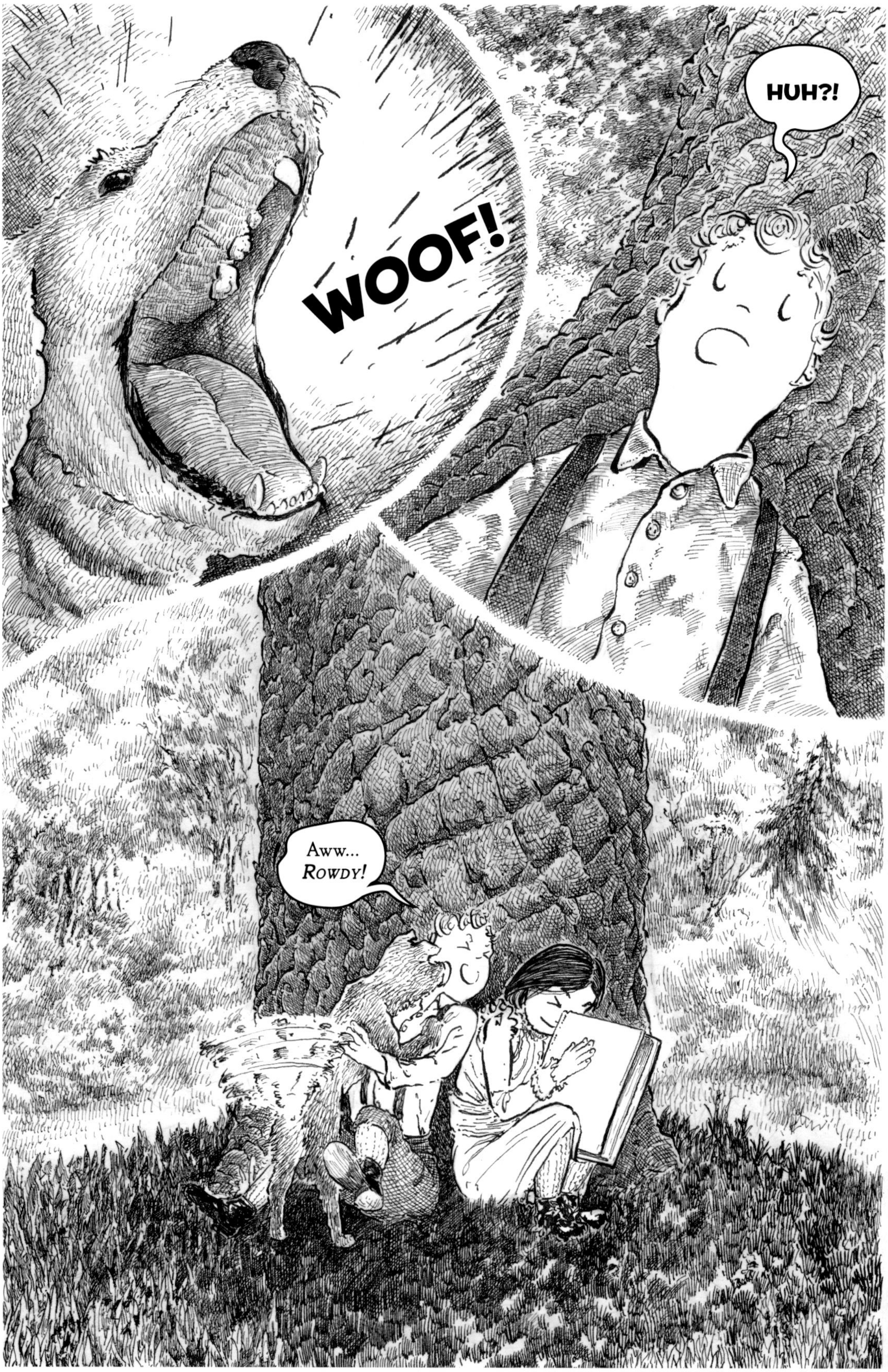
WOOF!
HUH?!
Aww...
Rowdy!

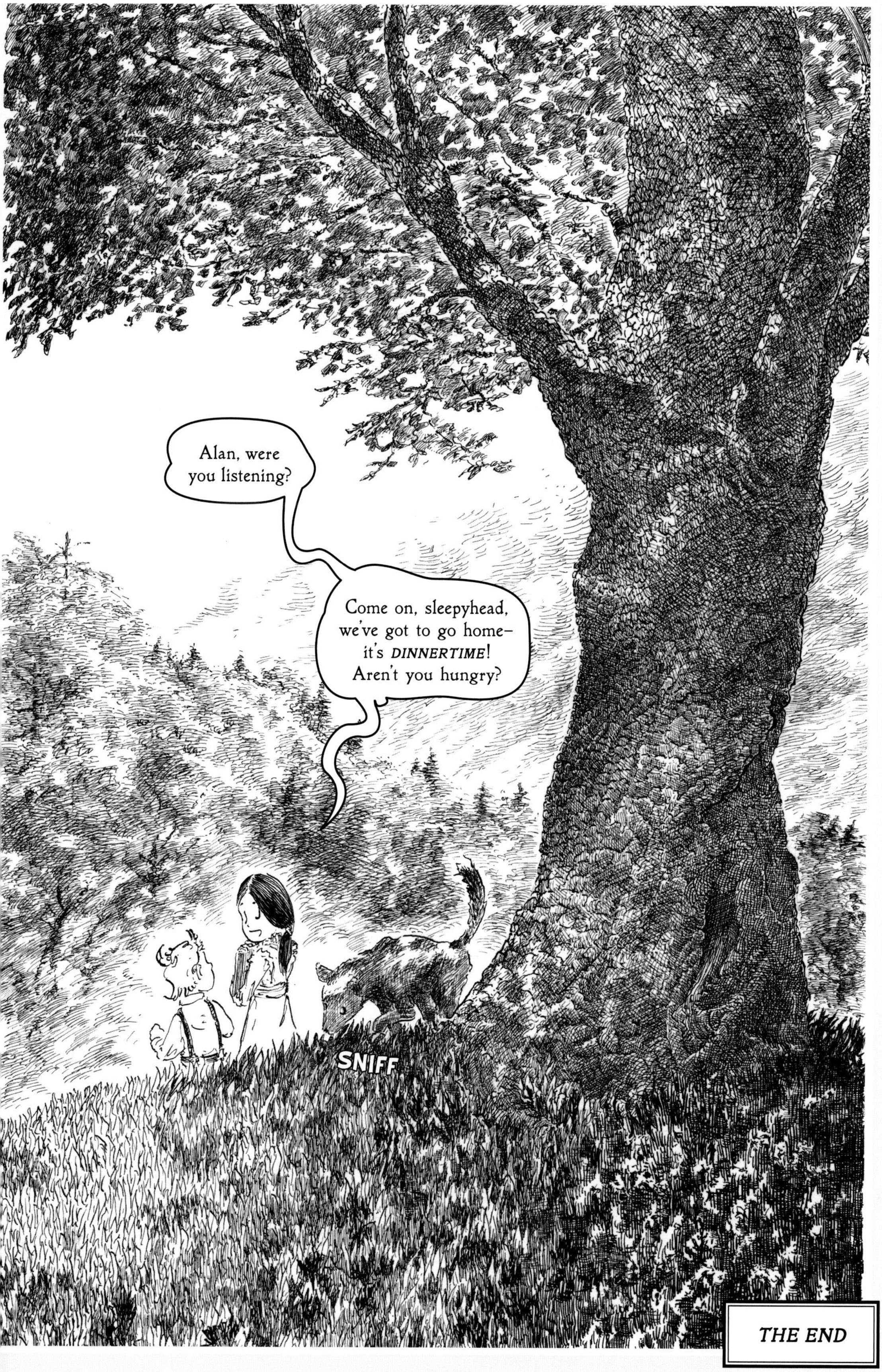
Alan, were you listening?
Come on, sleepyhead, we've got to go home— it's DINNERTIME! Aren't you hungry?
SNIFF
THE END

The Leah and Alan Adventures

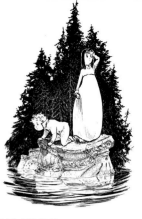

DAVID NYTRA has been drawing since he was old enough to hold a pencil. An artist who works in many media, including clay, wood, and animation, he lives in the small town of 100 Mile House in British Columbia, Canada. As a child, he loved books with many creatures in them and he has tried to fill his *Leah and Alan Adventures* with enough beasties to satisfy even the most demanding reader.

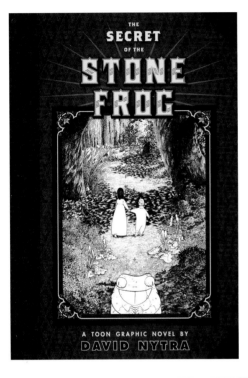

THE SECRET OF THE STONE FROG
A TOON GRAPHIC NOVEL BY
DAVID NYTRA

THE SECRET OF THE STONE FROG

David Nytra's award-winning debut book, a TOON Graphic.

When Leah and Alan awaken in an enchanted forest, they have only each other and their wits to guide them. In a world full of pet bees and giant rabbits, they befriend foppish lions and stone frogs. Learning to overcome danger, they find their way home—and their independence. David Nytra's breathtaking pictures break the boundaries of imagination, sending the reader on a wild flight of fantasy that tells a moving and universal coming-of-age story.

"The extraordinarily delicate and fine-lined art incorporates touches of manga aesthetic so that, like the story itself, it merges timeless narrative elements to craft something wonderfully innovative...A smashing success."

-Booklist

- ★ ALSC's Graphic Novel Reading List
- ★ Harvey Award Nominee
- ★ Nutmeg Book Award
- ★ New York Public Library's Children's Book List of 100 Titles for Reading and Sharing
- ★ School Library Journal's Top Ten Graphic Novels of 2012

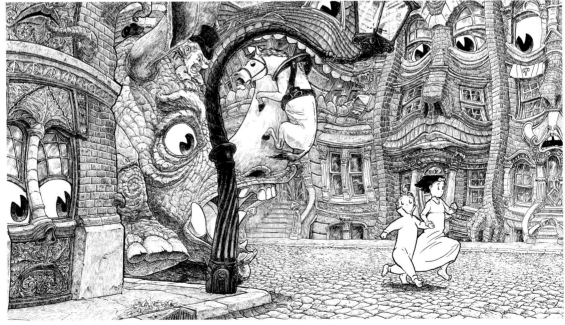

BEHIND THE STORY

Don Quixote

Don Quixote is a Spanish novel by Miguel de Cervantes, published in the early 1600s. It tells the story of an old nobleman who has read too many books about knights. He dons a suit of armor, names himself "Don Quixote," and finds a squire to help him on his own knightly adventures. In one episode, Don Quixote tries to attack a field of windmills that he thinks is a group of giants with huge swinging arms. This inspired the expression "tilting at windmills," which means attacking imaginary enemies. ("Tilting" comes from the medieval art of jousting.)

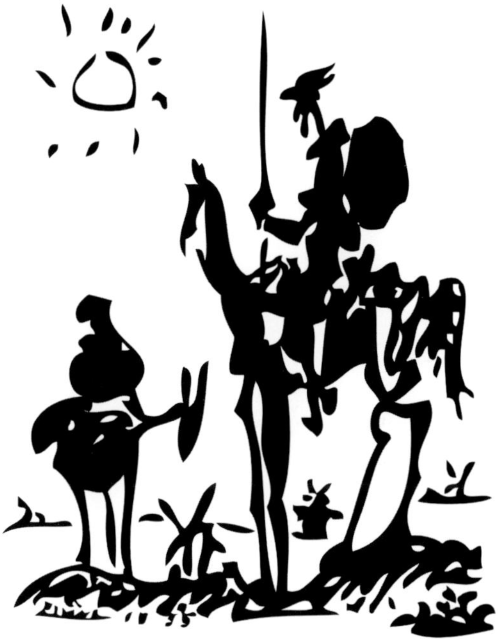

Pablo Picasso, "Don Quixote," 1955, *Les Lettres Françaises.*

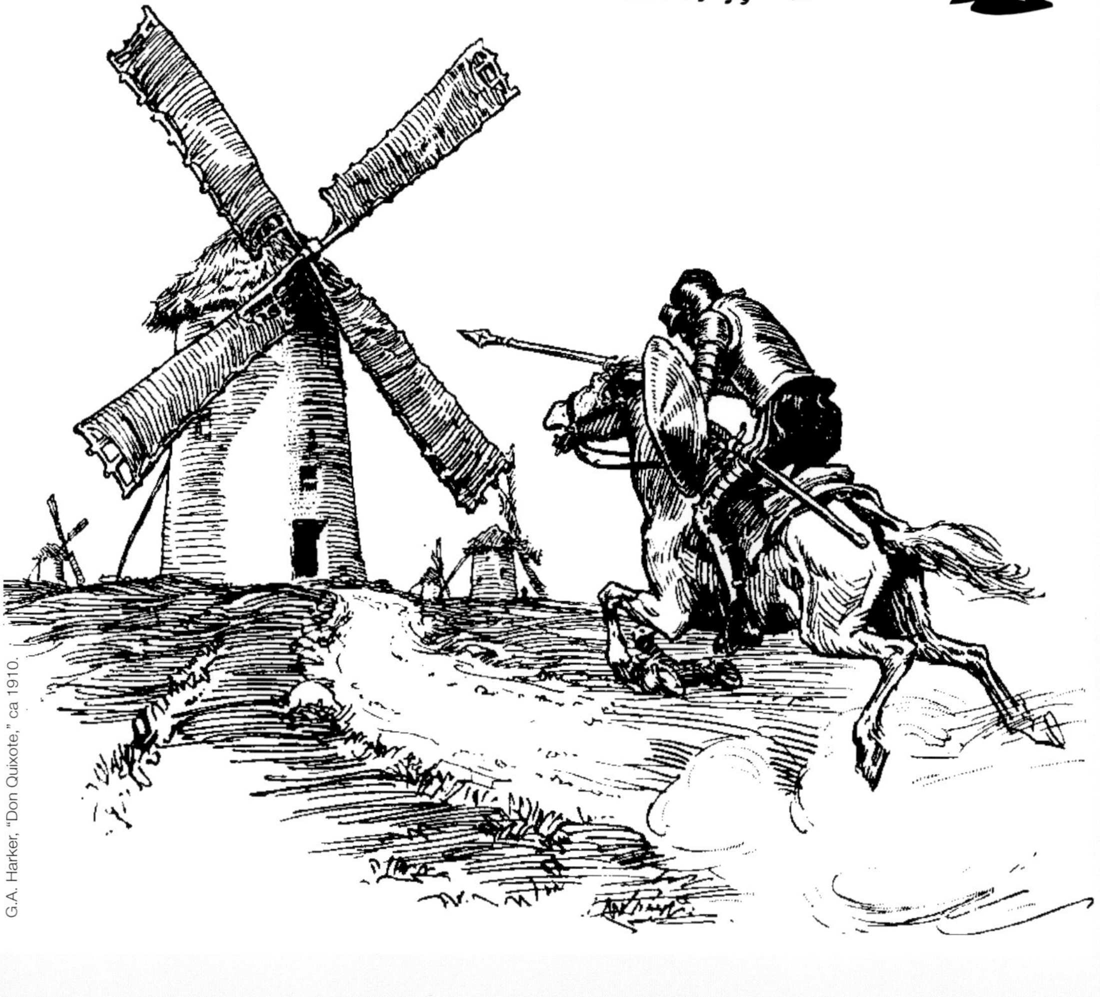

G.A. Harker, "Don Quixote," ca 1910.

Ziz, Behemoth, Leviathan

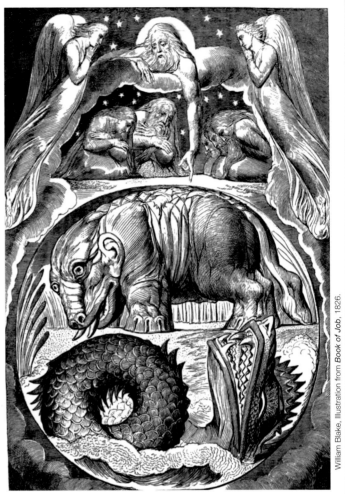

William Blake, Illustration from *Book of Job*, 1826.

An engraving of the Behemoth and the Leviathan by William Blake, 1826.

T he Ziz, the Behemoth, and the Leviathan are huge creatures from Jewish mythology mentioned in the Old Testament. Each rules over a specific kingdom: The Ziz rules the birds, the Behemoth the beasts, and the Leviathan the fish. The Ziz is a giant, griffin-like bird. Her wings are so large they can block out the sun, but they also protect the earth from wind. If one of her eggs falls from her nest, it causes earthquakes and flooding. No one knows exactly what the Behemoth looked like. Some scholars think of it as a hippopotamus, rhinoceros, dinosaur, or crocodile. The word now refers to any large or powerful being. The Leviathan is a sea monster, thought to resemble a giant serpent or whale.

Harley Bestiary, ca. 1230. The British Museum.

Bestiaries

A bestiary, or *bestiarum vocabulum*, was a medieval European book that listed and described all kinds of animals, including birds, with Christian moral lessons. Imaginary animals, like the unicorn and griffin, were included. Bestiaries were beautifully hand-illustrated as "illuminated manuscripts."

Dragon entry from the Harley Bestiary, *written in Latin ca. 1230.*

Pertelote

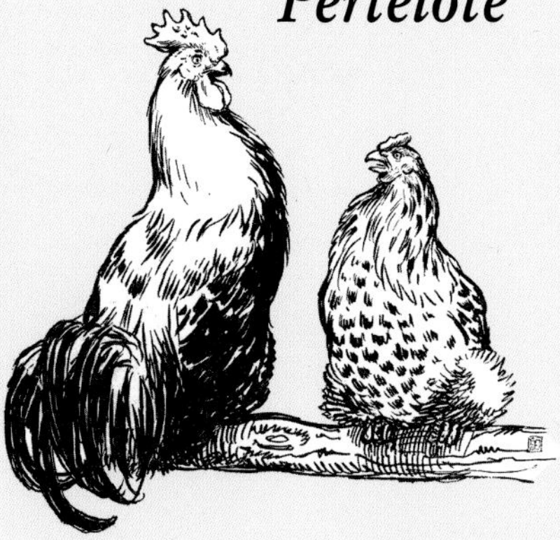

Frank Adams, "Chanticleer and Pertolette," 1915, *Children's Stories from the Poets.*

Pertelote is the name of a hen in *The Canterbury Tales*, a work of medieval literature composed in the late 1300s by Geoffrey Chaucer. It is one of the great works of English literature. The tales follow a group of religious pilgrims who tell each other tales to pass the time on their journey. In one story, a proud rooster dreams that he will be killed by a fox. His favorite wife, Pertelote, pays no attention to his fears. In the end, a fox does try to eat him but is outsmarted by the crafty rooster.

Sir George

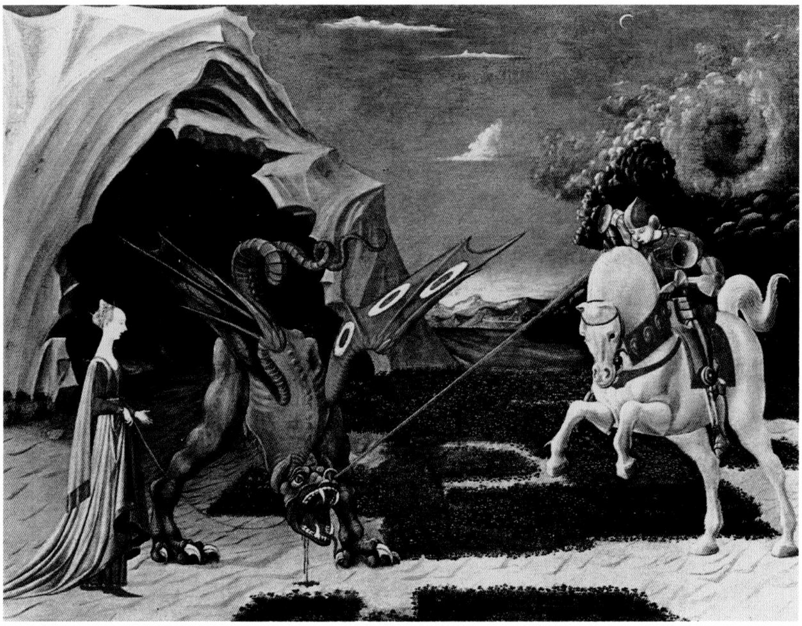

Paolo Uccello, "St. George and the Dragon," 1470.

Sir George may be related to Saint George, a soldier born in Roman Palestine in the late 200s, who became a Christian and was martyred. He appeared in stories of lives of saints in the early 900s. According to legend, Saint George saved a city from a huge dragon that was killing its young women. With only his lance, George killed the monster and rescued the king's daughter, its next victim. Saint George and the dragon have been painted hundred of times and appear on the coat of arms of many European cities and the country of Georgia. He is the patron saint of England, and his cross forms its flag.

The Man-eating Boat

The design of the Man-eating Boat seems inspired by canoes of Native Americans and Canadians of the Northwest Coast, which stretches from Alaska to northern California. Artists carve canoes from a single log and paint them with animal designs that often honor family members. For First Nations people, creating artistic objects is an important way to transmit beliefs, histories, and stories to future generations.

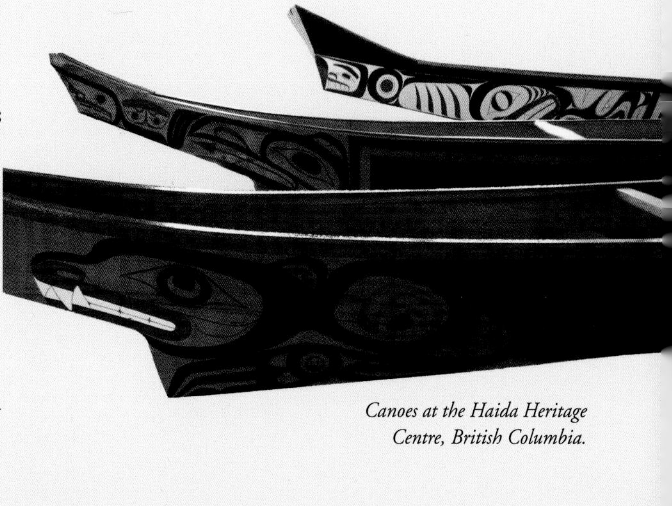

Canoes at the Haida Heritage Centre, British Columbia.